BR
OF THE
EMPIRE
D0014070

BRIDES OF THE EMPIRE

Three Romances Thrive among Christians of the First Century

DARLENE MINDRUP

ISBN 1-59789-105-3

Cover art by GettyOne

Published by Barbour Publishing, Inc., P.O. Box 719, Uhrichsville, Ohio 44683, www.barbourbooks.com

Our mission is to publish and distribute inspirational products offering exceptional value and biblical encouragement to the masses.

ecpa Member of the Evangelical Christian Publishers Association

Printed in the United States of America.
5 4 3 2

Dear Readers

As an avid reader of romance, when I became a Christian in 1979, I noticed that there was a severe lack of Christian romance books. I was frustrated that there wasn't something to replace the romances that I used to read that had become so ungodly. One day, I happened upon a **Heartsong Presents** special in our local Christian bookstore. I was so excited that I immediately bought several and then decided that maybe they could use more authors. (Boy, was I gullible!)

My love for history inspired the books that I wrote, and homeschooling my children helped me to find the inspiration for the stories as we studied. Now, my son is grown and proudly serving in the air force, and my daughter is married to a fine marine with two beautiful children. With the departure of my children, my husband, Allen, and I found ourselves with a lot of time on our hands. Nowadays I spend my time as part-time secretary of our church and working on the crafts that I love.

I will always be thankful to Barbour Publishing for giving me the chance to write. I love to hear from my readers, so please let me know if you enjoyed reading these stories as much as I enjoyed writing them.

God Bless,
Darlene Mindrup

The Eagle and the Lamb

To my mother who taught me to be the best I could be.
And to my beloved husband who believes that I am.

Prologue

The amazed murmurs of the crowd ascended slowly to a deafening roar. Parthians, Medes, Elamites, and Judeans all chattered and motioned frantically at one another.

Jubal Barjonah pushed himself forward angrily, his eyes coming to rest on the leader of the Galileans. What was his name? Simon, called Peter, that was it.

Twelve of them stood and faced the crowd, but it was Peter who addressed them.

"Fellow Jews and all of you who live in Jerusalem, let me explain this to you; listen carefully to what I say."

The crowd quieted, their attention focused on the speaker. He continued.

"These men are not drunk, as you suppose. It's only nine in the morning!" Jubal could hear several snickers in the crowd.

"No, this is what was spoken by the prophet Joel."

Jubal's startled eyes flew to Peter's face, his attention suddenly riveted. Jubal had studied the prophet Joel's writings for many years. He almost had a passion for them. They and the writings of Isaiah were his favorites. Peter's quoting of Joel was totally accurate, but how did that apply to this situation? Jubal's attention was caught once more as the voice went on, vibrant and full of authority.

"Men of Israel, listen to this: Jesus of Nazareth was a man accredited by God to you by miracles, wonders and signs, which God did among you through him, as you yourselves know."

There was no denying the man Jesus of whom he spoke was a fantastic magician. Jubal had seen the results of his "healings."

Peter continued, *"This man was handed over to you by God's set purpose and foreknowledge; and you, with the help of wicked men, put him to death by nailing him to the cross."*

Jubal felt a stab of guilt when he remembered his part in the debacle. He had been one of the crowd shouting for the crucifixion of the man they called Jesus.

As Jubal listened to Peter quoting from the Psalms of David, he felt convicted by the things he had to say. Could what he said be true? Was it possible that Jesus fulfilled the old prophecies?

Suddenly the writings of Isaiah came clearly to his mind. The false witnesses at the trial, Jesus' refusal to answer the charges. Struck and spit on, and still He did not open His mouth.

Jubal's face paled, and his heart started to thunder. What had they done? His mind twisted with the agony until he cried out with the others.

"Brothers, what shall we do?"

Peter replied, "*Repent and be baptized, every one of you, in the name of Jesus Christ for the forgiveness of your sins. And you will receive the gift of the Holy Spirit. The promise is for you and your children, and for all who are far off—for all whom the Lord our God will call.*"

Jubal pushed forward with the frenzied crowd, intent on reaching the speaker. The words of the mighty Joshua came to his mind. From this day forward, he and his house would serve the Lord.

Chapter 1

The sound of thundering hooves broke the silence of the still, peaceful morning. Two riders appeared on the brow of the hill. Though both were large and strong, one stood out as the more confident of the two. His black hair was cropped close to his head and glistened with the moisture from his perspiration. Bare muscular arms rippled against the short white tunic he wore so gracefully. Eyes as blue as the Mediterranean gave evidence of his Greek ancestry.

He and his steed matched perfectly. Both large and powerful. One barely under control, hooves stomping in frustration at being held in check.

"Easy, Orion," the rider soothed as he reached down to stroke the horse's neck. "We must remember our friends."

The friend in question quickly caught up, his breathing more labored than his companion's.

"For pity's sake, Antonius, can't you control that mangy beast?" he complained in irritation. "I thought we were on a hunt, not having a race."

Antonius glanced at his friend, his eyes roving over his already lathered horse. A fierce pride welled up inside Antonius. Orion was the best horse the Roman legion had to offer, but only because he belonged to Antonius personally.

Since Antonius's father had been a senator and had the ear of the emperor, Antonius had been granted special privileges. Orion was the one Antonius was the most grateful for. Already the stallion from Thrace had been instrumental in saving his life. More than once.

Orion was not lathered at all. Even now, after an hour of riding, it still took all of Antonius's energy to control him. Sliding from his mount, Antonius dropped the reins and stared about him.

"Come now, Flavius. Surely you are not tired."

Flavius dismounted also, brushing dark hair from his eyes. "As though I would admit it if I were."

Antonius grinned but jerked to attention when he noticed movement from the trees to his left. Motioning Flavius to silence, he reached for his bow and quiver of arrows. A glitter of excitement sparkled in his eyes as he took aim.

"What do you see?" Flavius whispered urgently, trying to peer in the direction Antonius was aiming.

"If I'm not mistaken, there's a deer among those trees. See the brown spot? To the left."

A slight movement caught Flavius's attention. "Shoot, Antonius, before he gets away."

The *twang* of the bowstring was the only answer Flavius received as Antonius's arrow whistled unerringly toward its target. A small *thud* was followed by a piercing scream that drained the blood from Antonius's face.

"By the gods!" Flavius whispered. "That sounded like a human scream."

Antonius followed the same direction as his arrow, leaping over rocks and roots. Pushing aside the shrubbery, he noticed a small clearing among the bushes. A small body lay crumpled at the edge of the perimeter.

Laying down his bow, Antonius went quickly forward, turning the body over when he reached it. A young girl lay unconscious before him, her breathing labored. The arrow had pierced her shoulder, and blood was flowing swiftly from the wound.

"Zeus!" Flavius's startled exclamation brought Antonius's eyes to his friend.

"Get my water bag," he snapped.

Flavius disappeared from view, returning a moment later with the bag. Antonius opened the flask and poured water over the girl's wound, gently probing with his fingers.

"I need to pull out the arrow, but I need something to stem the flow of blood first."

Flavius looked helplessly around. "What?"

Reaching down to the hem of his garment, Antonius quickly jerked off a piece of material.

"When I tell you, use this to put pressure on the wound."

Flavius nodded his agreement. Sweat beaded on Antonius's lips and face as he gritted his teeth and got ready to pull the arrow free. It was fortunate that the girl was unaware of anything happening to her.

"Now!"

Antonius jerked the arrow, and Flavius pushed the material against the girl's shoulder.

"Be thankful it's only a Jewish girl, Antonius. Otherwise, there could be big trouble."

Antonius pulled another strip from his garment to use as a bandage to tie the other piece in place. The girl's color was beginning to alarm him.

"She must be from somewhere close. We need to find her village and get help."

Lifting her gently in his arms, Antonius strode swiftly into the open. A piercing whistle rent the air, and Orion lifted his head, his ears perked forward. Another whistle and the stallion threw himself forward, hooves thundering toward Antonius.

"Take her, Flavius, and hand her up to me."

Antonius took the girl in his arms, settling her against his chest. Her head fell backward against his arm, and her eyes fluttered open momentarily. Dazed brown eyes gazed at him uncomprehendingly. A spark of recognition seemed to light behind her eyes and then faded.

"Who are you?" The whispered croak barely made it past her lips before her eyes closed again. *Thank the deities,* thought Antonius. This was not going to be a pleasant ride.

Flavius lifted Antonius's gear to his own horse and quickly followed. A much-used path told them in which direction to head, and they quickly came upon a small village. People came to their doors and stared with open hostility at the two Roman soldiers.

A young girl standing at the well turned startled eyes upward as Antonius paused beside her. Sudden fear filled her face, and she turned to run.

"Wait!" Antonius commanded, and the girl froze. "I need help."

The girl noticed for the first time the bundle held in his arms. Her eyes widened farther, and she stared up at him in horror.

"Is this girl from this village?"

The girl nodded her head, her eyes never leaving the figure of the wounded Jewish girl.

"Take me to her family," Antonius commanded again, and the frightened girl quickly turned to point the way. "I said, take me." Antonius had no time and was in no mood to knock on doors.

Orion picked his way along the main street, shying nervously as a door slammed behind him. The girl reached a house that was slightly larger than the rest they had encountered. From what Antonius knew of the Jews, the owner must be somewhat wealthy. *Probably a carpenter or a blacksmith.* Antonius felt a moment's disquiet.

Flavius pulled up beside him. "Uh-oh. This could be trouble."

Antonius gave him a silencing glance and turned when the door opened at the girl's knock. Another young girl stood in the doorway, her eyes widening in alarm when she saw Antonius and Flavius. The other girl spoke quickly to her, but Antonius couldn't understand what was being said. Turning, the girl fled back down the street from whence they had appeared.

"We need help," Antonius barked. The girl jumped slightly and disappeared from view. A moment later, the door opened wider and a large man appeared. His beard was white, which told of his age, but his body was large and powerfully built. *Definitely a smith,* Antonius decided.

"What can I do. . .Sara!" He leaped the distance to Antonius's horse, his hands flailing about helplessly. His eyes glared fiercely up at Antonius, who hastened to explain.

"An accident. My friend and I were hunting. . . ." Words suddenly failed him at the look of agony on the old man's face.

Reaching up, he gently took the girl from Antonius's arms.

"Simhah!" he bellowed, and the girl who had answered the door came quickly to his side. Seeing the girl in the old man's arms, Simhah paled.

"Don't just stand there! Make ready a pallet. Get some more water from the well. And have Pisgah run for the healer."

Turning, he strode away without so much as a backward glance. Flavius stepped his mount to Antonius's side.

"Come. Let us leave this accursed place. Her people will take care of her now."

Antonius barely heard him. His eyes were following the old Jew as he disappeared from sight. Whether he liked it or not, he felt compelled to stay. He had to make sure the girl was going to live.

"You go, Flavius. I intend to stay and see this through."

Flavius snorted. "Don't expect gratitude from these people. Like as not, they would just as soon split your throat."

The fierceness returned to Antonius's face. Flavius shook his head. The only time he had ever seen that look on Antonius's face was when he was getting ready to do battle.

"All right," Flavius sighed, "but I stay with you." He looked around him nervously. "I don't trust these people."

Dismounting, both men walked to the door. Flavius hesitated, but Antonius pushed his way forward, ducking his head to enter. When Antonius's eyes adjusted to the dim light, he could make out four figures in the room. There were two sections to the room, which had two floor levels, one about eighteen inches above the ground. It was there they had laid Sara and were bending over her.

The old man turned at their entrance, his shaggy eyebrows ascending toward his still-full hairline. Antonius could see the struggle going on within the man before he finally came toward them.

"Shalom."

Antonius nodded his head. "Peace be with you, also."

If the old man was surprised, he certainly didn't show it. Antonius thought that the man would have made a fine general. His bearing was almost regal.

The woman leaning over the girl turned to him in surprise. She rapidly fired her speech at him. He answered her quietly, but with authority. Her lips set in a grim line. Again she attacked him with her words, and again he answered quietly. There was no doubt she didn't like what her husband had to say. Her angry eyes rested on Antonius and Flavius briefly before she turned and addressed the old Jew again. This time when he answered, his voice rang with his displeasure.

The old woman rose from her place. "Yes, *adon*," she replied scathingly.

"Abigail!" He glanced at her angrily but turned toward the Romans. "Is there something more I can do for you?"

Antonius stepped forward, his eyes going to the girl on the mat. "Her name is Sara?"

The old man nodded, questioning Antonius with his eyes.

Before Antonius could form his next question, another old man arrived. He stopped suddenly, his eyes going wide at the sight of the two soldiers. His wizened face and long sideburns gave him a somewhat comical appearance, similar to a little monkey Antonius had once seen at a bazaar. Sara's father turned to him, motioning toward the still figure on the mat.

Antonius frowned as they began to converse in Aramaic, struggling to follow the words. His ability with the language was very limited since he came in contact with it so seldom. Still, he could understand some of what was being said.

"She will live?" he questioned.

The wizened old Jew glared at him. "It's a good thing you Romans are poor marksmen. A little farther to the left and she would not be alive even now."

"Hold your tongue, old man!" Flavius ordered. "Antonius is one of the finest marksmen in all Rome!"

Wizened brown eyes regarded them curiously. "My mistake," he told them and turned away to rummage in the sack he had brought with him. Pulling herbs from the bag, he concocted a poultice that he placed on the wound.

There was a disturbance at the door, and a young Jewish boy entered, a look of fear contorting his features when he saw the Roman soldiers. There was something vaguely familiar about him to Antonius, but he couldn't quite place him. Ducking his head, the boy turned to leave again.

"Dathan!"

The boy stopped, turning reluctantly toward the old man. He was obviously the son.

"Father."

"Where have you been? We have need of you," the boy's father told him.

"I had things to do."

Antonius watched with interest the sulky expression of the boy and the grim, set lips of his father. Lifting a goatskin bag, the old man handed it to the boy. "Go and get some water from the well."

The boy's eyes sparked with anger. "That's women's work! Send Simhah, or if she can't, send Sara."

The old man threw the goatskin at Dathan, launching into a volley of speech that Antonius had no hope of following. The boy's eyes grew wider, and his glance flew to Sara. His face paled. Taking the goatskin, he turned and fled. Straightening his shoulders, the old man turned to Antonius.

"The healer says that Sara's chances are good if she can make it through the night. She has lost a lot of blood, but she is healthy and strong."

Antonius wasn't sure if the old Jew was trying to convince himself more than

Antonius. Realizing that there was little he could do and that his help wouldn't be appreciated anyway, he prepared to leave. Fixing the man with an imperious eye, he told him, "I will return on the morrow."

All the inhabitants of the room watched in silence as Antonius and Flavius turned to leave. The door shut firmly behind them.

"Whew! I was beginning to wonder if we would get out of there with our lives," Flavius joked.

One dark eyebrow winged upward as Antonius looked him over.

"Surely a soldier of Rome is not afraid of a few old Jews."

Flavius snorted. "The old healer looked like he might be capable of putting a curse on you. The next time you go, be sure you take your shield with you to protect you from the daggers they throw with their eyes."

Mounting their horses, they wheeled around and headed out of the village. Antonius rode silently, his face as black as the thunderclouds that so rarely swept through the region. A tic worked continually in his cheek.

"Come now, Antonius," Flavius cajoled. "For the love of Poseidon, you didn't see the girl. It wasn't your fault."

"I'm a trained soldier. I know better than to launch at a target unless I know what the target is. If I were on the battlefield, it could have been one of my own soldiers." His voice quieted, and Flavius realized that he finally spoke of what truly bothered him. "She couldn't have been any older than Diana."

Flavius regarded him somberly but said nothing. They rode in silence until they reached the outskirts of the city. Flavius eyed Antonius warily, sensing his dark mood.

"Antonius, come to my house tonight. I know just the thing to cheer you up. I'm having a party. Galvus will be there, as well as Lucretius and Ovid." He glanced at Antonius slyly. "Helena will be there, also."

Visions of the fiery redhead came to Antonius's mind, as well as pleasurable memories of Helena's flirtatious manner. That she desired Antonius was all too clear, but something held Antonius back. Sometimes he wondered if she was as helpless as she seemed to be. Of course, this brought thoughts of Diana to mind. Frowning, he turned to Flavius.

"No, my friend. Tonight I will spend with Diana."

Eyes filled with understanding, Flavius nodded. "Then this is where we part. Give Diana my. . .I mean, tell Diana. . .tell her I said hello," he finally finished in a rush. Saluting, he turned his horse about and headed in the opposite direction.

Antonius's dark mood increased. Orion seemed to sense his reluctance and slowed his steps. Tonight he must face Diana. Tomorrow he must face an angry old Jew and, hopefully, a small Jewish girl. Straightening his shoulders, he kicked Orion's sides and hurried home.

Chapter 2

Sara awakened to almost stygian darkness. A strong odor of dill filled her nostrils. She was disoriented, so she lay still trying to remember where she was. What had she been doing? Slowly the events of the morning came back to her. Had it all been a dream? Trying to lift herself from the pallet, she felt an excruciating pain in her left shoulder. Moaning, she lay back. At the noise, a figure rose up beside her, almost frightening her senseless.

"Sara?"

The moon slivered a beam through the little window that was beside the door. Her father appeared within its beam, and even in the semidarkness, she could see the tiredness of his features.

"What happened?" Sara's voice was little more than a whisper. She stared around the room uncomprehendingly, a frown puckering her brow.

"Praise God!" Jubal went down on his knees, almost weeping with relief. He took Sara's hand gently into his large hands, stroking it gently. "You don't remember?"

The frown deepened as Sara tried to remember. She had been at her favorite hiding place, trying to work through some of her problems. The little copse in the woods was where she always went when she had a lot of thinking to do. Then there had been two horsemen. She had been fascinated by their fluid movements on their mounts, never having seen a Roman soldier before. And then the larger of the two had dismounted, and she had leaned closer to see him better. That was the last thing she could remember.

"I was in the woods, and I saw two Romans. Soldiers."

Her father laughed without mirth. "It would seem one of them mistook you for an animal. He shot you with an arrow. Ahaz has been hours attending you. Here, let me light the lamp."

Sara was touched. No one wasted oil at night. It was too precious a commodity. Her father must have been truly worried.

When he had lit the lamp, he brought the stand over and set it beside Sara's mat. He sat down beside her and took her hand once more in his. "You little *aton*," he told her gently. "You could be dead now because of your stubbornness."

Sara smiled slightly at the familiar term that only her father could use as an endearment. To be likened to a donkey was not usually complimentary.

"I have told you to stay close to the village and especially to stay away from the woods, and still you disobey."

The throbbing in Sara's shoulder intensified, and she moaned again. Her mind was becoming fuzzy with the pain, and she was having a hard time understanding what her father was saying. He leaned closer at the sound.

"Your pain is coming back?" He left her side and went across the room, returning with a bowl. Lifting her head gently, he placed the bowl against her lips. "Drink this," he told her.

Her throat felt parched, and she drank greedily.

"Not so much." Pulling the bowl away, he placed it on the floor beside him. He watched as the draught worked its way into her system, and her eyes closed softly. A gentle snore brought a slight smile to his face. As he watched her, his face began to cloud with his thoughts. The Roman said he would return on the morrow. His lips set grimly. Taking the lamp from the stand, he blew it out and felt his way familiarly to his own bed. He frowned. Time enough to deal with that when the situation arrived.

When Sara awakened again, the sun was shining brightly through the little windows of the house. She moved her head slowly, careful not to disturb her shoulder. Her mother was puttering in the kitchen, humming a tune she had heard at Cousin Bashan's wedding ceremony. Sara smiled slightly. Her father must have told her mother that Sara was well. At least as well as could be expected.

Slowly glancing around the room, she noticed her father's absence, as well as Dathan's. Pisgah came in the door quietly, her eyes going toward Sara's mat. A smile brightened her face.

"My lady! Sara is awake!"

Sara's mother whirled around, her face creasing into a smile at the sight of Sara's lively expression. She put down the bowl she was holding and came quickly to Sara's side.

"Daughter? How do you feel this morning?" She placed her hand against Sara's forehead, smiling again. "No fever. Thank God."

Sara reached up with her right hand, taking her mother's hand in her own. They smiled at each other, and Abigail wiped a tear from her eye.

"What do we have here?" Sara's father stood in the doorway, a load of wood in his arms. His smile beamed across to Sara. "My little aton is alive and kicking?"

He walked across the room and laid the wood beside the fire pit before coming back to where his wife stood. Placing an arm around Abigail's shoulders, he gave her a slight squeeze. "I told you, Mother, that God would take care of her."

Abigail smiled mistily up at him. "Indeed you did."

"Let's give thanks," he told them, and Sara closed her eyes as her father praised God for caring for her and asked that He continue to be with her. "In Jesus' name. Amen."

The rest of the day, Sara lay and watched her mother moving about the house.

The connecting door to the shop was open, and she could see her father busily working at the forge. Periodically he would come to the door and smile at her, then return to his business. Sara felt warmed by their love.

Around noon, when Sara thought she would die from boredom, she heard a horse approaching. Not the light donkey hooves of the villagers. This had to be a huge horse, if it fit the sound of the steps. She was just wishing she could get a glimpse of it when the steps stopped outside their door. Sara's mother and father exchanged glances before Abigail hurried to close the front door and then the connecting door to the shop.

Antonius dismounted, smiling wryly when he heard the door close. Looping the reins lightly around a bush, he started for the door. Before he could take more than two steps, the old Jew he had seen yesterday approached him from the side of the house. He said nothing, merely standing there staring at Antonius. There was no expression on his face, nor could Antonius see any in his eyes. He thought again what a fine general the man would make.

"I have come to see Sara," Antonius told him.

"Sara is fine. Except for the healing, which will take time."

"I will see for myself." Though Antonius hadn't raised his voice, the man knew nothing short of a full-scale war would deter him from his course. He stood silently, eyeing Antonius warily. Nodding his head, he turned and headed for the front door. Antonius quickly followed him.

Although he was not in uniform, Antonius was a commanding presence. Pisgah's eyes widened as he ducked his head and entered. Seeing her distress, Abigail handed her a jar.

"Go and fetch some water from the well."

The girl fled, glancing furtively over her shoulder.

Antonius's eyes went immediately to the mat in the corner. He could see the girl, Sara, staring at him with curious eyes. There was no fear in her countenance. He walked quickly to her side and stared down at her. Her face was pale, her dark hair matted around her shoulders. Only her large, dark eyes seemed to be alive. Antonius wondered briefly what the girl would look like cleaned and dressed properly, not in the brown color she seemed to favor.

"Hello," Antonius said softly, afraid of frightening her.

"Shalom," she told him. She stared at him, a slight frown puckering her forehead. "I have seen you somewhere before."

Before he could answer, her father stepped between them. "This is the soldier who shot you."

Antonius frowned at him but turned his eyes back to Sara. "It was an accident. I thought you were a deer. Your brown tunic. . ."

Sara nodded understandingly. "I was in the bushes where I ought not to have been. It was forbidden to me, and yet. . .I disobeyed." Her eyes pleaded with her father for forgiveness. His answering look assured Antonius, at least, that he would forgive the girl anything.

It was bad manners to ask, but Antonius was determined to stay, for a while at least. "May I sit?"

Abigail was affronted, but short of being rude, she had no choice. Taking a stool, she placed it next to him. Ignoring her outraged look, Antonius placed it closer to Sara. The stool was too little for Antonius's large frame, and he realized that this was done deliberately. Irritated, nevertheless he smiled with charm at Abigail. She blinked her eyes and turned away.

Antonius stared at Sara, his eyes going all over her and returning to her face. "I can hardly believe it." He shook his head wonderingly. "I thought for sure. . ."

Sara smiled gently. "That I would be dead?"

A flush spread across Antonius's face, but he merely nodded. "I have never seen such a quick recovery."

"Jewish healers have much knowledge of the body. They also have a secret weapon."

Antonius knew he was being baited, but he took it anyway. "What is this secret weapon?"

Sara smiled at him. "God."

Antonius leaned back and looked at her wryly. "Which god?"

Sara looked at him with wide, innocent eyes. "There is only one God."

Rather than get into a philosophical discussion with her, Antonius changed the subject. "How many are in your family?"

Smiling knowingly, Sara told him.

"And your brother?" The Roman was searching the room with his eyes, and Sara began to feel uneasy. Her mother must be having the same reaction, because Sara could see the knife she was using to cut the vegetables shaking in her hand. Her father had gone back to his workshop but kept them within sight.

"I know your mother's name is Abigail and yours is Sara and your father's is Adon, but what of your brother?"

"What makes you think that my father's name is Adon?" Sara asked in surprise.

"The day I brought you home—yesterday—I heard your mother call him that."

A hand to her mouth quickly covered Sara's mirth, but her eyes were alight with laughter. Antonius wasn't sure what he had said to cause her response, but the smile made the girl almost pretty.

"I take it I've said something wrong?"

Still smiling, Sara answered. "*Adon* is a Hebrew word for 'master.' My mother only uses it when she wants to irritate my father."

"Oh."

"Many Jewish women call their husbands *adon* or *baal*."

"And *baal* means?"

"Lord," she told him and watched his eyebrows lift to his dark hairline. "My father's name is Jubal Barjonah," she told him proudly.

"The way your mother said the word, I assume she didn't mean it as a term of obeisance?"

Sara shook her head. "My father doesn't wish to be called lord or master. He says there is only one Lord and one Master. My mother knows this, but. . ."

"I know. Just to irritate."

Sara nodded.

"And who is this Lord and Master?" Antonius wanted to know.

Antonius and Sara jumped when an urn clattered to the floor. Abigail leaned over to pick up the pot, giving Sara a warning look. The look was not lost on Antonius. His glance flicked from one to the other.

Turning back to Sara, he waited for an answer. Sara's eyes reluctantly met his. She was not ashamed of the answer, but her impetuosity may have endangered her family.

"His name is Jesus," she told him softly.

Sudden comprehension dissolved the rising suspicions in his mind. *Christians.* He glanced around at each of the occupants. No wonder they were so closed and suspicious. He had heard of the persecution of Christians. As yet it had mainly been local and between the different sects of the Jews. If this man was a Jewish Christian, then most of this village must be, also. Many Jews had moved to Ephesus because they could no longer trade with the Jewish community. Christians were as avidly hated by the Jews as they were by the Romans.

Nodding his head, his eyes made one more circuit of the room and returned to Sara. "I told my sister about you. She said she hopes the gods favor you with health." Sara frowned, and he hurried to continue. "I will tell her that your God has done so."

Antonius could tell the girl was beginning to tire, so he quickly got to his feet. Her eyes flew upward to his, and he looked searchingly into them, seeking he knew not what. He realized that even with the animosity of her parents, she had shown him nothing but kindness. He also realized that, for a while, he had been able to forget some of his own troubles. There was something about her. Something soothing. Relaxing.

"I am glad that you are better. I am also very glad that I didn't. . ." He hesitated before turning and striding to the door. He nodded his head to Abigail and Jubal before ducking and disappearing outside.

Sara strained to listen, waiting for the sound of the horse's hooves that would signal his departure. She felt an emptiness as she heard him ride away. Strange. What could a Roman mean to her? Sighing, she drifted off to sleep.

It was several weeks before Sara was back to her full strength. Her shoulder still pained her somewhat, but she had healed well. She never returned to the copse in the woods, and the Roman never returned to see her. Looking up at the vivid blue of the sky, Sara had to smile. She swung the empty water bag, glad to take from Pisgah the chore of fetching the water. Of course, Pisgah enjoyed the opportunity to gossip with her friends, but the job itself was a tedious one.

Since the well was on the outskirts of the village, one could easily see the main road from its location. As Sara drew the bucket up, she noticed a column of dust rising from the road in the distance. *Roman soldiers.* Her heart leaped foolishly in response. She couldn't imagine the Roman coming with a squad of troops. Realizing that it would not be good for her to be caught here, she quickly filled the bag and hurried home.

Her father was grinding a sickle when she peeked her head in his shop. "There's a group of Roman soldiers heading this way. About twenty, I would say."

Jubal left his grinding wheel and joined his daughter at the door.

"They're still a ways off."

"Could be passing through," her father told her absently. "Find Dathan."

"Yes, Father." Sara hurried to the fields where she found her brother. His tools lay beside him, and he was lying on the ground, staring up at the sky.

"Father wants you," she told him.

Dathan jumped, getting quickly to his feet. "Now what?"

Sara hurried after him, reaching the house only seconds after Dathan. Since her mother was still at the weaving loom, Sara assumed her father hadn't mentioned the soldiers. Still, Jubal came frequently to the living rooms with one excuse or another.

Just when Sara had breathed a sigh of relief, there came a pounding on the door.

Chapter 3

Jubal glanced around the room before going to the door and opening it. His face paled when he found himself confronting a Roman soldier. Behind the soldier stood several other soldiers, the feathers in their helmets quivering in the breeze.

"Is this the house of Jubal Barjonah?"

"Yes." Jubal looked in confusion from one soldier to another. "What can I do for you?"

Sara felt a lump form in her throat. It must have been because she had told the Roman that they were Christians. Her heart started thumping erratically, sudden fear for her family almost overwhelming her.

Slowly the soldier unrolled a scroll. His eyes quickly surveyed the occupants of the room before he started to read.

"This house and all of its possessions are hereby confiscated in the name of Callus Phibeas, soldier of Rome, in payment of the debt owed to him by one Dathan Barjubal."

Dathan leaped to his feet, his eyes darting to and fro, seeking a means of escape. Finding none, he turned pleadingly to his father.

"I didn't mean to!" He fell on his knees before Jubal. "Please!" He glanced up at his father, his voice becoming angry. "It was a trick!"

Until that moment, Jubal had hope that this was some kind of mistake. That hope faded fast in light of his son's behavior.

"My son, what have you done?" There was no fear in the strong voice, only a desire to know the truth.

Dathan hung his head, his hands clenching and unclenching at his sides. His voice was barely a murmur that Sara had to strain to hear.

"A gambling debt."

A sternness settled over Jubal's visage. He turned to the soldier. "How much?"

The Roman laughed, a mercenary light coming to his eyes. "More than you have, old man."

"How much?"

The smile left the soldier's face at the lack of respect in the old man's attitude. Handing Jubal the document, the soldier smirked when he saw the old Jew pale, his eyes widening in alarm.

"But that's impossible!" Jubal turned to his son. "How is this possible?"

"This property is hereby confiscated and will be sold to pay the debt." The soldier smiled a malicious smile. "Including all the residents and servants of this residence."

The look that passed through Jubal's eyes caused the soldier to step back hastily. Turning, he snapped his fingers. "Take them," he commanded, and the guards moved forward as one.

Sara knew her father would be a match for any two men, but when five fell upon him, she knew he had no hope of winning. Everywhere was chaos. Pisgah and Simhah were being led outside in shackles, fear contorting their features.

Dathan tried to flee, but a huge Roman soldier slammed his fist into the side of Dathan's head, sending him sprawling senseless to the floor. Abigail screamed, clinging to Sara. A soldier reached for Sara, leg irons dangling from his fingers. For the first time, the horror of the moment penetrated her shocked senses. She pushed her mother toward the door.

"Run!" she screamed, pain tearing through her scalp as a soldier grabbed her hair and jerked her backward. She knew it was useless to fight, but she had to try. The soldier grinned down into her face as another soldier applied the shackle to her ankle.

Sara was led outside where her mother was bent weeping over the prostrate figure of her father. He was bound hand and foot, lying semiconscious on the ground. Blood dripped from his head and his mouth, a large bruise beginning to swell his eye.

Abigail was crying softly, while Dathan moaned, his face buried in his hands. Sara watched helplessly while the soldiers ransacked their home. She began to plead with God for their salvation, never expecting it to come in the form of a tall Roman on a large white horse.

Antonius paused, his brow furrowing. Kicking his horse forward, he pulled to a stop at the entrance to the house just as a tapestry flew out the door, barely missing the horse. Orion reared, and it took all of Antonius's skills as a horseman to stay seated astride the frightened beast. By the time he had regained control, the leader of the soldiers was at his side.

"What goes on here?" Antonius roared with anger, his voice quivering in his wrath.

The soldier paled considerably, his Adam's apple moving rapidly up and down. "Tribune! I'm sorry! We didn't see you here." He tried to take hold of Orion's bridle, and the horse lashed out with his teeth, barely missing the man's fingers.

Reaching down to calm the high-strung horse, Antonius's eyes circled the yard, coming to rest on Jubal and his family. Sara was gently helping her father to his feet.

"You haven't answered my question, Soldier. What is going on here?"

Motioning to Dathan, the soldier explained about the gambling debt. "Since he can't pay it, I have been ordered to confiscate this property and all of its occupants."

Antonius arched an eyebrow. "The debt is that large?"

Handing Antonius the scroll, the soldier waited for permission to continue. Instead, Antonius handed the document back. His gaze rested on Sara a moment, a sudden glitter entering his eyes. Reaching into a bag on his saddle, he pulled out a smaller bag, its contents jingling slightly. He motioned the soldier over and thrust the bag into his hand. The soldier lifted puzzled eyes to Antonius.

"Payment of the debt," Antonius told him.

"Sir?" The soldier was beginning to doubt the tribune's sanity, but he didn't dare question him further.

"I am buying this property."

Jerking his head up in surprise, the soldier opened his mouth and then closed it again. "But, Tribune. . .an auction. . .these are not. . .my orders." He stopped, unable to go on.

"Whose orders?"

"Callus Phibeas."

Antonius stared at him until the soldier dropped his eyes. "Since when has Callus had enough rank to issue orders?"

Flushing angrily, the soldier lifted his head. "It's a signed, legal debt."

"Agreed. And now the debt has been paid," Antonius told him, his voice laced with steel. "Should Callus have any questions, send him to me." The last four words, uttered in such a tone, caused the soldier to swallow hard. As the soldier turned to go, Antonius stopped him.

"Wait. What is your name?"

Lifting his chin, the soldier turned to answer. "Marcus Trajan."

Antonius nodded. "Marcus, see that Dathan is sent to the galleys."

A moan caused Antonius to turn his head. Dathan was on his knees, rocking back and forth in the sand. Sara's pleading brown eyes caught his attention. Tightening his lips, he turned back to Marcus. "You have your orders."

"Yes, Tribune." Still, the soldier hesitated. "What of the others?"

"Release them."

Remembering the battle between five of his finest men and the old Jew, Marcus was hesitant. "But. . ."

"I said, release them."

Marcus motioned to the two soldiers nearest him, who hastened to obey. Antonius Severus was a wealthy and powerful nobleman, not to mention a tribune of Rome's army. Let Callus deal with him, if he had a mind to. As for Marcus, he hoped he never found himself in such a predicament again.

They released all except Dathan, who was still sobbing on his knees in the sand. The soldiers hauled him to his feet and led him screaming away.

Sara felt her heart start to pound when Antonius's eyes fastened on her.

"Get your things together. You're coming with me."

"No!" Jubal stepped forward, placing himself between his daughter and the Roman. His huge hands clenched into fists, but Antonius was unmoved.

"Hear me, Jubal Barjonah. You have a wife to worry about. See to her and leave Sara to me."

Jubal's face turned red with rage, and Antonius knew that if he couldn't calm the man, someone might get killed.

"Listen to me, Jubal, for Abigail and Sara's sake." Antonius could see the old man struggling for control, and he continued. "I have need of Sara. I believe she can help me with my sister. I know you are angry about Dathan, but he brought his problems on himself. I will not explain my actions to you in this regard. I am taking Sara with me, but you need have no fear for her safety. I do not beat my slaves."

"It is not beating that concerns me."

Antonius was taken aback by the man's forthrightness. A sardonic smile touched his lips as his eyes raked Sara from head to toe. Sara squirmed under his perusal, feeling like a lamb that was found wanting.

"You have no need to fear on that score, either. I have a preference for voluptuous blonds, not skinny Jews."

Sara felt her anger beginning to rise. Realizing that she was in a precarious position and could further hurt her parents, she swallowed down the hurt the tribune's words had caused her.

Antonius stared hard at Jubal. "We will speak again, but right now, I have more pressing matters to attend to."

Jubal was torn, standing rigidly in front of Antonius. His eyes flashed fire that ignited an answering spark in Antonius's.

"Have it your own way." Antonius snapped his fingers, and several of the guards stepped forward.

"Wait!" Sara flung herself forward, laying a pleading hand upon her father's arm. "I will go with him."

Jubal stared into Antonius's face. Not so much as a muscle twitch revealed any of the Roman's thoughts.

"What of us?" Jubal finally managed to ask.

Antonius gazed levelly into Jubal's worried eyes. "This property belongs to me now, as do you." He nodded his head toward Abigail and the servants. "As do they." Sara couldn't miss the note of warning in his voice. "Take care of this property as though it were your own, and if Sara serves me well, someday it will be again."

A puzzled look passed between Sara and her father. Antonius sighed impatiently. He laid a hand on Jubal's shoulder and felt the old man stiffen at his touch.

"I don't want your house or you or your servants. I have plenty of my own. But

I have need of her." He nodded his head at Sara. "I promise you I will take care of her and that no harm will come to her while she is with me." He placed his hand on the eagle crest of his shield, the crest that represented Rome. "On my honor as a Roman soldier."

Although Jubal had no faith in Roman soldiers, or their oaths, somehow he believed this one. *He would make a good Jew,* Jubal thought. *Strong. Fierce.*

Sara went quickly to get her few possessions. Her eyes filled with tears as she realized that this could very well be the last time she ever saw her family again. Looking around the rooms where she had known so much happiness brought a lump to her throat. *Please, God,* she thought, *take care of them.*

Antonius spoke to her father for several minutes before he mounted his horse again. Had he told her father what was to become of Dathan? When Sara returned to his side, her bundle of clothes under her arm, Antonius reached down and lifted her to the saddle in front of him. A familiar feeling washed over Sara as he wrapped his arms around her and lifted the reins. Touching his feet to the horse's sides, they leaped forward. When Sara looked back, she saw her father and mother in each other's arms. Her father looked frail with his grief. Sara had never seen him that way before, and she felt his pain as her own. Turning around, she kept her eyes forward.

They rode in silence for some time before Sara finally dared to ask a question. "Tribune?"

She regretted questioning him when he leaned forward to hear her, his cheek brushing against hers. Her heart jumped, and her breathing became shallow.

"Yes?"

Swallowing her fear, her voice came out hesitantly. "My brother, Dathan. Must he be sent to the galleys?"

Antonius leaned back and looked down at the girl in front of him. All he could see was the brown silk of her tresses hanging long and straight in front of him. He was almost tempted to run the strands through his fingers. Bringing his thoughts up short, he tried to answer her question without hurting her. He had remembered where he had seen Dathan before, after he left her home. In Ephesus, at the legionnaires' headquarters. Gambling with the soldiers.

"Your brother has a lesson to learn," he told her calmly. "I have seen your brother when he gambles."

Sara jerked her head around in surprise. Antonius stared down into her large brown eyes for several seconds. "Oh yes, Sara." The huskiness of his voice caused a fluttering in the pit of her stomach. "He has the sickness. When he gambles, nothing else matters. Not you. Not your family. Not anything."

"But he's only a boy," she told him softly.

She watched as his eyes dilated to black obsidian. He snorted, and Sara turned away, unable to withstand the scorn she saw in his face.

"When I was his age, I had already joined the Roman legion and saw my first battle."

Orion shifted beneath him, and Antonius took a moment to adjust his position, pulling Sara more securely against him.

"Because of Dathan, your family has lost everything and are slaves of a Roman. You are here with me now, not knowing what I have planned for you." Antonius could feel her breathing deepen and almost laughed aloud. "I would have died before I let such shame come upon my family."

"Perhaps so," Sara agreed. "But I fail to see how the galleys will accomplish anything. It can't change what has already transpired." There were tears in her voice, though she held her body rigidly erect, and he could not see her face.

"Some of my soldiers have had the same sickness," he told her roughly, not unmoved by the tears. "The only cure for them is to get them as far away from the temptation as possible. There will be no time to think of such foolishness where your brother is going, and maybe it will help him to realize just what he has lost."

Sara thought of her brother in the bowels of a ship, day in and day out, never seeing the sun. Every day, rowing, rowing. Chained to others doing the same. Her heart cried out with the pain, and tears flowed freely down her cheeks. *Poor Dathan.* So full of life. So impetuous. What would become of him? For that matter, what would become of her?

She could see Ephesus laid out before her as they slowly approached the city. She had only been here twice with her family, even though they lived close. Instead of excitement as she had felt before, she felt only dread. Somewhere down there among the ports, her brother was being chained in a hold. Somewhere down there was her future, but the only future she could see was filled with sorrow. Without realizing it, she leaned her head back against Antonius's chest.

The sudden warmth of Sara's body against his brought Antonius's thoughts sharply back to the present. It suddenly came to Antonius just what she must be going through. The fear she must be feeling. The thought of someone doing something so barbarous to Diana almost made his blood boil. He felt a moment's guilt until he realized that he had done all of this for Diana. Pulling Sara tighter against him, he tried to let her know that she was safe. He had snatched her from her home and family, sent her brother to the galleys, purchased her home in less than ethical circumstances, and yet through it all she had maintained her composure. She certainly had no reason to trust him. Suddenly he felt very protective.

"You have nothing to be afraid of, Sara," he whispered in her ear and felt her shiver. Mistaking the response, he pressed his lips tightly together. He decided he needed to give her time. He remembered the time he had spent in her company. For the past several weeks, his thoughts had returned to her from time to time, wishing at times that he could be in her presence. Just being around her had brought peace to his troubled soul, if only momentarily. When Diana's condition had worsened, he remembered the healer who had treated Sara. Although he had some of the finest physicians in Rome attending to Diana, they had been able to do nothing. Desperate, Antonius had decided to seek the healer out. Instead, he had come away with Sara. In time she would see what he needed her for, and maybe, just maybe, she could help Diana. Firmly he pushed the guilt feelings aside and tried not to think too much about the future.

Chapter 4

Antonius led his horse through the backstreets of Ephesus, bypassing any would-be gossips. He went through large wooden gates set inside six-foot-high concrete walls that surrounded his outer garden. A servant was waiting when he stopped his mount, taking the reins from Antonius, who had to smile. Only Gallus could handle the huge stallion, and he no more than a boy of fourteen. They had forged a bond between them, precipitated by the boy's love of anything equine.

Sliding from the saddle, Antonius reached up, placing his hands around Sara's tiny waist and helping her to dismount. He patted Orion before releasing him to the boy's custody. "Be sure he is fed, watered, and brushed down." Antonius knew he didn't need to remind the boy, but it was part of a long-standing game the two played. As usual, the boy's lips pushed out in a pout and he told the horse, "One day I will take you away from such a mean master."

Sara's eyes widened in shock. She glanced at Antonius, only to find him grinning at the boy. Realizing that this interplay between the two was not serious, she smiled slightly. It was good to know that Antonius had a sense of humor and treated his slaves like people instead of like dogs.

Glancing around her, Sara was awed by the large villa. Huge Doric columns rose majestically upward, ending at a roofline that gave the front entrance a spatial elegance. Antonius led her through the open door into the atrium, where the bright light of the afternoon sun shone through the opening in the ceiling. Brightly colored wall paintings and cold marble floor tiles decorated the room. Sara had never experienced such wealth in her life, even though among the Jews, her father was considered a wealthy man.

Antonius watched her silently, knowing that whatever the circumstances, she would find a way to adjust. "Come, Sara," he told her. "I will show you around while I explain certain things to you."

She regarded him soberly. "About your sister?"

He nodded. "That and other things."

They went through a large doorway supported by Composite columns into the peristyle. A fountain tinkled in the center of the courtyard, surrounded by trees, shrubs, and flowers. The color and beauty almost took Sara's breath away. Sunlight spilled through a large opening in the ceiling. Leading her to a bench near the fountain, Antonius motioned for her to sit.

"Anyone who resides at this house is welcome to use the peristyle, but only if the area is not being utilized for some reason." He motioned toward the other end of the courtyard, and Sara could see another garden through another opening.

"That is the fruit and vegetable garden. You are allowed there anytime."

Sara understood. With each word he uttered, she felt more and more the shackles of bondage. He made very clear the differences between them.

Sitting down next to her, Antonius picked a flower and began to slowly pull it apart. "My sister is dying," he told her, and Sara could hear the pain in his voice. "The doctors say there is nothing more that can be done." He sighed in frustration. He looked at Sara before he turned his attention back to the flower, dropping a petal on the ground. "They're not even sure what ails her."

Sara's eyes clouded with sympathy. "I'm sorry."

Antonius turned to her and smiled wryly. "Are you? After all that I've done? Why should you care about a Roman?"

Taking her time before answering, Sara looked up at the sky through the opening in the ceiling and stared pensively at the feathery clouds drifting above them. Oh, to be on the hillsides watching the sheep graze, their soft bleating echoing across the knolls.

"It is true that I have no love for the Romans," she told him softly. "But neither do I hate them."

Antonius watched her, his eyes sliding from the straight dark hair, across skin bronzed by the sun, to the sandals on her feet. His gaze returned to her face and rested there. She had a flawless complexion and shimmering brown eyes that seemed to see into his soul. She could not be called beautiful, even by her own countrymen's standards. Still, there was something that caused a person to want to be close to her. A gentleness. A peacefulness that seemed to come from within.

He noticed again the sheen of her dark skin. No Roman woman would be caught dead with skin of such a color. It seemed too plebeian. Roman women took pains to make sure that their skin was creamy and white. Antonius found the contrast rather stimulating. Shaking his head, he turned away.

"Come. I will introduce you to my sister."

Standing, he helped Sara to her feet, which she found rather disconcerting. He held her hand a moment longer than necessary, though Sara could tell it was without conscious thought. Letting go of her hand, he brushed a hand through his dark hair, breathing out a long sigh.

"Sara, I need to explain something to you. I brought you here not only to be a servant—I already have more than I can use—but to be a friend. A companion for my sister." He stared into her eyes, willing her to understand. "She's very lonely. It's harder for her than most because for so long she was the toast of Ephesus, even at her age. She had many friends and plenty of them men. Now, no one comes to see her, except perhaps my friend Flavius."

He could tell by her puzzled expression that she didn't understand what he was trying to say. He tried again. "People in Ephesus are concerned with their health. We have an abundance of physicians to attend to their needs, but they have a tendency to fear what they cannot understand."

Sara looked up suddenly, catching the intent look of Antonius's eyes. Hers were filled with comprehension. "Is your sister's illness contagious?"

"No."

"You know that for certain?"

"Yes," he told her adamantly. "No one else in this house has been ill, nor I for that matter, and Diana has been ill for some time. Ever since. . ."

He stopped suddenly, and Sara wondered what he had been about to say.

"Come. I will introduce you, then we will talk again."

Sara followed him up the staircase that led to a balcony above. He stopped outside a door and tapped gently.

"Come." The voice was muted, but sadness laced the one word.

Antonius opened the door and went inside, Sara close on his heels. The room was darkened against the afternoon sun. A figure reclined on the bed, but it was too dark to tell much about it. Sara assumed that it was Diana.

"Antonius!"

A thrill ran through Sara at the intensity of the greeting. Happiness, longing, and desperation, all rolled into one. It was obvious that Antonius was Diana's whole existence.

Diana buried her face in her hands and started weeping softly. "Oh, Antonius! Where have you been? I called and called, but Decimus said you had gone."

Antonius went to her and gathered her gently in his arms. Diana clung to him as he tried to soothe her distress. Sara felt a lump in her own throat. What must Diana's life be like that a visit from her own brother was what she longed for with every fiber of her being?

"Come now, little dove," he remonstrated softly. "You'll make yourself ill. Dry your eyes and see what I have brought for you."

The sobbing stopped instantly, but Sara could see the sheen in the eyes lifted to Antonius's face.

"What have you brought me?"

The childlike cadence of the voice were all the more surprising when a servant came in and pulled back the drapes from the window, and Sara could see the figure in the bed for the first time. Blond hair, the color of the sun in the afternoon, was matted around a porcelain white face that had to be at least as old as Sara. Blue eyes that were almost violet turned to regard Sara.

Antonius motioned Sara into the room. "I have brought you a companion." At Diana's startled look, he continued. "Now you need never be alone again."

Sara felt her heart sink. Was she to be the slave of a lonely, ill girl who had nothing to live for, it would seem, except her brother? Sara felt compassion for the girl but wondered if she, too, would be required to stay in a dark bedroom all day. Flicking her eyes around the room, Sara was conscious of marble tables, chests carved from cedar, and silk draperies that bespoke of wealth and luxury. A gilded prison, but a prison nevertheless. She chastised herself for her selfishness. What would Jesus have her do? With the question came peace. She would do whatever she could to make Diana's days happier.

Diana opened her mouth to say something but stopped. She turned to Sara, and a sudden smile lit up her features. Sara felt a twinge of envy. With her hair combed and dressed properly, Diana would be remarkably beautiful. Diana's eyes took on an animation of their own.

"Hello." Her voice had brightened considerably. Sara searched her eyes and found only warm friendliness. She returned the girl's smile and felt something pass between them.

"I know we will be friends," Diana told her, and Sara believed her, relaxing visibly.

Antonius watched the exchange with satisfaction. He had done the right thing. He knew it now, though he felt a slight pang when he remembered Abigail's face as he had ridden away with her daughter. Arrogance quickly resurfaced. What did it matter? They were only Jews, while he as a Roman soldier had a job to do. He had been on the brink of a decision that would have altered his life completely. Now he felt like he could postpone what he considered to be the inevitable. Someday he would have to resign his commission in the legion to stay home and be with Diana. How much longer she had, he didn't know, and his heart sank when he thought of life without her. Every time he had been sent away, when he returned, he found Diana much worse than when he had left. It would take weeks to get her back to normal. At least as normal as possible in her circumstances.

Releasing Diana from his arms, Antonius rose from the bed. "I will leave you two to get to know each other. I have some things that need my attention."

Diana clung to his hand, staring imploringly up into his face.

"It's all right," he told her quietly. "I will be in the office. I have to go over the shipping lists with Abijah. I will be close by if you need me."

Reluctantly Diana released his hand. When Antonius reached the door, he turned back to Sara. "I will speak to you later, after Diana is settled for the night."

Sara nodded, swallowing hard when the door closed behind him. She turned to Diana, who was watching her curiously.

"You are not Roman. Nor Greek for that matter."

"No," Sara explained. "I am Jewish."

"Ah. A slave?" she questioned.

Sara hesitated. "I suppose you could say so."

Diana quirked an eyebrow and looked remarkably like her brother. "You're not sure?"

Again Sara hesitated. "I consider no man my master."

Diana's eyebrows flew upward, her mouth quirking with humor. "It's obvious you've never had a lover."

Color suffused Sara's face. Thinking carefully before answering, she finally told Diana, "No. That is true. But that is not what I meant. Actually, what I meant to say is that I already have a master."

"Of course you do, silly. Antonius."

"No." Sara was being drawn into a conversation she didn't think she was ready for. Somehow, this did not seem the right time. "I serve my God."

"Oh!" Diana relaxed. "Is that all? Which one?"

"To the Jews, there is only one."

Diana wrinkled her nose. "Sounds boring to me. But it doesn't really matter. I no longer believe in deities anyway. I have asked healing from them all, paid a large sum of money, even, and still nothing." She settled herself back on the bed, her face filled with despair. "You may serve your God, Sara. I suppose it doesn't hurt to have faith in something." The desolation in her voice convinced Sara that there was nothing left for Diana to believe in. In time, perhaps Sara could share God's love with her. Even the apostle Paul had shared the good news with the Romans. Could she do any less?

"My lady," Sara asked hesitantly. "Would you like me to dress your hair?"

Diana turned her head lethargically on the pillow. "What for? There's no one to see me."

Sudden inspiration made Sara pause. "There's Tribune Antonius."

Diana thought about it. She supposed that with everything Antonius did for her, the least she could do was look presentable. It had been a long while since she had cared anything about her looks. Antonius would love her anyway, but still some measure of pride returned to her.

"Yes, Sara. That would be good. Have Decimus bring some water."

Sara smiled. "Yes, my lady." When Sara opened the door, she found a young man waiting outside. He quickly got to his feet. Although he was young, his handsome features bespoke of early manhood. His short white tunic showed to perfection his strong, muscular body. Blond hair shimmered in the afternoon sun, and his clear blue eyes regarded her expectantly. Sara assumed that he was required to stay there in case Diana needed anything.

"You wish for something?" he asked quickly.

"I need water to wash my lady's hair." The boy's eyes lit up, and it was clear to Sara that Diana was liked by the boy. "Can you find me some fragrance for the rinse water, and some olive oil?"

"Right away, my lady." He turned and hurried away.

Sara went back into the room. "Where are the brushes, my lady?"

Diana frowned at her. "You needn't call me 'my lady.' I don't want you to seem just another servant. I want us to be friends. Call me Diana."

Refusing to consider what the tribune might think of such an arrangement, Sara nodded. Diana motioned to the dressing table. "You'll find the brushes and things over there."

A tap at the door signaled the return of Decimus with the water. He went to the corner and set the urn next to a small marble tub. Going to the door, he turned. "If there is anything else, I am right outside." He closed the door quietly behind him.

Sara went to Diana and helped her to sit up in bed. Taking the brush, Sara began to gently stroke Diana's hair, starting at the bottom and working her way up. Eventually her hair was free of tangles. Although Diana's hair was long, it was thin and dull, an obvious sign of ill health. Sara had done her best to make sure she didn't hurt the girl, knowing that her head would be sensitive after such a long period without care. Since Sara found no evidence of lice, she assumed that someone had washed Diana's hair before, or maybe her sickness hadn't been that long.

Pulling a chair carved from Lebanon cedar over to the marble tub, Sara prepared to wash Diana's hair. She kept up a constant flow of chatter that required little effort on Diana's part but helped her to relax.

Sara helped Diana to the seat and began to gently wash her hair. She rinsed it with clear water that turned a dirty brown as it flowed through Diana's hair. Deciding to wash it several times, Sara had to first ask Decimus to bring more water.

When the rinse water finally ran clear, Sara took a towel and began to pat the hair dry. She poured a measure of oil from the cruse and began to massage it into Diana's scalp. As she worked her fingers through Diana's hair, she began to hum a tune that her mother had sung to her as a child. The soothing melody helped Diana relax, and soon she closed her eyes.

"That feels wonderful, Sara. I don't know why I never bothered before."

Taking the brush, Sara first washed it in some water before using it to brush out Diana's hair again. Finally her golden tresses lay curling against her back, the olive oil giving it extra shine.

"Would you like to change outfits, my. . .Diana? This one is a little wet."

Submitting patiently to Sara's ministrations, it wasn't long before Diana was settled back against the pillows on her sleeping couch. Sara decided that enough had been done for one day. Diana was tired, but already she looked like a changed girl. A feeling of accomplishment engulfed Sara. Given time, Sara knew she could come to love this unhappy Roman girl.

The soft, regular breathing told Sara that Diana was asleep. Taking Diana's soiled tunic, she went to the window and pulled the drapes a little. Enough to keep out most of the light, but not enough to give it the tomblike appearance it had before.

Opening the door, she found Decimus waiting expectantly.

"Could you empty the water?" she asked him, and he nodded his head, going past her and into the room. Picking up the tub, he started to pass Sara, his eyes quickly surveying the sleeping figure. A smile crossed his lips fleetingly.

"What do I do with the soiled tunic?" she asked.

He turned his look full upon Sara. "Just leave it by the door on the balcony. I will see to it. The master wanted to see you when his sister fell asleep." His eyes went back to the bed. "She doesn't stay awake very long at a time. She's very weak. What you've accomplished today is a miracle."

Following him back down the stone balustrade, Sara wondered if perhaps he might be right. Had her Lord sent her here for a purpose? Like Paul who was in chains himself and still managed to win most of the household of Caesar to the Lord? The thought was disturbing. And what of the tribune? What part did he have to play in all of this drama? The house seemed suddenly sinister. There was much of the evil one at work here, but praying to the Lord helped to push back the darkness. For the time being, she would be a light in this house. She would try not to be afraid, and she would try her best to show the Way to these infidels. Already she was beginning to love one. She prayed fervently that she would not love the other.

Chapter 5

Sara entered the bibliotheca behind Decimus. She stared around her at the large number of papyrus scrolls that rested in cubicles in the walls. Manuscripts seemed to be on every available surface. Sara had heard of such libraries before but had never seen one.

Antonius was leaning over a table when they entered. He straightened up and motioned Sara forward. His eyes were questioning, so Sara answered him. "Diana is asleep."

He nodded. "And? What did you think?"

"She seems very fragile and lonely. Other than that, I know very little."

Decimus interrupted. "My lady allowed her to wash her hair. And she changed her tunic, also."

Antonius looked at Sara in surprise. "How did you manage this?"

Sara shrugged. "I merely suggested it."

"I have suggested this also, but she has never done it for me," Antonius told her.

"Perhaps you didn't have the right incentive," Sara told him mysteriously.

"And that is?"

Even Decimus seemed intrigued, waiting for her to answer.

"I only suggested that she might wish to look nice for you, Tribune."

Antonius felt humbled by Diana's love, but he was also filled with exhilaration. Sara had managed to do in a few hours what he and the other servants hadn't been able to do in months. Fortune had smiled upon him when she led him to Sara that day. He would have to arrange a sacrifice to the gods. Perhaps Fortuna, goddess of luck.

He turned to Decimus. "From now on, when Sara is with Diana, you no longer need to wait outside her door. But when Sara needs something, be prepared for her call."

"Yes, my lord."

Decimus and Antonius exchanged glances, smiling at each other before the boy left the room. Sara watched him depart.

"Decimus. . . Is he a slave, also?"

Antonius felt uncomfortable. "Yes." The short, clipped word told Sara that he would say nothing more on the subject. If Sara wanted to know anything more about Decimus, she would have to find out from Decimus himself.

Rolling up the papyrus he had been examining, Antonius used it as an excuse to turn away from Sara's accusing eyes. Her censure bothered him, but she asked him a different question from what he was expecting.

"When did Diana become sick? Was she visiting out of the country?"

Antonius shook his head. "No."

He seemed disinclined to speak further, so Sara pressed harder. "It would help me, Tribune, to know how to deal with her sickness. What do the doctors say?"

He waited so long to answer that Sara thought he wasn't going to. Finally he looked at her angrily. "They say she is under some kind of curse from the gods."

"That's it? That's all they say?"

Antonius nodded his head. Putting away the last scroll, he motioned to the doorway. "Let's go into the atrium where it's cooler, and I will try to explain things."

Sara followed him through the doorway and into the atrium. For the first time, she noticed the scenes depicted on the wall hangings. Various gods played among the heavens and the earth, while people gave offerings. Other scenes depicted the battles of the Roman army. Sara shivered with distaste. Noticing her response, Antonius hid a smile.

"Perhaps the peristyle would be better."

Sara followed him through the marble portals to the seat beside the fountain. He motioned for her to be seated, but he stood before her, trying to gather his thoughts.

"Almost a year ago, my sister was engaged to a Roman noble. They were very much in love, but shortly after their engagement party, he was killed when a horse threw him. He was a friend of mine, also." He stopped, and Sara watched his eyes glaze over at the remembered pain. "For a time, Diana refused to see anyone. Even me. She hid in her bedroom and would scream if anyone so much as tried to come near her. I called for the physicians, but they needed to examine her to see if there was anything more than grief wrong with her." Slowly he sank to the bench beside her, a faraway look in his eyes.

"And was there?" she questioned, even though she thought she already knew the answer.

He glanced at her uncomprehendingly. "What? Oh. . .not that they could find. One physician left a draught for her to take to help her sleep. It was the first sleep she had had in almost a week." He leaned his head in his hands. "I thought her mind was gone. I have seen this happen before when someone lost a loved one."

Sara was becoming suspicious. "And did she take the sleeping draught again?"

Antonius glanced at her impatiently. "Only when she couldn't sleep. What are you trying to say?"

"I'm not trying to say anything. I was just wondering."

"Well, you can ask questions of the physician when he comes tomorrow,"

Antonius told her. "He comes once a week to care for her."

Sara decided to try again. "And how is she after the physician leaves?"

He took a moment to think about it. "Quiet, I suppose you could say. Very lethargic. But she sleeps better."

"She is sleeping well now," Sara reasoned, and he looked at her in wonder.

"That's true, but then she sleeps a lot anyway."

"Then why should she need a sleeping draught?" she demanded softly.

Antonius jumped to his feet. "Look, Sara, I don't have all the answers. I just have to trust the physicians to do the best for her. Let's not speak of this anymore tonight." He lifted Sara to her feet. "Let's go and check on Diana, and then you can have something to eat. You must be starved."

Again Sara marveled that he would care so much for a mere slave. She walked up the concrete stairs with him to the balcony that surrounded the peristyle. He went to Diana's door and knocked softly. When there was no answer, he quietly pushed open the door and peeked inside. Sara followed him into the room and had to smile at Diana's figure curled up asleep. Antonius laid a hand against her cheek and sighed with relief.

"There's no fever. Sometimes she has bouts with fever and nausea. But not tonight."

Antonius picked up the tray of food beside the bed that was for the most part untouched. Sara wrinkled her nose at the disgusting blend of greasy foods.

"Tribune, is that the kind of food she always eats?"

Frowning, Antonius studied the tray. "Is there something wrong with the food, too?" he asked sarcastically. "Tell me, are you a Jewish healer, as well as the old man?"

Sara shook her head. "Ahaz has taught our people much about different healing balms and herbs, but he is the master. It doesn't take a healer to realize that greasy food might be indigestible to a sick stomach."

Antonius seemed to ponder what she said. Shrugging his shoulders, he told her in exasperation, "The physicians said she needed the fat."

"I see."

Two little words with a wealth of condemnation. Antonius whirled on his feet and left the room. When he reached the balcony, he told Sara, "Go and get something to eat, and then return to Diana. Sometimes she wakes during the night and is frightened."

Gritting her teeth at his arrogant tone, she followed him down the stairs. "The kitchen is through there," he told her coldly, and Sara wondered what had made him so angry. There was no way she could know that her questions had made him feel remiss in his duty to his sister. He decided that tomorrow he would ask more questions of the physicians.

Sara ate a solitary meal of dates and oranges. She had very little appetite, and the emotional turmoil of the day was beginning to catch up with her. When she returned to Diana's room, she found that Decimus had placed a sleeping couch in the room for her. Sara smiled slightly at his thoughtfulness. He couldn't know that all of her life she had slept on a mat on the floor.

She went to the water urn in the corner and freshened herself before going to the couch and throwing herself on her knees. She leaned against the bed, her heart nearly breaking with her grief. Prayers went swiftly up on behalf of her parents and Dathan, and she asked God to take care of them. She prayed for Diana, that God would heal her body and her soul. She prayed that Antonius would be a kind master. Lastly she prayed for herself. Peace settled down around her, soothing, and she knew that God was with her. That was how Decimus found her the next morning, still on her knees.

Sara could hear voices coming from the peristyle, so she hastily turned her steps away and headed instead for the kitchen. She had made friends with Bacchus, the kitchen cook. He was kind but could become very angry if someone so much as hinted that there was something wrong with his food.

"Bacchus, what kind of food would you fix for someone who was very ill if you had the choice?" Sara asked him.

"Humph. No one has asked me, but if they did, I would tell them that soups and broths and fresh fruit would be the best thing."

Sara nodded. "I knew you were a wise man."

Bacchus puffed up at the praise. This little Jewish slave was intelligent for a woman. Already in the week she had been here, she had made some subtle changes. Changes he heartily approved of.

Decimus entered the kitchen. "Sara, the master wishes your presence in the peristyle."

Heart thumping fearfully, Sara went quickly, only to find Antonius with another man. She hesitated in the doorway, but Antonius motioned her to come in.

"Sara, you probably don't remember my friend Flavius, but he was with me the day I shot you with the arrow."

Flavius stared at the girl curiously. She looked nothing like the little girl they had found on the hillside. He couldn't know that Antonius had ordered her to wear more colorful clothes, refusing to let her wear the brown she favored that made her look so colorless. Indeed, Flavius found her rather attractive, in a strange sort of way.

"I have told Flavius about the change you have wrought in Diana, and he thought maybe Diana might be inclined to see him," Antonius told her. "Go and find out if Diana will have a visitor."

"In her bedchamber?" Sara blurted. Color flamed into her face when Antonius smiled mockingly and Flavius burst out laughing. Turning, she fled up the stairs and entered Diana's room, slamming the door behind her. These Romans had no shame whatsoever. Was nothing sacred to them?

Diana was sitting up in bed, her hair curled becomingly around her slender shoulders. Although Sara had managed to make some change in her appearance, Diana was still lethargic and had very little energy to do much of anything. Sara was beginning to form some opinions of her own, having watched proceedings for the last week.

She still shivered when she thought of the day the physician had come. He had given Decimus the sleeping powders that Diana used almost every night. Sara was horrified when he pulled a container from his bag and took out little insects. Making an incision on Diana's arm with a small knife, he placed the insects on the cut where they greedily fed off Diana's blood. As each insect became gorged, he removed it and put another in its place. Covering her mouth, Sara ran from the room.

When she returned, Diana lay pale and listless against the covers. Going to her side, Sara took Diana's hand in her own, gently stroking her palm and wrist. Diana smiled slightly.

"Not used to a little blood, Sara? Don't worry, you soon will be."

Sara refrained from comment. There was no way she could ever become used to such a gruesome sight. And if there was any way possible, she intended to prevent it from happening again.

That had been almost a week ago, and Diana seemed better today. But the physician would come again tomorrow, and then it would start all over again.

"My lady, there is someone here who would like to see you."

Diana's face registered her surprise. "Who would want to see me?" she asked sarcastically. "No one has cared enough before."

"Perhaps they would have if they thought you wanted it," Sara answered.

"I don't wish to see anyone. Except Antonius." Sara turned to leave the room so she could deliver the message, but before she reached the door, Diana stopped her.

"Wait! Who is it?"

"His name is Tribune Flavius, my lady," Sara told her and watched her eyes spark with interest.

"Flavius? Here?" Her face took on a faraway expression, and she smiled slightly. She quirked an eyebrow at Sara. "He was in love with me at one time, you know. Before. . ."

Watching the frown forming on her face, Sara hurried to turn her thoughts. "So, do you wish to see him?" Diana hesitated so long Sara decided she must not have heard. About to repeat the question, Diana suddenly turned wistful eyes to her.

"I would like to change first." Sara smiled with pleasure and hurried to the chest that held Diana's colorful array of tunics.

"Let me have the royal blue tunic and the soft blue *palla*," Diana suggested. "At least they will not make me look so ill."

Sara helped her replace her tunic and then wrapped the palla around Diana's shoulders and waist.

"Would you like me to braid your hair?" Sara asked her.

Excitement began to sparkle in Diana's eyes. Sara rarely saw that look. Only when Antonius came to visit.

"Yes, braid my hair. There are some pearls on my dressing table that you can use, also."

When Sara returned to the garden, she found Flavius waiting expectantly.

"She will see you now, Tribune."

His brown eyes ignited with joy in response, and Sara thought that he was a most handsome man. She smiled softly at him and then turned her eyes to Antonius. He was thunderstruck. Sara had to stifle a grin.

Antonius turned to Sara, his mouth open in surprise. "What magic did you use to accomplish this?"

Sara frowned at him. "Not magic," she stressed, "just love and encouragement."

Both Flavius and Antonius regarded her somberly. Antonius knew that what she said was true, for he had noticed a bond forming between his sister and Sara. It was hard to imagine, but they truly seemed to love each other. Like sisters. Sara could get Diana to do things that even Antonius couldn't manage. Antonius felt a twinge of jealousy.

"I'll come with you, Flavius," he told the young man.

Sara followed both men up the stairs. They paused outside Diana's chamber, but Sara motioned them inside. The drapes were opened wide to receive the full morning sun, which gave a glow to Diana's blond hair. Although it was still thin from her illness, it glowed with the care Sara had been giving it.

Diana looked pale but beautiful. Flavius couldn't take his eyes from her, and Antonius stared with awe at the transformation. He glanced at Sara, who was staring with pride at Diana.

Flavius went forward, taking Diana's hand in his and raising it to his lips. "You look truly beautiful. Worthy of Aphrodite herself," he told her softly.

Diana blushed at the compliment, and the color made her look healthier, adding a touch of innocent beauty to her face. "Flavius," she murmured, "I have missed you."

Sara could see him swallow hard, his eyes roving restlessly over Diana's face. "If that is so, lovely one, but say the word and I will be by your side every day."

Diana gave a trill of laughter. "And what would Caesar have to say about that? Far be it from me to cause one of his most loyal officers to desert."

Antonius stepped forward. "Diana, it is good to see you looking so well." He could see the dark circles under her eyes, the translucency of her skin, but there was life in her eyes. He began to have hope. How much of this was due to Sara who tended her constantly?

"If you don't mind, I have some things I need to discuss with Sara," Antonius informed them. Placing a hand on Flavius's shoulder, he gave it a squeeze. "I will see you later."

Flavius barely noticed their departure, and Antonius grinned at Sara. She preceded him out the door but left it open behind her. Antonius's mouth quirked and he shook his head slightly. The girl was a definite innocent.

Sara followed Antonius through the atrium, her eyes averted from the wall hangings she so despised. He took her through to the triclinium, an adjoining room that was sometimes used when they entertained guests for a meal. It had been a long time since this room had been occupied, but Antonius knew it would be less offensive to Sara's decided ideas of purity. He motioned her to be seated on a small chaise, and he sat down next to her.

"Sara, I don't know how you have managed to wrought such a transformation in my sister in such a short time, but I want you to know that I am truly thankful." He hesitated, his eyes searching hers. Sara waited patiently for him to continue. Something was bothering him, and eventually he would tell her what it was. She began to feel a little apprehensive, but he finally continued. "I want to repay you in some way."

That she was amazed was an understatement. She searched his face for some clue to where this conversation was leading but could find none.

"I am a slave, Tribune. I expect no payment," she told him softly.

He waved his hand in dismissal of her statement, frowning in annoyance. "Neither Diana nor I see you as such."

Sara was confused, cocking her head slightly. "Then how do you see me, sir?"

He watched her so long that Sara thought he wasn't going to answer. "I didn't bring you here to discuss how I see you. I brought you here to tell you that tomorrow I will take you home to visit your parents."

Sara's face filled with delight, and forgetting herself, she threw herself into Antonius's arms, hugging him joyously. When she would have pulled away, Antonius held her more firmly. He grinned at her as her face suffused with color.

"Perhaps I should take you to see your parents more often," he teased.

"Please, Tribune," she begged, struggling for release. Antonius bent and kissed her nose before quickly releasing her. In an instant, his demeanor changed from playful to serious.

"We have to assure Diana that we won't be gone long. I don't want everything undone that has already been accomplished. If this can't be done, then we cannot go."

Sara's heart sank. Although Diana seemed slightly better, she still had bouts of depression and would burst into tears at the least little provocation. Sara was afraid to even ask. Fortunately the way was made clear when she and Antonius returned to Diana's room and found Flavius on the verge of departure.

"She's very tired," he told Antonius. "She needs to rest now."

Antonius could see Diana's eyes starting to glaze with fatigue, but still she tried to maintain a facade.

"Don't forget, Flavius," she told him in a coquettish voice. "You promised to spend time with me tomorrow."

Flavius smiled, taking her hand to his lips again. "I will be here even if I have to take on Caesar himself," he told her teasingly.

After the two men left, Diana quickly began to droop. Sara rushed to her and helped her ready herself for sleep. Sara would wait until later to discuss Antonius and her trip to see her parents. She begged God to let nothing happen to hinder them. The only problem she was having was the thought of being alone with Antonius again. Remembering the feel of his arms around her, she buried her face in her hands. "Please, God," she begged, "don't let this happen to me."

Chapter 6

Sara felt the exhilaration of riding in a chariot for the first time. Antonius had chosen this means of transportation because Sara didn't know how to ride a horse. And although it may have given him some pleasure to have her in his arms again, he didn't think it would be pleasurable for Sara.

It had been easier than either Sara or Antonius had believed to leave the villa, partly, they were certain, because of Flavius. Diana had been more animated than Antonius had seen her in a long time. Perhaps Sara was right and Diana was beginning to heal, if not physically, then at least mentally. Antonius had assured her that they would return before the physician's visit that afternoon.

Sara pressed herself closer to the front of the chariot, trying to ease herself away from Antonius's form. He smiled slightly, recognizing the maneuver. His pride was somewhat affected since he had never had a woman turn away from him before. He decided to tease her a little. Using a flock of cranes as an excuse, he leaned forward and pointed them out to Sara. He felt her body stiffen as his chest pressed against her back. Antonius grinned. She had nowhere else to go.

"Tell me, Sara," he whispered in her ear. "Did you leave someone behind when I took you away?"

Choosing to misunderstand him, she snapped in irritation, "Of course I did. Isn't that who we're going to see?"

He ignored her displeasure. "I mean, a man. Did you not have someone you were attached to?" he asked her softly, his breath brushing against her ear. He felt her shiver and grinned again.

"I had no one," she told him stonily.

Antonius decided to relieve her of her misery and pulled back, adjusting the reins in his hands. The beauty of the day filled him with vitality, and taking a deep breath, he lifted his eyes heavenward, giving thanks to the gods. As though she could read his thoughts, Sara spoke with the same exhilaration.

"God has truly smiled upon the earth today."

"*Your* God?"

Sara pressed her lips together. "I have told you. There is only one God."

"That is your belief. We Romans believe a person should be allowed to choose whichever god they desire."

"How kind," Sara told him, her voice dripping with sarcasm.

Antonius frowned. Although he had meant what he told Sara about not seeing her as a slave, he still felt aggravated by her lack of respect.

"Why should anyone believe in your God over the others?" he asked her.

"Tell me, Tribune. How do you picture a god? Is he not all-powerful?" she queried.

"Of course."

"How is it then that your Roman gods can be destroyed by one another? Punished by one another for their misdeeds?"

Antonius chose to answer her question with one of his own. "And your God cannot be destroyed?"

"No," she told him seriously. "He has been since before time and will continue after time ceases to be."

He tried to puzzle out what she was saying. "And you believe only one God could create the whole earth? And everything in it?"

"One time," she told him, "I went to a wedding banquet. Several of the women—aunts, sisters, cousins, mothers—were trying to prepare the feast. Each had their own idea of how it should be done. It was total chaos."

Antonius smiled wryly. "I have seen this, also. I get what you are trying to say. If more than one being tried to create the same thing, we would have the same result."

"Your gods are capricious," she reiterated. "My God is unchanging. His word is His oath, and nothing can cause Him to break His word. He is a loving God who cares for His people."

"And if your God cares for you so much, then why are you a slave?" he asked her derisively.

Sara had no answer. She had asked herself the same question over and over, but she had faith that God had put her where she was for a purpose.

"No answer, Sara?"

"No one knows the mind of God, Tribune. If we did, He wouldn't be God."

For the rest of the journey, Antonius thought about what she had said. As they neared her village, he could feel the rising excitement emanating from her. He followed the path he remembered, turning away from the spot where he had first encountered Sara that fateful day. Unerringly he made his way to Sara's front door. Both the front door and the shop door were closed against the increasing heat from the sun.

Things seemed too quiet, and when Sara would have jumped down, he held her back. His soldier's instinct told him something was seriously wrong.

"Stay put," he commanded.

"But. . ."

"Do as I say, Sara. If you get out of this chariot, I'll have you flogged."

Sara paled at the threat, swallowing down her anger and impatience. Antonius got out of the chariot and cautiously approached the house. He knocked on the door, waiting for a response. None came. Sara was frightened. She, too, could sense that something was amiss.

Antonius applied his shoulder to the door, and it creaked open on its leather hinges. He peered into the gloom.

"Sara. Come here."

She was at his side in an instant. He nodded his head toward the corner, and she could see a figure lying on a mat. Pushing the door open wider to let in the light, Sara could make out the figure of her mother, her eyes closed.

"Mother?" Sara's voice echoed eerily around the room. Quickly she went to Abigail and laid a hand against her forehead. Bending closer, she was startled when her mother suddenly opened her eyes.

"Sara?"

Sara could barely understand her, her voice was so faint. "Yes, Mother. It's me. What has happened to you? Where is Father?"

Instead of answering, Abigail closed her eyes again. Sara looked at Antonius in alarm. "My mother is ill."

Sensing a presence, Antonius whirled quickly to face the door. Jubal stood in the opening, his eyes on Sara. He was thinner than when she had left a week ago, and he looked like an old man. His shoulders were bent as though he were carrying the weight of the whole world on his shoulders.

"Sara? You have come home."

His tired voice was the last straw for Sara. She threw herself into her father's arms and burst into tears. "What has happened here? What's wrong with Mother? What's wrong with you?"

Although his strength had been diminished, Sara felt as though he would surely crush her ribs.

"My baby," he whispered over and over.

Antonius was stricken with remorse. Had he been responsible for all of this? When he remembered the strength of the old Jew, his regal bearing, and then saw the way he was now, he wanted to cry himself. He gave a discreet cough.

"Sara, perhaps your mother has need of the old healer?"

Sara looked up, realizing that she had forgotten the tribune's existence. She knew he was probably right.

"Father," she pleaded. "What is wrong with Mother?"

Jubal looked past her to Abigail. "She has been that way since the day the two of you were taken away." He glared at Antonius. "She has lost all will to live."

Antonius swallowed hard, turning away. "Sara, go for the healer."

"He has already been here," Jubal told him. "There is nothing he can do."

Antonius jerked his head up. Where had he heard those words before? Is that what all physicians said?

Sara went to her mother, sitting beside her on the mat. "Let me talk to her. Alone, please."

Antonius nodded, but Jubal seemed disinclined to leave. Antonius motioned outside. "I need to speak to you," he told Jubal.

After they left, Sara took her mother's hand in her own. She started humming softly the song her mother used to sing to her when she was a child and afraid.

"Mother," she urged softly. Abigail opened her eyes again and smiled.

"Am I dreaming, Sara?"

"No, Mother. I have come home."

Abigail's face wrinkled into confusion. "I don't understand."

"The tribune brought me home to see you. He has been very kind to me."

Sara went on to tell her mother about Diana and life at the villa. "So you see, Mother," she concluded, "God must want me there for a purpose. I haven't been harmed in any way. In fact, I have been treated as though I were a friend instead of a slave."

Abigail smiled. "I need to ask the Lord's forgiveness. I didn't trust Him to take care of you." She lifted a hand to stroke Sara's cheek. "If He has a purpose for you, then He must also have one for your brother."

"Yes, Mother," Sara choked. "And for you and Father, as well."

When Jubal and Antonius came back, Antonius looked from Sara to her mother. "She is resting better now," she told both of them.

Antonius nodded. "Your father needs to speak to you. I will wait outside." He paused. "Better yet, I will allow you time with your family, and I will come back for you later." He clicked his heels together, bowed, and left.

By the time Antonius returned, Sara had managed to get her mother to eat some food. After all they had to say to each other, Sara knew that her parents would be all right now. Whatever Antonius had said to her father had brought the color back to his face and the pride back to his eyes. Sara had prayed with her mother and could tell it had brought her peace. Still, Sara was reluctant to leave them.

Sara was surprised when Antonius told her parents, "Sara may come and see you at least once a week."

Her mother had smiled then. It was the hardest thing Sara had ever had to do, to walk away from her family just then, but she knew Antonius would never leave her behind. Because of Diana.

Antonius helped her into the chariot and took up the reins. Before he could snap the whip, Sara laid her hand over his. He looked at her questioningly.

"Tribune, I would like to see Ahaz before we leave."

"The healer?" he questioned.

Sara nodded her head. Antonius hesitated but decided that she must want to consult him because of her mother. He owed her that much.

"Show me the way."

Sara led him down the street and out past the village. They hadn't gone far when

Sara motioned for him to stop. Antonius looked at the mud hut with distaste.

"Here?"

Sara nodded and started to get down from the chariot.

"I will go with you," he told her.

"No!"

Antonius pulled back in surprise, sudden suspicion bringing a frown to his face.

"Ahaz will not talk to me if you are there," she told him placatingly. She waited for his permission, looking everywhere but at him.

"Go then," he snapped. "But be quick."

When Sara returned, she was clutching a bag in her hand. Antonius helped her into the chariot.

"What is that?" he wanted to know.

"Some things Ahaz gave me." Antonius stared at the bag doubtfully, so Sara placed the bag out of sight. "Ahaz has always shared with the people of my village the things that he grows. Herbs, spices, various plants."

"For medicines?"

"Sometimes," Sara replied. "Bacchus told me that he likes to experiment with various spices and herbs, so I thought I would bring him some."

Antonius grunted an answer, taking the reins in his hands and deftly applying the whip. They were silent on the return trip, each thinking their own thoughts.

Gallus took the reins from Antonius, who turned to help Sara alight from the chariot.

"Go and see how Diana is. I will be along in a minute."

Sara found Diana in much better spirits, though her face was extremely pale.

"Oh, Sara! I'm so glad you're home. Where's Antonius?"

"He said he would be here shortly," Sara told her.

"Please, Sara," Diana begged weakly. "Could you massage my scalp like you do? I have a fearful headache. If it wasn't so early, I'd take my sleeping draught now."

Sara frowned but went to Diana and released the ivory bone pins from her elaborate hairdo. Slowly Sara began to massage her scalp, humming a tune as she did so. Sara could feel the tension begin to drain out of Diana. She was unaware of Antonius watching from the doorway.

"Oh, that feels good," Diana sighed. "You have magic hands."

Sara laughed. "I don't know about that, but my father used to enjoy me doing this for him."

"How was your family?" Diana wanted to know.

Sara sobered. "My mother was ill. My father. . .he seemed all right when we left."

Antonius entered the room and came to stand close beside Sara. She felt suddenly clumsy, though Diana didn't notice any difference.

Decimus knocked on the door. "My lady, the physician is here."

Sara felt Diana stiffen beneath her fingers. "You don't need to see him, if you don't want to," she told Diana.

"Of course she does," Antonius intervened. "If you can't be sensible, leave the room."

"Tribune. . ."

"I said, leave," he commanded, taking her by the arm and forcibly removing her from the room.

Sara paced up and down the balcony until the physician left. Going swiftly into the room, she found Diana much as she had previously. Sara's lips tightened when she saw the bandage where the physician had bled her again. Diana's eyes were glassy.

"Sara," she whispered. "I think I want to sleep now."

"Yes, Diana," she answered softly, her eyes filling with sympathy. "I will get things ready."

After Diana was asleep, Sara hurried to the vegetable garden behind the house where she knew she wouldn't be interrupted. Throwing herself to her knees, she began to pray fervently. She felt a measure of peace when she finished, her eyes swimming with tears as she lifted them to the dusky sky.

When Diana was asleep, Sara was free to do as she chose. Tonight, however, something told her to stay close to Diana, so she busied herself picking up in Diana's room. When she finished, she pulled a chair close to the bed, leaving one lamp lit so that she could see if Diana needed her.

How long Sara had been sitting there she didn't know, but darkness had veiled the night with its cloak. Crickets began to chirp in the peristyle below, their familiar cadences seeping in through the open door. The night was warm, and very little air came into the room. Diana became restless, moving her head from side to side. She started to moan softly, becoming even more agitated. Sara got up and leaned over her, putting a hand to her cheek. Diana's skin was extremely hot.

Sara went out to the balcony and called Decimus. He must have been close by, because he was at her side almost instantly.

"What is it, Sara?"

"Diana has a fever," she told him and noticed that worry lines creased his brow. "I need some cool water."

"I'll get it right away."

Sara hurried back to Diana. She felt her forehead and became instantly worried herself. Her fever was climbing.

Decimus entered the room with a bowl of water and brought it to Sara. "How is she?"

"Not good. Her fever is getting worse, and so is her restlessness. If she gets worse, she may harm herself, flailing about like she is."

Decimus left the room and came back quickly, carrying a soft drape of material.

He found Sara trying to hold Diana down. Taking the material, he wrapped Diana in its folds tightly, which only caused her to become more agitated.

"Antonius! Antonius!" she rasped.

"What should we do, Decimus?"

Decimus stood worrying his bottom lip with his teeth. "I think I had better go for the master. He left word with Abijah where he would be in case anything happened." His voice lowered. "I have never seen her this bad before."

Sara hesitated. She couldn't handle Diana alone; she hadn't the strength. In her delirium, Diana possessed surprising strength herself. "I think we should send Abijah. I need you to help me with Diana."

"Abijah is not here right now. He went to his brother's house, but he told me where to find the tribune."

"I will go then," Sara told him, but Decimus was already shaking his head. Diana fought the covers, managing to get her legs free and kicking out angrily. It took all Decimus had to wrap her snugly again. He looked at Sara worriedly.

"Perhaps you are right, but if you go out at night alone, the master will have my hide."

"What choice do we have?" she remonstrated with him. "I don't have time to argue with you. Tell me where to find the tribune."

Sara found herself hurrying through the dark streets of Ephesus, praying wildly as she flew along. Her prayers were answered, because she reached the house she was looking for unmolested. She only had time to take in the fact that this villa was almost as large as Antonius's. Pushing through the gates, she climbed her way to the door, pounding furiously upon its solid wooden surface. She waited breathlessly until she heard a sound from the other side.

The door opened slightly, and light spilled out into the darkened courtyard. A servant peered out, trying to focus on Sara's darkened figure. His eyes squinted slightly, his face drawing into a frown when he realized the woman before him must be a servant.

"What do you want?" he growled, inching the door closed to a mere crack.

Sara released a breath, wringing her hands in the folds of her tunic. "Is Antonius Severus here?"

Recognition flashed momentarily in the servant's eyes, but he made no answer. His mistress had made it quite plain that nothing was to interfere with her party, especially not where Antonius Severus was concerned.

"Please," Sara begged. "I have to see him. His sister is very ill."

The servant opened the door wider, torn by his desire to please his mistress and the sure knowledge that Antonius would have him flayed if he ever found out that he had refused to bring him knowledge of his sister. As he stood hesitating, a figure approached from the street, stopping when he recognized Sara.

"Sara? What are you doing here?"

Sara turned to him with relief. "Tribune Flavius, I must speak with Antonius. He left word with Abijah that he would be here."

Flavius was instantly alert, his eyes searching her face. "Is it Diana?"

"She's very ill. Her fever is making her delirious, and she continually calls for Antonius."

Face pale, Flavius turned to the servant. "What are you waiting for?" he snapped. "Get Antonius!"

"Yes, my lord."

Flavius waited with Sara, watching the man's back disappear into the anteroom where Helena held her parties.

"How bad is she?" he asked quietly, and Sara could hear the desolation in his voice. *He must love Diana very much.* She wondered if Diana knew.

Antonius appeared, quickly covering the distance to where they stood. A beautiful redhead followed in his wake, clutching his arm when he would have left.

"Antonius! Where are you going?" she demanded petulantly.

"I'm sorry, Helena. I must go to my sister."

"For the love of Poseidon, why must you always attend your sister? What good will it do? She's going to die anyway."

Sara was shocked at such coldness, especially coming from one with such flawless beauty. She saw Antonius's eyes darken with anger. He shook her hand off as though she were some vile thing. Sara could see that Tribune Flavius was just as outraged, his fists curling at his sides. Antonius would have left without a word, except that Helena tried once more.

"I'm sorry, Antonius," she told him in her most seductive voice. "I didn't mean it. It's just that I have missed you so much." She stroked her hands up his arms and curled them around his neck. Antonius remained still, his arms hanging at his sides.

Helena's full red lips curled into a pout. "Oh, Antonius. You have become such a bore lately."

Reaching up, Antonius removed her hands from his body and gave her a slight shove. "In that case, Helena, I will not bother you with my presence ever again."

Antonius took Sara by the arm and pulled her down the steps. Sara could hear Flavius turn to follow them. He looked over his shoulder and gave Helena one final parting shot.

"The same goes for me, Helena."

When they reached the street, they could hear Helena's angry voice.

"You'll be back, Antonius."

Antonius and Flavius exchanged glances. Flavius shrugged his shoulders, a grin splitting his features. "I feel like a fly that has just had a narrow escape from a spider."

Antonius nodded his head in agreement, but his attention had already turned toward Sara.

"What's happened?"

Taking a breath, Sara explained Diana's condition. Antonius listened in silence, his face becoming a grave mask. "Flavius, will you go for the physician? Tell him it's urgent."

Flavius saluted once, then disappeared in the opposite direction, his figure quickly swallowed up by the darkness. Sara was panting, trying to keep up with Antonius, but she said nothing. She was just as anxious as Antonius to reach the villa.

Antonius went quickly to Diana's room and found Decimus kneeling beside the bed.

"Decimus?"

The boy jumped quickly to his feet. "My lord," he sighed with relief. "She is still burning with fever. I have bathed her face constantly; that seems to soothe her some, but she continually calls for you. I have never seen her this bad before."

Antonius sat down on the bed, pulling the wrap from Diana's body. Taking her firmly into his arms, he held her tightly and began to talk to her soothingly. Slowly she started to relax until her head rested against his shoulder, her eyes closed.

Decimus moved by Sara to fetch more water. She laid a hand on his arm.

"Decimus? You were praying?" she asked him in a soft whisper.

He looked at her in surprise. "Yes, my lady."

"May I ask in whose name you were offering for Diana's life?"

Decimus pressed his lips together, straightening his shoulders. "I asked in Jesus' name," he answered her just as quietly.

Sara smiled at him then, her eyes locking with his. "His will be done," she agreed. They stared at each other several seconds, probing each other with their eyes, realizing that they had a common bond.

At a sound below, they turned to see Flavius ascending the stairs rapidly, the physician following in his steps. Sara felt her heart sink at the sight of the rotund man. She disliked him intensely, realizing that some of her dislike stemmed from her own prejudice. He was nothing like Ahaz. Ahaz cared for the people he ministered to. This man did little and charged exorbitant prices.

The physician pushed past Sara and Decimus, going to stand beside Antonius. He pulled back Diana's eyelids and let them drop back into place. He was silent a long time. Finally he spoke.

"She's too far gone," he told Antonius. "There's only one thing left for me to do."

Chapter 7

The silence in the room was almost oppressive as each person tried to take in what the physician was trying to say. Sara's eyes widened in alarm. She didn't trust this physician.

"What can you do?" Antonius asked him quietly, his eyes never leaving Diana's prostrate form. He cuddled her gently, burying his face in her golden hair.

"I can make a mixture of hemlock and allow her to die quietly and peacefully." There was a total lack of emotion in the physician's voice.

"No!" Four voices rose in unison, making the one word thunder through the room. The physician jumped in surprise.

"She would feel no pain," he told them placatingly. "She is so far gone now that she probably doesn't even know what's going on around her."

"My lord," Decimus begged. "You cannot allow this!"

Sara's eyes burned with anger, but she said nothing, allowing Antonius time to think. Surely he would not consider such a suggestion.

Flavius stepped closer to Antonius, reaching out a hand to Diana and running his fingers through her hair. His eyes roved her face, but he addressed himself to Antonius. "Think carefully, my friend. Life is too precious to be taken lightly."

If anyone knew that, it was Antonius. Even though he was a trained soldier, he still had a difficult time taking a life.

"I know what you are saying, but I have to think of Diana."

"Tribune," Sara interrupted. "Surely there is another way."

Antonius stared at her in anger. "What would you suggest? Praying to that caring God of yours?"

The physician started to unpack his bag. "There is one more thing I might try," he told Antonius. Antonius's eyes filled with hope. "I can try to bleed her heavier. If I remove enough fluid, then perhaps her humors will come into alignment."

Antonius laid Diana back against the bed. He stared at her a long time before he finally stood and began pacing back and forth. He knew little about medicine, and what he had seen so far had not impressed him. But either way, Diana was going to die. Pain like he hadn't experienced since his parents' death many years ago clutched at his heart. He had been the sole caretaker for Diana since she was twelve years old. Had it only been five years since his parents' death? It seemed so much longer. He felt much older than his thirty years.

Sara placed an urgent hand against his forearm. "Please, Tribune. Don't let him bleed her anymore."

"You have a better suggestion?" he snapped, jerking his arm from her.

She answered him quietly but firmly. "Our scriptures teach that life is in the blood. As a soldier, surely you know that to be true."

Antonius hesitated. What she said made sense. When a soldier was weak, you tried to stop his bleeding, not inflict more. Still, Xanthus was one of the finest physicians in Rome.

"My lord, I must protest." Xanthus threw Sara a murderous glance. "I am trying to keep her alive. What does a plebeian know of medicine?"

Forgetting her position, Sara whirled toward him, her eyes shooting brown sparks. "You are killing her! You with your rich foods and bloodletting. You care not for Diana. You care only for your fat purse!"

"Sara!" Antonius's eyes told her more than words that she had gone too far. Concluding that punishment was inevitable, she decided she had nothing to lose.

"Please, Antonius," she begged. "Let me care for her."

Antonius was as much surprised by Sara's use of his name as the fact that she disobeyed his order for silence. Xanthus drew himself up angrily, spearing Sara with a daggered glance.

"You? What do you know about medicine?" he asked her scathingly.

"He has said she will die anyway," Sara gritted. "What is there to lose?"

"I'll tell you what there is to lose," Xanthus argued. "The difference between dying with dignity and dying without pain."

"Enough!" Antonius thundered, and Sara knew better than to disobey. She must let him decide for himself. His strong will and arrogant pride would never allow him to submit to a woman if he felt backed into a corner.

"Take Decimus and go to the garden," he told her quietly.

Her eyes pleaded with him, but he turned away. Sara would have liked to slap the smirk from the physician's face. Dropping her head, she quietly left the room, Decimus close on her heels.

"Flavius, take the physician to the bibliotheca and show him some of my manuscripts. I'll be along shortly."

"Of course. This way."

Xanthus would have argued, but the strange glitter in Tribune Flavius's eyes kept him silent. He could feel the rage emanating from the young soldier.

When Antonius was alone with Diana, he sat down beside her on the bed. She was so still. So pale. She looked as though a breath of wind would blow her away. He frowned. She hadn't seemed so, just this morning. She had seemed lively, anticipating a visit from Flavius. Could Sara be right? He remembered how quickly Sara's wound had healed. Was that why she had stopped to see the old healer today? Could she have been seeking his advice?

One thing was for certain. Xanthus had no love for Diana, and Sara did.

When Sara left Diana's room, her eyes were filled with tears. Decimus came up behind her and laid a hand on her shoulder.

"He will not do it."

Sara wished she could feel as certain. "How can you be so sure?"

"I know him. He's not capable of such a thing."

Sara sighed, lifting her eyes to the stars. "Decimus, Satan has many ways of making something evil seem right."

"Then let us pray together that our Lord Jesus will not allow Satan to so deceive Tribune Antonius," he answered confidently.

For several moments, all was quiet in the garden except for the soft petitioning voices of both Sara and Decimus. As always, when Sara took her troubles to the Lord, she felt a sense of peace envelop her. When they had finished praying, Decimus led Sara to the seat near the fountain. He sat down next to her, folding his hands between his legs. His head drooped, and he stared somberly at the ground.

"You love Diana, don't you?" Sara asked him softly.

He nodded his head. "But not in the way you think. When I was brought to Ephesus as a captive seven years ago, I was only ten years old. The master's parents were alive then." He paused, picking a dried flower petal from the ground and twirling it through his fingers. "My lady was also ten at the time. Her father had come to the market to purchase a slave. He wanted someone strong. A man. My lady noticed me among the others and felt sorry for me. She pleaded with her father to choose me." Here he stopped, a grin spreading across his face at the memory. "Her father could refuse her nothing. She was the light of his life. So. . . here I am."

Sara smiled. She could imagine Diana being imperative and spoiled even at that age. "You became friends?"

Decimus nodded again. "She was the sister I left behind," he told her quietly.

All was peaceful and quiet in the garden save for the rushing water of the fountain. Sara looked up at Diana's door. It was hard to imagine that only a few feet away a battle was going on for the soul of a young girl. Sara began to pray harder.

When Antonius entered the library, he found Xanthus warily watching Flavius, who was twisting his dagger in his hands. Antonius hid a grin. Flavius was making his feelings all too apparent.

"Flavius, will you bring Sara to me? And you may as well bring Decimus, too."

Flavius sheathed his dagger with an extra-loud snap and left the room. Before long he returned, Sara and Decimus close behind. They searched Antonius's face for some clue to his decision but found none.

"Xanthus," Antonius began. "I respect your profession and have been pleased with your services," he lied, "but I have decided to allow my sister to die on her own." He swallowed hard.

Sara went limp with relief. *Thank You, Lord!*

The physician nodded his head in understanding. Not many people would choose such a hard way, but some simply could not let go. This he understood, and he found no offense.

"If you need me further, Tribune, you have only to call."

"Thank you." Antonius raised an eyebrow at Decimus, who interpreted his look correctly. "Will you see that Xanthus receives his payment?"

"Yes, my lord."

When they left the room, Antonius turned to Sara. "If there's anything you can do, do it. But I want you to understand that if she dies painfully, I will hold you personally responsible."

"I understand. May I have total responsibility for Diana? Her diet, everything?"

Antonius sighed, pushing his hands through his hair. He looked at Flavius, who looked just as intently back at him. He nodded his head. As Sara was about to leave the room, Antonius took her by the arm. Although he held her lightly, his hand felt like a shackle of steel, his eyes menacing in their severity. "Remember what I said. I don't want her to suffer."

"I love her, too," she reminded him quietly, and he loosened his hold. Nodding her head at Flavius, she left the room.

Sara made a mixture from the herbs Ahaz had given her and added it to a bowl of water. After mixing it together, she then tried to spoon some into Diana's mouth. Little by little, the brew went down her throat. Taking a cloth, she dipped it into the cool water Decimus had brought for her and placed it on Diana's forehead. She then settled herself in a chair beside the bed, prepared for a long night's vigil.

Periodically throughout the night, Diana would become restless and start to moan, rolling her head back and forth. Sara would then give her more of the herb mixture and replace the compress with a cool one. Then Diana would settle down again for several hours.

The sun was beginning to send its first fingers of light into the semidark room when Sara's head started to nod. Diana hadn't awakened in hours. Head dropping to her chest, Sara jerked awake. Blinking sleepy eyes, she got up and went to Diana, laying a hand against her cheek. Her breathing was deep and regular, and Sara could tell the fever had broken and the worst was over.

She opened the drapes wide to let in the morning light, knowing that it wouldn't bother Diana. Her sleep was too sound. The herbs Ahaz had given her had helped to alleviate the fever, but she wouldn't mention them to Antonius. She sensed that he would not approve.

Antonius had left word that he would sleep in the room next to Diana's and that he should be called if there was any change. Sara went to the door and found Decimus asleep on the balcony in front of the threshold. She smiled softly. Let the boy sleep. She would go to Antonius herself.

Stepping over the sleeping lad, Sara moved carefully and quietly to the next door. She tapped lightly but got no response. Opening the door slowly, she found Antonius asleep, still sitting up on the couch, his head drooped to one side and his dark hair spilling across his forehead. He looked so childishly innocent that Sara felt her heart melt at the sight of him. Crossing the room, she lightly touched his shoulder.

In one quick movement, she found herself pinned beneath him on the couch, his eyes glittering strangely down into hers. Her eyes opened wide in fear, her heart pounding loudly in her chest.

"Tribune!" she squealed in fright. "It's Sara!"

For a moment, his eyes remained unfocused, then slowly he relaxed. He shook his head slightly to clear it, releasing her wrist from his crushing grip.

"Sara?" He looked down into her face, one part of his mind registering the fear he saw there. "Sara." His voice softened, and he lifted a hand to stroke down her cheek. Her wide eyes stared back at him, and Antonius felt himself move as if in a dream. He lowered his head, bringing his lips softly down on hers.

The moment his lips touched hers, Sara felt her mind begin to spin. Without realizing it, she returned his kiss, her lips telling him of her innocence. Antonius knew he should have pulled back, but a strange fire was beginning to warm his blood. He pressed closer, his lips becoming more demanding.

Warning bells went off in Sara's mind. She tried to push Antonius away, but his strength was too much for her. She tried to turn her head away but found herself unable to move. Using the only weapon available to her, she began to fervently pray.

"My lord?" Decimus's voice from the doorway brought Antonius back from the yawning precipice he had so nearly tumbled into. He pulled back quickly, running a hand through his hair in agitation.

"Sara!" Antonius was at a loss for words. He leaned back, and Sara hastily climbed from the couch. She would have just as hastily exited the room, but Antonius stopped her.

"Wait!" Sara froze with her back still to him. "What is it, Decimus?" he wanted to know.

Decimus glanced from one to the other, casting his eyes to the floor. "I was looking for Sara," he answered quietly. "I couldn't find her in my lady's room and wanted to find out how my lady was doing."

Both men fixed their attention on Sara. "The fever has broken, and she is sleeping quietly. That is what I came to tell you, Tribune." Sara's eyes were also cast downward but flew up at Decimus's whoop of joy. She had to smile when she saw the joy that radiated from his face.

"I will go and bring you something to eat," he told her happily, skipping across the balcony.

Sara would have followed, but again Antonius stopped her. "I would have a word with you." She heard him move behind her and felt herself tense up. Antonius saw her body stiffen and clenched his jaw in frustration.

"Sara." He laid a hand on her shoulder and felt her jump slightly. Gritting his teeth, he dropped his hand. "I'm sorry about what happened just now. I didn't know what I was doing. I would never hurt you. Surely you know that."

She didn't answer him for a moment, and when she did, it was to change the subject. "Diana is much better this morning. Her fever is gone, and she was sleeping peacefully when I left."

"I heard you tell Decimus."

"Is there anything else, Tribune?"

Antonius sighed, turning away. "Not for the moment. I will be along to see Diana as soon as I have visited the baths and cleaned up some."

"Yes, Tribune."

For the rest of the day, Sara attended to Diana. Her lack of sleep was beginning to tell on her, and she started to droop wearily. Decimus found her patting water onto her face to keep awake and convinced her to lie down on the other sleeping couch to rest. At first she protested, but when Decimus told her he would stay in the room also, she relented. Within moments, she was asleep.

Although Diana awakened periodically, she was awake for only minutes at a time. Sara knew that what her body needed the most was time to recuperate from all the bloodletting, so she didn't worry too much about Diana's diet. She did, however, send word to Bacchus to prepare some broth for Diana's nourishment. Decimus returned with a tray holding a bowl of broth, and resting in a small urn was a blue hyacinth. Sara laughed aloud.

"What is so funny?" Decimus was clearly puzzled.

"Bacchus is letting me know that he approves of Diana's diet," Sara told him.

Decimus raised an eyebrow, clearly unconvinced. "I hope this works."

Sara took his face between her hands and smiled into his eyes. "What I want from you, my brother, are your faithful prayers."

He grinned back at her. "I have never stopped."

Releasing him, she stepped back. "Someday, Decimus, I would like to learn how you came to know the Lord."

"And I you."

They smiled at each other before parting company, and although Decimus stayed close by, Sara had no need of him again that day.

The next three days followed a pattern. Diana would awaken periodically, and Sara would give her some broth, bathe her, brush her hair, and let her go back to sleep. Antonius would come in the evening to check up on her, and Sara's heart never failed to miss a beat whenever he entered the room.

He would sit and hold Diana's hand, even when she was asleep, and talk to her about many things. Sometimes he would bring some of his Greek manuscripts and read her poetry. Sara would sit enthralled, though she didn't think anything could compare with the psalms of David.

Color was beginning to come back to Diana's cheeks, and Sara attributed that to Bacchus's cooking. He truly did know how to feed an invalid.

Five days after Diana's collapse, she opened her eyes, and they regarded Sara clearly for the first time.

"What time is it?" she asked, trying to lift herself up on the bed pillows.

Sara hurried to her side. "You must stay put. You have been very ill."

"Have I? Where's Antonius?"

"I'm not sure, but he's here in the villa somewhere. Do you want me to send for him?"

Diana lay back down. "Not right now. For some reason, I'm famished."

Sara smiled with pleasure. "That is wonderful news. What would you like to eat?"

"I'm so hungry I could eat Orion," she joked.

Sara's trill of laughter reached Antonius, who was coming up the steps. He hurried the rest of the way, entering Diana's room and almost knocking Sara over. He grabbed her arms to keep her from falling, clenching his teeth when she jerked away.

"Tribune," she told him in a breathless voice, "Diana is much better this morning."

"So I can see." He smiled widely at Diana, going over and sitting on the couch beside her. She was almost emaciated, bones protruding from her shoulders. "We have Sara to thank for your life," he told her.

Diana looked from one to the other. "Someone will have to tell me what has happened. I seem to be missing something."

For the rest of the day, Diana spent her time between eating and periods of sleep. She was better than Antonius had seen her in a long while, and he thrilled at her increasing intervals of wakefulness.

Whenever he tried to express his appreciation to Sara, she would mumble something about her God and flee. With rising irritation, Antonius realized that if he wanted to have a conversation with Sara, he was going to have to demand her presence in some way. A stubborn light came into his eyes, and his shoulders straightened with assumed arrogance. *So be it.*

Chapter 8

"Antonius?"

"Hmm?" Antonius raised his eyes reluctantly from the scroll he was perusing. He glanced at his sister, noting with pleasure that she had lost much of her skeletal appearance and was beginning to fill out healthily. *Sara's doing, no doubt.* Since she had taken over Diana's care, Sara had been as bristly as a bear.

He remembered bringing Diana a special delicacy of hummingbird tongues only to be faced by a wrathful Sara reminding him of his promise to allow her complete control of Diana's care, including her diet. At first he had been angry, then amused. He certainly couldn't fault the results.

His sister's bright blue eyes stared out at him from a beautiful face framed by the gold of her now full and shiny hair. She worried her bottom lip with perfect white teeth.

"What do you think of Sara and Decimus's God? Do you think it's possible there could really be only one God and that He really cares about His people?"

Antonius frowned. "Now what's going on inside that pretty little head of yours? What brought this on?"

She wrinkled her nose, turning her attention out the window. The day was beautiful, and the cobalt blue of the sky was an almost exact duplicate of the eyes studying it. Diana regarded the vivid colors of the warm morning solemnly.

"I almost died, Antonius," she told him softly.

He felt fear clutch his heart as he remembered that night. Diana was the one person he loved most in all the world, and he had almost lost her. So many happy memories linked them inextricably together.

"I would have thought that would make you all the more grateful to be alive. Ready to live your life to the fullest."

Diana turned her gaze back to him and regarded him solemnly. "If I had died, Antonius, where would I be now?"

Antonius got impatiently to his feet, brushing a hand haphazardly through his hair. He began to pace to and fro.

"What do you want me to say?"

Diana sighed gently. "You have so much knowledge at your fingertips, and yet you can't answer such a simple question."

"Simple!" He blew out his breath in frustration. "Man has studied that question since the beginning of time."

"And?"

"Diana!" He paused, struggling for an answer. His mind seemed to go blank. "What do you think?"

"I think you're trying to throw this back on me." She grinned. "I'm not the one who spends hours poring over dusty old manuscripts." Diana watched through prideful eyes of love how Antonius was struggling to give her a satisfactory answer. He had always been her mentor. So calm and sure in a crisis, yet here he was, floundering over a theological issue.

"Sara and Decimus have both told me of their belief in a place called heaven for the saved, and hell for the unsaved."

Antonius glared at her in aggravation. "Well, I wouldn't put too much faith in their religion. Their leader was a carpenter who was nailed to a cross."

"They told me this, also," she answered softly.

"If He were God, how could this happen?" he remonstrated logically.

"They say He allowed Himself to die for our sins, so that we could live forever with God."

"What utter nonsense!" Antonius would have a word with Sara and Decimus when they returned from visiting Sara's parents. "Listen to me, love." Antonius's voice was soft with reassurance. "What grievous sins could you have committed to warrant eternal punishment? You've always been kind and loving."

"But it's more than that," she told him, and he rolled his eyes heavenward.

"For the love of Poseidon! Can we change the subject?" he begged.

Diana watched her brother, her lips twitching with amusement. He looked like a caged lion, and just about as approachable.

"I'm hungry," she acquiesced, and grinned openly when he sighed with relief.

"I'll tell Beatrice to bring us a tray," he told her, hurrying through the door.

When Beatrice entered with the tray, Antonius glanced over it skeptically. How could Diana be gaining weight and health from such a selection of food? He set the tray down on the marble table next to Diana's couch, raising an inquiring brow.

"There doesn't seem to be much of sustenance," he grumbled.

Diana laughed joyously. "Oh, Antonius, if you could only see your face. Sit down, and let's eat. I'm starved!"

Shaking his head, Antonius sat down across from her. He bit into the delicately seasoned fish, chewing slowly. His eyebrows winged upward.

"This is really good!" he said in surprise.

Diana said nothing, merely handing him portions of the fruit mixture and nuts. Her eyes danced merrily as she watched her brother consume his food with obvious enjoyment.

"Here, try these. They're my favorite." She handed him a small cake and watched his eyes widen in surprise when he bit into it.

"What's in this thing? It's delicious."

Diana sucked the honey from her fingers before answering. "Chopped dates, almonds, honey, things like that."

She reached across, dabbing at the honey dripping down his chin. This was almost like the time they were children and she and Antonius had gone on a picnic.

"So my brother, what are you studying today?" She indicated the scrolls he had been studying earlier. Diana wondered at the sudden color that rushed to his face. Antonius turned his eyes away before answering, thereby missing the grin his sister threw his way.

"Actually, I've been reading some of the writings of Josephus."

"And who is Josephus?"

"Josephus is a Jewish historian and statesman."

"Ah."

Antonius noticed the grin and frowned. "Don't look at me like that."

"Like what?" Diana asked innocently.

"Oh, never mind," he answered in exasperation, wiping his hands on the wet towel provided and rising to his feet.

"Where are you going?"

"I have work to do," he told her gruffly.

Diana's eyes darkened, and the smile left her face. "You said you would keep me company until Sara returned," she pouted.

"Diana," he answered softly. "You don't need me to stay with you. You are well now, both physically and mentally."

"But I get so bored," she complained. "Sitting here day in and day out. I still can't walk!"

Brushing a hand through her hair, he tugged gently, forcing her to look at his face. "That will come with time."

"But I'll go crazy here alone. I have nothing to do."

Antonius thought for a minute. "How about if I carry you out to the peristyle? You could sit in the shade by the fountain. Would you like that?"

"Oh yes!"

Antonius had to smile at her childlike enthusiasm. Reaching down, he lifted her effortlessly into his strong arms and carried her down the steps to the garden. Settling her comfortably on the bench, he called for Beatrice.

Beatrice came quickly at his call, lifting her eyes demurely to his. What he read in her eyes was anything but demure. Frowning, he brusquely instructed her to see to Diana's needs, then quickly turned on his heel and left. The purple trim from his short tunic gave color to the otherwise white robe. His skin was burnished by the sun, as was most of the Roman legion, and his build was that of an athlete. Many a heart had been lost at the altar of this young Roman. Two pair of female eyes watched him stride away: one brown pair with regret, the other pair with amusement.

"I'll call you if I need you, Beatrice," Diana told the girl.

"Yes, my lady."

Diana leaned her head back, basking in the warmth of the sun shining down through the peristyle roof. Eyes closed, she smiled at the feeling of euphoria that enveloped her. Why had she not thought to come here before? For a long while, she sat thus, enjoying the freedom from the monotony of her room. She had missed so much the last several months, holing herself up in her room. Refusing to live because Ledo had died. Strange, she could barely remember his face. How could this be if she was so much in love?

"Surely the goddess Aphrodite has chosen to descend from Mount Olympus and grace the earth with her beauty. My eyes are blinded by such a radiant vision."

Diana had jumped at the first word, her heart thumping with fright. She turned now to greet her visitor, a smile blazoned across her face.

"Flavius! You flatterer. You scared me half to death."

"That wasn't my intention," he assured her. "But seeing you sitting here. . .so lovely, so. . .alive."

Diana laughed. "Oh, Flavius! It does feel good to be among the living again!" She cocked her head to one side. "But if you are looking for Antonius, he has gone to his office."

Flavius's voice came back soft and low. "No, I didn't come to see Antonius. I heard you were almost well again, and I had to come see for myself." His voice became husky. "You are more beautiful than ever."

Color flooded Diana's cheeks, and she turned her head away. "So what is happening in the legion? Are you still to remain in Ephesus, or will they be sending you elsewhere?"

Flavius sat down beside her, staring at the water tumbling in the fountain. "I have decided to resign my commission," he told her, and her eyes widened in surprise.

"Why?"

He glanced sideways at her, his eyes dark and unfathomable. "A legionary cannot marry, and I have a desire to do so."

Diana felt the color drain from her face. Turning away from him, she clutched the front of her palla, closing her eyes against the pain.

"How nice," she told him and was surprised that her voice sounded so normal. "As for me, I plan never to marry," she told him airily and missed the hurt that flashed through his eyes. "I could never leave Antonius."

"But. . .surely someday Antonius will want to marry?"

"Who will want to marry?" Antonius asked as he walked into the garden, catching the last of the conversation. "What am I missing here?"

Flavius rose to his feet. "Nothing," he answered quietly. "We were just discussing marriage."

"Whose?" Antonius wanted to know.

"Never mind," Diana told him quickly, and Antonius's eyes narrowed when he noticed her pale face. "I'm tired, Antonius. Could you carry me back up to my room?"

"Allow me." Flavius reached down and lifted her into his arms. Biting her lip, Diana turned her face away from Flavius. She could feel the pounding of his heart and realized that, in a way, she affected him as he did her. But now he was to marry. He had said nothing to her. Perhaps he had confided in Antonius. For years now, she had considered Flavius a special friend, but it hadn't occurred to her until now just how much she had grown to love him. He had always treated her with gentle respect, much like Antonius treated her. Tears shimmered in her eyes. Suddenly she no longer wished to be treated like a sister, but she couldn't tell Flavius that. He would feel awkward to know that she had fallen in love with him.

Setting her down on the couch, Flavius leaned toward Diana, his eyes searching hers. Diana sighed with relief when Antonius walked in the door.

"Is there anything you want me to do for you, Diana?" Antonius asked.

"If you would close the drapes for me, I think I would like to take a nap."

Doing as she asked, Antonius then walked to the door, motioning for Flavius to follow. Reluctantly Flavius backed toward the door, his eyes never leaving Diana's face. Pivoting abruptly, he left, and Diana could hear his sandals clicking against the concrete. Burying her face in her pillow, she wept bitterly.

Sara reached up with her hand and gently touched the mezuzah on the doorpost before entering her parents' house. She walked across the dirt floor to the three sitting on mats at the low table.

"You found Ahaz well?" Abigail asked her.

Sara grinned. "Have you ever known him to be otherwise? He gave me more herbs and spices." She held up the bag for their inspection.

Decimus turned to Jubal. "If not for Sara, Diana would have died. God worked a miracle through her."

Jubal nodded his grizzled head. "Some good has come from this situation."

Sara smiled at him and looked at her mother. "I wish you could meet Diana. She really is a wonderful person. And so beautiful."

"King Saul was a handsome man, and look what happened to him. Beauty of the heart is what matters," Abigail answered.

Decimus was staring hard at Sara before he turned to her mother. "I must agree."

Sara smiled wryly at them. "I know what you are saying, but it would be nice to have beauty such as Diana's."

Her father snorted. "What does a Roman who is willing to own slaves know of beauty?"

"Father," Sara argued. "It was forcefully brought to my attention that in times past when the Israelites were conquerors, they owned slaves, also."

Her father glowered at her but couldn't argue the point. Sara had been unable to, either, when Antonius first brought it to her attention. "To the victors go the spoils," he had told her.

Decimus broke into her musings. "We need to get back soon."

Sara nodded her head in agreement. Darkness would soon descend, and it wouldn't be good to be caught on the roads after dark.

Decimus stood to his feet while Sara kissed her mother good-bye. Jubal and Abigail followed them out to the end of the road.

"I'm glad the tribune kept his word," Jubal told Sara. "It's made all the difference in the world, being able to see for ourselves that you haven't suffered."

Sara's eyes filled with tears. "Keep praying for Diana."

"We will," Abigail answered for her husband. She hesitated a moment before laying a hand on the side of the cart. "Sara, if you could find out anything about Dathan. . ."

"I'll try, Mother." Abigail stepped back from the cart, nodding her head. It was all Sara could do.

Decimus clicked to the horse and they were off, Sara watching until her parents were a mere speck in the distance. Decimus didn't miss the sheen in her soft brown eyes.

"I like your parents."

Sara gave him a wobbly smile. "Yes, they are the best parents a girl could have."

A distant look came to Decimus's eyes as he stared off in the distance at the rising columns of Ephesus. "I wish I could remember more about my parents."

"Do you ever want to go back?"

"To Britannia?"

Sara nodded.

"I used to think about it a lot. Now. . .I don't know. It's been seven years since I've seen my parents and my home. I don't even know if they are still alive."

Sara felt sorry for him. At least she still had her parents and, with Antonius's kindness, was able to visit them often. She thought she would have died if she had been in Decimus's place.

Thinking to lighten the mood, Sara smiled coyly at Decimus. "And is there another reason you are reluctant to leave? A girl, perhaps?"

He glanced at her sharply before turning back to the road. Color mounted to his cheeks, and Sara grinned.

"Aha! I thought so. Who is she?"

Decimus remained silent, so Sara began to guess. "Bithnia? No? How about Beatrice?"

Decimus threw her a look of such scorn that Sara burst into laughter. The rest of the journey, they teased each other back and forth, laughing gaily at one another's jokes. Decimus pulled the cart into the courtyard, laughingly lifting Sara out beside him.

Antonius saw them from the window of the bathroom. He leaned against the sill, his eyes narrowed. Decimus still hadn't removed his hands from Sara's waist, and she was still laughing at something he had said. Antonius watched them broodingly, his thoughts far from pleasant.

Drying himself, he quickly put on a clean tunic, deciding to leave off the toga. He needed to talk to Sara about Diana. About this religious thing. When they entered the atrium, Antonius was waiting.

"I wish to speak with you, Sara."

Sara glanced at Decimus, who shrugged his shoulders, his eyes suddenly filled with worry. Sara followed Antonius through the atrium to the bibliotheca. This seemed to be his favorite room in the house, and Sara realized that it was probably due to his thirst for knowledge. He was forever studying the scrolls in the library and purchasing new ones to pore over at his leisure.

He stood still in the doorway, motioning for her to precede him. To do so would bring her in close proximity to his body. She stopped, unable to bring herself to move forward.

"Sara?"

Her eyes flew to his, and she could see the amusement lurking there. The man knew the effect he had on her and was deliberately testing her will. Lifting her chin a notch, Sara looked straight ahead and passed through the doorway, brushing against his chest as she did so. When her eyes went to his again, his were veiled, all traces of laughter gone.

Swallowing hard, Sara turned to address him. "Yes, Tribune?"

Antonius forgot what he had intended to say. Suddenly the whole religion issue seemed so trivial. A look of irritation crossed his features.

"Why must you always call me Tribune?"

Sara looked at him in surprise. "But that's who you are."

"You called me Antonius once." His husky voice sent shivers up Sara's back, even as hot color flooded her face.

"I didn't mean to. I. . .I forgot myself for a moment. It was not appropriate, and I hope you will forgive me."

There was no denying the earnestness of the plea. Antonius nodded his head slightly in affirmation, his mind not completely on what she had just said. "Then why do you not call me master?" he demanded softly.

Sara dropped her eyes to the floor. "I have only one master."

She heard him move but kept her eyes fixed on the blue inlaid design of the marble. Antonius reached out, placing a palm against her cheek, lifting her chin none too gently with his thumb. Sara quailed beneath his look. His eyes glittered dangerously, and Sara's heart started to pound in response, her eyes widening in alarm.

"Who, Sara, do you consider your master?" he asked in a softly ominous voice.

Sara had to swallow twice before she could answer. She realized how fiercely possessive Antonius could be about things he considered his. Take Orion for instance, or even Diana. But it had never occurred to her that he might become angry over a slave.

"My Lord, Jesus Christ, is the only one I will ever consider my master," she told him in a quavery voice.

She watched the dawning comprehension on his face and felt the tension leave his body. A slight smile quirked his lips to one side.

"Ah, I remember now. Your religion." His eyes roved her face before settling on her parted lips. Her chest rose and fell rapidly with a mixture of fear and her awareness of him as a man. "I have no problem with you worshiping your God in any way you choose. Just remember one thing. You belong to me." He punctuated each of the last four words by tapping her lips with his thumb.

Sara's lips thinned with anger. Jerking herself free, she stepped away from Antonius. She saw his face tighten with returning anger.

"Is that all you wished to talk to me about, Tribune?"

"No." He stared at her silently, his blue eyes smoldering in his anger. "What is going on between you and Decimus?"

Sara's head flew upward and she gaped at him in complete shock. "Decimus?" She frowned, struggling to find some meaning behind the question. "Decimus and I are friends. We share the same Lord."

"Make sure that's all you share," Antonius told her coldly.

Sara placed her hands on her hips in exasperation. "Decimus is like a brother to me!"

Antonius watched her in irritation. She was so truly naive, especially where men were concerned. He felt the anger drain away.

"Sara," he told her gently. "Decimus does not look at you in such a way. Decimus sees you as a woman. The woman he loves."

The color fled from her face, and she stared at him in anguish. "No. I don't believe you."

Sighing, Antonius took a step toward her, his lips thinning with displeasure when she backed away. Sara lifted her eyes slowly, encountering the hard blue glare of his penetrating gaze. His eyes captured hers and held her mesmerized against her will.

"Come here, Sara," he commanded gently. Sara shook her head, taking another step backward. The room was quiet save for the sounds coming from the courtyard below.

Antonius was aggravated that Sara always seemed so frightened of him. Beatrice would have fallen gladly at his feet. Sara, however, always found reasons to avoid his presence. It bothered his ego more than a little bit, though he wouldn't for the world admit it, even to himself.

"Sara." This time there was a definite note of authority in his voice, but Sara refused to move. Antonius realized that she was truly afraid of him. It radiated from every pore in her body, and he realized that he was the cause. Something about him frightened her, though he had never laid a hand to her. He frowned in annoyance.

"If I command you to do so, you know you will obey." Antonius wasn't nearly as sure as he sounded. Even from that distance, Antonius could see her body start to tremble. He continued to watch Sara, a well of irritation bubbling up inside him. He could force her, he knew, but what would that accomplish? She would be more frightened of him than ever. Without knowing why, he suddenly turned away.

"Send Decimus to me," he snapped, and Sara bit her bottom lip. Was Decimus to be punished because of her? As she turned away, Antonius called to her softly. She remained motionless, her back to him.

"You needn't be afraid of me, Sara. I wouldn't harm you."

Her voice came back to him small and still. "Perhaps I am more afraid of myself." With that, she quietly departed the room.

Antonius stared after her in surprise. The girl was a definite enigma. Just when he thought he had her figured out, she threw something surprising in his face.

Chapter 9

Sara was kneeling in the vegetable garden behind the villa when Decimus joined her. She glanced up quickly but turned away before her eyes had more than a moment to rest on Decimus's confused face. She had always felt comfortable around Decimus. . .had always felt toward him the way she would have liked to feel toward Dathan. But in a few short words, Antonius had destroyed the camaraderie she felt with Decimus. She was uncomfortable and unsure how to make matters right. Was it true? Did Decimus love her more than as a sister, or was it a figment of Antonius's imagination?

Decimus knelt down beside her, tearing ruthlessly at the weeds in the cucumber patch. His features drew into a frown, his eyes sparkling with suppressed anger.

"Antonius has forbidden us to mention religious matters to Diana. He says if he hears of it again he will have us both flogged."

Sara heaved a sigh of relief. So Antonius hadn't mentioned their conversation to Decimus. She was able to look at him more fully, forgetting her own distress in the face of his.

"Did he say why?" she asked softly.

He continued to pull at the weeds, and Sara noticed a tear wend its way down his cheek. Brushing at it impatiently, he turned toward Sara.

"I would defy him if not for you. I cannot allow him to punish you." He gritted his teeth fiercely. "But how can I not talk to Diana when she is so close to accepting the truth?"

Sara laid a hand gently on his arm. "There will be a way. Remember what the apostle Paul said. Slaves must obey their masters. To defy Antonius is to defy God Himself."

Releasing a pent-up breath, Decimus turned to her and gave her a rather wan smile. "How did you get to be so wise?"

Sara laughed. "I have had a good teacher. The best. My father once heard the apostles speak. It so filled his heart that he has spent the rest of his life trying to share it with others."

Decimus looked at her thoughtfully. "I wonder if my parents have ever heard the salvation message."

"Someday, Decimus, you must take it to them. I believe God has prepared you for just such a message. You have a way about you. People trust you."

He looked hard into her eyes. "Do you trust me?"

Sara reached down to pull a cucumber from the vine, even though she could tell it wasn't quite ripe. Her face flooded with embarrassed color. "Of course I do. You are the brother I never had."

He watched her quietly before turning away. "I thought you had a brother."

Relieved to change the subject, Sara told him about Dathan and their life together. He had always been rebellious and selfish, always avoiding work and seeking pleasure wherever he could find it.

Beatrice walked into the garden. "Sara, my lady wants you."

Sara got quickly to her feet, reaching down a hand and squeezing Decimus lightly on the shoulder. "Things will work out. You'll see. Just trust God."

When Sara walked into Diana's room, she could tell that she was extremely upset. A leftover supper tray sat untouched on the table beside her. Diana's hair was mussed and her clothes wrinkled. Sara hadn't seen her look like this in a long while.

"My lady? You wanted me?"

"I'm going crazy up here! Where were you?" Her voice was almost frenzied, tears shimmering just below the surface of her eyes. It was almost as though they were back to the first step again.

Sara's forehead wrinkled in bewilderment. "I was in the vegetable garden trying to find something special for your meal, but I see Bacchus has already sent it up."

"I don't want anything to eat. Take it away," she commanded imperiously.

Unsure just what had brought about the change, Sara did as she was told. She watched Diana cautiously, hoping that the young girl would confide in her.

"Sara?"

"Yes, my lady?"

"If your God cares so much about you, why does He let bad things happen?" There was a decided anger behind the curiosity.

Sara took a deep breath. Antonius had forbidden her to speak about such things with Diana, and to defy him would be a sin. But wouldn't it be more of a sin to remain silent? The apostle Peter had been forbidden to speak the gospel message, had even been sent to prison when he refused to remain silent. Could she do any less?

"No one knows the mind and ways of God," she told Diana firmly.

"Is that a convenient way of saying you don't know?" she asked sarcastically.

Sara blushed, but her eyes remained unyielding in their intensity. "No, it is just a way of saying I don't always understand. Sometimes things happen that we don't understand, but eventually they work out for God's purpose."

"Can you give me an instance?"

Thinking hard, Sara finally began to tell Diana the story of Joseph and his rise to power in Egypt. Diana sat enthralled, hanging on every word. When Sara finally finished, Diana looked at her skeptically.

"Is this a true story?"

"Yes, my lady."

"Humph," Diana responded autocratically. "Better to be the slave of a Roman than of an Egyptian."

"Better not to be a slave at all," Sara rejoined softly.

"Tell me another instance," Diana demanded, and Sara began to tell her the story of Queen Esther. Again Diana was captivated by the story. Her eyes became dreamy, a look of such longing in them that Sara was surprised. What was she thinking? Was she remembering her fiancé of time past?

"So God could be using us for His own purposes?"

"It's possible," Sara answered her quietly. "But like I said, I don't know all the answers."

Diana settled back against the cushions, staring off into space. "How can you get God to change someone's mind?"

"What?"

Diana's eyes, filled with purpose, focused intently on Sara. "How can you reach this God of yours?"

Unsure of just what to do, Sara remained absolutely immobile, biting her lip in indecision. She sat down next to Diana and took her small white hand into her own rough brown one.

"Listen to me, Diana. There's a whole lot more to this than you know. Let me try to explain."

For the next hour, Sara urgently related the salvation story to Diana. For some reason, she felt that it was imperative to make her understand. They argued back and forth. Diana was reluctant to give up the desire for action on her part. Perhaps if she made a sacrifice to Aphrodite, Flavius would change his mind about his bride and choose Diana instead. She mentioned nothing of this to Sara, and yet Sara sensed more behind the questions than Diana was divulging.

Finally Diana sat back exhausted. "But He's a Jewish God! What does He care about Romans?"

"He loves everyone, Diana; they just don't know it. He is not a Jewish God. He is not a Jew. He only chose the Jewish people because at that time they had more of a heart for Him. He needed a race of people to bring His Son into the world. He chose the Jews, but He could have just as easily chosen another people. Now that His Son has come, He doesn't need to keep a set-apart people. He still loves the Jews, but most of them have rejected the Son He sent to them in love."

Diana shook her head slowly from side to side. "How could they? After all that He did for them?"

"Many of the Jews are still waiting for a warrior king. Someone to help them reclaim what they have lost. They don't understand how great His love is. God is love," Sara finished softly.

When she left Diana's room, Sara still didn't know if Diana truly understood, but she felt she had made a step in the right direction. Sara had brushed Diana's hair and helped prepare her for bed. Whatever had been bothering Diana earlier seemed to have been pushed aside for the time being.

Antonius stared around him in aggravation. All the noise and confusion were getting on his nerves, and he longed suddenly for the peace of the villa.

"Don't look now," Flavius interrupted his thoughts, "but the spider has entered and seems to be looking for a particular prey."

All eyes were riveted on the voluptuous redhead threading her way through the throng of people. Antonius had to admit she was well worth looking at, but an image of pure brown eyes suddenly filled his mind. Whatever had made him think of Sara? Shrugging his shoulders, he plastered a smile on his face as Helena stood before him, her emerald green eyes sparkling with intent.

"So, Antonius," she purred. "I haven't seen you in a long while. I've missed you."

Antonius lifted a cynical dark eyebrow. "I find that hard to believe, Helena. The last time you talked to me, you assured me I was quite boring."

Color suffused her face, and Antonius was impressed. He had assumed Helena had forgotten how to blush a long time ago.

"Only a plebeian would remind me of such a thing," she told him angrily.

Flavius burst into laughter. "And there you have it, Antonius. That should effectively put you in your place."

Helena glared angrily at Flavius. "Why don't you go find someone else to talk to and let Antonius and I exchange apologies."

Flavius pressed his lips tightly together to keep from laughing at Antonius's thunderstruck expression. He got quickly to his feet, patting Antonius on the back. "See you later, old friend."

"I could get you for desertion," Antonius hissed angrily for Flavius's ears alone, which only caused the young man more merriment.

Helena slid down on the cushions next to Antonius, leaning close against his side. She slid one hand suggestively up his arm before latching on to it possessively.

"I hear Diana is much improved. I'm pleased. Now you won't need to run off so often."

Antonius felt the sweat begin to break out on his brow. This party of Gaius's was turning into a show fit for the Circus Maximus. As a soldier, Antonius had faced death many times. Without fear. But this woman clinging to his arm made his mouth go dry with trepidation. How could he have thought her attractive? He must have been blind!

Again Sara's image floated into his mind, and he shook his head in anger to rid himself of the picture. Sara didn't approve of such parties, and she certainly wouldn't approve of the different people draped over couches in various stages of undress. What she would most disapprove of would be the men with the men and the women with the women. He could almost see her disapproving scowl. Suddenly he felt very unclean. Helena stared at him in surprise when he rose quickly to his feet.

"Excuse me, Helena. There is something I have to do."

"Can't it wait?" she pleaded. "We could go to my house if you have had enough of the crowd." Her voice lowered suggestively. "I could help you relax."

Swallowing hard, Antonius shook his head. "Perhaps I will see you again," he told her dismissively and knew he would feel her wrath sooner or later. He headed quickly for the exit, not breathing until he reached the outside. He released his breath slowly, feeling as though he had just barely managed to escape with his life.

The afternoon sun warmed his face as he lifted it to the sky, dragging in deep, clean breaths. Flavius followed him out the door. "Is it just me, or have these parties begun to pall?"

Antonius looked at him wryly. "You didn't have to leave on my account."

"Why not?" Flavius wanted to know. "I only went on your account."

Antonius grinned. "Well, do me a favor the next time I'm tempted to go. Remind me that I might run into Helena."

Flavius shivered melodramatically. "The gods forbid!"

As they walked out the gate, Antonius turned to his friend solemnly. "What's happening to us, Flavius? All of a sudden, I seem to be on the outside looking in."

Nodding his head in agreement, Flavius smiled at his friend. "Maybe we're just getting old."

Antonius blew through his lips. "Speak for yourself, old man." He shook his head. "No, it's more than that. I find myself condemning things I used to participate in. The parties are only a part of it."

"Perhaps you've had your head in those dusty old manuscripts too much lately."

"Then what's your excuse?"

Flavius grinned wryly but shook his head. Antonius stared at him, a sudden illumination lighting up his eyes. "A woman!"

Color raced up Flavius's neck, spreading across his face and into his hairline. Antonius laughed aloud, drawing the attention of several passersby. "As I live and breathe! Why didn't you mention it to me? Who is she?"

Before Flavius had time to answer, Antonius placed a hand on his arm. Looking at him, Flavius found Antonius's eyes focused elsewhere, a frown on his face. Following the direction of his gaze, Flavius noticed Sara hurrying along on the other side of the street. She was deep in conversation with the boy at her side. When she broke into laughter, Flavius noticed the thunderclouds forming in Antonius's eyes.

Flavius's eyebrows flew upward as he watched the little drama unfolding before him. A sudden suspicion caused him to narrow his eyes and follow Sara's movements more carefully. Surely not. Antonius in love with a slave? And the girl wasn't even pretty. There had to be another explanation, but what he saw in Antonius's eyes he had seen before in others. Stark jealousy.

"I have something to do," Antonius told him absently. "I'll talk to you later."

Flavius watched Antonius cross the street and head in the direction the pair had disappeared. Shaking his head, he turned in the opposite direction. At least Antonius had been sidetracked from further questioning him about the woman in his life. How could he tell Antonius that the woman was his own sister? Antonius believed that they had a brother-sister relationship. Flavius shook his head. There was nothing brotherly about the way he felt for Diana. Someday he would have to face Antonius with a declaration of his love for Diana, but at least the time had been postponed. He sighed with relief.

Antonius followed Sara and Decimus through several alleyways and past the marketplace. He had assumed they were going to the market, but their basket was full of goods, and they were going in the opposite direction of the villa. His thoughts heavy with suspicion, he stayed close without being seen.

Antonius stopped when they stopped. Decimus put his hands on Sara's shoulders, his face intent on what he had to say. Sara seemed to be arguing with him, and Decimus finally nodded his head in resignation. When Sara would have passed him to enter the dirty apartment, he reached out a hand and stopped her. Bending down, he kissed her cheek, and Antonius felt the pain in his jaws from clenching his teeth together.

When Sara had gone inside, Decimus stood watch at the door. Antonius watched until the sun started to descend before Sara returned. When she came outside, Antonius noticed that her basket was empty. He frowned, trying to assess the situation. Something was going on here, and it definitely didn't make sense.

Antonius ducked into an open doorway when they came his way, their heads close together as they discussed something. He stayed hidden until they were far enough ahead of him for him to feel comfortable with the fact that they didn't suspect they had been followed. Drifting along the streets in their wake, he followed them back to the villa.

Sara was in the peristyle gathering flowers for Diana's room when she looked up and found Antonius watching her. The blue of his eyes was almost hidden by the black of his pupils, his face cast in granite. He stood so until Sara began to feel uneasy with his perusal.

"You wanted something, Tribune?" she asked him uncertainly.

"Where were you today?" he demanded coldly, and Sara could feel a knot forming in the pit of her stomach.

"I. . .I went to the market."

"Alone?"

Flushing, she looked down at the flowers in her arms. "No. Decimus was with me."

Antonius came to stand before her. She could feel the rage vibrating from his body. She sensed his unleashed violence and began to tremble.

"You went only to the market?" he insisted, his voice tinged with frost.

Sara bit her lip, wondering where these questions were leading. Had Antonius somehow found out about her and Decimus? And if so, how? She pulled in her breath, trying to relax. They had done nothing wrong. Not really.

"Answer me, Sara. Or should I call Decimus?"

Sara's head flew up, and Antonius's lips pressed together at the fear he saw there.

"You don't need to call. I am here." Both Sara and Antonius turned to watch as Decimus came through the back garden entrance. He walked purposefully, coming to stand beside Sara. His eyes lifted defiantly to Antonius.

"What were the two of you doing at the market?" Antonius bit out savagely.

"Shopping," Decimus told him calmly.

Quick as a flash of lightning, Antonius had the boy by the front of his tunic, lifting him clear off the ground. Sara screamed, trying to pry them apart. Antonius's eyes glittered with rage, and Sara feared for Decimus's life.

"Tribune! Please!"

"What's going on here?"

Antonius dropped Decimus to the ground, where the boy began rubbing his throat. Sara bent to him, but her eyes were raised upward in astonishment. Antonius stood transfixed, his eyes locked on his sister, who was leaning against the balcony with all her strength. In a moment, Antonius was up the stairs, lifting her gently in his arms.

"What do you think you're doing?" he demanded fiercely.

"I heard Sara scream. What's happening? What were you doing to Decimus?" Diana's voice rose higher and higher.

"Shh," Antonius begged. "You'll upset yourself."

"I'm already upset," she told him. "I want to know what you were doing."

Antonius's eyes flashed downward to where Sara was still leaning over Decimus. Both of them were staring in horror up at Antonius, who was feeling more than a little foolish at the moment. He hadn't even given them time to explain.

"Both of you come up here. Now!"

Sara helped Decimus get to his feet, and Antonius watched as they began to ascend the stairs. They looked like a pair about to face the execution squad. Antonius smiled grimly. No, he hadn't given them a chance to explain, but he would now. And it had better be one good explanation.

Chapter 10

A Christian! Are you out of your mind?" The thunder of Antonius's wrathful voice echoed throughout the room.

Diana sighed. "Sit down, Antonius, and stop roaring at me like a lion! Let me explain."

Antonius whirled on Decimus. "This is your doing! By the gods, I should have the skin stripped from your back."

Decimus remained still, the only outward show of emotion the paling of his face.

Sara opened her mouth to speak, but Diana interrupted angrily. "You'll do no such thing! Decimus had nothing to do with this."

Antonius fixed his eyes on Sara, their hard glitter giving evidence of the rage he had worked himself into. "Then it must be your doing."

Again Diana intervened. "It was not Sara's doing nor was it Decimus's. It was my own decision. You cannot blame them for answering the questions I asked of them."

"Can't I?" Antonius's voice was more frightening in its quietness than his previous ranting. His eyes glowed almost obsidian, and Sara felt herself swallow in fear. "I seem to remember commanding them not to speak of religious things to you."

Diana tried to rise from the couch, leaning heavily on the table next to it. Antonius became instantly alarmed and went to her, trying to get her to settle back down again.

"If you won't sit down, then I'll stand up," she told him firmly.

"All right! All right, I'll sit down," he relented, and Diana collapsed back with a sigh of relief.

"Decimus, you and Sara may leave," she told them.

"No!" Antonius was back on his feet in an instant.

"Antonius," Diana pleaded. "I would rather speak with you about this alone."

Staring down at her, Antonius felt some of the anger drain away. Whatever had happened, Diana was much like the girl she used to be. A sparkle in her eyes gave evidence of the life that again flourished within her. She had almost died, and now here she was, vibrant and full of purpose. And she had walked. Praise the gods. Or should he thank Sara's unseen God?

"Go," he told them without taking his eyes from his sister. "Decimus, you will wait for me in the bibliotheca."

Sara and Decimus exchanged glances. "As you wish, my lord."

When they had gone, Antonius turned back to his sister. "You have a lot of explaining to do. And what is this about you becoming a Christian? It's. . .it's preposterous. I forbid it, Diana!"

"Antonius," she told him softly. "You can't forbid me to believe what I believe. As the head of our family, you have the right to forbid me many things and command me to do others, but you cannot control what's in my mind. Nor in my heart."

What she said was true, and Antonius felt the anger returning as he felt his own helplessness. He needed to be calm if he wished to sway Diana from this way of thinking. She could be as stubborn as he was at times. Taking a deep breath, he sat down beside her, taking her hand in his own.

Diana reached up with her other hand and laid it against his cheek. "Before you say anything, let me tell you something. I didn't just believe overnight. I've given this a lot of thought. I've had enough time, that's for sure. I started asking questions, I guess, years ago. Maybe when Decimus first became a Christian himself. We talked about it a lot."

She slid her hand down, wrapping it around his hand with her other. "Decimus is not a Jew."

"I'm aware of that," he told her irritably.

"But he accepted a Jewish God. That intrigued me. We spoke of it often. Then Sara came to us, and. . .well, you know what happened. I owe her my life."

Antonius jerked to his feet, pacing the floor like a caged lion. He pushed his hands through his hair, dropping them helplessly to his sides. "She has filled your mind with all kinds of nonsense."

"No, Antonius. She has not. She only answered the questions I asked of her. I figured this out for myself."

For the first time, Antonius noticed a difference about his sister. She looked more mature, more in tune with her emotions. He was suddenly filled with foreboding. He had no idea what this change meant for their lives.

"What have you figured out?" he asked her quietly.

"That of all the gods and goddesses, of all the religions, of all the beliefs, this one makes sense."

Antonius went and sat down by her side again. Sighing, he looked deeply into her eyes to see if he could read the truth there. "How does it make sense that a God who loved His people would treat them the way He has? Their race has been almost completely destroyed."

"Antonius, do you remember the time you and Father disagreed about the way you should live your life? You wanted to join the legion, and he wanted you to take over his business enterprises."

"I remember," Antonius told her grimly, thinking back to that time that had caused the first real breach in their father-son relationship. He had wanted to please his father, but he had wanted to please himself more. In the end, Antonius had his way, but it had left a sour taste in his mouth.

"He could have commanded you, but that would only have driven you farther away. God is like that."

"Diana. . ."

"Wait. I'm not finished. Romans believe that the Christian religion is abhorrent. Detestable. But what could be so wrong about a faith that teaches you to love everyone, even your enemies? Imagine if everyone embraced this philosophy."

Antonius turned to her in anger. "Not everyone will. It's impossible."

"With God, all things are possible, but you're probably right. That's not what I'm asking. What if I were? What is so bad about such a thing?"

Antonius began massaging his forehead with his hands. "This religion preaches anarchy."

"Rubbish! How can this be so when the scriptures teach that a slave should obey his master?"

His head snapped up, and he glared at her. "If this were so, why did Sara disobey me and continue to fill your head with such foolish notions?"

Diana smiled. "Fortunately for me, Sara has a different master."

"So I've heard," Antonius returned dryly.

"Jesus taught His followers to obey the laws of the land, as long as they didn't conflict with God's own laws."

"I can't believe you've fallen for this!"

Diana pressed her lips grimly together. "All right, Antonius. I'll make you a challenge. Find some of the old scrolls of the Jewish prophets. Read them. Study them. Use your mind. Then. . .then your heart will follow."

Antonius decided that he was getting nowhere. Maybe she was right. If he could find something in the Jewish scriptures to convince her, she might be more reasonable.

"All right," he told her. "I'll do that, but in the meantime, I want you to keep this quiet. Romans have always hated Jews, and the winds stirring among the people are not favorable to them. I command you to be silent about this. Worship this Jewish God if it brings you pleasure, but do it quietly."

"Whatever happened to Roman tolerance of all religions? Is Rome so afraid of the truth?"

Antonius decided to ignore her. "As for this other matter, I will not have you giving away our food to all the riffraff of this city."

"But. . ."

Getting to his feet, Antonius went to the door and threw it open. "Sara!" he bellowed.

Sara must have been in the peristyle below, because she came rapidly to his side. "Yes, Tribune?"

"Come in. I want you to hear what I have to say."

Sara followed him inside, glancing with trepidation at Diana's tense face. He closed the door and leaned his back against it.

"I was just telling my sister that I refuse to feed the entire poor population of this city."

"You called them 'riffraff,' I believe," Diana answered him sarcastically. "Would you consider General Titus to be such?"

Antonius frowned. "What are you talking about?"

"Do you remember General Titus, Antonius?" she asked him quietly.

"Of course I do. My first command was under him. What does he have to do with this?"

"He's one of the 'riffraff' I've been helping."

"That's not possible! He's a retired general. Rome takes care of its own."

"Not when they're Christians," Diana told him quietly and watched the color leave his face. A hurt look came into his eyes, and though Sara felt pity for him, she realized he would not appreciate her concern. She dropped her lashes to hide her feelings.

Diana got slowly to her feet, holding up her hand imperiously when Antonius and Sara would have rushed to her assistance. She walked slowly, falteringly, across the space to her brother's side. Touching his arm gently, she lowered her voice placatingly. "Please, Antonius. We have so much. You are willing to give food to marble idols, why not to living people?"

Antonius stared at her for what seemed an eternity. Sara was not aware she was holding her breath until Antonius sighed, laying his palm gently against Diana's cheek.

"Very well," he told her, and a bright smile broke across Diana's face, only to vanish a moment later when he continued. "But you will not deliver the goods yourself, and I will not have Sara wandering around that section of the city. Send Trophus."

"But. . ."

"I forbid it, Diana." For all its quietness, steel threaded his voice.

Diana set her lips mutinously, giving back glare for glare. It was easy to see the resemblance between brother and sister when they stood thus. Reaching down, Antonius lifted Diana into his arms and carried her back to her couch. Straightening, he stroked a hand down her cheek and turned and walked out of the room.

Antonius entered the bibliotheca where Decimus stood staring out the window. The boy turned at his entrance, his eyes veiled. Clearing his throat, Antonius reached for a scroll that was on his desk. Curling it, he then placed it carefully in a case and held it out to the boy.

Decimus stared suspiciously at the container, one eyebrow ascending to his blond hair. "You wish me to deliver this, my lord?" he asked, reaching slowly for the scroll.

"It's yours," Antonius told him shortly. "Your freedom papers."

Decimus jerked his hand away, his eyes opening wide. "You are giving me my freedom?" he asked, suddenly suspicious. "Why?"

Antonius frowned in annoyance. "That's a stupid question to ask. Take the scroll."

"Not so stupid, my lord," he replied quietly. "Why now?"

"I want you away from Diana. I don't want her head filled with your heathenish religion."

Decimus shook his head slowly. "You had that scroll prepared before you found out about Diana's commitment to Christianity."

Antonius felt rage begin to bubble inside at the familiar use of Diana's name. Taking a breath, he tried to regain control.

"Think carefully, Decimus," he gritted. "I am offering you your freedom. You can return to your people. Your country. I had it in mind to send you away with enough money to help you get started in your new life. You have served this family well."

"And if I don't wish to leave?"

The quietly spoken question caused Antonius's eyes to darken, his face becoming a hard mask.

"You will not stay here," he told him ominously. "You can leave here a free man, or you can leave here a slave—but you will leave."

Decimus bit his lip in indecision. Antonius was in a towering rage; that was all too clear. Maybe when he calmed down, he would regret this action, but the Lord only knew when, or if, that might be.

"And what of Sara?" he dared to ask.

Flames ignited in Antonius's eyes, and Decimus took a step backward, though Antonius himself had not moved.

"Sara has nothing to do with you."

"I love her," Decimus told him quietly. "I cannot leave her here. I want to marry her."

Decimus sensed more than saw Antonius's rising anger. He thought he understood, and that understanding gave him the strength to continue. "She is a Christian, too," he told Antonius reasonably. "Surely you don't want her around Diana."

"Don't push me, Decimus."

Swallowing hard, Decimus decided he might as well go all the way. He had nothing to lose. "May I speak to Sara?"

A muscle worked convulsively in Antonius's jaw. Decimus thought for sure that Antonius was going to refuse his request. Instead, an unusual calm seemed to settle around him. "Go ahead, but Sara will remain here. Be sure you make that clear to her."

Decimus found Sara in the peristyle, staring up at the risen crescent moon. Stars filled the dark expanse of the sky. Torches were lit in the garden, and though he could not see her face clearly, he could tell she was smiling.

"What makes you so happy?" he asked her softly. "What are you thinking about?"

She jumped slightly, turning her head quickly in his direction. "You startled me," she told him breathlessly, a smile returning to her face. "I was just thinking how God works in such mysterious ways."

Decimus sat down beside her. He pulled a hibiscus blossom from its bush and placed it gently in Sara's hair. She frowned at him uncertainly.

"What bothers you, Decimus? I see worry in your eyes."

He looked away from her, trying to gather his scattered thoughts. "Sara, Antonius has given me my freedom."

Sara's eyes went wide in shock, the color draining from her face. Her eyes flew swiftly around the peristyle before returning to rest on Decimus's face. Suddenly her face came alive with joy.

"But, Decimus, this is wonderful! Now you can go home to your people. You can tell them about God."

Sighing, he buried his face in his hands. "It's not that simple."

Totally confused, Sara placed a hand gently on his down-bent head. "I don't understand."

Brushing his hands back through his hair, he lifted his head and stared intently into her eyes. "I won't leave you. I told him I want to marry you."

Sara sat back in stunned amazement. She couldn't think of a thing to say. It had never occurred to her that Antonius might be right in his assessment of Decimus's feelings. She had thought it a case of mistaken imagination on Antonius's part.

"What did he say?" she asked softly, suddenly fearful of what might be coming. She had no desire to leave. She loved Decimus, but not like he wanted.

"He said to make clear to you that you cannot leave." Decimus gritted his teeth in impotent anger. He had been trying to think of a way, but he kept coming to the same conclusion. Either he left a free man or he would leave sold to someone else. The pain of it caused tears to come to his eyes. He turned away from Sara, not wanting her to see.

Sara watched him thoughtfully. She could sense Decimus's pain, but she could not help her own relief. She never meant to hurt Decimus, and though she didn't take his feelings lightly, neither did she believe him in love with her to the extent that he seemed to feel.

"I cannot marry you, Decimus," she told him softly, trying to shield him from more pain. "I don't love you the way you mean. Not the way my parents love each other." His shoulders slumped in defeat, and Sara felt torn. Stroking his back in slow-moving circles with her hand, she began to reason with him. "I told you God had a purpose for you. I told you that one day you would go home and spread God's Word. Now that time has come."

A tear slid down Decimus's cheek, and Sara gently wiped it away. "Someday you will meet the woman God meant for you to marry, and you will be glad you waited."

He shook his head vehemently. "Never!"

Sara hid a smile. He sounded so much like a hurt child.

Suddenly he turned to her, his eyes alive with hope. "I could ask Diana to release you, also."

"Antonius has the final say in this family. What would he say?" Sara was unsure just why Antonius refused to let her go with Decimus, and she was unsure why it made her feel excited inside that he was so unwilling to let her go. She thought his reasoning probably had something to do with Diana.

Decimus turned away. "You want me to go?"

"Oh, Decimus! Part of me will cry for your loss, but the other part of me thrills for your release." She took his face between her palms and smiled gently into his eyes. "Go with God. And don't forget your little Jewish sister."

Decimus gave a halfhearted attempt at a smile. "I could never forget you." Turning away, he sighed and got to his feet. "I'll tell Antonius that I accept his offer."

Sara watched him walk with bowed head from the garden, and her heart ached for him. It occurred to her that she knew just what it was like to love someone who didn't love you back.

Decimus took the scroll from Antonius. He watched him silently. Using his newfound freedom, he decided to say what needed to be said. "Sara is a very special woman. I hope that she will never be hurt."

Antonius recognized the threat in Decimus's voice, but surprisingly he felt no offense. "I have no intention of hurting her," he told him quietly.

Nodding his head, Decimus began to twirl the scroll in his hands. "May I say good-bye to Diana?"

Again Antonius took offense at the use of her name. Then it suddenly occurred to him that Decimus and Diana had been more than slave and mistress. They had been friends. Would Sara ever get over her fear of him and feel that way, too? He nodded his permission. Reaching his hand into the gold box on his desk, he pulled out a small bag of money. He held it out to Decimus, who did nothing toward taking it.

"Please," Antonius told him. "For Diana. She would be very distressed if she knew you wouldn't take it. You deserve it."

Slowly Decimus took the bag, clenching it in his hand. He stared at Antonius a long moment before he turned and walked out of the room.

Chapter 11

Over the next several weeks, Antonius found himself watching Sara more and more. He looked for her whenever he entered the villa and found himself disappointed if she was not around. He began to call her to him in the bibliotheca, supposedly to discuss some of the Jewish writings he had managed to buy.

At first, Sara was reluctant. But as Antonius shared the writings on his scrolls with her, she began to relax and look forward to those times. As a child, her father had read from the old scrolls, but Sara had been too little at the time to remember much. Now she found herself fascinated by the writings of the old prophets.

Antonius would watch her eyes light up when he read particular passages, and he would wonder what had caused her response. She would patiently answer his questions, but he could tell she was holding herself back for some reason.

Sara began to explain to him the meanings behind the prophecies and their fulfillment in the man called Jesus Christ. It still made no sense to him that a god would allow His Son to be crucified on a cross, the cruelest, most detestable form of punishment there was. Any argument he had, though, was met with reasoning and logic from Sara. She had an answer for everything. It amazed him that a woman could speak so intelligently.

On this particular day, they were lightly arguing about the attributes of deities.

"If this Jesus was God, how could He have died?" Antonius wanted to know.

"It was because He was God that He had to find a way to live as a man. He allowed a part of Himself to become mixed with a human so that He might better understand us. Our temptations, our desires. There was nothing He didn't experience. But because He was God, when the time came for His mortal body to die, He was still able to overcome death."

Sara frowned at his cynical smile and decided to try again. "Romans claim that the emperor is a god, is this not so?"

"That is so," Antonius agreed.

"And yet Augustus, Tiberius, and Caligula are all dead. And someday Claudius will die, also. If he were a god, he wouldn't need the food tasters and the bodyguards."

Antonius would have argued, but he couldn't. She was right. But how did that make her God any different then? He had died, also.

"I know what you're thinking," she told him softly. "But there is a difference.

Jesus allowed Himself to die so that we might live. He died, but He arose again. He overcame death. Over five hundred people witnessed this."

Surprised that she could read his mind so well, Antonius turned away and looked out the window. He had been reading some of the Jewish prophecies that had predicted the downfall of the Jewish people. Some of the conquerors were predicted by name over a hundred years before that king was ever born. It was uncanny.

He had spoken with some of the soldiers who had been in Jerusalem when the man Jesus had been crucified. The stories they told him made his blood run cold. Since Antonius himself had only been ten at the time, he didn't remember very much about the man who had caused such an uproar in the Roman republic.

One of the centurions who had been in Jerusalem at the time and had served Pontius Pilate was himself now a Christian. What kind of attraction could this religion have that so many people would flock to it even in the face of persecution? The thing that upset Romans so much was the fact that it taught equality for everyone.

"May I go now, Tribune?" Sara's soft voice interrupted his thoughts. "It is almost time for lunch, and Diana wanted to have it in the peristyle."

He nodded his head and watched her walk gracefully toward the door. "Wait!"

She stopped and looked at him inquiringly. "Yes, Tribune?"

He crossed the space to her and stood looking down into her expressive eyes. "Do you still miss Decimus?" he asked her quietly and studied her face intently.

She dropped her eyes, but he lifted her face by cupping her chin in his large, rough palm.

"Do you?" he wanted to know.

"Very much," she told him truthfully. She had longed for her friend to confide in many times. She missed his company when preparing baskets of food for those whom Diana chose to help. She missed his laughter that so many times helped her over her own periods of depression. And if she were not mistaken, Diana missed him just as much.

Antonius rubbed his thumb gently over Sara's lips and saw the fear return to her eyes. Was she so afraid of him, or was she, as she had said, afraid of herself? He decided to find out.

He lowered his mouth to hers, holding her firmly when she would have moved away. When his lips met hers, he let out an unconscious sigh. This is what he had longed to do for some time now.

Sara tried to hold herself rigid beneath the onslaught to her senses. Her mind clouded, and reason seemed to be slipping away. When Antonius wrapped his arms around her, she found herself leaning into his kiss, returning it with a fervor she didn't know she possessed.

Antonius was surprised at Sara's capitulation. Feelings he had never felt before swirled through his body, capturing his mind and his heart. Suddenly he longed for something more. He realized that what he felt for Sara transcended the physical, causing him to yearn for things he hadn't known existed. But what it was, he wasn't quite sure. These feelings were new to him.

He lifted his lips from Sara's and slowly dropped his arms to his sides. Feeling him withdrawing, Sara came back to her senses. She looked into Antonius's eyes and saw the veil that descended over them to hide his thoughts. Her face flooding with color at her forwardness, she turned and fled.

"Antonius, I would speak to you about something."

Antonius grinned at his friend, pulling Orion to a stop. Flavius reined in his mount also and sat chewing on his lip. For the last several miles, Flavius had been utterly preoccupied. Antonius had wondered if he would share what was troubling him or if he would keep it to himself.

"Well?" Antonius encouraged.

Flavius's eyes scanned the horizon in every direction, refusing to meet Antonius's eyes that were beginning to fill with suspicion.

"Is it about this unknown girl you refuse to share with me?"

Color flooded Flavius's face, and he felt his heart pound with trepidation. "You already know her," he told Antonius quietly.

Antonius stared at his friend, his mind trying to figure out the person to whom Flavius was referring. Obviously Flavius feared his wrath. Suddenly his eyes widened, and he turned on Flavius. "Not Helena!"

Flavius glared at him. "By the gods, Antonius. Give me credit for having some sense."

Antonius looked perplexed then. "For the love of Poseidon, tell me."

Gaining his composure, Flavius lifted his chin firmly, staring boldly at Antonius. "I am referring to Diana."

Antonius felt his mind go blank with incredulity. His sister? His little Diana? She was but a child! He felt his anger begin to rise and as suddenly dissipate. Sara was as old as Diana, and hadn't he been seeing her in much the same way?

"How long has this been going on?" Antonius asked him angrily.

Flavius frowned. "There's nothing going on."

"Then what are you talking about?"

Sighing, Flavius dismounted and began walking toward a little copse of trees. "If we're going to discuss this, let's do it in the shade."

Dismounting also, Antonius followed Flavius and joined him where he sat on a fallen tree. He realized that Flavius looked as though he were about to face a gladiator and not his best friend.

Antonius sighed. "Let's hear it, Flavius."

"I love Diana, Antonius. I have for a long time." He swallowed hard before continuing. "When I thought she was going to die. . .I thought I would die, also," he finished quietly.

Antonius could well understand his feelings. Leaning his elbow on his knee and putting his cheek in his palm, Antonius turned to Flavius.

"So just what exactly are you saying, Flavius? You momentarily caught me off guard, but I am rational now." He smiled wryly, and Flavius returned his smile.

"I want to marry her."

Something flickered briefly in Antonius's eyes. "Have you spoken of this to her?"

"Once," he answered softly, and Antonius wondered at the pain in his voice. He sat up straight.

"And did she reject you?"

"Not exactly."

Antonius became exasperated. "Well, speak up, man. What did she say?"

Flavius picked up a stick from the ground and began to break it into little pieces. His forehead creased in a frown. "She said she would never marry. That she couldn't leave you."

Surprised, Antonius stared hard at his friend. "She told you this? Did she tell you that she didn't love you?"

Flavius shook his head. "No. We didn't speak of love."

"What? You aren't making sense, Flavius."

"The last time I came to your house, I told Diana I was resigning my commission so that I could get married."

Sudden understanding caused a grin to spread across Antonius's face. "I assume you didn't say to whom you wished to get married?"

Frowning at him, Flavius pressed his lips together. "How could I?" Turning away, he lowered his head and dropped the pieces of stick to the ground. "She didn't give me a chance," he finished lamely.

Antonius laughed, pounding Flavius on the back. "I think maybe you two were at cross-purposes, my friend. I'm not sure if Diana loves you in the same way, but I think she might."

Flavius glanced up quickly, hope filling his eyes. "You truly think so? And this would be all right with you?"

Antonius answered him softly. "I can think of no one whom I would rather have for a brother. Come to dinner tonight, and maybe together we can convince my sister of this, also."

"It must be her decision," Flavius warned.

"Agreed."

"I can't marry you, Flavius." Diana stood trembling between her brother and Flavius, tears shimmering in her eyes.

"What?"

"Antonius." Flavius's warning stopped Antonius in his tracks. His fists curled at his sides. What was going through his sister's mind now? He had seen her eyes fill with joy when Flavius spoke of his love, then the joy had faded and turned to sorrow. One thing he was convinced of. Diana loved Flavius as much as he loved her.

"I don't understand," Flavius told Diana softly. "Do you not love me?"

Diana struggled with an answer that wouldn't bring down the wrath of her already sensitive brother. That Flavius loved her was more than she had ever dared to hope. Weeks ago she would have flown into his arms at such a declaration of love as he had given her. But now she was a child of Christ. If she told him so, she knew his eyes would fill with loathing. But she would not deny her Lord. He had made a remarkable change in her life already. Believing she had lost Flavius to another, she had found solace in the peace that Jesus had brought to her life. Although she had hurt, she hadn't hurt nearly as badly as she would have before she found Him. She couldn't turn her back on Him now.

Flavius came to Diana, lifting her bowed head. He looked seriously into her misty blue eyes. "If you tell me you don't love me, I will never mention this again. But I would always like to remain your friend."

The simple words that would leave her life intact refused to be said. She couldn't deny her Lord, but neither could she lie and deny her love for this wonderful man.

"I love you, Flavius," she told him tenderly and watched the joy that filled his face. "But I can't marry you."

"I don't understand." He frowned in confusion. "Is it because of Antonius? Because he has already agreed."

Diana looked at her brother and knew that her answer would displease him. He had such a volatile temper, and she knew she was about to light the fire within him. "I can't because I'm a Christian," she told Flavius, though her eyes never left her brother.

Flavius stared at her, dumbfounded. "By the gods!" he whispered, suddenly dropping to the couch behind him.

No one spoke, and the eerie silence became oppressive. Finally Flavius brushed his hand through his dark hair, lifting his eyes to stare broodingly at Diana. He seemed to suddenly come to a decision. Getting up, he went to Diana and took her by the shoulders. She dropped her eyes in embarrassment, not able to see the loathing she felt sure would be there.

"Look at me, Diana," he commanded gently, and she raised her eyes slowly to his. His brown eyes were aglow with his love, and Diana caught her breath. "I don't care what religion you choose, or what god you choose to worship. I want to marry you anyway."

Diana felt her heart beat rapidly in response to his words, and tears came to her eyes. He still loved her, even though she admitted her Christianity. If she married him, could she win him to her Lord? Could she, by example, show him the true way? And if he never believed, what then? Would it make a difference? Couldn't two people who truly loved each other live together in harmony even though they had different beliefs? *No, they couldn't,* her mind told her, and she realized that Satan was giving her a full taste of his power. How easy it would be to give in.

"I can't marry you, Flavius. I can't." Diana pushed his hands away and fled the room, Sara close on her heels.

Flavius stared at Antonius uncomprehendingly. "I don't understand."

"I think I do," Antonius told him grimly. "These Christians are as zealous in their beliefs as are the Jews. When they believe something, they hold to it fiercely."

"But Diana. . ." Flavius shook his head in confusion.

"Listen to me, Flavius," Antonius muttered. "Diana has been corrupted by these Christians. She needs to be removed from their influence."

Flavius glared at him. "Isn't Sara a Christian, also?"

Antonius drew up his shoulders, his face becoming a bland mask. "Leave Sara to me."

"But what can I do? You heard her say she wouldn't marry me!"

"She will if I decide it," Antonius answered firmly.

Flavius watched the feelings chasing themselves across Antonius's face. He shook his head. "I can't force her, Antonius. She would only hate me in the end."

"I don't think so. You heard her say she loves you."

"She loves me now, but what of later?"

"If you can get her to forget this Christianity business, there will be no problem."

Flavius sighed. "And if I can't?"

Antonius smiled wryly. "I have faith in you, my friend."

Flavius lifted an apple from the supper tray, turning it slowly around in his fingers. Putting it back, he turned to Antonius. "Very well. What do we do?"

"Leave the arrangements to me." Antonius clanged the bronze gong sitting on the table, and Beatrice entered the room. "Send Sara to me," he told her.

Sara came moments later, the thin blue material of her tunic drifting around her. Her sandals clicked across the marble floor as she came to stand before him. Lowering her eyes respectfully, she inquired, "Yes, Tribune?"

"Sara, I am sending you to your parents for a while."

Her eyes flew up in surprise, and Antonius felt himself drawn into their deep brown depths. "You will go tomorrow and return in a fortnight."

She gave him a puzzled look but quickly lowered her eyes. She was filled with apprehension, wondering what Antonius was up to now. She knew it had something to do with Diana and Flavius, and she was reluctant to leave but had no choice. And it would be good to stay with her parents for a while.

"Yes, Tribune. I will make ready," she told him softly.

It suddenly occurred to Antonius that Sara would be gone, and he would not see her for a while. He missed her when she was gone for a few hours. What would it be like when she was gone for two weeks? Maybe during that two weeks he could rid himself of his obsession with her. Whatever happened, things would be changed when she returned.

Chapter 12

Sara touched the mezuzah slanted on the doorpost that contained the sacred writings of the Shema and thought about the words it contained. "Hear, O Israel: The LORD our God, the LORD is one. Love the LORD your God with all your heart and with all your soul and with all your strength."

She spread her fingers softly against the mezuzah and wondered if that was possible for her now, because no matter how hard she tried to deny it, she knew that Antonius held a large portion of her heart.

He was coming for her today, and her heart was already pounding just thinking about it. She remembered his soft kiss and how she had unashamedly responded to it. Color rose to her cheeks. She must forget. He was a heathen who worshiped stone idols. Why had God let this happen to her? Why couldn't she have loved Decimus instead?

Entering the house, she found her mother singing in the kitchen. Sara smiled. For as long as she could remember, she had enjoyed the sound of her mother's lilting voice going about her daily duties. She laid the water bag on the table.

"Did you hear any news at the well today?" her mother asked curiously.

Sara thought about the reaction of the villagers, many of them her friends. They were suspicious of her, and with good reason. They couldn't understand how she could be happy serving a Roman. Frankly she couldn't understand it herself. She should be miserable, and yet she longed to return.

"Hannah is getting married," she told her mother, picking up a knife and helping her remove the seeds from the dates.

Her mother looked surprised. "To whom?"

"Daniel Barjamin."

"Jamin's son? Little Daniel?" Abigail shook her head. "It seems that our children marry younger and younger."

Sara grinned. "Mother, you know that you were only fifteen when you married Father."

"And how old is Hannah?"

"The same age as I am," she returned with humor.

Abigail again shook her head. "Seventeen. How is it possible? The time has flown so quickly. You need to think of marrying soon yourself."

The smile left Sara's face. "I am a slave, Mother. Had you forgotten?"

Abigail looked stricken. "I'm sorry, Sara. It's been so much like old times that

I had forgotten." Her face became solemn with her thoughts.

Regretting her sharp words, Sara hugged her mother. "Let's not think of it right now."

Her mother looked sad for a moment. "But you have to go back today."

Sara decided to change the subject. "Father is finished with Ahaz's sickle. I thought I might return it to him."

"I'm sure your father would appreciate it."

Laying down the knife, Sara went through the connecting door to her father's shop. She found him bent over the forge, sweat pouring down his bare back. At fifty years of age, her father still had an athlete's build. No doubt from working the forge, day in and day out.

She laid her hands on his shoulders and began to briskly massage his muscles.

"I have missed your touch," he told her. "Your mother is far too gentle."

Sara laughed. "Don't let her hear you say that."

Her father smiled wryly. "That's for sure. She'd probably strip the skin from my hide the next time."

"I thought I'd take Ahaz his sickle," Sara told him.

"Good idea. He's too old to come for it, and I'm too busy to bring it to him. Besides, I'm sure he'd like to visit with you."

Sara grinned. "I'll be back before long."

Taking the sickle, Sara started walking down the street, heading for Ahaz's house. She smiled as she thought of the old man. He had always been like an uncle to her, complaining that she was always under his feet. From the time she had been able to walk, she could remember being fascinated by Ahaz and his potions and mixtures.

She tapped at his door, touching the mezuzah before she went inside. "Shalom," she told him.

"Shalom, Sara." He grinned back. "What brings you to see an old man?"

"I brought you your sickle."

"Ah. Then bring it in and have a seat."

Sara joined him at his table, sitting on the mat provided. Although the structure was crumbling, it was clean inside.

"So, tell me of Ephesus," he commanded softly.

Sara shook her head slightly. "So many idols. So many unhappy people. They look for hope in their marble statues and find only emptiness."

"And what of you, Sara?" he asked. "What have you found?"

Color filled her face, and she dropped her eyes to the floor. "I have found many friends. Many of them belonging to the Way."

Ahaz nodded his head wisely. Sara knew that he could probably tell more from what she didn't say than from what she did. He got to his feet and ambled slowly to the door, peering up into the hills.

"What are you looking for?" Sara asked him.

"Nopet hasn't yet returned."

Sara hid a smile. The old man's love for his ewe was well-known by all the villagers. Everyone kept an eye on her, knowing how lost the old man would be without her. Nopet. Honey from a honeycomb, he called her. His pride and joy.

"Would you like me to go look for her?" she asked.

He watched the sun starting to descend from its zenith and paused before answering. "There are still several hours before sunset." He spoke absently, as though he had forgotten Sara was there.

Sara got up from the mat and laid a hand on his shoulder. "I will go look for her. She can't be far."

She went up the hillside behind Ahaz's house, knowing that it was a favorite grazing place for the old ewe. She couldn't find the sheep, but she found several fresh tracks. Deciding to follow them, Sara wandered down a well-trod path that ended at the bottom of a hill. She could see the tracks cross over and begin to ascend on the other side. As she followed the trail, she lost track of time, not noticing that the sun was quickly descending to the horizon. She forgot everything in her fear for the ewe.

Coming upon a small pool of water, she could see where the ewe had stopped to drink. As she bent down to examine the tracks to find which direction the sheep had gone from here, she noticed another set of tracks. They looked like dog tracks, but larger. A shiver chased down her spine. *Wolves.*

Getting up quickly, she hurried in the direction of the tracks. It never occurred to her that her life might be in danger. Her thoughts were centered on little Nopet.

She came out on the edge of the hillside, looking down over a small valley. Rocks jutted precariously in several directions, making several ledges. Sara carefully went from ledge to ledge, looking over their sides. Her breath caught in her throat at the deep gorge that ran about three hundred feet below her. A rushing stream of water snaked off to the west, and as Sara followed it with her eyes, she noticed how far the sun had set.

Knowing that Antonius would probably be at her house by now, she got quickly to her feet. She glanced helplessly around, trying to decide what to do. She would just have to go back. Someone else would have to come look for Nopet. Probably the little ewe was already home, being cuddled by her worried owner.

She started to climb back down the way she had come when she heard a sound coming from her left. She froze, her heart beginning to thunder in panic. The sound came to her again. A soft bleating. She hurried toward the sound, her feet slipping and sliding on the rocks.

When she reached the area where she thought the sound had come from, she could see nothing. She waited, hoping to hear it again. After what seemed an eternity, she again heard the soft bleating coming from below her. Lying down, she leaned far out over the ledge. Below her, Nopet lay on the rocks, her head lifting pitifully as she cried for help.

"Oh," Sara murmured. "You poor little thing."

Now what was she to do? Even though the lamb was small, she was still fat and would be too heavy for Sara to lift off the rocks. She would have to go for help. As Sara turned to go back from the ledge, she could hear a cracking sound coming from beneath her. Her eyes opened wide in alarm; but before she could scramble to safety, the ledge gave way, and Sara felt herself tumbling through space. A scream ripped from her throat, only to be silenced as her body hit the rocks below.

"Antonius, if you love me, don't make me do this."

Antonius turned away from the tearful face of his sister. He was beginning to feel like a monster. "It's because I love you that I'm making you marry Flavius."

"I can't believe Flavius agreed to this," she murmured, almost to herself.

"Let's just say that I talked him into it. I can be most persuasive when I need to be," he told her, and she flinched at his arrogance.

"Oh, I know that," she told him angrily. "Sometimes you are like Satan incarnate."

"Satan?" He had never heard that term before.

"The evil one who controls the world," she explained.

Antonius felt as though he had just been sliced in his heart by a dagger. Could she really believe that of him? He was only doing what he thought best. He loved her and wanted to see her happy.

"I thought your Christian God controlled the world," he told her wryly, the hurt evident in his voice.

"In the end, He does. But Satan has control of everything evil. In the end, God will triumph over Satan, but in the meantime, we must suffer with Satan's presence."

"How have you come to know so much in so little a time?" he demanded.

Diana dropped her head, refusing to answer.

"No matter," he told her firmly. "When you and Flavius are married, he will take you away from all of that. You will have children and learn to be a good Roman wife."

"Nothing you can do can take me away from the love of God," she answered him softly.

Frustrated, Antonius picked up his mantle. He struggled with something to say that would make her understand just how much Flavius and he loved her. "Tomorrow, Diana," he told her. "You will marry Flavius tomorrow. The arrangements have all been made."

He watched her for any sign that might show a softening in her attitude, but he found none. Sighing, he turned and left.

The sun was beginning to descend from the noon sky when he headed outside the city. Leaving Ephesus behind, he breathed deeply of the fresh air. Though Ephesus was beautiful, reputed to be second only to Rome, it was filled with the stench of rotting humanity. Having never considered himself a moral man before, he wondered at the change in his attitude.

He had never taken part in the city's wild orgies. In fact, he had allowed himself to feel somewhat superior to those who chose to participate. Now he realized that by condoning their acts, he was just as bad. Why had he not seen it before?

He had recently read the book of Hosea in his Jewish collection of scrolls. It appalled him that Hosea's God would command him to take an adulteress as a wife. But perhaps Hosea's people thought as little of adultery as did the Romans. He, on the other hand, would probably kill his wife if she did such a thing.

But Hosea's God had talked to him about the Israelites worshiping idols. He told them they would be destroyed because of it. He said an eagle was over the house of the Lord. Could He have meant Rome? Was Rome being used to punish the Israelites? And if so, would Rome then be destroyed by her own corruption?

He pulled his chariot to a halt in front of Jubal's house. Descending from it, he headed for the side of the house where Jubal had his shop. He knew they would be expecting him. He had sent word.

He found Jubal bent over the forge, his muscles rippling as he pumped the bellows. Antonius was impressed with the strength of the old man, though at fifty years of age, he wasn't too old. Antonius fervently hoped he looked as good at that age. Many a legionnaire would envy this man his body.

"Shalom, Jubal," he told the man as he entered the shop.

Jubal turned his head at the Roman's entrance. No matter how hard he tried, he couldn't help but like the young officer.

"Shalom."

"Is Sara ready to leave? My sister has missed her greatly."

Jubal turned back to the forge. "Sara isn't here right now. She went to visit Ahaz."

"I see. Do you mind if I sit?"

Jubal nodded toward the stool in the corner. Antonius made himself as comfortable as possible and struck up a conversation with the old Jew.

They talked about many things, finding much that they had in common. Antonius was surprised to see dusk beginning to settle on the land. He frowned. "Sara should have been back by now. It will be dark and too late to return to the city."

Jubal looked up from the forge, a sudden frown creasing his brow, also. "You're right. Perhaps she came back, and we didn't hear her."

He went to the connecting door and yelled for Abigail. She came quickly to his side, drying her hands on a towel.

"Has Sara returned?" Jubal asked, concern lacing his voice.

She looked past him in surprise at Antonius. "I thought perhaps they had already gone."

"Without saying good-bye?" Antonius asked sarcastically, getting rapidly to his feet.

Abigail and Jubal exchanged worried glances. Taking off his leather apron, Jubal turned to Antonius. "I'll go look for her."

"I'll go, too," Antonius answered him, suddenly anxious.

Following Jubal to Ahaz's house, Antonius kept a constant watch along the road. When they reached the mud hut, Jubal pounded on the door.

"All right, all right. Don't break down my door."

Ahaz opened the door, squinting in the late afternoon light. "I thought you were Sara."

Jubal's face drained of color, and Antonius felt a tight knot of fear clutch at his heart.

"Where is Sara?" Jubal demanded.

"She went to find Nopet," the old man answered him worriedly. "But that was hours ago."

"Which way did she go?" Antonius demanded and reined in his impatience when the old man squinted his eyes at him.

"Ah. The Roman," Ahaz wheezed. "Come to claim your property? More like come to find your master." The old man suddenly cackled with mirth, and Antonius frowned in annoyance. What was the old man talking about? It took a great deal of control to keep his hands from the old man's body.

"She went that way," Ahaz told them, pointing up the hill.

Antonius was already headed up the hill before Jubal caught up to him. "Tell me about this countryside," Antonius prodded.

"Up higher, the hills become rocky. There's a deep gorge that has been carved out by a running stream. I don't think Sara has ever been this way before."

Jubal's worry mirrored his own. Antonius took a deep breath, climbing the hill quickly. When he reached the top, he wasn't even breathing hard. Turning to Jubal, he found the old man had easily kept pace with him. Before long they found Sara's tracks.

"She's following an animal's tracks," Antonius said in surprise.

"Nopet is Ahaz's ewe."

"She's trying to find a stupid sheep!" Antonius was suddenly, inexplicably filled with anger. He would throttle the girl with his bare hands when he found her.

"She's very special to Ahaz," Jubal answered him placatingly, recognizing the growing anger. Was he angry because he was worried or because Sara was making him late?

"There are wolf tracks here, also," Antonius told him worriedly.

"Then let's go. We haven't long until it will be too dark to see."

They followed the tracks, coming to the place where Sara had been lying on the ledge. The tracks ended abruptly, and there was no other sign.

Antonius was the first to hear the bleating of the ewe. Lying down, he leaned over the ledge. "I see the ewe," he told Jubal. "But I don't see. . .wait. . ."

Pushing himself carefully over the edge, Antonius gripped for handholds among the rocks. Slowly he lowered himself down as the last rays of light peeked over the mountains, leaving them in sudden darkness.

"Is she down there?" Jubal asked anxiously.

"Yes. She's unconscious. It looks like she hit her head on the rocks."

Antonius stared around him in the dark. He could barely make out the shapes of the hillside and could hear the water rushing below in the gorge.

"Jubal, there's no way to get her out of here without some rope. You need to go for help."

Jubal looked around him in the gathering darkness. The moon was gibbous in the sky, which afforded him some light, but not much. He wasn't sure he could find the same place in the dark.

"I'll be back as soon as I can," he told Antonius, turning to hurry down the hill.

Antonius knelt beside Sara. He could feel the stickiness in her hair and knew that it had to be blood. Taking off his mantle, he wrapped it gently around Sara as best as he could without moving her. He was afraid to move her body without being able to see the extent of her injuries.

Sitting down beside her, he took her head gently in his lap. He brushed the dark strands from her eyes, his fingers softly tracing her cheekline. He felt along her shoulders and let his hand rest on her chest. The faint beating of her heart was reassuring, and he sighed with relief.

As he sat in the dark, he could feel himself being watched. Glancing up, he could see yellow eyes peering at him from above.

"No, my friends," he said softly. "She belongs to me."

Chapter 13

Antonius didn't know how long he sat in the dark, cradling Sara's head in his lap, waiting for help. He petitioned every deity he was familiar with, and some he was not so familiar with. Finally he lifted his face to the night sky, glaring at the fiery stars over his head.

"All right, Sara's God, whoever You are. Wherever You are. She's in Your hands. She tells me You love her and that nothing happens without Your will. What did she ever do to deserve this? Hasn't she been hurt enough? Some protector You are. Twice she has almost died."

He looked down at Sara's prostrate form and felt a lump forming in his throat. When had he begun to care so much? How had it happened? What was there about this girl, so unworldly and naive, so lacking in physical beauty, that had touched his heart?

Sighing, he leaned back against the rocks, unmindful of the sharp edges digging into his back. What was he to do now? He wanted Sara more than anything he had ever wanted in his life, but he knew she would never come to him willingly. Was that what made her so intriguing? Was it a desire to possess something that he couldn't have?

She stirred him physically like no woman ever had, yet he had barely touched her. They had exchanged a few kisses, nothing more, but he longed for more. The very scent of her roused thoughts in him that Sara would consider most inappropriate.

What was most unusual was the love of knowledge they both shared. He could talk to her for hours and know that she was just as desirous to learn more as he. Most of the women of his acquaintance were interested only in the games at the Colosseum or the theater or other such mindless occupations. Sara not only understood what he read from his scrolls but could converse with him intelligently about them.

His hands stroked gently over her forehead. The blood seemed to have stopped flowing, and Antonius lifted his eyes heavenward again. "Thank You," he whispered, almost sure to which deity he was expressing his gratitude.

Sounds from above alerted him to the presence of the rescue crew. Torchlight brightened the area above his head, and Jubal's face peered at him from over the ledge.

"How is she?" he questioned anxiously.

"She's alive; more than that, I don't know."

"I'm coming down."

A rope snapped out from the ledge and quickly unwound as it was lowered toward Antonius. Jubal followed the rope, his large form a suddenly reassuring presence to Antonius. When he reached Antonius's side, he bent down, taking Sara's hand in his. His hands swiftly scanned her body, searching for other signs of injury. Finding none, he leaned back on his heels, sighing in relief.

"She hasn't awakened?"

"No," Antonius told him, gently lowering her head and getting to his feet.

"I've brought help. Let's get her out of here and back to Ahaz's," Jubal told him.

It didn't take long for them to get Sara to the top of the hill. Antonius and Jubal hurried down the hillside, not waiting to see if the men were able to get to Nopet. Antonius carried Sara in his arms, sweat beading his brow. Jubal was impressed with the young Roman's surefootedness, even in these parts that were unknown to him.

Jubal touched the mezuzah on the doorpost, following Antonius inside. The darkened interior was lit by one small lamp, the smoke drifting upward to a crack in the ceiling. Ahaz rose from his mat, hurrying to their side.

"What happened?" he questioned.

Antonius and Jubal exchanged glances before Antonius strode across the room and laid Sara against the mat in the corner.

"Nopet fell over a ledge. Sara must have tried to help her," Jubal explained.

The old man's face paled as he hurried over to where Antonius had placed Sara. "And Nopet?"

"The men are trying to get her out. I don't know if she's been hurt or not," Jubal told him.

Kneeling beside Sara, Ahaz began to investigate her injuries. He lifted her eyelids gently before turning to Antonius. "She hasn't awakened at all?"

Antonius shook his head. "I'm not sure how long it's been since she fell, but the time I was with her, she remained unconscious."

Ahaz glared at Antonius. "How is it, Roman, that ever since you have been around Sara, she seems to have become unusually accident-prone?"

Rising to his feet, Antonius gave the old man a murderous look. "What are you saying, old man?"

Before Ahaz could answer, Sara moaned softly, turning her head slightly on the mat. Antonius knelt quickly by her side, stroking her dark hair gently from her cheeks and pushing it out of the way. Sara's eyes fluttered open, and she gazed uncomprehendingly at Antonius.

"Antonius?"

Antonius. Not Tribune. Antonius smiled widely, his blue gaze focused on Sara's face as realization returned, and with it her usual reticence.

"What happened?" Sara frowned, trying to recall. "Nopet?"

Jubal came and bent down beside his daughter, taking her hand gently in his own. He grinned. "Perhaps next time Ahaz won't send a donkey to retrieve his lamb."

Sara smiled, trying to sit up. Her head began to reel, and the room started to spin. Moaning, she lay back on the mat.

Antonius and Jubal focused their attention on Ahaz, their questions in their eyes. He was already preparing one of his concoctions and refused to look their way. Going to Sara, he bent and helped her to drink the brew. Within minutes, she sighed, released from the pain.

"She hit her head, or something hit her head. I don't know which. Regardless, the only injury I can find is to her head. Everything else seems to be fine."

"Aren't you going to give her something to make her sleep?" Antonius wanted to know, distressed that Sara would be suffering from the pain. Her face was so white, and she lay quietly, her eyes opening and then drifting closed again.

Ahaz frowned at him. "No. She needs to be awake so that she doesn't drift into a deeper sleep than that from which she has already awakened. I have seen it happen before." Ahaz sat down next to Sara, settling himself comfortably on the mat. "We have a long night ahead of us. I need to make sure Sara stays awake."

Jubal was torn. He knew his wife would be frantic with worry. "I need to tell Abigail, but I will come back."

"I'll stay," Antonius told him firmly.

Although Sara was awake, she was in a surreal world with no thoughts of her own. Her mind drifted in and out of focus, and she felt unusually free from any worries. Even her father's anxious face caused nothing more than a slight feeling of regret.

"She's fortunate," Ahaz told them, "that she landed among the grass. It was thick enough to prevent her serious injury."

"God protected her," Jubal declared, a song of thanksgiving rising to his lips.

Antonius felt the hair prickle on the back of his neck as Jubal recited words that Antonius had read among the Jewish scrolls. Words from their king David.

Jubal left shortly with a promise to return. Antonius made himself comfortable across from Ahaz, the only thing separating them being Sara's prostrate form. Antonius shifted uncomfortably as Ahaz continued to stare at him. The old man made him nervous. It was almost as though he could see inside his mind.

Ahaz hurried to the door when he heard a disturbance outside. Flinging open the portal, he let out a cry of joy as a sheep was thrust into his arms by its disgruntled rescuers. Thanking them profusely, Ahaz hurried to lay the sheep down and inspect it for injuries. Finding no serious ones, he began to scold the ewe gently even as she hurried to what was, Antonius supposed, her favorite corner. Only when the ewe had settled for the night did Ahaz turn again to Sara.

As Ahaz ministered to Sara, Antonius watched him warily. There was something on the old Jew's mind, and Antonius had no doubt Ahaz would come out with it sooner or later. Time passed slowly, and Antonius chafed at the inactivity. He felt like he should do something.

"Relax, Roman. There's nothing we can do now except wait."

Antonius studied the man curiously. "You don't like me, do you?"

Ahaz snorted. "I suppose you're all right. For a Roman."

One dark eyebrow winged its way upward. "Such praise might go to my head. You should use it sparingly."

This was met by a cackle of laughter. Antonius recognized the wisdom behind those deep brown eyes and realized that he would like to have this man's respect.

Ahaz began to speak in Aramaic to Sara, trying to keep her awake. He would switch periodically to Greek and then to Hebrew. Antonius recognized the tactic. Sara would have to try to concentrate on what he was saying, which would help her to stay awake.

Antonius stared at Sara's pale face. When her eyes switched to him, she smiled slightly, and Antonius felt his heart respond.

"You are so handsome," she whispered, and Antonius raised his eyebrows, his glance flicking to Ahaz.

"She's unaware of what she's saying. The drug I gave her confuses the mind but relieves it of pain."

Antonius frowned. Her whispered words had filled him with happiness, but now he wasn't sure. What did she really think of him? Did she know how much he cared for her? Did she feel the same? She responded to his kisses, but that was only a physical reaction. Antonius knew he wanted more. Much more.

Smiling down into Sara's eyes, he decided to take a chance. "As you are beautiful," he told her softly, bending forward and touching his lips to hers. When he lifted his head, Sara reached her hand up and gently stroked her fingers down his cheek before letting her hand fall limply back to her side. Closing her eyes, she sighed softly. Antonius leaned back, content for the moment to leave things as they were.

Ahaz opened his mouth to speak but was startled into silence when thundering hoofbeats passed the old hut. Antonius went to the door, recognizing the jingling of Roman *cingula* as the horses went by. He opened the door quickly, but they were already rounding the bend. Frowning, he closed the door and returned to sit beside Sara. Although her eyes were dazed, they were focused on him.

What were Roman soldiers doing here and at this time of night? His eyes met those of Ahaz, and he saw the same question mirrored in their mysterious brown depths.

It was only moments later when they heard the horses returning. Jumping to his feet, Antonius reached the door just as the horses stopped outside. Before he could release the latch, someone started to pound furiously on the door.

Antonius flung the door open and stepped back in surprise when Flaviu strode past him and into the room. Taking off his helmet, his gaze scanned th room before coming to rest on Antonius.

"I heard what happened. Will she be all right?" He nodded his head in Sara direction.

"It would seem so." Antonius smiled wryly at Ahaz. "It appears that Jewis people have hard heads."

"Not any harder than your sister's," Flavius told him, clearly aggravated. Ther was something more in his attitude, and the smile left Antonius's face.

"What's wrong?"

Sighing, Flavius pushed a hand through his dark hair. "Diana has disappeared."

The color drained from Antonius's face. "What do you mean, she's disap peared?" he asked hoarsely, grabbing Flavius by the front of his cape.

Flavius pulled a small scroll from his belt. "She left this for you. She sent on to me, also."

Antonius took the scroll and quickly unrolled it. His eyes scanned the brie message, and Flavius could see them darken with his anger.

"What did yours say?" Antonius demanded.

Flavius rubbed a hand across his face, raising pain-filled eyes to Antonius "She says that she cannot marry me and that it would be wrong before her God t do so. I have had soldiers discreetly searching the city for her all evening."

Antonius gritted his teeth in frustration. "How can she have disappeared Where could she have gone? She wasn't well enough to have walked far."

Antonius thought back over the last two weeks. Diana had worked hard ever day, practicing her walking. She had seemed almost driven in her efforts to ge back on her feet. Now he understood why.

Antonius glanced back at Sara. He had to find Diana, but how could he leav Sara like this? Fear began to worm its way through him as he realized that he migh possibly lose one or the other. Ahaz could see the indecision in Antonius's face an got up from his mat, ambling across the room until he reached Antonius's side.

"Sara will be fine," he told Antonius. "All she needs now is to rest. He strength will return before many days, though her head may ache much longer."

Antonius sighed with relief. Going to Sara, he hunkered down beside her. "I will return for you in three days," he told her softly, letting his hand slide down he arm and squeeze her hand.

She watched him with unfocused eyes. Frowning, Antonius knew there wa nothing more he could do here right now. He would find Diana and then com back for Sara. Getting quickly to his feet, Antonius strode past Flavius and out th door. Flavius turned swiftly on his heel and followed.

"I brought Orion from the old man's house."

Antonius nodded, swinging himself to the horse's back. "Let's go!" he commanded.

When they reached the villa, Antonius dismounted, handing the reins to Gallus. He turned to Flavius. "Have you no idea where she could be?"

Sliding off his own mount, Flavius shook his head. "I hoped that you would."

Antonius leaned against Orion. "By the gods, Flavius, what's happening? Everything is going to ruin. Nothing's the same."

Flavius felt Antonius's pain, realizing in that way they had something to share. "I don't know, Antonius. Why would Diana run away? She said she loved me."

Antonius didn't answer. What could he say? He was only now beginning to understand himself. At first he had thought that Sara's God wasn't a very strong God since He hadn't been able to protect her from the things that were happening to her. After talking with Diana, he wondered if perhaps these things were caused by the one Diana called Satan instead. Perhaps this Satan was trying to destroy Sara and her family, and instead, Sara's God had intervened on their behalf. He had witnessed some incredible things where Christians were concerned.

A sudden thought occurred to Antonius. "Do you have any idea where General Titus lives?" he asked.

Flavius looked surprised. "General Titus? I haven't heard his name mentioned in years. Why do you ask?"

"Come inside and I'll explain. Then we'll see if we can find him or one of these other Christians. Maybe Diana is hiding out with them."

Antonius knocked at Jubal's door and waited. Moments later, the door opened, and Abigail faced him. She stood back wordlessly and waited for him to pass.

Sara was sitting by the counter in the kitchen, slicing cucumbers into a bowl. She looked up, her face suffusing with color.

"Tribune. I'll only be a moment." She placed the knife on the counter and got to her feet.

"Take your time."

Antonius watched her gather her things together, going to her mother and hugging her. A gash on her forehead was surrounded by a huge purple bruise, and Antonius winced involuntarily.

"Are you sure you are recovered?"

Sara came to stand before Antonius, her head bowed. "Yes, Tribune."

Antonius felt irritation rising in him. She had called him Antonius before, had even told him he was handsome, now here she was, back to calling him Tribune. Perhaps it was her mother's presence, or perhaps she had been told of her words to him and now was embarrassed by them.

He handed her into the chariot as Jubal came from the side of the house. Jubal's eyes went from one to the other before coming back to Sara. "Take care, Sara."

She smiled back at him. "And you."

Antonius walked back to Jubal and held out a small leather pouch. Jubal looked at him questioningly even as his hand reached for it.

"For you," Antonius told him before turning on his heel and rejoining Sara in the chariot. Wrapping his arms securely around her, he lifted the reins, slapping them against the horse.

Sara felt almost glad to be returning. She had missed Diana, but she had missed Antonius more. She could feel his tenseness and knew that something was wrong. He had been almost cold. Distant. Was it something she had done?

"Diana is missing," he told her without emotion.

Turning her head sharply, Sara stared at him in surprise. "How? When?"

"The day I came to get you. You know nothing of this?" His blue eyes showed his uncertainty.

She shook her head. "No, Tribune." Turning back to the front of the chariot, Sara offered a silent prayer for Diana's safety. She turned back to Antonius.

"Have you looked for her?" she asked and then realized what a foolish question that was.

"Sara," Antonius told her softly. "Diana ran away from marrying Flavius."

"Oh." Sara saw they were rapidly approaching the city, and her mind was trying to think quickly what to do. Had Diana gone to fellow Christians to hide out? They would have understood her plight and been willing to help her. Antonius must be hurting abominably. He loved Diana. But then why would he try to force her into marriage? It didn't make sense.

When they arrived at the villa, Antonius handed her down. "You are free to do as you please until I can find Diana. I'll be in the bibliotheca if you need me."

Turning, he strode away. Sara watched him go with some misgiving. He was hurt, but he was angry, too. She went inside only to find the whole villa in a state of mourning. Everyone loved Diana, and everyone was concerned.

Deciding to see if what she had supposed was correct, Sara took a cape and slipped out the side gate. So intent was she on her mission that she failed to notice the figures who slipped out behind her. Hurrying through the streets, she came to the rundown section of the city. She went to the apartment that she had been to so many times with Decimus. Knocking gently, she went inside.

"Sara!" Diana ran to her, throwing her arms around Sara and hugging her tightly. Tears flowed freely from both of their faces.

"Diana! Antonius is worried about you."

Diana drew back slightly, her eyes filling again with tears. "I know. I'm sorry, but I had to leave. I couldn't go through with it."

"What happened? I knew you were supposed to marry Flavius, but I didn't think you would run away."

Taking her by the hand, Diana pulled her over and had Sara sit near the window.

Facing the room, Sara smiled at General Titus and his wife, Callista.

"Welcome, Sara," General Titus told her, handing her a cup of *posca*. Sara took the watered wine and smiled her thanks, turning back to Diana.

"You have been here all this time?"

Diana nodded, dropping her hands to her lap. "Antonius must want to kill me."

Sara sighed. "I don't know about that, but when he brought me home today, he was very quiet. More so than usual."

Diana and Sara exchanged stories when General Titus and his wife left the room. That Diana was miserable was obvious, though she tried not to show it. Her lovely blue eyes were dulled with worry. Sara wondered why Antonius had sent her away when he was planning Diana's wedding. Did he think she would try to stop it?

Someone knocked on the door, and Callista went to answer it. Sara and Diana smiled at each other. General Titus was a kind and helpful man. Many people found their way to his door, and he helped them all, even if it meant giving them his last denarius. Diana had been only one of many.

Callista opened the door, her breath drawing in sharply in surprise. Diana and Sara rose quickly to their feet, only to find themselves staring into Antonius's cold blue eyes. Sara realized then that he must have followed her here. Flavius stood to his side and slightly behind him. Seeing Diana, he pushed past Antonius and came to stand before her.

"Why?"

The one word held such a wealth of hurt that Sara felt her throat close tightly. She looked past Flavius to Antonius. He was so unmoving, his face revealing nothing.

General Titus came back into the room, stopping in midstride. His eyes widened in surprise and then filled with welcome. "Antonius! It's been years!"

Antonius felt some of his anger evaporate. Christian or no, this man had at one time been like a father to him, and Antonius had loved and respected him. Glancing around at the tenement apartment, clean but so obviously a hovel, Antonius felt Rome's betrayal of one of her best, due to this same pagan religion that Sara embraced.

"General Titus," he acknowledged. "I've come to fetch my sister."

There was silence in the room until Diana finally broke it. "I'll get my things," she said softly to no one in particular.

"I'll come with you." Flavius followed her from the room.

Feeling uncomfortable, Sara turned away from Antonius's dark perusal. She went to Callista and hugged her. "Thank you." Looking into her eyes, Callista knew that Sara wanted to say more, but something held her back. She gazed over Sara's shoulder at Antonius and raised her brows but said nothing. Turning to her husband, she said, "Should you not offer Antonius some posca?"

"Thank you, but I haven't time," he told her softly.

Callista stared at him, her lips tilting up in humor. "It may be some time before your sister returns," she told him.

Antonius looked over her shoulder to the hallway where his sister and Flavius had disappeared. He could hear what amounted to a heated argument, and his eyes came back to Callista's face. His lips quirked in humor. "You could be right."

"Come in then and have a seat, boy," the general told him. "We have a lot of catching up to do."

Antonius sat in the seat indicated, motioning for Sara to sit beside him. Reluctantly Sara did as she was bidden. She was very aware of Antonius and the arm he draped over the couch behind her.

"I understand you've become a Christian?" Antonius cut right to the heart of the matter. He respected this man more than he had any other, save his father. His question invited an explanation.

General Titus explained how his conversion had come about. His eyes gleamed intensely as he focused his attention on Antonius. "I have never seen anything like it before or since. The sun refused to shine for three hours. The earth shook, and rocks were split apart everywhere."

The words so softly spoken caused a chill to race down Antonius's spine. If anyone else had told him such a thing, he would have scoffed, but not at this man. Antonius knew him too well.

"You were in Jerusalem when this happened?"

"Yes. I was there with my soldiers to help still the threat of insurrection. But God had other plans for my life."

"Does this God have a name?" Antonius inquired, impressed despite himself.

"Some call him Jehovah. Some, El Shaddai. There are many names for Him," the general told him.

"Like Zeus and Jupiter?" Antonius asked skeptically.

General Titus laughed. "No, my friend. Each of His names means something special in Greek, Aramaic, and Hebrew. His names explain who He is at certain times. Sometimes He's the Father chastising His children, sometimes the Judge passing sentence."

Antonius nodded in understanding. "I see."

Sara looked at him in surprise, because it sounded as though he really did understand. Her heart began to beat harder. Could he possibly understand it all? *Please, God, let him believe.*

Diana and Flavius entered the room, and Antonius noted the defeat etched across his friend's face, his shoulders slumped in dejection. Diana was being stubborn, no doubt. His lips thinned in anger. He would handle this matter at home.

Getting to his feet, Antonius pulled Sara swiftly to hers. Placing a hand on the small of her back, he propelled her toward the door.

Diana turned at the door, tears in her eyes. "Thank you for taking me in. May God bless you." Turning, she fled outside.

As the general and his wife watched the four walk away, General Titus turned to his wife. "Come, Callista. I think we have some heavy praying to do."

Chapter 14

Antonius watched his sister and Flavius out the window of the bibliotheca, tempted to intervene. The same scenario had been performed for the last two weeks. Every day, Flavius came to see Diana, and within a short period of time, they were in a heated argument. Then Flavius would leave, only to return the next day and try again.

Shaking his head, Antonius decided not to interfere. This was something they had to work out for themselves. After talking with Diana, Antonius realized how distraught she was over the thought of marrying a man who didn't share her faith. He had finally granted permission for her to decline the marriage. It had been hard to do. Flavius had been extremely hurt. He had refused to give up, and Diana loved him enough to try to win him to her way of thinking.

Diana was vociferously arguing her cause when Flavius suddenly swooped forward and kissed her on her surprised mouth. Color flew to Diana's cheeks, and Antonius had to grin. *Atta boy, Flavius. Keep her off balance.*

Antonius turned at a sound from the doorway. Sara stopped on the threshold and stared at him questioningly. He felt his heart squeeze within him. This was something else that was going to be hard to do.

"You wished to see me, Tribune?"

"Come in, Sara." Antonius motioned her forward. "There's something I need to discuss with you." His eyes roved over her, taking in the colorful yellow tunic she wore. She looked like a butterfly in the sunshine.

Sara felt her heart start to pound. What had she done to cause such a look on Antonius's face? Something was terribly wrong, and she had no idea what it could possibly be.

Antonius couldn't bring himself to look Sara in the face, so he busied himself rolling up scrolls and putting them away in their cubicles. With his back to her, he leaned heavily against the carved desk. "Sara," he began reluctantly, and Sara became more concerned. She had never seen him so unsure of himself.

Sighing, he turned to face her, leaning back against the desk. "I've made inquiries to find out about your brother, Dathan. I had it in mind to have him set free."

A smile spread across Sara's face at the news, her heart suddenly filled with joy. Dathan coming home! The smile left her face as rapidly as it came. Antonius didn't look pleased at all. "You couldn't find him?" she asked hesitantly.

His eyes met hers briefly and quickly flicked away. He motioned her to a seat, coming to kneel in front of her when she slowly lowered herself into it.

Antonius licked suddenly dry lips, taking one of Sara's hands in his own. He began to absently stroke her wrist with his fingers, not realizing the effect he was having on her.

"I only know of one way to tell you this," he told her firmly, his eyes fully meeting hers for the first time.

"Dathan is dead," he told her softly, his throat closing around the words. He felt her begin to tremble, her eyes growing wide with horror. Slowly she shook her head from side to side.

"No! It can't be!"

Sara's mind began to whirl with her confusing thoughts. *Dathan dead!* How was it possible? Surely God had a purpose for his life. He couldn't die this young, he just couldn't. Feelings of guilt overwhelmed her. She hadn't been the kind of sister she should have been, and truth to tell, she had loved Decimus more than her own brother.

Now she could never make it up to him, never ask his forgiveness. She felt somehow to blame. Staring into the intense blue eyes in front of her, she felt her anger begin to boil. Hadn't she told Antonius that Dathan was just a boy? He couldn't be expected to survive such harsh conditions as the galleys.

Black anger clouded her reasoning as she continued to stare at Antonius. He was to blame. He was the one who had put these things into motion and brought such a disaster upon her brother.

"It's your fault," she told him tonelessly.

Antonius released her hands, drawing back at the pain she inflicted with her words. He had already fought with his own feelings of guilt, his own self-condemnation. But there was more that Sara needed to know. There was more to the story.

"Sara."

"No!" Sara jumped to her feet, almost knocking him to the floor where he was still kneeling. When he reached out to her, she drew back sharply and stared at him with loathing. "You killed him. You murdered him!"

"Enough!"

"I hate you!" she gritted through clenched teeth.

Sara was beyond reasoning, beyond fear of retribution. Lifting her hand, she violated all the laws of Rome and struck her master a resounding blow across the cheek. Turning, she fled from the room.

Antonius stared after her in surprise, his hand covering his cheek, where a red mark was beginning to show. By all rights, Sara had forfeited her life with such an action. He could have her fed to the lions in the arena or even crucified if he so chose. He shuddered at such a possibility.

Although he was angry at Sara's refusal to listen to his explanation, he understood her feelings. She had every right to accuse him. He hadn't given any consideration to anyone's feelings when he had taken Sara from her home and sent Dathan to the galleys. He hadn't cared whom he hurt as long as he got his way. *Just like Rome.* The words echoed in his mind and left him no peace. He would give Sara time to recover, and then he would try again.

Sara paused outside the bibliotheca, suppressing the shudder that ran through her. Antonius had demanded her presence, and she thought she knew why. She had been foolish to slap him, and her rash action may have cost her her life. Taking a deep breath, she entered the room.

She was surprised to see Diana standing next to the desk where Antonius sat, her eyes full of compassion. Sara walked over and stood in front of Antonius, her head bowed respectfully.

Leaning across the table, Antonius laid a scroll in front of Sara. "Take it," he commanded, remembering another time.

Sara lifted her eyes to his and saw his pain reflected there. What had he to be hurt about? Thinking the scroll her death sentence, her fingers trembled as they reached forward and clasped the document.

"Antonius is giving you your freedom, Sara," Diana told her joyfully. "I'm going to miss you something fierce, but what he's doing is right."

Sara swallowed the knot in her throat. She didn't care that he was freeing her or even that she wasn't to be punished for her actions earlier. Only one thought stood out clearly in her mind. He was sending her away.

Diana wrapped Sara gently in her arms and hugged her close. "We won't say good-bye, because I intend to see you again every time I get the chance. You must come to my wedding, also."

Looking up, Sara questioned Diana with her eyes. Color filled Diana's cheeks and made her look more beautiful than ever.

"Flavius is coming around to my way of thinking. It may take some time, but I won't give up. God is supreme, and His Word won't come back empty, so Flavius doesn't stand a chance. When that happens. . .then we'll be married," Diana finished softly.

Antonius got to his feet and came around the desk to stand beside them. He reached out a hand but let it drop to his side.

"Get your things together. We'll leave for your home within the hour."

Confused, Sara turned away. She had told him she hated him and had slapped his face. She had blamed him for the death of her brother and called him a murderer. And he was giving her her freedom. She had expected to be punished and, instead, had been rewarded. Isn't that what was known as grace?

Her heart breaking, Sara gathered her things together while Diana chatted to her. What did she expect? She had been a servant, nothing more. She had been wrong when she thought Antonius cared for her. Maybe he had, just a little, but she had destroyed that with her thoughtless words.

Antonius helped Sara into the chariot after she and Diana hugged each other, clinging together as friends. He wrapped his arms firmly around her, taking up the reins.

"I'll miss you," Diana yelled as they drove away.

Tears that had been held back now struggled for release. Believing herself unobserved, Sara let them trickle in masses down her cheeks. She should be glad she was going home, and in a way she was, but her heart felt torn apart by her confusing feelings regarding Antonius. She blamed him for the death of her brother, and yet she couldn't resolve that with the man she had come to know and love.

Antonius watched the tears wending their way down Sara's cheeks and felt his chest constrict painfully. He wanted to take her in his arms and hold her close, begging her forgiveness. But now wasn't the time or the place, and he had things to settle with her parents. He prayed that they would listen before condemning him.

They reached Sara's house as the sun was beginning to set. Lifting her down from the chariot, Antonius watched as she walked away, head held high. A smile twitched his lips. Stubborn to the end.

Antonius followed her into the house, knowing that Jubal would be through with his business for the day and that he would be preparing for supper.

Abigail and Jubal rose to their feet in surprise, Abigail's eyes locked on her daughter's distressed face. Raising her eyebrows, she sought the reason from Antonius.

"I must speak with you," he told them quietly while Sara set about putting her things away. Antonius followed her with his eyes, wanting to reach out to her. Comfort her.

"Have a seat," Jubal told him, "and share our supper."

"I need to get some water," Sara told them desperately and fled out the door. Antonius started to rise and go after her but realized her parents were waiting. Lowering himself back to the mat, he sighed heavily.

Sara returned to find her mother in tears, her father preparing to come after her, and Antonius gone. She had been gone several hours, and though darkness had descended, she couldn't bring herself to come back. She had lain on the grass watching the stars appear and wondering at God's will for their lives. *Oh, Dathan, Dathan. Are you with God?* Remembering his life, she doubted it and felt even more sorrow.

Laying the empty water skin on the table, Sara went to her mother and tried to comfort her, only to realize that she was not wailing as the Jewish people normally did for their dead. Though her eyes were filled with tears, there was joy and acceptance there, also. Perplexed, she turned to her father.

"Antonius told us that you didn't let him explain about your brother's death," he told her sorrowfully. "Perhaps you should have listened."

"Listened! What could he say that could bring Dathan back? What could he say that would take away his guilt in this matter?"

"Dathan is with God," her father told her quietly, and she curled her hands into fists at her sides.

"How can you say that? You know how he lived!"

"But I also know how he died," he told her angrily, "and if you would listen, you would see the hand of God in all of this."

Her father watched her struggling to comprehend his attitude and realized that he had failed her in this regard. He should have trusted God and not blamed the Roman for his son's own foolishness. "Sit down, Sara," he commanded quietly.

Sara sat on the mat next to the table where Antonius had been, the food forgotten. She picked up a date and began to twirl it in her fingers. Her father looked tired but somehow jubilant. She had missed something by staying away. Something important.

Her father sat across from her, crossing his legs. He began to explain to her what Antonius had told him about Dathan's death.

Dathan had been assigned to the galley of a Roman warship. There had been ninety-nine other rowers, besides himself and the drummer. When the warship had gone to the aid of a grain ship coming from Alexandria that was being attacked by pirates, a fierce battle had ensued. The warship had rammed the pirate ship, but in doing so had busted open its own hull, causing the Mediterranean to rush in. Although Dathan had been one of the first freed, he had refused to leave without helping the others. He had gone down with the warship, still trying to free the other slaves.

Tears poured freely down Sara's face, and she was filled with an acute pride in her brother. Her mother was sobbing softly in the kitchen area as she put away the supper dishes.

"I'm proud to know that he would die to save others," she told her father softly. "But what of repentance?"

Jubal smiled at his daughter. "One of the slaves told Antonius when he was questioned that shortly after Dathan arrived, he started talking to them about God's love. He sang hymns while he rowed and praised God whenever he had the chance. Many of the slaves who died with the ship died in the Lord, thanks to Dathan. He. . ." Jubal choked on the words, and Sara went swiftly to him.

"It's all right, Father."

Jubal hugged his daughter close, burying his face in her neck. He sobbed quietly for the loss of his only son.

"I don't know how or why Dathan repented, but God has allowed us to know that he did." Jubal pulled back from his daughter and looked seriously into her face.

"And I will thank God every day for sending the Roman into our lives."

Sara felt her heart lurch at his words. She had blamed Antonius for her brother's death, when in all probability, he had saved his eternal life. What would have happened if Dathan had continued on the path he had chosen? Thank God for Antonius's wisdom. Thank God for Antonius's heart. Now how was she ever going to be able to apologize and ask forgiveness?

Sara sat alone in the copse in the woods, knees drawn up under her chin. She was so still that a fallow deer entered the woods without suspecting her presence. She smiled slightly.

It had been a long time since she had come to her favorite spot. Her thinking spot. Not since the accident with Antonius. Sighing, Sara closed her eyes and brought his image to mind, but the only image she had was of blue eyes filled with hurt and pain. It had been several weeks, and still the memory wouldn't go away. When she opened her eyes again, he was standing not more than twenty feet away. Thinking she was seeing a vision, she hastily closed her eyes and opened them again.

He was still standing there, more handsome than ever. His short white tunic was trimmed with purple, the color of the aristocracy, and his leather belt emphasized the leanness of his waist.

"I thought I might find you here," he told her quietly. She looked for some kind of emotion but found nothing. Why was he here?

He walked over and sat down on the log next to her. Though he didn't look at her or touch her, still she felt herself firmly attached to his presence.

They didn't speak for several minutes, each concerned with their own thoughts. It was Sara who finally made the first move toward reconciliation.

"I was hoping I'd see you again and have the chance to apologize. To ask your forgiveness."

He looked at her then, his face registering his surprise. "You have nothing to apologize for. I'm the one who should be apologizing." He leaned his head forward, pushing the palms of his hands against his eyes. "Can you ever forgive me?"

Sara's heart went out to him. She could see now what she hadn't seen at a distance. Tired lines radiated out from around his eyes, and he was thinner than before. His face was almost haggard.

"I forgave you a long time ago," she told him softly. "My father told me about Dathan. I'm sorry I misjudged you. Please forgive me for the awful things I said. I let my Lord down terribly in my words and my actions."

Antonius let out his breath, turning to face her. "I think you're more like Jesus than you know," he replied, then smiled at Sara's astonished reaction. His smile faded as he continued to stare at her, his eyes resting on her lips. Suddenly he jumped to his feet and began pacing.

"Zeus! With my arrogance, it's a wonder God didn't strike me down dead. What

I wanted, I took." He looked down at her, and his voice quieted. "Even you."

Sara looked away from him. "My parents have helped me to remember that everything that happened was by God's will. I have a tendency to forget that."

Antonius knelt in front of her, placing a hand on each side of her on the log. He was so close that Sara could smell the fragrance of sandalwood he used after his baths. She tried to move away, but there was no place to go.

He leaned forward until his lips were mere inches from her own. "As long as you don't forget me," he told her softly, huskily.

Sara's heart pounded furiously. What was he trying to say? Did he care for her after all, or was he trying to assuage his feelings of guilt?

"I could never forget you," she answered him softly.

A fire seemed to ignite behind his eyes, and she thought he was going to kiss her. Instead, he leaned back, a dubious expression crossing his face.

"And what exactly do you remember?" he asked doubtfully.

Sara's lips twitched. "I remember a man who loved his sister so much he would do anything for her. I remember a man who tried to help his friend find happiness with the woman he loved. I remember a man who freed my parents when he had no need," she finished softly. "Why didn't you tell me?"

He turned his face away, embarrassed, but Sara reached out and gently turned it back so she could see his eyes. His hand went up to cover hers, holding it in place against his cheek.

"I wanted to, but I didn't want you to feel beholden to me."

Sara's forehead creased in a frown. "I don't understand."

Letting go of her hand, Antonius rose to his feet, pulling Sara up and into his arms. He bent forward, kissing her gently on the nose.

"I love you, Sara," he told her. "I want to marry you, but I didn't want you to marry me because you felt you owed me. I freed you for the same reason. I wanted to make sure that what I felt for you was real, not just something physical whenever I was around you."

Sara stared up at him, her mouth open in surprise. How many times had she dreamed those words, prayed for this moment. She loved Antonius with all of her heart, but she couldn't marry him. Only in her dreams, her fantasies, but never for real. Diana realized the danger and stood firm against the temptation; how could Sara do less?

She tried to pull away, but Antonius wouldn't let her. Did he know that just by holding her he could cloud her thinking? Every time it had been harder and harder to deny him.

"I can't marry you, Antonius," she groaned softly.

His brow furrowed, and his eyes lit with anger. "What do you mean, you can't marry me? Are you trying to tell me you don't love me? Because if you are, I don't believe you."

Swooping down, he kissed her passionately and felt her body melt into his embrace. Getting no resistance, Antonius gentled his kisses, reveling in Sara's response. He lifted his lips slowly from hers and stared intently into her eyes.

"Now tell me you don't love me."

Sara's body was trembling all over. Her legs would not support her and if not for Antonius's arms, she would have found herself on the ground. She leaned her forehead against his chest and could feel his heart pounding with a rhythm to match her own.

"I don't deny that I love you." Her voice was muffled against his tunic, and Antonius had to strain to hear her. "But I can't marry you."

Realizing she meant what she said, Antonius jerked her back to face him. His face colored angrily, and his fingers bit into her arms.

"By the gods! You can't mean it!" He shook her none too gently. "Why?"

Sara saw the pain in his eyes, and her own filled with tears. "I can't marry you for the same reason Diana wouldn't marry Flavius. You're not a Christian."

Dawning comprehension brought a sparkle to Antonius's eyes, and his fingers relaxed their hold. "Is that the only reason?" he wanted to know, and Sara nodded her head.

"And what if I tell you that Flavius and Diana are to be married in three weeks?"

Sara jerked her head up in surprise. Had Diana given in after all? Had the temptation been too great? Poor Diana. She tried to push out of Antonius's hold, but he still refused to let her go. There was laughter in his eyes, and Sara felt her temper begin to rise.

"I'm not Diana. I won't marry a man unless he's a Christian."

"Then marry me," Antonius demanded softly.

Ceasing her struggles, Sara stared at him in amazement. "You?"

"Yes, me." He saw the doubt filling her eyes, and he began to shake his head. "No, Sara. Not just to marry you. I've learned a lot about Jesus in the last few months. Before, He was just a story about an insurrectionist. Now I know the truth. I've spoken to many people who witnessed His death, including General Titus, and I can't doubt their words." He rubbed his finger gently against her cheek, across her nose, and up her other cheek. "But even more than that, I've seen what He can do in someone's life after His death. Take Diana, for instance."

Sara felt as if her heart would burst with happiness. Oh, God had truly blessed her life. Now she understood what the apostle Paul had meant when he said that all things worked together for the good of those who loved God.

"Beloved," Antonius whispered, pulling her more firmly into his embrace. "Marry me."

Eyes shining, Sara shyly lifted her lips to his. Antonius marveled at her sweetness and how a few words had changed her from a fighting vixen to a soft lamb.

His body responded to her show of love, and his kiss deepened. For the first time, Antonius felt like he had come home, welcomed by the one whom God had chosen for him from the beginning. He was awed by God's patience, His goodness, and His love.

Things would not be easy, but with God's help, all things were possible. Antonius reached for Sara's hand, clasping it firmly in his own. He smiled down into her face, kissing her softly on her lips. Then turning, they walked out of the forest together.

Epilogue

Sara stared out her bedroom window at the sun rising over Ephesus. The beautiful columns of the Artemesion shone whitely against the morning sun, its pink rays spreading their fingers across the sleepy city.

How could someplace so beautiful be so full of evil? Everywhere, Satan had a grip on this city. A citizenry who prided themselves on their tolerance of other religions and their belief that they were more civilized than other races, and yet they sent hundreds to die in the arenas for their amusement.

Antonius came up behind her, sliding his arms around her already swollen waist. She sighed as he began to nibble on her earlobe and leaned back against him.

"Couldn't you sleep?"

Sara shook her head. "I'm worried, Antonius."

He sighed heavily. "As am I. Now that Nero is Caesar, I think things are going to become much worse for the Christians."

"What can we do?"

Antonius turned her in his arms, kissing her lightly on the nose. "I think it's time that I take you and the baby to safety. When things change, maybe we can come back."

Sara felt the beginnings of real fear. "But where can we go?"

"I thought we might go to Alexandria, in Egypt."

Sara's mouth dropped open. "So far?"

"That's the point, beloved," he told her patiently. "Although it is an important city, it's far enough from Rome to be relatively safe. Your parents have agreed to come with us."

Smiling brightly, Sara hugged him. "How did you manage that?"

Antonius laughed. "I reminded Jubal how close Alexandria is to Jerusalem. Your father has a desire to see his home again."

Suddenly sobering, Sara turned back to the window. "Before now, the only people who persecuted Christians were the Jews. Now it seems everyone is against us. Why? We preach nothing but peace and love. How can anyone hate those things?"

Resting his chin against the top of her head, Antonius sighed. "People don't want to be reminded of their sins. They want life to accept them as they are, no matter how depraved they might be."

"Perhaps God intends us to spread the Word. If not for this persecution, wouldn't you be content to remain safely here in Ephesus?"

Antonius agreed. "I don't know why these things have to happen. I don't know why a good man like General Titus and his wife, Callista, had to be slaughtered in the arena. I only know that we have to trust in God."

"And Diana?"

"She and Flavius have agreed to come, also."

"Thank God," Sara sighed in relief.

As the sun rose brightly in the morning sky, Antonius made arrangements for his family to leave Ephesus. They would travel a long way and become pilgrims in a strange land, but the Lord would always be with them.

Not long after they left Ephesus, Rome burned, and along with it much of what was still human and moral. Nero chose to blame the Christians, though there were those who said it was actually Nero himself who ordered the destruction.

Far away in the land of Alexandria, Sara gave birth to a son and named him Zephaniah, because God had protected him from the evil and destruction of Rome.

Edge of Destiny

To my children, Dena and Devon, who have given my life focus.
May God always hold them in the palm of His hand.

And to Anita Johnson,
who has taught me the true meaning of friendship.

Chapter 1

Decimus Antigonus stood on the edge of the milling crowd and felt his stomach coil with revulsion. As large as the city of Rome was, how had he managed to be at this particular spot during this moment in time? Would that he were anywhere else in this whole stinking city.

"I am bid ten denarii. Do I hear more?" The crusty slave master spread out his toothless smile over the crowd.

"Eleven denarii." The speaker threw an angry glare across the gathering throng, challenging a man on the other side.

The man looked calmly back, his obsidian gaze unblinking. His robes denoted his occupation, a priest in one of the temples.

As the afternoon sun beat down upon his back, Decimus studied the dark-eyed priest. Knowing what the man had in store for his unfortunate victim, Decimus felt a wave of pity. Whether they were male or female, most of the slaves in the temples were destined for prostitution.

"Twelve denarii." The priest's cool voice and dark look sent a shiver down Decimus's back. Evil seemed to emanate from the man in waves.

Murmurs broke out among the crowd. Obviously a war was going on over the girl standing on the auction block. The slave dealer standing beside her smiled his gapped grin, and his eyes began to gleam.

Decimus's eyes went to the girl standing resolutely on the platform. Small of stature, thin, and emaciated, he could find no reason for the avid bidding.

Then his eyes lifted to the girl's face and held. The only feature that redeemed her face from plainness was the pair of large brown eyes that gazed out at the crowd fearfully. Dark lashes swept down to once again obscure her eyes and the terror that was lurking there.

The bidding had reached twenty denarii. Decimus stared in surprise at the young girl. What did these men see that he could not? True, her coloring was unusual. Blond hair very much the color of his own topped a rather petite frame that looked as though a good gust of wind would blow it away. Blond hair and brown eyes were indeed a striking combination, but for twenty denarii?

For a moment, the girl's eyes lifted and stared straight into his own, and then Decimus knew. Purity and innocence reached out to him, touching his very soul. Surely the angels in heaven must have such eyes. How had such a girl managed to make it to the slave market of Rome and still retain such innocence?

The girl's vulnerability touched Decimus on the raw. Flicking a glance across the crowd, he could see the merchant's face as the priest continued to outbid him. The man wanted the girl badly, that much was obvious. The hotness of his gaze as it roved the girl's body caused a slow boil of anger to erupt inside of Decimus.

Looking across at the priest, Decimus could see no change in his demeanor. The priest was as cool and confident as ever. When the priest looked at the girl, it was for an entirely different reason. As a temple prostitute, the girl would bring a fortune, at least until her purity was stripped away by the atrocities committed there. The desire to possess such innocence would be overwhelming to many of the men of Rome who were sated with the sins of this life.

The crowd had become almost hushed as the contest continued. A third man had entered the bidding. Decimus recognized one of the more prominent senators of Rome, the purple trim of his tunic giving evidence of his aristocracy. One look into the girl's eyes, and the senator had entered the fray.

Decimus glanced back at the girl. Her body was visibly shaking. *If only she would keep her eyes down,* he thought to himself, for there was little else to recommend her.

Where had he seen eyes like that before? A sudden image came to his mind of a young Jewish girl with brown hair and dark brown eyes, much the same as those he had just seen. *Sara.*

Decimus felt a tightening in his chest. *Sara.* A slave girl in his previous master's house. A slight smile touched his lips. Sara had no looks to speak of either. Her beauty had come from within, but that inner loveliness had been so great that Decimus the slave had fallen in love. That sort of beauty of spirit could only come from the Spirit of God. Seeing the girl on the auction block, Decimus realized that she and Sara had much in common.

The ache in Decimus's chest grew even tighter. He still loved Sara. He had asked her to marry him, but she had refused. She had told him that his love was a brother's for a sister. Not so, for hadn't he stayed faithful to her memory all these years? But was her memory as clear in his mind as it once was? He was no longer sure. He had not seen Sara for almost five years, and his feelings were confused.

"Thirty denarii," the slave merchant cackled gleefully, bringing Decimus abruptly back to the present. "Do I hear more?" Rubbing his hands together, he glanced from the portly merchant to the priest. *The senator must have the upper hand,* Decimus decided.

Obviously both the merchant and the priest were reaching the end of their resources. Sweat was beaded across the merchant's brow as he wrung his hands in agitation. Only the priest remained unaffected. The senator was smiling smugly. Only a miracle would save the girl now.

Decimus's heart ached for the girl. Whichever way she went, she would be misused and abused, her innocence defiled. *God, help her,* he pleaded.

His thoughts were interrupted by a woman making her way through the crowd. Her bright yellow palla would have drawn attention even if her regal bearing had not. She wasn't old, but neither was she young. In her youth she had probably rivaled Aphrodite in beauty. She went to the senator and touched his arm, turning to see where his attention was focused.

When the senator looked down at her, his face was immediately filled with shame. Decimus could see even at this distance the love that glowed from his eyes as he beheld who must have been his wife. She frowned reproachfully at him before she turned and walked away. The senator flicked a brief look at the slave girl before turning and hurrying after her.

So much for the senator. Decimus would much rather have seen the girl go to him than to either of the others, but God had apparently saved at least one Roman from the sin of adultery.

Now the priest's eyes were gleaming with an unholy light. Decimus knew that although the priest would probably have more money than the merchant, too much spent on one slave could cause him to be punished. He couldn't have defeated the senator, but the merchant was another matter.

The girl was devoid of color, her lips trembling noticeably. A tear was coursing a path through the dust on her cheek. In her innocence, was she aware of what was intended for her? The anger within Decimus began to churn. Grinding his teeth together, his gaze again went from merchant to priest.

The crowd had grown larger, and although no one else had entered the bidding, many were taking sides. The chattering around him grew unbearably loud, and the press of unwashed humanity against him from all sides made Decimus want to retch. He should leave. He had a very important appointment with a man who could help him leave this accursed city. Still, something held him in place.

The merchant glared angrily at the priest, his color an alarming puce. The priest gazed back at him impassively.

So, the priest had won. Decimus felt his skin begin to crawl as he recognized the symbol of the gold necklace glinting in the sunlight. A snake curved round a pole. The symbol of Aesculapius, the god of healing. People went to the temple of Asklepios and allowed snakes to crawl all over their bodies, hoping for healing. Decimus closed his eyes tightly. Were all Romans insane? If only they could know the *true* Healer, the one who heals the spirit. Many of the diseases of these people came from their own immoral lifestyles.

"Going once."

The slave merchant's voice brought Decimus back to reality. So what price had the priest paid? He had missed the last bid.

"Going twice." The slave trader glanced hopefully at the merchant and then over the crowd. Although the girl had already brought what amounted to a fortune in terms of slave prices, he still hoped for more. "Surely you can see the worth of such a piece. She has much to offer."

When Decimus glanced at the girl, he found her staring back at him. Her luminous brown eyes seemed to reach into his very soul and found him lacking. Sadly she lowered her eyes, submissively accepting her fate.

Without realizing it, Decimus found himself moving forward to the fringe of the crowd. The slave master was raising his hand for the final call. The merchant had turned away, pushing through the crowd, his face as scarlet as the tunic he wore. The priest stared impassively at the girl, his eyes glowing black.

Decimus felt helpless as he watched the slave trader's hand raised to its utmost. Cold sweat broke out across his forehead. *Forget it,* he told himself angrily. *She's nothing to you.* Why should he feel such agony over an unknown slave girl?

"One hundred denarii." The crowd around Decimus parted, surprised faces turned his way. A rippling murmur ran through the mob.

For the first time since the whole procedure began, Decimus saw the priest's face become animated. His mouth dropped open, his jaws working convulsively. His eyebrows flew toward his receding hairline, and his eyes lost their impassivity. He glared in angry surprise at Decimus, who was no less surprised himself.

After one startled glance at Decimus, the slave trader asked again for a higher bid. The heat from the sun seemed to intensify as Decimus felt the sweat break out on his palms. After what seemed an eternity, the priest swung angrily away, and the slave trader turned back to Decimus.

"My lord, she is yours," he announced hesitantly, his look passing over Decimus's worn clothes. Since leaving Ephesus, Decimus had dressed in rags, hoping to convince any would-be robbers that he was too poor to be bothered. Now everyone in the crowd would know that was not so, and Decimus knew that among such a crowd there would be cunning thieves and robbers.

Lifting his chin, Decimus strode forward, stopping in front of the podium. He jerked his money bag from inside his tunic where it had rested peaceably for years. He still had much of the money Antonius had given him when he sent him away with his freedom. If he kept this up, though, his fortune would dwindle away like the sands of time.

Decimus handed over the coins to the slave trader, making sure he received his bill of sale and slave papers. Now he was really aggravated with himself. What was he going to do with a slave? Especially a scrawny little girl.

For the first time since he had opened his mouth and uttered those preposterous words, he looked at the girl. Although her lashes veiled her eyes, a slight smile curved her lips, and her trembling had ceased.

What was she thinking? That she was safe with him? How could she be so accepting of her fate?

His mind wandered back to when the Romans had invaded his homeland of

Britannia. He did not know if his family were even still alive. The last he had seen of his family was his father lying in a pool of blood, his mother's prostrate form over his father, and his sister being shoved from one Roman soldier to another while they laughed at her torment.

He had tried to come to her defense, but a young lad of ten had very little strength compared to a seasoned Roman soldier. Decimus had managed to draw blood from one hearty specimen with his teeth before he was knocked senseless.

Many beatings later, he had finally been cowed. Most of the scars were still visible across his back. Even now he squirmed when he thought of his cowardice. He had been born a warrior, one of Britannia's aristocracy. Wouldn't it have been better to die a free man than live as a slave?

But stay. If he had died then, he would never have heard the good news of Christ. No, even now he would rather be a slave who knew Christ than a free person who was a slave to sin.

But this girl. What had she undergone to stand there so meekly willing to succumb to her fate, and what was he to do with her now? He should have minded his own business and bypassed the crowd, but curiosity had gotten the best of him.

Now here he was, expected at a meeting—a rather dangerous liaison at that—and he was encumbered with a female slave! *God, what am I to do now?*

Decimus helped the girl down from the platform, avoiding her eyes. Long blond hair draped demurely across her cheeks. Why was her head not shaved? Obviously she hadn't been sent to the baths as slaves usually were before they were brought to market.

He tapped his foot impatiently while the slaver removed the iron leg bands. Taking the girl by the arm, Decimus propelled her none too gently through the crowd. His one aim was to get as far away from the central market as quickly as possible. The snickers that followed him sent waves of color washing across his face.

When they were clear of the marketplace, Decimus pulled the girl to a stop in the shade of an apartment building. He glanced quickly around to see if they had been followed. Seeing no one, he turned his attention back to the girl.

Her face was bent submissively down while her fingers toyed with the frayed cord around her waist. The rough brown wool of her dress could barely be called a tunic. As his eyes moved over her, he noticed other things he hadn't seen before. She was barefoot and bleeding. Decimus bent to inspect the sores on her feet.

"You're hurt."

"It's no matter, my lord." Her voice flowed over him in gentle waves.

Decimus allowed himself to look into her eyes. As he expected, their light spoke volumes. Shaking his head, he quickly got to his feet.

"We can't stop here. Someone may be watching." He looked at her skeptically. He hated to cause her more pain, but they couldn't stay here. "Do you think you can keep up with me? We're going to have to move fast."

"I am strong, my lord," she answered softly. "I will keep up."

Grunting, Decimus started to turn away before he remembered something. "I don't know your name."

"Chara, my lord. My name is Chara."

Decimus said nothing for a moment. Finally he nodded his head. "Chara," he said, seeming to test the word on his tongue. "That's a beautiful name." She didn't answer, and he frowned. "One other thing. Don't call me 'lord'. Do you understand?"

She glanced up at him in surprise before quickly looking down again. "What shall I call you then, my l–?" She stopped, biting her lip in confusion.

"My name is Decimus," he told her softly.

Frowning, she answered him slowly. "I. . .I cannot call you by your name!"

"It's my name, and it's what I prefer." Decimus began to feel impatient.

"But I am a slave. It's not proper."

"Look." Decimus brushed a hand in agitation through his tousled blond locks. How could he explain to the girl without sounding like some raving lunatic? "You're not a slave. I mean. . .well, you were. . .but you're not. I don't want a slave."

Her head remained bent, and her voice seemed small and far away. "You don't want me?"

Rolling his eyes heavenward and releasing a sigh, Decimus was at a loss for words. *God, help me. If You wanted this, I need some guidance.*

He looked uneasily around him. "We'll have to talk about this later. Right now we have to get out of here. Are you sure you can walk?"

"Yes."

Taking her again by the arm, Decimus began to hurry her toward the other end of the city. The sundial at the town square had shown him that the hour was later than he expected. The sun would be going down quickly, and he still had a long way to go.

When they reached a high white wall, Decimus slowed his steps. Glancing around him again, he opened the gate in the wall and ushered Chara ahead of him. Flowering hibiscus lent their color to the already fading blooms of other flowers. Summer was full upon them, as was evidenced by the dry petals of the wilting leaves. A marble fountain splashed in the center of the enclosed garden, shaded by a large olive tree.

Decimus led Chara to a marble bench beside the fountain. "Wait here," he told her.

He was gone only a moment, returning with an elderly gentleman dressed in the tunic of the Roman aristocracy. Gentleness emanated from the older man's serene face, and a smile lit his features.

"Ah, Decimus. So this is the girl."

Decimus nodded. "I have no idea what to do with her, Antipus. My foolish impulsiveness has imperiled our plans."

Antipus shook his head. "Not at all, my friend. It would take only a moment to rectify the situation."

"I don't understand."

Antipus motioned toward the villa. "Come inside, and let's discuss it. It's much too hot out here."

Decimus looked down at Chara. She was still sitting with head bowed, hands clutched together in front of her. Laying a hand on her shoulder, he realized that he was hesitant to leave her.

"Chara is hurt," he told the old man. "She needs tending."

Instantly concerned, Antipus moved to Chara's side. His eyes missed nothing in their quick perusal.

"Of course. I didn't realize." He motioned again toward the villa. "Bring her into the atrium. It's cooler there." Noticing her dirty, disheveled appearance and bloody feet, he paused. "Wait. Better yet, bring her to the baths. I will have one of my servants tend to her while you and I talk."

For some reason he couldn't fathom, Decimus was reluctant to give over care of the girl to someone else. He felt responsible, for one thing, and her obvious fright was another. She had quickly lifted her eyes to his and then dropped them just as quickly, but he had read the fear there. She seemed to trust him even though he had given her no cause, and such faith humbled him.

Reaching down, he scooped the girl into his arms. "Tell me where to go."

Antipus had already started for the house. "Follow me."

He led them through the peristyle and into the atrium. Lush potted plants filled the room, making it seem as though the garden outside spilled over to the inside. Following Antipus through the hallways, Decimus was struck by the opulent surroundings. Antipus must be one of the higher officials of Rome, and a very wealthy man. He frowned but kept his thoughts to himself.

The baths were just as luxurious, and profuse potted plants again gave an impression of the airy outside. Pungent scents of sandalwood, myrrh, and a host of other odors he couldn't name filled the steamy air.

Gently he set Chara on her feet, keeping an arm around her for support. When he glanced down at her, he found her eyes studying his face, but she quickly dropped her gaze.

Antipus clapped his hands, and a young girl entered the room. She glanced from Decimus and Chara back to Antipus.

"Take the girl and see to her needs," Antipus told her. "She has need of a clean tunic, and see that she gets anything else she may want."

Nodding, the girl came quickly to Chara's side. "This way, my lady."

Chara's head flew up in surprise. "Oh, but I'm not. . ."

"It's all right," Decimus interrupted her. He had no idea what was going to happen or what role the girl might play over the next few days, but he wasn't taking any chances. The less said, the better. "Just do as she says."

When Chara quickly dropped her eyes to the floor, Decimus grew exasperated. Perhaps it was the proper posture for a slave, but it was beginning to get on his already taut nerves. He would have to speak to her about it, but for now it would have to wait.

He followed Antipus from the room and back along the corridors to the atrium. It was definitely cooler in here. Although the open roof allowed the sunshine into the room, the shade from surrounding trees cooled the air as it blew gently through the open portals.

Antipus indicated that Decimus have a seat, and Antipus sat down across from him. He reached for a silver gong sitting on the table, giving it a gentle *clang*. In answer to his summons, a young man entered the room with a tray of refreshments.

"Please, help yourself," Antipus told Decimus.

Decimus was surprised when his stomach rumbled. "Thank you." He reached for a peach and a knife.

Antipus settled back against the cushions of his seat. "Now, tell me exactly what happened and how you came to possess a slave."

Getting his thoughts together, Decimus regaled Antipus with his tale from the moment he had entered the market until the time he had fled. Antipus's lips twitched with amusement.

"It's not funny, Antipus," Decimus protested. "What am I going to do with the girl?"

"Settle down, my friend. As I said before, it would take but a moment to set her free. She can remain here, if you like."

For some reason, Decimus was reluctant to commit himself to such an action. He knew it was the right thing to do; then why did he hesitate? Instead, he changed the subject. "What was your idea for getting me out of Rome?"

The old man pursed his lips, taking his time before answering. Lifting a pear from the plate, he began to methodically cut it into sections.

Decimus could barely contain his impatience. He felt like ripping the fruit from the man's hands and demanding an explanation. He managed to control himself, but only just.

Antipus leaned forward, his expression serious. "One of the main problems we have with leaving the country at this time is that the Romans have learned that Christians won't lie or deny their Lord."

"And?"

"Patience, my friend. If you would let me explain without interrupting?"

Leaning back, Decimus forced himself to relax. "I'm sorry. Please continue."

"The Romans also know that a Christian won't own a slave."

When Decimus opened his mouth, Antipus fixed him with a look, and Decimus subsided.

"The soldiers have become devious in their ways of sniffing out Christians. Anyone who boards a ship is asked if he is one." He leaned forward to emphasize his point. "But if you board a ship and they know you *are* a slave, they will likely not bother you."

Decimus rose slowly to his feet. "Are you suggesting that I become a slave to escape Rome? Because if you are, you must be out of your mind! I will never again bow to the yoke of any man, nor will I ever subject anyone else to it." He shook his head angrily. "No, Antipus, I will never be any man's slave again, nor do I ever intend to own one."

Antipus raised his brows. "But you already do."

Sinking back onto the couch, Decimus put his head in his hands. He had already forgotten this afternoon's fiasco. "What a mess I've made of things."

"Decimus, listen to me. I know how you feel, and I admire you for it. No one could fault you for your compassion where the girl is concerned. Probably I would have done the same in your situation." He grinned. "I have done so on occasion myself, purchasing slaves here or there and then giving them their freedom." He watched Decimus carefully. "None of the servants in my house are slaves. They have all been granted their freedom and may leave anytime they choose."

Surprised, Decimus searched the old man's face for the truth of the statement.

"Chara will be safe with me." Antipus suddenly sobered. "I wish I could say the same for my own wife. The more I become involved with clandestine Christian affairs, the greater the risk of detection. I would ask that you take my wife with you—but that would certainly bring notice to me, and it's not yet time. I need to help as many others as I can to escape from this city. I'm not sure how, but I'll find a way." He stared thoughtfully at his twisted fingers. "My only fear is for the safety of Agrippina. As my wife, she will be subject to the same punishment I receive."

"What of Chara then? What would happen to her were you to be arrested?" Decimus queried in concern.

Antipus glanced up. "What? Oh, yes. She would be sold on the slave market again as would any others in this household." He smiled without mirth. "Of course, my servants know that if anything happens they are to run as far and as fast as they possibly can. I wouldn't wish any of them to become lion feed, nor a human torch in Nero's gardens, for that matter."

"Nero is an animal," Decimus declared vehemently.

"No," Antipus answered gently. "Nero is a devil. If I believed it possible, I would say he was Satan incarnate." Shaking his head sadly, his eyes took on a preoccupied look. "What has happened to the glory of Rome? What went wrong? That the people can worship a man as a god. And such a man! Someone who would kill his own mother and wife and then marry a prostitute. Is anywhere safe from such a madman?"

"Rome has tentacles everywhere, but less so in Britannia," Decimus declared. "I don't remember much about my birth country, but I know it is far enough away that Rome has less concern with it."

"I wouldn't be too sure," Antipus answered. "Since Nero forced Seneca to commit suicide, more and more his generals have the ear of the emperor. They have been stirring up trouble, for they are hungry for conquest."

The young serving boy entered the room. "There is someone to see you at the door, my lord."

Antipus got quickly to his feet. "Ah, the person I've been waiting for. Bring him in."

Decimus came to his feet, the blood draining from his face as the young boy reentered the room, followed by a Roman soldier, impressively dressed in all his regalia.

Chapter 2

Chara felt the warm, scented waters of the bath drift soothingly around her as she stepped down the stairs into the tiled bath. The young girl who had helped her with her things was lifting a cruse of oil for inspection.

"Would you like a violet scent when you are finished, my lady?"

Instead of answering her, Chara asked a question of her own. "What is your name?"

The girl smiled shyly. "Candace, my lady." Again she held up the cruse, raising her eyebrows questioningly.

What would Decimus have her do? Intuitively Chara knew something important was going on in the other room. Decimus had spoken of plans, and both men seemed worried that there might be danger. He had deliberately stopped her from revealing to Candace that she was, herself, a slave.

Still, it had been a long time since Chara had been showered with such attention. And how long had it been since she had a real bath? She felt the luxurious sensation of the water swirling around her and reveled in the feel of it. There was no telling how long it would be before she had such a chance again.

"The violet scent would be nice, Candace, but do you think you could leave me alone for a while?"

Candace didn't seem surprised. "Of course." She motioned to a small gong beside the pool. "Just ring that when you're finished, and I will come."

Left on her own, Chara allowed the thoughts she had been holding at bay to surface. Closing her eyes tightly, she prayed for continued strength. God had been merciful to her thus far, but what did her future hold? Why was she being tried in such a way?

Tears trickled down her cheeks as she thought of her loving mother who had so recently died. Pain washed through her as she once again relived the last eight months.

Her mother had been sick for so long, and her stepfather had taken to drinking and carousing. He had once been an educated and cultured man, but now he would come home at all hours in a drunken stupor, and always her mother forgave him and tried to care for him. But she had been too sick herself.

And Franco, her stepbrother, had only made matters worse. Ever since Chara and her mother had entered the household, Franco had hated her. Perhaps he considered her a usurper who would one day cause him to lose some of his inheritance.

Whatever the reason, he had made Chara's life pure misery. But she had refused to tell her mother, knowing that it would only cause dissension and hard feelings.

Then her stepfather had died. In a drunken daze, he had managed to fall from the dock into the river. No one had known. Some fishermen found him one morning washed up on the bank.

After that, her mother's health declined even more. Chara attributed that to the fact that upon his father's death, Franco had made it quite clear that Chara and her mother were there only on his forbearance. Chara squirmed at the memory.

And then one morning, Chara had gone into her mother's room with her breakfast tray only to find that her mother had died peacefully in the night. Chara grieved, but she had little time to mourn, for Franco had let Chara know that he wanted nothing to do with her, and he began to make her life as hard as possible.

"You're so ugly no decent man would want you," he told her. "And I'm certainly not going to be responsible for you the rest of your life." After that, she had been relegated to the role of servant.

One night Franco had been unusually friendly and invited Chara to dine with him. Although Chara was suspicious, she didn't want to offend him, so she reluctantly accepted. Her stepbrother had been charming, lulling Chara into a false sense of security. Perhaps he had had a change of heart. It was only later that she found out he had slipped a potion into her drink that would make her sleep.

When she awakened, she found herself in leg chains far from her home of Gaul. Franco had sold her to a slave trader heading for Rome. The journey had been long and arduous, the heat unbearable. The only thing that had saved her from rape was her constant illness.

Chara realized early that something about her seemed to appeal to a particular breed of men, the kind she had no desire to attract. She knew it was not her looks, for she had none to speak of, but something about her drew them nevertheless. She hadn't had to worry about Tarus, the slave trader, for his interest lay elsewhere. He preferred the young boys, and Chara felt sympathy every time Tarus stopped to buy new slaves and a young boy was among them.

Then they had reached Rome, and Tarus decided that, rather than spend extra coins on sending the slaves to the baths, he would just stop in the marketplace and hold his own auction.

Chara had learned well the ways of a slave; Tarus had seen to that. When the auction had begun, she kept her eyes demurely on the ground. She had glanced up once to encounter the gaze of a ruddy-faced merchant, his bright red tunic matching almost to perfection his complexion. She shivered with distaste when he looked into her eyes. His own had grown large, a strange gleam coming into them.

When she heard a second voice entering a bid, she had let curiosity get the best of her and she looked at the man. His black gaze had rested on her only a moment, but she had felt defiled. His robes told her that he was a priest. And she shivered at what he probably had in mind for her. Her mother had told her appalling stories of the Romans and their temple prostitutes.

And then she had seen Decimus. His angry blue gaze had stared into hers, and she felt her heart lurch within her. He was handsome, strongly built. His blond hair shone in the sunlight. Without knowing why, she had longed for him to be the one to purchase her. Realizing from his ragged appearance this could not be so, she still gave way to her imagination. Something about him drew a response from Chara, and she realized that she was making a peremptory judgment. He could be a madman for all she knew, yet there was an indefinable quality about him that spoke of character well hidden.

When a third man had started to bid on her, she had felt mortified with shame. Each man had telling eyes, and what they said caused her to become almost faint with trepidation. She had prayed harder.

In the end, it had been Decimus who had purchased her after all. One hundred denarii! How could he afford so much? His clothes had led her to believe he was just an impoverished bystander. She had hoped for him to purchase her, but now what? What did he have in mind for her?

Pain washed through her when she remembered him saying that he didn't want her. Wasn't that what Franco had told her? But if Decimus didn't want her, why had he paid such an exorbitant price? It didn't make sense, but Chara knew one thing for certain. God had cared for her from the beginning, and He surely wouldn't desert her now.

Lifting the silver wand, Chara rang the gong.

Antipus saw the expression on Decimus's face and hastily tried to reassure him. "It's all right, Decimus. Galla is a friend."

Decimus glanced suspiciously from one to the other. Galla stepped forward, extending his arm. Looking from Galla's face to the extended arm, Decimus slowly reached out his own. Galla clasped Decimus's forearm with his hand, and Decimus hesitantly returned the pressure.

Looking relieved, Antipus motioned for them to be seated. "Galla and I have a plan for getting you out of the city."

Decimus's eyes narrowed. "Why would a Roman soldier want to help me escape from the city?"

Galla regarded him steadily. "Because I am a Christian, too."

"A Roman solider who is a Christian?" Decimus studied the man warily. "I hope you'll excuse me if I'm not quite convinced."

Smiling, Galla turned to Antipus. "I think our young friend needs some persuading." He turned back to Decimus. "Just what would it take to reassure you?"

Confused, Decimus looked from one man to the other. He shrugged his shoulders helplessly.

Antipus intervened. "Really, Decimus, we only want to help you. Would Marcus have sent you here otherwise?"

Shaking his head, Decimus eyed the other two suspiciously. "I'm sorry, it's just that. . ."

"You are right to trust no one," Galla told him. "Christians are dying every day in the arena because of their faith in their neighbors and even their own families."

"Please, gentlemen, we haven't much time," Antipus interrupted. "Let's have a seat and discuss all the particulars."

Decimus sat, but his body remained tense. The only reassurance he had that these men were genuine was the word of a close friend. If he couldn't trust these men, he knew of nowhere else to go.

"Decimus has a problem," Antipus told Galla. "He found himself the possessor of a slave today."

Galla's eyebrows rose. "A slave?"

Color flew to Decimus's cheeks, and he hurried to explain the situation. Galla sat back thoughtfully. He looked at Antipus. "Could he not leave the girl with you?"

"I have already suggested that," Antipus told him. "Anyway, I have a plan that might get Decimus out of the city, and perhaps a few others, as well."

Galla listened to the old man's suggestion. Pinching his lips between his thumb and finger, he considered a moment. "Your idea has some merit. No one would question a centurion about his slaves." Galla contemplated Decimus, his eyes sparkling with mirth. "And how would you feel being the slave of a Roman centurion?"

Decimus's eyes flickered briefly, but he refused to be baited. "How would I get to Britannia? I have no idea how to get there from here."

Surprised, Galla looked from Antipus to Decimus. "Didn't Antipus tell you? I'll be taking you."

Equally surprised, Decimus glared back at him. "You? Why ever would you be taking me to Britannia?"

"I see Antipus hasn't told you very much."

Antipus smiled slightly, shrugging his shoulders. "I thought I would leave that to you."

Nodding, Galla turned back to Decimus. "Britannia is my home."

Though he was taken aback, Decimus remained silent.

"At least it was the home of my father, and my grandfather and great-grandfather before that. It would take too much time to explain the whole situation," Galla told him. "Let me summarize for you. Many years ago, Julius Caesar penetrated my great-grandfather's homeland. My grandfather's father was impressed with the man, but he was also afraid. He sensed that the man had a destiny which would bring him into contact again with Britannia. Later, my grandfather and my father met Claudius, who decided that Britannia would be an asset to Rome. Claudius annexed it into the empire, and for the most part treated my people well. My father decided to accept Claudius's offer of serving in the Roman army."

"He was actually willing to fight against his own people?" Decimus interrupted incredulously.

"At that time, peace had been made with Britannia. Claudius made treaties with some of the tribes, and my father was a wise man. He understood the way the winds were blowing, and he knew there would be no stopping the Roman war machine. By serving Rome, my father was planning for the future. But he never forgot Britannia, and he never let me forget it either."

Decimus nodded in understanding. "So when your father retired, he was granted automatic citizenship, and then when you were born, you were considered a Roman citizen by birth."

Galla nodded. "Correct. And since I have the *privilege* of being a Roman citizen, I have learned much about Rome."

"You're spying for Britannia?"

Sighing, Galla pressed his lips together. "No, I'm not. My father served Rome faithfully, as have I. But since Claudius's murder by his own wife, Rome has become barbarous, wanton in its destruction. Rome is no longer the democracy it was intended to be. It has become vile and depraved. It's time for me to go home. Rome is on its last leg, and the people of Britannia have a chance of regaining what was once lost. I want to help. I also wish to tell them about my Lord, Jesus Christ," he finished quietly. "I have some leave time coming to me, and I wish to visit the home of my father and grandfather."

Decimus couldn't fault the man's logic. He watched him closely, and he liked what he saw. His allegiance was to God, not to Rome. Not even to Britannia. There was strength of purpose in Galla's face. Here was a man of integrity.

"So, what do you say, my friend?" Antipus inquired. "Are you ready to leave Rome? Are you ready, like Galla, to go west and north—and spread God's Word?"

Decimus took his time answering. His look passed from one man to the other. Finally he nodded his head. "I'm ready!"

"Praise God!"

Three pairs of startled male eyes turned toward the doorway. Chara stood silhouetted within its frame, her hands clutched together in front of her. Her changed appearance was remarkable. A clean white tunic softened her emaciated frame, and her golden hair shone brightly with the reflected light of the now lit torches.

Galla's eyebrows winged upward as his eyes traveled over the young girl standing before him. He turned to Antipus for some answers, but Decimus was already moving forward. He stopped in front of Chara, his eyes full of questions.

Chara's luminous brown eyes returned his look, her face animated with joy. "You know my Lord Jesus!"

Decimus frowned. "What?"

"I heard you just now." She smiled radiantly at Galla. "You know Him, too."

Decimus glanced at Antipus, then at Galla, his look returning to Chara. "You're a Christian?"

Her smile transformed her plain features. "Yes! Oh, praise God that you are one, too. I knew when I saw you in the crowd that there was something different about you." Realizing what she had just said, color flooded Chara's cheeks. Quickly she dropped her eyes to the floor.

Galla looked at Decimus, his lips quirking with humor.

"She's the girl I was telling you about," Decimus told him, his own face coloring with embarrassment.

"The slave?"

Grinding his teeth together in exasperation, Decimus glared at each man in turn. "She's not a slave!" Noting their dubious expressions, he amended his statement. "Well, at least not for long."

Galla was studying Chara, a strange expression on his face. Decimus felt heat run through his body, while at the same time he felt an icy thrill in his midsection. Was this Roman truly a friend? Could he really be trusted? A moment ago he had thought so, but now he wasn't so sure.

Antipus felt the tension emanating from the young Briton and immediately tried to soothe the troubled waters. "Come in, child. Have a seat."

Chara looked to Decimus for permission. Nodding his head, he watched as Chara crossed the room with a rather stiff gait. Remembering the sores on her feet, Decimus followed her and knelt before her. Gently he lifted one foot and then the other, placing them carefully back on the floor.

"The sores don't seem as bad since they've been washed."

Chara murmured her agreement, trying to restore her breathing to normal. The touch of Decimus's hands, so gentle yet so firm, had sent pleasurable tingles running up her legs.

Galla crossed to the couch, taking a seat beside Chara. His encompassing look wandered from head to toe. "So, little sister. How do you come to be in such a position?"

"It's a long story, my lord."

Taking one of her hands, Galla smiled charmingly at her, his soft brown eyes inviting her confidence. "If you are indeed a sister, then surely you know that no man has the right to be called Lord, save one."

She smiled into his eyes, feeling for the first time in a long while the freedom to do so. "I'm afraid I have been conditioned to speak so."

"And rather well, I might add," Decimus grunted, somewhat bothered by the exchange. His look wandered over the soldier, and Decimus realized that Galla was not much older than himself. Until now, the thought hadn't occurred to him that the Roman was a mighty handsome specimen, even with that scar running down his cheek. His bronze skin spoke of his health, and his dark, curling hair added to his lean good looks.

Chara told them her story, leaving nothing out. Decimus felt rage begin to bubble inside him. How could any man do that to his own sister, even if she was only a stepsister? If Decimus could have reached the man at that point, he would have gladly flogged him within an inch of his life. He was struggling with shame at such unchristian thoughts when Chara spoke again.

"I hold him no ill will. I can see God's hand in all of this. I was too afraid to leave, even though I knew I wasn't wanted. With Franco, my fear made me more a slave than when I was with Tarus. This way I was forced to leave." She smiled at Decimus. "Now I understand why God has led me here."

Decimus turned away, unwilling that any should see his embarrassment. He was bothered that the girl seemed to have fixated upon him as her personal deliverer.

"Still," Galla spoke gruffly, his hands clenched into fists on his lap, "I would be hard pressed not to hold a grudge."

Antipus thought it time to intervene. Already darkness had descended, and they still had resolved nothing. He addressed Chara. "My dear, we have a plan for getting Decimus out of the city, and Galla, as well. I can see now that I must include you, too."

Suddenly fearful, Chara stared wide-eyed from one to the other. She had the strangest desire to take Decimus's hand and cling to it. Flustered at her unusual reaction, she dropped her lashes over her telling eyes.

"Do you know what is happening to Christians here in Rome?" Antipus asked her gently.

She shook her head solemnly. "I'm afraid that until a few months ago I was rather isolated and protected."

The old man sighed. "Well, I won't regale you with all the gruesome details. Let's just say that Rome has become a very unhealthy place for Christians. Especially since almost a third of the city burned, and many people place the blame on the Christians."

For the next several hours, they discussed the details of getting the three out of Rome. Galla would have had no problem on his own, but the others would surely be suspect. As slaves, however, perhaps they would not be bothered.

When they finally agreed on a plan, Antipus rose from his seat. "It's almost midnight. I have had my servants prepare rooms for all of you for the night. You are welcome to stay as long as you wish. Please make yourselves at home. If you need anything, just call one of the servants."

Galla rose with him. "I thank you for the hospitality, but I'm afraid I must decline. I am expected at the garrison." He turned to Decimus. "I'll leave you to make arrangements about clothing for the girl and yourself. Remember, by the time we reach Britannia, cold weather will be setting in."

Decimus nodded. "I'll see to it."

Antipus followed Galla out the door, leaving Decimus and Chara alone. Decimus picked up a marble statue of a horse and began to twirl it nervously in his fingers. Finally he cleared his throat.

"We have assumed that you wish to go with us to Britannia, but if this is not so, you have only to say."

"You forget that despite what you say, I am still a slave," she answered quietly.

Placing the statue back on the table, Decimus frowned. "Just for the moment." He stopped, remembering the plans they had just discussed. He was bothered more than a little bit by the fact that Chara would be considered the property of the Roman. That troubled him more than the fact that *he* would be considered so, also.

Chara looked down at the floor, allowing her hair to fall forward over her cheeks. She said nothing for a long time, and Decimus took the time to study her. Although her face was hidden from view, the rest of her was clearly visible. She didn't look more than sixteen, though her incarceration could have added years to her appearance. How old *was* the child?

Her hair shone golden after her bath, even lighter than he had at first believed. She had the coloring of someone from Germania, and he wondered about her ancestry. The white tunic which hung on her slender figure only added to her air of untouched purity. Bones protruded from her shoulders. Again Decimus felt rage boil inside. Such a gentle girl, yet she had endured so much. Compassion stirred within him, and something else as yet indefinable.

Antipus returned, followed by two servants. "Dagon will show you to your room, Decimus, and Candace will show you yours." He smiled at Chara. "You have had a rough day. I hope you sleep well."

She returned his smile. "Thank you. Thank you for everything."

"I also wish to thank you," Decimus told Antipus before following Dagon out the door.

When they reached the top of the marble staircase, Decimus stopped, turning Chara toward him. "You will be all right?"

For a moment, she stared deeply into his eyes. Placing her hands gently on his shoulders, she raised on her tiptoes and softly kissed him on the lips. "Thank God He sent you into my life."

Decimus was moved despite himself. He didn't want to be responsible for this girl, and yet here he was, making plans for her to go with him to Britannia. He didn't want to feel anything for her, and yet he had been stirred by her guileless kiss. Letting go of her shoulders, he turned and quickly exited, following Dagon down the corridor.

Chara watched him walk away, a sinking sensation in the pit of her stomach. She had made him angry by being so forward. Her face colored crimson as she realized what she had done. How could she have acted that way? She was normally painfully shy, yet with Decimus she felt like a flower beginning to newly bud, slowly opening to the world around it. Shaking her head, she turned and followed Candace to her own room.

Candace lit a lamp and pulled the draperies. Chara studied the room, awed by such wealth. Even her stepfather had not had such luxuries, and he had been a wealthy man.

When Candace left the room, Chara made ready for bed and slid between the silken sheets. She nestled snugly into the bedding, almost purring with contentment. She did not know what the future held for her, but she had learned to take one day at a time, and for now she would enjoy every moment of such luxurious living.

Closing her eyes, she began to pray. She didn't get far before tiredness overcame her and she drifted off into a dreamless sleep.

Chapter 3

Decimus spent the next several days scouring the marketplace for suitable clothing. Since the warm Mediterranean climate was predominant most of the year and it was the middle of summer, only linen tunics were to be found.

He finally found what he was looking for at a little stall in a back alley near the docks. Placing his denarii on the counter, he rolled the wool tunics into a ball. Ever on the watch, he kept his eyes and ears open.

When he returned to the villa, he found Chara waiting for him in the garden. "You found what you wanted?"

Decimus nodded. "Pretty much so. I still need to find fur-lined cloaks if possible. If not, we may have to wait until we reach Gaul to purchase them."

He laid the bundles on the bench beside her. "How are your feet this morning?"

Smiling, she held out one small foot, now encased in a leather sandal, for inspection. "Much better, as you can see. They are almost completely healed."

A half smile touched Decimus's lips. "It's fortunate that the first part of our journey will be by sea. You shouldn't have to do much walking." Moving the bundle of clothing aside, he sat down next to her. He twisted his fingers together, eyes focused on the ground. When he cleared his throat, Chara gazed at him expectantly.

"Is there. . . I mean, do you. . ." He paused, turning slightly away from her. Picking up a dry flower petal from the ground, he started crumbling it to pieces.

Chara waited, her soft brown eyes wandering over his features. He took his time before finally asking what was uppermost in his mind. "When we get to Gaul, is there anyone you wish to see?" His eyes found hers. "I mean, is there family you wish to. . . ?"

Chara was already shaking her head. "There is no one. I have nowhere to go, if not with you."

Decimus considered her for a long time, then got up and started pacing in front of her. Running a hand in agitation through his hair, he came to an abrupt halt. Kneeling beside her, he tried to decide how he could explain certain things to her. She was such an innocent that she would probably have no idea what he was talking about.

"Chara. . ." Again he stopped. Before he could begin again, Antipus came into the garden.

"Well, hello. How did things go at the market today?"

Decimus sighed in relief. Perhaps Antipus would know a way to tell Chara the things that needed to be said. He would ask him later.

Decimus rose to his feet. "Things went well. I found most of what I needed."

"Probably cost you a few denarii, hmm?"

Grinning, Decimus confirmed it with a nod. "The old reprobate who sold me the woolen robes knew he had me in a tight spot. He was a smart old donkey."

Antipus laughed. "Probably Bacchus. He's the wiliest merchant in all of Rome. If you can't find what you are looking for anywhere else, Bacchus is sure to have it."

"Have you heard from Galla?" Decimus wanted to know.

Antipus turned an inquiring look on Chara and motioned to the bench where she was seated. "May I, my dear?" Smiling her consent, Chara moved to the side to allow Antipus to be seated. "No," he said, "he hasn't sent word to me."

Decimus sighed. "How long will it be, Antipus? The longer we stay, the better the chances of being caught and sent to the arena."

"Patience, my friend. Everything in good time. In the meantime, make yourself at home here. Agrippina and I welcome the diversion from our monotonous life."

"Your lady is a wonderful person," Chara told Antipus softly.

He smiled, touching Chara's cheek with his palm. "She certainly has fallen in love with you. She seems to think of you as the daughter we never had."

Chara didn't feel it her place to inquire, but her eyes held a question.

"No, child," Antipus told her. "Agrippina and I have no children of our own." Pain was in his eyes when he looked away. "It was just not to be. Now, well, now I thank God. Children would be just one more worry, more people for whose safety I would fear."

Thinking to deter the old man from his melancholy thoughts, Decimus pulled a small statue from his sack. He handed it to Antipus. "I found this at the market and thought that I would like you to have it. A small way of saying thank you."

Antipus held the statue cupped in his palms, and his eyes filled with tears. A shepherd was carrying a lamb over his shoulder, his staff in his hands. Even such a small statue was intricately carved and detailed so that the man's features were clear. His chin was thrust forward in determination, yet his eyes were filled with joy. Decimus had marveled at it when he saw it at the idol merchant's stall. It was indeed a work of art.

"Just like our Lord," Antipus told them softly.

Decimus silently agreed. Those had been his same thoughts when he had spotted the shepherd among the other idols. When he looked at Chara, her eyes were fixed intently on the statue. She glanced up at him and smiled, and Decimus caught his breath. When she smiled with her eyes like that, she was almost pretty.

Feeling foolish for such a flight of fancy, Decimus scowled and turned toward the villa. "There are some things I need to attend to before this evening." Bowing, he left them.

Chara followed him with her eyes. When he was out of sight, she turned back to Antipus. He was regarding her solemnly.

"You love him?"

Eyes wide, she would have denied it, but she wasn't sure that she could. "How can one tell after such a short time?" she remonstrated.

He smiled that gentle smile of his. "Agrippina and I knew the minute we laid eyes on each other. We were fortunate that our parents allowed us to marry, since we came from different backgrounds."

"You love her very much." It was a statement and not a question.

"Is that so surprising? We're old, but not yet dead. Agrippina is the other half of the clay that the Lord used to create me. I have never desired another."

Chara looked away. "I hope God has such a thing in store for me."

Antipus patted her hand. "He does, my dear, He does. So never settle for second best. You'll know if he's the right one. Sometimes people know right away; other times love grows slowly like the unfolding of a flower."

Getting up, Antipus waited for Chara to rise, also. They made their way slowly back to the villa, and Chara thought how much she had grown to love this man and his wife in just the few days she had been here.

Agrippina met them in the atrium, smiling at her husband. "Beloved, can you spare me your charming companion?"

The elderly man arched a brow, cocking his head at Chara. He grinned, giving her a wink. "Well, if I must."

Agrippina's gaze followed her husband across the atrium. When she turned back to Chara, they still glowed with her love.

"I wondered if you would show me that intricate stitch you were telling me about. I have decided to use it to trim Antipus's tunic that I have had made for his birthday."

Chara smiled. "He'll be pleased."

While Agrippina was engrossed with her stitching, Chara took the time to study her. Her hair was piled on top of her head in an elaborate style that the Romans loved. Although it was streaked with gray, there was still much black showing through. Her face was unusually devoid of wrinkles for one of her age. Although Agrippina was slightly plump, she still had a fine figure for an older woman.

Chara longed to grow old with a husband of her own, but her stepbrother had pointed out to her time and time again that she had no looks and that no man would want her. She didn't want to believe him—but she did.

Candace knocked on the doorpost. "My lady, supper is ready."

Agrippina looked up in surprise. "Oh my goodness! Is it *that* late?" Apologetically she squeezed Chara's hand. "Oh, my dear, I had no idea. And you just sat there patiently. Please forgive me."

When Chara and Agrippina descended the staircase, they were arm in arm, laughing together. Decimus watched them from below and marveled again at how lovely Chara could look when she laughed. Her eyes lost their veiled look and took on a special radiance. Each time he saw her, something seemed to tug at his heartstrings a little more. He shook his head in irritation. He was letting his imagination run away with him. Sara was the one he loved, the one he had longed for with every fiber of his being for years now. Hadn't he? Closing his eyes, he tried to picture her face, but no image came to mind except that of a young blond girl with artless brown eyes. Sara's hair had not been blond.

Decimus gritted his teeth in frustration. This was going to be a long journey, and he needed to keep his wits about him. He surely didn't need his mind filled with confusing thoughts.

After the meal, Antipus excused himself, saying that he needed to attend a party in honor of Senator Secubus. "Secubus is an old friend," he told them, lifting his mantle from the stool in the hallway. "It would seem odd if I didn't attend."

Agrippina folded her hands in front of her and gave her husband a skeptical look. "Beloved, be careful."

He frowned at her. "I'm always careful, Agrippina. You know me."

"Yes, Antipus, I do. That's what causes my concern."

Decimus grinned as the old man threw his wife a disgusted look. After Agrippina closed the door behind him, Decimus stepped forward and put a hand on her arm. "My lady, could I have a word with you?"

Surprised, she glanced first at Chara. "Of course."

She followed him into the triclinium, where Decimus shut the doors carefully behind them.

Chara stared at the closed doors, knowing a moment's disquiet. What did Decimus wish to talk with Agrippina about? Was he going to suggest that she, Chara, remain in Rome after all? A knot formed in the pit of her stomach. Realizing that she could do nothing, she made her way to her room to prepare for the night.

A soft, warm breeze stroked against her face as she stood leaning against the balcony. Turning her face into it, she closed her eyes, smiling with contentment. She had always loved the wind blowing against her face. Her mind turned to a psalm of David that she had heard long ago, and she remembered that the psalmist had called the wind "God's breath." When the breeze drifted against her, she felt loved. Protected. If only she could always feel like that.

A noise from below indicated someone's presence. As she watched, Decimus came from the villa, his head bowed in thought. Chara watched him walk to the fountain and lean against it. His handsome face was creased with worry. What preyed so heavily on his mind?

Sensing someone watching him, Decimus turned and looked up. They stared at each other a long moment before Chara turned away.

When Decimus closed his eyes that night, a vision of Chara standing in the moonlight, her hair flowing like a golden halo around her head, filled his mind. He fervently hoped Agrippina could make Chara understand the things he couldn't bring himself to tell her.

When Chara left Agrippina's room the next afternoon, she was a wiser, and less naive, young lady. Her cheeks burned at the things Agrippina had shared with her. A young woman must always be aware that her actions can be misinterpreted by men; a young woman traveling alone with men is in a precarious position; a young woman in such a position must take extra care not to appear to be encouraging unwelcome advances. Had it been Decimus's idea to have Agrippina tell her all these things? She felt mortified. Was it because of the innocent kiss she had bestowed upon him that first night?

Chara's cheeks filled with color when she came upon Decimus in the atrium. His wide-eyed innocence convinced her, however, that he had had nothing to do with her enlightening conversation with Agrippina.

"You've been with Agrippina?"

Embarrassed, Chara looked away. "Yes. She had some things she wished to discuss with me."

"Indeed. I hope it was nothing too serious."

The color deepened in her cheeks. "No! No, not at all."

Decimus hid a grin. "Would you like to come with me to the market today? I have most of what we need for the journey, but there are some things that perhaps you need for yourself?"

Chara smiled brightly. "I would love to come. Let me tell Agrippina."

They wandered through the market, listening to the merchants hawk their wares. Everywhere the crowds surged around them, the clamor of different languages mixing together into a cacophony of sound. Decimus stopped at a booth and purchased two peaches. "Hungry?" he asked.

Chara shook her head. "No, but they look delicious."

"We'll save them for later."

As they meandered through the crowds, Chara began to feel happy. For a time she could forget that Rome hated Christians, she could forget that she was a slave, she could forget that her life was in danger. For a time she could pretend that she and Decimus were just a couple of. . .what? Friends?

"You were smiling a minute ago. Why the frown now?" Decimus demanded softly.

Chara looked away. "It's nothing." She stopped, eyes growing wide with fear. Decimus followed her look and encountered the eyes of the merchant who had bid against the priest at the market. The merchant's look roved boldly over Chara's form that in the past week had begun to fill out slightly.

Head thrown back in anger, Decimus glared at the man with cold blue eyes that glittered dangerously. Finally the man looked away, but not before throwing Decimus a murderous look.

"Let's go back to the villa," Chara begged softly. The afternoon had been ruined.

Decimus tilted her chin, and her fears subsided at the calm look on his face. "You don't have to worry about men like that. I will let nothing happen to you. I promise."

She smiled wryly. "You shouldn't make promises you might not be able to keep."

He remained silent, knowing she was right. Taking her by the arm, he turned her in the opposite direction. "Maybe you're right. Maybe we should return to the villa."

Opening the gate that led to Antipus's villa, Decimus ushered Chara ahead of him. Once inside, they both seemed reluctant to part company. Instead, by unspoken consent, they wandered across the courtyard, pausing at last in front of the fountain.

Chara sat on the marble bench, but Decimus remained standing. He studied her face slowly, and Chara bent her head, embarrassed. Franco's critical words were never far from her thoughts. What did Decimus see when he looked at her? Was she only a responsibility to him? Seeing her reflection in the water, she knew it could not be otherwise.

"Hello."

Both Chara and Decimus glanced up, Chara smiling when she recognized Galla. He strode across the yard, motioning to the villa.

"I've been waiting to speak to you. You've been gone a long time." There was a question in his statement.

Bristling at the Roman's arrogance, Decimus took instant offense. This man didn't own him. At least not *yet*. "We were searching the market for any last-minute items we might need for the trip."

Galla's eyebrows flew up at the surly tone of voice. "It wasn't my intention to pry, or to suggest anything improper. I merely wondered if there had been some kind of trouble."

Feeling ashamed of his outburst of temper, Decimus shrugged. "Nothing important. We saw the merchant who was trying to buy Chara, but he didn't accost us in any way."

Galla's searching gaze flicked over Chara, but he could find no sign that she was upset or harmed in any way. Whatever had happened, the young Briton seemed to have taken care of the situation.

"I need to speak with you and Antipus. The time for our departure seems to be approaching more rapidly than I had anticipated."

Decimus gave him a questioning look but waited until Chara rose from her seat and followed them inside. A strained look about Galla's mouth didn't bode well for Decimus's peace of mind.

Antipus joined them in the triclinium, as did Agrippina. When they were all seated, Galla began to explain. "I'm not quite sure what has happened, but the army has ordered the search for Christians to be intensified." He looked at Antipus somberly. "It seems that it has come to the generals' attention that certain men within the Senate are following this 'vile sect,' as they call it."

The color drained from Agrippina's face. She reached for her husband's hand. He clasped his fingers with hers and began to knead them gently. "Are there any names being mentioned?" he asked quietly.

"Some," Galla answered. "But not yours that I'm aware of."

The fear in the room seemed a tangible thing, leaving a sour taste in Chara's mouth. What were they to do now?

Galla rose. "There will be room for three others to go with us, but that's all I can arrange." He looked at Chara. "I'm afraid that I must insist that the others be all men. Anything else would be suspect."

Antipus nodded his head. "Agreed. I only wish. . ." He stopped, looking at his wife.

"Don't even think of it," she told him firmly. "My place is with you, and I will not leave, no matter *what* you manage to arrange."

"Beloved."

Agrippina rose to her feet. "I will hear no more about it." Quickly she left the room.

Antipus was shaking his head. "She's a headstrong woman," he told them softly, "but what a woman."

Decimus felt the helplessness of the situation. "You have to leave, Antipus. It's no longer safe for you here."

The senator looked at him sadly. "Where would I go? I'm too old to be a missionary to Britannia. Besides, I may have nothing to fear. Whatever the circumstances, God will take care of me." He smiled at them. "And if it is my time to die, then no power on earth can stop it. Frankly, if not for Agrippina, I would be eager for death, for then I will see my Lord."

The room was silent. Galla and Decimus exchanged glances. Shrugging his shoulders, Decimus rose to his feet to stand beside Galla. "When will we leave?"

Galla sighed. "I'm still not sure, but you need to be prepared to leave at a moment's notice. Have your things packed and ready."

Antipus got to his feet. "I have something for you. Wait here."

He left the room and returned shortly with a large cedar box. It had an inlaid mosaic design of pressed silver. Lifting the lid, Decimus could see that it was full of coins. Antipus lifted out a small bag and handed it to Galla.

"This is my contribution to your mission work in Britannia. Since I can't come myself, I want to have a part in spreading the Word."

Galla opened the bag curiously. His face paled, and he glanced at Antipus in stunned disbelief. "There are several talents' worth of gold here!"

Antipus nodded. "One hundred, to be precise."

Decimus's legs gave way, and he dropped to the couch behind him. He was speechless. What a fortune!

Galla tried to hand the bag back to Antipus. "I can't take this. It's too much!"

"No. You have no idea what you will face when you reach Britannia. But one thing we know for certain, Roman currency is used there, as well as everywhere else." Pushing Galla's hand away, Antipus smiled at him. "You have no idea where you will be able to find work or how you can make a living. Take it." He smiled at Decimus. "It's for all of you, including Chara and the other three men whom I will choose to send with you."

Galla's voice was hoarse as he gave Antipus his sincere thanks. He handed the bag to Decimus. "You take care of it. I have to return to the garrison and then to the palace. I must keep my eyes and ears open." His look was intent. "Remember, have your things ready."

Decimus felt a cold finger of foreboding slide down his spine. "I'll see to it right away."

Galla nodded. Turning, he gave Chara a half smile before he rapidly exited the room.

Antipus watched him go. He stood staring after him for several moments before he turned back to Decimus and Chara. "I must go see to Agrippina."

After he left the room, Decimus slowly rose to his feet again, taking a deep breath and releasing it slowly. He turned to Chara. "We need to get our things together."

She didn't answer right away. When she finally looked at him again, there were tears in her eyes. "What of Antipus and Agrippina?"

Pressing his lips together, he avoided her eyes. "I don't know. All we can do is pray."

"Can't we. . ."

"No," he interrupted angrily. "We cannot *force* someone to do something they don't wish to do. In the end, we are all responsible for our own actions."

A tear trickled down Chara's cheek, and she rose slowly to her feet. "I'll see to the packing."

Decimus noticed the tear and felt his own frustrations mount. Why was God allowing this to happen to the people who loved Him most? Why were such evil men allowed to live and prosper, yet the obedient suffered? He had no answer.

He wanted to reach out and take Chara in his arms and soothe away her hurt, but how could he when he didn't know how to make it right? What words of comfort could he offer when he had so many questions of his own?

He watched as Chara walked out of the room, her head bowed low. Sighing, he clenched the bag of coins. A veritable fortune. But what good was money if you died before you could use it? Tucking the bag into his belt, he followed Chara from the room.

Chapter 4

That evening Antipus had three guests for supper. Each man was a Christian, and each had his own story to tell.

Caleb was a slave of Judea who had been in hiding for some time, ever since his master had been killed in an accident involving a chariot. Caleb was a Jew, but a converted Jew who now served the Lord Jesus, and when the opportunity had presented itself, Caleb fled to other Christians who were willing to hide him until they could conceive of a way to get him out of Rome. Although the authorities weren't looking for him, per se, they were always on the watch for runaways. Especially someone who would prove useful in the arenas.

Caleb hated his slavery, but he had felt compelled to serve his master well, since the apostle Paul had commanded it. But upon the death of his master, Caleb had fled. Since the one who owned him was now dead, Caleb was not waiting around for someone else to take his place. He had done his duty, and now he considered himself free.

Then there was Thomas, a Greek. He had been set free from slavery years before when he had saved the little girl of his master from drowning. Since she was an only child and dearly beloved, they had repaid him with his freedom.

He had remained with the family as a servant, doing what they had purchased him to do, teaching their children Greek and Greek literature. Thomas was a very learned man, a man of letters.

And last, but not least, was Trophimus, a very young Roman who had recently witnessed his parents' death in the arena. Although Trophimus's father had been an influential man, not even that had been able to save him when it was discovered that he was a member of the Christian sect.

Chara felt drawn to the young boy. He couldn't have been as old as her own eighteen years of age, and he seemed even younger than his chronological age. She smiled gently when she was introduced and felt a decidedly motherly urge to protect him.

As they dined on pheasant and fish from the Mediterranean, they got to know one another. Antipus explained Galla's plan for getting them out of the city.

Caleb's dark eyes flashed. "You expect me to sell myself to a Roman? Willingly?" He rose to his feet, and Chara noticed the man's powerful build. Although Caleb was probably middle-aged, he was a commanding presence. "Never!"

Antipus frowned, motioning for him to be seated again. "Galla is a Christian, and although he feels slavery to be wrong, still he is willing to purchase all of you for a short period of time."

"How kind!" Thomas's voice dripped with sarcasm.

Antipus sighed. "Let me try to explain this better. Galla, being a Christian, will not lie. Now, if you are going to accompany him on this trip, you will need to be just what he says you are. His slaves. If you have a problem with this, let me know now and I will arrange for someone else to take your place. God knows, there are enough Christians willing to leave Rome."

"But a Roman? How do we know it's not a trick? How do we know we can trust him?" Caleb was clearly unconvinced.

Trophimus spoke quietly. "Antipus is a Roman, too. What matter if he be Roman or not? In Christ, aren't we all the same? This is what my father taught me." He glared at Caleb, but there were tears in his eyes. "Unless my father died for nothing."

The room grew quiet, and each member felt convicted by the young man's words. Clearing his throat, Antipus rose to his feet. "I have made arrangements for Caleb and Trophimus to remain here. You will be safe, and we can easily locate you in case we have to expedite things. Thomas, we know where to locate you, but we must know of your whereabouts at all times. If you are called upon to leave in a hurry, we don't want to have to leave someone behind." His warning was clear.

After the meal, everyone separated to their assigned rooms. Murmured conversations could be heard as they ascended the stairs, the fear evident in their quiet voices.

As Chara was about to go upstairs, Decimus placed a restraining hand on her arm. "I need to talk to you a moment. In the peristyle."

Surprised, she followed him out into the garden. He had taken great pains to avoid being alone with her lately, and she wondered at his motives now. Still, she followed him to the bench and seated herself, staring up at his pensive face.

Decimus cleared his throat. It was important to him that he make her understand his position and where she stood in all of this chaos. "Chara, you know that I don't wish for you to remain a slave." He stopped when her head dropped forward, blond hair hiding her face from view. What was she thinking? In the short time he had come to know her, he realized that this woman was completely devoid of conceit. She was lacking in confidence in herself or anything about herself. He knew that if he said the wrong thing, she would retreat inside herself where he would have trouble reaching her.

"I hope you will understand when I tell you that I cannot give you your freedom just yet."

Her eyes flew to his face, but she remained silent.

"When I. . ." He paused, finding it hard to utter the words. "When I sell myself to Galla, everything that I own becomes his by right of possession." He watched her face closely. "That includes you."

Wrinkling her forehead, she spoke for the first time. "I don't understand. What are you trying to say?"

"Galla decided it would be easier all around if I retained possession of you instead of giving you your freedom before he purchased it back. He thinks that this would be the best way in case anything happens to him."

Chara smiled. "If he thinks it best, then I have no qualms. I trust Galla completely."

Decimus frowned. She was so frustratingly innocent. Although he liked the Roman, he still wasn't sure he trusted him completely.

"He will *own* you."

"As you own me now?"

Decimus brushed his hand through his hair in exasperation. How could he make her see? "That's different."

"How so?" She looked at him skeptically, and he had to refrain from gritting his teeth.

"He. . . I. . . There's a difference."

"I don't see how." Rising to her feet, she laid a hand against his arm. "I understand your feelings, but I trust Galla. He's done nothing to prove otherwise."

Decimus sighed. "I don't want to see you hurt or anything to happen to you. I have considered you my own responsibility for some time now. It will be hard for me to relinquish that chore to someone else."

He could feel her withdraw from him even though she made no movement. Her eyes grew distant. Now what had he said? Every time he talked to the girl, he felt he was treading on eggshells.

"Have no fear," she told him angrily. "Whether owned by you or someone else, I will obey." Turning, she hastened across the garden.

"Chara!"

She froze at the command in his voice. He walked up behind her. His hands moved as though to reach for her shoulders, but he didn't touch her.

She refused to look at him. "May I go now? I have things to attend to."

Sighing, Decimus dropped his hands to his sides. "Yes, you may go." He watched her walk away, her head bent low. Raising his eyes heavenward, he threw up a petition on her behalf and then one for himself and then, while he was at it, for them all.

Three days later, Chara and Candace were crossing the hallway when a furious pounding shook the door. They exchanged fearful glances before Candace slowly went to the door and opened it just a crack. She fell backward as Galla pushed his way in.

"Where's Decimus?"

Chara felt her heart drop. Galla spotted her and came quickly to her side. "Get your things. I have to get you out of here."

"What's happened?"

"They arrested Antipus today. Where's Agrippina?"

Fear clutched Chara's insides. "She went to the marketplace."

He gritted his teeth with frustration. Raking his fingers through his dark hair, he fixed his eyes intensely on Chara. "Get the others. We have to move you now."

"But what of Agrippina?"

He shook her slightly. "Get the others!"

Conditioned to obey, Chara fled upstairs. Galla followed her with his eyes before turning to Candace, still clutching the door. "Tell the other servants. Antipus has been arrested."

Eyes wide with fear, Candace turned to obey. She turned back, tears in her eyes. "What will happen to him?"

Galla pressed his lips together. "I don't know, but it doesn't look good. Nero's generals have never particularly liked Antipus. Antipus is too pure a man in Nero's debauched empire. He shows Nero up for the depraved lunatic that he is."

Candace hastened away to tell the others. Galla knew that Antipus had given each of the servants money just in case such an event would happen. Pray God they would find places of refuge.

Decimus came quickly down the stairs to meet him. "Chara said that Antipus has been arrested?"

Galla nodded. "I have to move you to a different location. Thomas will be safe for the time being, but soldiers will be here, probably within the hour."

"We're ready. Caleb and Trophimus are getting their things, and then we will be ready to leave. Where will you take us?"

"A man who lives close to the docks is a Christian sympathizer. He will hide you in one of his warehouses until I can make different arrangements." Galla glanced around him. "It won't be as comfortable as this, but it should be safe. Right now the soldiers are searching only private residences. It hasn't occurred to them to look in the storehouses and such."

"Thank God for that!" Decimus turned as Chara hurried down the steps. She had a large bundle clutched in her hands.

"Is this all you have?" Galla wanted to know.

Decimus nodded. "I thought it best if we take only what we can use. We can purchase other things as we have need of them."

Trophimus came down the stairs followed by Caleb, each carrying a bundle. A faint raise of Caleb's eyebrows asked the question they all wanted to ask.

"There's a wagon at the back gate," he told them. "You will be taken to your new hiding place." Galla stared intently at each one. "Remember, each one of your lives is dependent on your cooperation with each other."

Galla let the warning sink in before ushering them out to the courtyard and through the gate. A wagon was waiting there, almost filled with baskets of grain. Galla opened one basket that was empty and motioned for Chara to get in. Decimus lifted her to the wagon and helped her inside.

Each person in turn got into one of the baskets, all except Decimus.

"You will be the driver." Galla gave Decimus instructions on where to find the storehouses and told him to ask for a man named Aureus. "He'll take it from there. God go with you."

Decimus climbed into the wagon. Lifting the reins, he turned to Galla, and they stared at each other a long time.

"God keep you safe," Decimus told him.

"And you," Galla answered softly.

When Decimus reached the warehouses, he had no trouble locating Aureus. The docks were a bubbling hive of activity. Merchants hastened to and fro, checking on the progress of their imports and exports. People were everywhere, yet no one seemed to take particular notice of the wagon and its driver.

Aureus met Decimus at the door to one of the warehouses, opening wide the portal and motioning Decimus inside. Pulling the door closed after him, he met Decimus at the back of the wagon. Together they opened each basket and helped its occupant to alight.

Aureus's eyes opened wide at the sight of Chara, her blond hair swinging around her shoulders as she climbed down from the wagon.

"A woman?" he questioned.

Decimus didn't answer him. "Where do we go from here?"

Dragging his gaze from Chara, the old man motioned toward the back of the storehouse. "This way. It isn't much, but you should be safe here. At least until Galla makes arrangements otherwise."

They followed him through the semidarkness, their eyes slowly adjusting to the dimness. Although Aureus looked elderly, his spry movements gave the impression of a much younger man. His head was bald on top with a curl of white ringing the edges. When he smiled, his teeth were yellow, and a few were missing.

"You'll have to make arrangements between you on what to do with the young lady. There will be little privacy here."

Chara colored hotly, remembering her conversation with Agrippina.

"We will manage something," Decimus told the man, not unaware of Chara's embarrassment.

Nodding his head, Aureus turned to leave. "There are provisions over there." He motioned to a corner where several baskets and chests were stacked. "Help yourselves. I'll try to stop by daily to see if you need anything."

"How long?" Caleb didn't appreciate the tomblike darkness and stuffy atmosphere, though he knew he could survive anything as long as it wasn't for an extended period of time.

Aureus continued on his way, shrugging his shoulders. "Don't know. You'll have to wait for Galla."

They heard the door slide closed behind Aureus as he exited. Decimus turned to the others. "Well, let's see what we have here."

They opened baskets and chests and found, among other things, bed linens and pillows. Decimus looked around him, trying to figure some way to afford Chara some privacy. Taking one of the blankets, he arranged it between some stacked crates of goods, improvising a small room.

He grinned at her. "Your quarters, my lady."

Smiling, Chara thanked him and put her bundle down in the rough shelter. It wasn't much, but his thoughtfulness pleased her.

Trophimus dropped his own bundle in the corner. Crossing his legs at the ankles, he lowered himself to the ground. He leaned back against the wall and closed his eyes.

Decimus watched Caleb do the same. He wondered how long they would all have to stay here, but more than that, he wondered what was happening to Antipus and Agrippina.

He looked behind the blanket barrier he had constructed for Chara and found her on her knees, her lips moving rapidly in silence. Going over, he dropped down beside her and took her hand in his. She glanced up in surprise.

"I thought I would join you, if you don't mind."

Giving him a half smile, she bowed her head again.

Galla listened to the conversations going on around him, all the while trying to see into the senate chambers. He could hear the loud discussions but couldn't see any of the speakers. Frustrated, he pushed his way forward.

"Senator Secubus, we all know that you and Senator Antipus are close friends. Perhaps you share this odious religion of his?"

There was a threat hanging in the words.

"I have always been loyal to Rome! How dare you, Fendicus, try to trap me in this same vile net you have managed to spread out to others." Secubus's angry voice reached clearly into the hall. "Perhaps you have something yourself to hide."

Instead of being angry, Fendicus's voice was low and compelling. "You can't transfer suspicion to me, my friend. *I* am not the one helping Christians to flee Rome."

"And you think Antipus is?"

"We have proof," another voice intoned.

There was silence for a full minute. "What proof have you, Trinian? The word of a beaten slave?"

"No, Secubus. The word of a perfectly healthy, but *loyal*, servant of Rome. A servant in Antipus's own home."

Galla gasped softly. Someone in Antipus's house was a traitor and had informed the government of Antipus's activities. Galla leaned weakly against the wall, closing his eyes. What had he done? He should never have invited Antipus to be a part of his clandestine activities.

His eyes flew open. Did they then know of his own part in these proceedings? If not, they surely would soon. Who was the informer? Galla felt a murderous rage well up inside him. A good man might possibly die because of someone else's perfidy.

Turning, he quickly forced his way through the press of people and headed for the street. He hadn't much time. He had to act quickly.

It was dark when the door slid open again. The stillness on the docks compared to that of the activity this morning was disquieting. The refugees remained absolutely immobile until they recognized a whispered voice.

"Decimus?"

"Here." Decimus made his way to Galla's side. "What news?"

Galla shook his head solemnly. "It's not good, I'm afraid. There was a spy in Antipus's house."

A soft gasp caused both men to spin quickly around. Chara stood silhouetted in the moonlight from outside. Decimus took her arm and quickly moved her aside.

"And what of my lady?" she queried softly.

Galla shook his head. "I don't know."

"What do we do now?" Decimus wanted to know. "We can't stay here. Surely they must know about you."

"I'm not sure if they do, but you're right. There's always that chance." He lifted the papers he held in his hands. "I've brought the papers to make the purchase of the three of you as slaves." He looked at Chara. "Has he explained about you?"

Chara nodded. "If anything happens to you, I will still be his *responsibility*.

Galla's eyebrows raised slightly at her surly tone of voice, and he glanced at Decimus, who merely shrugged his shoulders. Who knew what went on in the minds of women?

Galla followed them to the back of the shelter and nodded to Trophimus and Caleb. "I've sent word to Thomas. He should be here soon. Right now, let's get on with business and I will explain my plans."

When the arrangements were finalized, Galla took the papers and carefully rolled them up. Placing them inside his breastplate, he then motioned for them all to get seated. Before he could explain, the door to the outside opened again. Galla doused the lamp, and everyone became still.

Soft footsteps came hesitantly toward them, stopping periodically. "Is anyone here?"

Decimus sighed with relief. "Thomas."

Thomas joined the group, clutching a bundle. Galla proceeded to explain the events of the afternoon to him, and Thomas nodded sadly. "I know. I heard from one of the servants that Agrippina has been taken into custody, also."

"Do you know where they are being held?"

Thomas hesitated so long Decimus thought he wasn't going to answer. He nodded slowly. "They are in the dungeons below the arena."

"Dear God!" Chara buried her face in her hands.

"What can we do?" Decimus wanted to know.

"There's nothing we can do." Galla's quiet voice brought Caleb to his feet.

"We have to do something! We can't just let them die!"

"Will it help Antipus if we all die? Would that make him happy?" Galla was angry, not only with Caleb but also with himself. He felt impotent, unable to do anything. As a trained soldier of Rome, he found this unacceptable and frustrating.

"Is there nothing we can do?"

Galla stared grimly at Chara's tear-streaked face. "Pray."

"What will *you* do now?" Decimus wanted to know.

Galla turned away. "I have to return to the garrison. I will make arrangements to sail two days from now."

"What if they arrest you, also? What if they know that you've been helping Antipus?" Decimus had no idea what would become of them if the soldier were taken, also. He felt his frustration begin to mount.

"Aureus will try to find a way to get you on board a ship going somewhere. You still have the money Antipus gave us?"

Decimus swallowed a knot in his throat. "Yes."

Galla nodded, then quickly turned and left.

"Two days." Trophimus sighed. "Better get some sleep while we can. Who knows what the morrow will bring."

"God knows, Trophimus," Chara told him. "If He cares enough to know the number of hairs on your head, then He is concerned with your whole life."

Trophimus smiled weakly. "I know that in my heart, but sometimes my head gets in my way."

"You're not alone," Thomas told him, sitting next to him. "I, too, struggle with doubts when a good man like Antipus suffers and an evil one like Nero doesn't."

"You forget," Chara told them, "Antipus's suffering will only last a short time, but Nero's an eternity unless he repents of his wickedness."

Decimus helped Chara to her feet and led her to the cubbyhole they had made earlier. He looked long into her face, his eyes tracing the paths her tears had left on her cheeks. She looked so little, so helpless. Without giving it any thought, he pulled her gently into his arms and held her close. He could feel her sobs begin again.

"We'll be all right," he told her softly.

Her voice came back to him, muffled by his tunic. "But what of them?"

He knew to whom she was referring. "I don't know. We'll have to wait and see."

He held her close a moment longer, then gently pushed her away. "Try to get some sleep."

Nodding, she turned away from him, pulling the blanket closed behind her.

Chapter 5

When Galla joined them at the docks two days later, his face looked haggard, his mouth tight. Decimus knew something was terribly wrong, but Chara was the one who asked the question they were all afraid to voice.

"Any news?" Her soft voice trembled slightly.

His gaze went to Decimus, who read the grim message there. Moving closer to Chara, Decimus placed an arm around her shoulders.

"Antipus and Agrippina were sent to the arena yesterday with about thirty others."

Chara felt her legs give way beneath her. Thankful for Decimus's support, she leaned against him, and he lifted her in his arms and strode to her cubbyhole, laying her gently on the blanket. Chara turned her face against the bedding, her sobbing echoing eerily in the warehouse.

Decimus joined the others. "What now?"

"I've arranged passage for tomorrow. Myself and five slaves. When I get here tomorrow, be ready to attach yourselves to my retinue. Make it seem as though you are entering the docks with me."

They all nodded in agreement. Decimus considered the Roman a moment, noticing that for all his strength, his muscles were shaking. Was he as afraid as the rest of them? Or was he worried about something else?

"Was your name implicated with the others?"

Galla shook his head. "No, and since it wasn't, I have a pretty good idea of who the perpetrator was. Antipus mentioned that one of his menservants was visiting family these last few weeks. Undoubtedly the scoundrel wanted to be out of the house before he went to the emperor's generals with his betrayal, and his story about his family was just that—a story. Because he was not here these last weeks, he did not find out about my connection with Antipus. Or yours. I hope his guilt rests heavily on his shoulders." Galla's eyes gleamed, and Decimus wondered if he was considering retribution.

"I'll leave you now. Be ready when I return on the morrow." He turned away but then turned back. His eyes went to the corner where quiet sobs could still be heard. "Will she be all right?"

Decimus followed his look. His heart went out to Chara, for she had really loved the old man and his wife. They had treated her as a beloved child. "Only time will heal such wounds."

Glancing back at Decimus, Galla nodded his head. He walked out the door and gently closed it behind him.

"I hope he wasn't followed." Caleb's voice was tense.

"Why should he be? He said he wasn't suspected." Thomas turned away and went and sat near Chara's cubicle. Trophimus followed him, his eyes flicking toward Chara's blanket and then away.

"I could go crazy cooped up in here." Caleb grabbed an orange and began to peel it.

"Better here than in the dungeons below the arena," Decimus told him roughly.

The hours seemed to drag by. Periodically Caleb would get up and begin to pace. His constant restlessness was beginning to wear on Decimus's already tattered nerves.

Darkness descended, and still nothing happened. Chara remained quietly in her cubicle until hunger drew her forth. The others watched her discreetly as she found some dates and began to chew them. Decimus rose and went to her.

"Are you all right?" he asked her softly, noticing her swollen, red eyes.

She nodded her head slightly before lifting her eyes to his. The pain he saw there mirrored his own. "Why couldn't they have come with us? Why?" She looked at him without really seeing him. "Antipus will never see the beautiful robe Agrippina was making for him."

Turning, she went back to her pallet and lay down. Closing her eyes, she tried to sleep.

Decimus found it impossible to sleep himself. Finding a comfortable position next to the door, he decided to keep watch. They had to be ready when Galla returned.

The moon rose golden and full, a lovers' moon. Decimus smiled wryly. The moon was just the same as the night he had left Antonius's villa. And Sara.

Closing his eyes, he leaned his head back against the wall. He should never have left Ephesus. Instead of solving his problems, it had escalated them.

At times he longed for the days when he had served in the house of Antonius, for though he had been their slave, he had been happy with Diana and her family. In his heart, Antonius's sister had become the sister he had left behind in Britannia. He missed Diana as much as he had missed Sara.

He frowned. *Had* missed? Did he not miss Sara now? Where were the feelings he had thought were so intense? Now when he remembered Sara, he remembered more the things she had said than the way she looked. He could remember one time when they had sat and discussed the scriptures, arguing the finer points of the Law. As a Jew, Sara knew so much more about the scriptures than he did. Always, Sara had put God's will before her own.

Faint fingers of vermilion were creeping across the predawn sky when Decimus roused the others. Quickly gathering their things together, they waited and watched from the door for Galla's arrival. The docks were soon brimming with activity. With so many people, they should be able to blend in easily.

Before long, they spotted Galla winding his way through the crowds of people. He was followed by four wagons and several servants carrying loads of goods. When he drew close to the warehouse, Decimus and the others slipped in among the wagons, following Galla as he headed for a large cargo ship at the end of the pier.

Normally cargo ships allowed many passengers to travel on their open decks, but this particular ship showed no signs of such activity. A Roman soldier strode down the dropped plank to meet Galla as he came to a stop. "Centurion." He nodded.

"You made room for my goods and slaves?" Galla's voice betrayed none of his trepidation. Now he would know if his name had been implicated with the others.

The soldier looked around at the array of wagons and servants. His eyebrows rose. "I was told there would be *five* slaves."

"As there are. These other servants are here merely to help load the trade goods meant for Britannia."

The soldier looked at everything carefully before tipping his head. "Your quarters have been arranged. Your slaves can find room on the deck."

Galla motioned to those standing near. "Start loading." He turned to the soldier. "Show them where to stow these things."

"Aye, Centurion." Slapping a fist against his chest in salute, he turned and preceded them up the gangplank.

When they reached the deck, Chara stayed close to Decimus to avoid being trampled by the hurrying sailors as they scurried to their tasks. Everywhere was pandemonium, yet there was purpose in each sailor's face and order in the way they proceeded. Obviously they knew what they were about.

Galla froze as several soldiers came up the steps from below ship. "What are they doing here?" Decimus whispered.

"I have no idea, but I'm about to find out."

He crossed the deck quickly, and Chara leaned closer to Decimus. Without thinking, he put his arm around her. They waited in silence until Galla returned.

"They have been sent to help guard the ship from pirates. Apparently the raidings on the seas have increased, and Nero's army is determined that these supplies get to their troops in Britannia. It seems Roman spies have heard word of another Briton uprising brewing." He rubbed his chin thoughtfully. "I've wondered why General Agabus was so anxious to help me reach Britannia. *Trade goods*, he said."

"You think he has an ulterior motive?" Decimus inquired.

"I do now," Galla answered him calmly. "I'm afraid we're faced with another problem right now, though."

Decimus waited for him to elucidate.

Galla's eyes were probing the ship and its occupants. His look settled on Chara. "Have you noticed there are no other women?"

Surprised, Decimus and Chara looked around at the hubbub of activity. Decimus and Galla exchanged glances.

"What do we do? Will there be no other female passengers?"

Galla shook his head. "Every nook and cranny is being used to store supplies going to Britannia. And then there's the soldiers, as well."

"How many soldiers are there?" Decimus was beginning to feel strangely uneasy.

"Only about twenty. They needed to save the room for the supplies. It looks like they're planning for a campaign, though, and somehow I have become a part of it. General Agabus probably didn't think that I would be bringing a woman, and since she's a slave, I doubt he would have cared anyway."

Chara glanced up at Decimus, worrying her bottom lip with her teeth. Decimus sighed. "What do we do now?"

"Chara will have to stay in my quarters."

Decimus felt heat surge through his body at the suggestion. Noticing the ominous gleam in the young Briton's eyes, Galla shrugged. "It's the only way to protect her. Look around you."

Decimus looked. Many of the sailors and soldiers had stopped to stare at Chara. Some were nudging others, their whispers and ribald laughter reaching across the distance. Decimus felt the heat in his body intensify. Helplessness again caused his temper to flare.

Galla's lips pressed tightly together. "You had better get a grip on your jealous possessiveness, Decimus. I won't have you jeopardizing our plans." Taking Chara's arm, he propelled her across the deck and below.

Decimus watched their progress, stunned at Galla's assessment of the situation. Was he jealous? *Ridiculous!* One had to really care for someone to be jealous of them. He cared about Chara but not *that* way. Deciding that the Roman was imagining things, Decimus went to find the others.

Three days at sea and still the beautiful weather held. Chara lifted her face to the salty breeze and smiled with contentment. Free from Rome, at least for the most part. She looked around her, watching several of the Roman soldiers lolling about on the decks. Many eyes turned her way, and Chara shivered.

Decimus joined her at the rail, a half smile curving his lips. "You look well."

Chara returned his smile. "I am."

"No seasickness?"

She grinned. "None. I wish I could say the same for poor Trophimus."

Decimus turned his head in the direction of the young Roman. Trophimus had spent the better part of the last three days hanging his head over the side of the ship. Decimus smiled in sympathy when the young boy slowly made his way across deck and dropped down on his pallet.

He turned his eyes back to Chara. He was hesitant to ask her anything about the sleeping arrangements that had been made between her and Galla, but he had to know.

"You and Galla. . ." He could not think how to phrase his question.

Chara glanced at him and then away, refusing to say anything unless he specifically asked.

Decimus cleared his throat. "Things are well?"

Taking pity on his obvious distress, Chara looked him full in the face. Her soft brown eyes hardened perceptibly. "Galla treats me as a sister. He has given me the bunk in his cabin, and he sleeps on the floor by the door."

Decimus looked away, embarrassed. "He protects you well." He felt aggravated that he was not the one watching out for Chara. After all, didn't she belong to him? He caught his thoughts up short. What was he thinking? He didn't own the girl. Not really. No one could really own another person, especially one who already belonged to God.

Decimus stared at a dolphin in the distance. "How do you come to know so much about Christianity?"

Blinking her eyes, Chara needed a moment to collect her thoughts after such an abrupt change of subject. She followed his look, smiling at the dolphin that was shortly joined by others.

"My mother taught me."

Decimus raised an eyebrow quizzically. "And how did she know so much? Gaul is a long way from Judea."

"My mother was a young girl living in Galilee at the time Christ was there."

Decimus's eyes widened. "Did she actually get to see Him?"

Chara nodded. "He spoke to the multitudes, of which she was one. She was only seventeen at the time and a slave in the house of a Roman official. She went to hear Him speak one day. She realized there was something different about Him. She said He spoke with such power and authority one couldn't help but believe Him."

"What did He speak about?" Decimus asked curiously.

"Love, mainly. Loving each other and *especially* loving God."

"But at that time, Jesus preached only to the Jews. How did your mother come to hear Him?"

Chara shook her head. "No, He spoke to the crowd. Many among the crowd were Gentiles. Perhaps He *was* only speaking to the Jews, but many others heard Him, also."

Decimus glanced back to sea, his blond hair tossed in the breeze. "I wish I could have heard Him."

Chara agreed. How wonderful to have actually heard the voice of the Master, to have actually seen His face. She turned to Decimus and smiled. "True, that would have been wonderful, but thank God we now have the message of salvation, as well as the Jews."

Decimus returned her smile. Reaching up, he pushed her hair behind her shoulder, letting his hand slide down her arm.

"What goes on here?"

Decimus and Chara jumped. The Roman soldier who had saluted Galla stood behind them, glaring at them. His coldly gleaming eyes went over Chara's flushed countenance. "You there, you dare to dally with your master's slave? He'll have you horsewhipped." His eyes went boldly down Chara's slender form. "I can't blame you, mind. But the centurion is not one to take an infraction lightly."

As the soldier's eyes continued their inspection, Decimus's hands curled at his sides. He took a step forward, but Chara quickly placed a hand on his arm.

"We were doing nothing wrong."

"I'll bet," he sneered contemptuously, and Decimus had the urge to strike him. Unconsciously he stepped forward. Suddenly he was jerked around. Surprised, he came face-to-face with Galla.

"Is there a problem?" Galla asked softly. No one was fooled by the quietness of his voice, least of all the Roman soldier.

Snapping a salute, the soldier motioned to Decimus and Chara. "I found them together. The man seemed to be making free with his hands."

Galla turned to Decimus, his eyebrows going upward. Decimus felt himself flush with hot color, embarrassed and angry.

"We were doing nothing, my lord, except talking," Chara told him quietly.

"Go to our quarters," Galla told her. She looked from one to the other, then hastily did as he commanded. Decimus felt himself growing angrier by the minute.

Lifting his hand, Galla struck Decimus a blow across the face that sent the young man reeling. He turned an accusing face toward Galla, who motioned his head slightly to his left. Decimus looked that way, surprised to see several Roman soldiers standing there. Understanding dawned, and Decimus dropped his eyes.

"I will speak with you about this later. Go below and make yourself useful."

Galla watched Decimus walk away and hoped that he understood why he had done what he did. Galla couldn't afford to lose the respect of these Roman soldiers. He and the others had a lot at stake here. He turned to the men. "Be about your business."

They quickly dispersed, and Galla went to his quarters.

After that, Decimus was careful to keep his distance from Chara, although whenever she was on deck, Galla made a point to be with her. For the most part, she remained in the cabin, safely out of sight.

The weather changed as they grew closer to Gaul. The winds increased, and the sea grew choppy. Trophimus, who had recovered from his seasickness, once again took to the rails.

Galla found Decimus unlacing the ropes from the sails. Bending down, Galla gave him a hand.

"I haven't had time to apologize for the other day—nor to explain." He kept his voice soft for fear of being overheard.

Decimus continued his work without looking up. "Not necessary." He rolled the sails, lashing them tightly in place. Finally he looked at Galla and smiled slightly. "I've always had a rather violent temper."

Galla smiled back, relieved that Decimus showed him no ill will. Decimus rose to his feet. "My temper is something the Lord and I are working to change." His voice was barely louder than a whisper.

Galla rose also and said in an equally soft voice, "Sometimes a temper is not such a bad thing. Many a battle has been won by sheer anger. I—"

A shout interrupted his words. "Ship on the horizon!"

Turning in the direction the lookout indicated, men scurried to the rails, straining their eyes to see.

"Can you make anything out?" the captain wanted to know.

"I can't tell yet," the lookout hollered back down. "It's still too far."

Tension mounted as the ship drew closer. Finally the lookout yelled to the captain. "Pirates!"

There was instant pandemonium. The captain gave the orders to raise the sails again, and the sailors jumped to obey.

"What are you going to do?" Galla asked the captain, his attention focused on the rapidly approaching ship.

"We're too loaded down to outrun them without the wind at our backs. We'll have to try to go with the wind."

"That will take us off course."

"It's the only chance we have," the captain told him grimly.

"Turn starboard!" the captain yelled, and Decimus could feel the instant change in the movement of the ship. "Set sails!"

The sails billowed out instantly, filled with the strong wind. They were now headed off course at a rapid rate, and yet still the pirate ship gained on them, little by little.

"Arm yourselves!" Galla commanded, and the soldiers hastened to obey. They quickly gathered swords and javelins and took positions on the port side of the ship.

The pirate ship was close enough for Decimus to make out individual figures on the decks. He counted at least fifty men. The Roman ship was outnumbered, he realized, but not badly.

Decimus noticed Chara among the men lining the rails. Quickly he crossed to her side. Taking her by the arm, he hurried her down the steps to Galla's quarters. "Stay here!" he commanded, and his voice brooked no argument.

Chara sank to the bunk, listening to feet pounding above her head. What was happening up there? Could they withstand an attack? Sliding quickly to her knees, she began to fervently pray.

At the rails, Galla watched intensely as the ship drew closer. He prayed to God that his people would be kept safe. What irony to flee death sentences in Rome only to meet their deaths at the hands of pirates. He knew his men were strong and competent and might win the day, but *someone* was bound to die in the skirmish. He prayed that Chara would be spared.

A fiery arrow flew across the water, falling short of its intended target. Others followed, arriving closer each time.

Decimus gritted his teeth as he prepared to defend himself. He had never been trained in the art of self-defense, and though he knew less about using weaponry, he wielded his sword with a determination that surprised Galla.

Suddenly the pirate ship veered off. The Roman ship's occupants hurried to the port side as the pirate ship put distance between them.

"What happened?" Decimus asked Galla under cover of the confusion.

"I don't know!" He was as confounded as the rest of them.

"Ship off the starboard!"

All eyes turned in time to see a Roman triple-banked warship slide around from their left. Its three rows of oars sliced effortlessly through the water, adding momentum to the wind that suddenly filled their sail.

The Roman warship rapidly cut the distance between itself and the pirate ship. As it drew closer, Decimus could see the soldiers as they prepared for battle. The pirate ship was hopelessly outnumbered.

Before long, the warship overtook the other. Their speed had been rapid, and they were so far away by this time that Decimus could barely see the figures of men running to and fro. A plank was dropped from the Roman ship to the pirates', and troops surged across.

"Poor lost devils," Galla commented softly.

Decimus watched as fire filled the sails of the pirate ship. The battle was over almost before it began.

"Drop sails!" the captain bellowed. "Man the oars!"

The ship moved sluggishly against the wind. Before long, they were back on course.

Decimus went to Galla's cabin and found Chara curled up in a ball on the bunk. Her eyes were frightened, and her lip trembled noticeably. She was clutching Galla's dagger in her hands.

Decimus's lips twitched. "Are you going to use that on me?"

Giving a sharp cry, she threw the dagger to the bunk and ran across the room, throwing herself into his arms. "Thank God, you're safe!"

He pulled back from her enough to look into her face. He shook his head slightly. "No. Thank God, *we're* safe."

Decimus explained what had happened, and Chara sighed, leaning her forehead against his chest. His warm arms tightened gently around her, trying to impart some measure of consolation.

Chara gave a prayer of thanks to God for their safety. She felt comforted by the warmth of their embrace, and her trembling slowed, then ceased altogether. Leaning back against Decimus's arm, she smiled into his face, suddenly realizing how dear he had become to her.

Decimus returned her smile, thankful himself for their safety. They had come so close to dying. What would have become of Chara if the attack had not been thwarted? As he continued to stare down into her eyes, the smile slowly slipped from his face. His gaze fastened on Chara's parted lips.

Chara could feel the pounding of Decimus's heart beneath her palms, and her own began to race in response. Slowly he moved his face closer to hers until their lips were only a breath apart. Without knowing she had moved, Chara leaned closer, closing her eyes as their lips met.

As Chara melted into the embrace, she slid her hands up around Decimus's neck. Warmth spread through her unlike any she had ever known. If only this moment would never cease.

Decimus suddenly broke the embrace as he heard thundering footsteps along the passageway. Galla slammed into the room.

"Are you all right?"

Chara nodded, her face suffusing with color. Galla grinned at her, unaware of the tension in the room.

"Well, at least one good thing came of this. Trophimus is no longer seasick."

Chara forced a laugh while Decimus smiled lamely. He was watching Chara intently, though Galla noticed nothing of their exchanged gazes.

"We shouldn't have any more problems with pirates. A Roman legion is patrolling the area. Apparently they want these ships with supplies to Britannia to arrive intact."

"How long until we reach Massilia?" Decimus wanted to know.

"Soon. Another four days, perhaps less if the wind changes."

Decimus turned to Chara. "And when we reach Massilia, you will have your freedom."

Chapter 6

Chara stared morosely at the approaching port of Massilia. Typical of ports anywhere, the docks were alive with activity. The hot sun's rays reflected against the tile roofs of the buildings.

Although the sun was warm against her skin, Chara felt cold inside. What would become of her now? Decimus promised her freedom upon reaching Massilia, because this far from Rome, Christians were in less danger.

Crazy man! What did he suppose she should do with her freedom? Find work somewhere? She let out her breath in frustration. Obviously he wished to be free of her. Free from his *responsibility*.

Galla joined her at the rail. "Why such a pensive look on such a beautiful day?"

Chara smiled slightly. "What's to become of me, Galla? Where do I go from here? Trophimus, Caleb, and Thomas will have no problem finding work. They are strong and skilled, but what of me?"

Before he could answer, a soldier approached them, snapping a salute. "Centurion, the captain wishes to speak to you. He's below in the cargo hold."

Galla nodded, watching as the soldier turned and abruptly left them. He looked at Chara. "I'll talk to you later. Will you be all right?"

She smiled slightly. "I'll be fine. Go ahead."

The ship was sliding into the dock, the smoothness of it showing the sailors' expertise. Chara watched as the plank was dropped and men scrambled up in a surging horde.

Sacrarii carried their loads from wagons, waiting their turns at the scales. A *stuppator* balanced on scaffolding, ready to caulk the ship that had just entered the dock. Chara marveled at his ability to twist and turn, never losing his balance.

So intent was she on watching the scenes around her that Chara failed to hear Decimus come up behind her. She jumped when she heard his voice.

"I haven't seen you for a few days."

Chara glared at him. " 'Twas not by *my* choice."

He had the grace to blush. True, he had avoided her for several days, ever since the attack on the ship. He hadn't known what to do or even what to think. His thoughts were even now in a turmoil about what to do with Chara.

"Chara, we need to talk."

Chara noticed the way Decimus refused to look her in the face. She felt her anger begin to rise. Well, he needn't bother worrying about her. She could take care of herself. He needn't worry that she would beg for his attention.

Galla was hurrying toward them, his lips set in a grim line. He pulled up beside Decimus. "Have you seen Thomas?"

Decimus frowned at the urgency of his tone. "Yes, he went below to see about our provisions."

"I'll go find him. You find Trophimus and Caleb and bring them to my quarters. Chara, you wait for us there. Hurry!"

Decimus didn't wait to ask questions. He hurried in the last direction he had seen the young Roman and the Jew. Chara watched them both disappear from sight and hastily went to the cabin to wait for them.

Galla was the first to arrive with Thomas, followed shortly by the others. Decimus closed the door behind them, and they all looked to Galla for an explanation.

"We have a problem. The soldiers will be accompanying me all the way to Britannia."

Chara dropped to the bunk. Decimus's eyes grew wide. "They will be coming with *us*?"

Galla nodded. "There's more to it," he told them grimly, going over and sitting next to Chara. "It seems that I am not entirely free from suspicion after all and that there is some question as to my *loyalties*. Captain Caltupa wasn't supposed to tell me this, but he has known me a long time."

"What does that mean for the rest of us?" Caleb wanted to know, his suspicions rising.

"It means," Galla told him tersely, "that you have to come with us."

Thomas surged away from the wall where he had been leaning. "To Britannia? Not if my life depended on it!"

Galla glared at him. "What about *six* lives?"

All in the room stared helplessly at Galla as the meaning of his words penetrated.

"Is there no other way?" Trophimus questioned.

"I have thought of a way for you to still have your freedom, but it will be risky." Galla waited until he was sure that his words had sunk in. "I will still give you your letters of manumission. I had them prepared before we left Rome. I will also give you part of the money that was given to us for this mission. As we travel overland, you are free to slip away."

"Just like that?" Caleb asked incredulously. "What happens if we're caught?"

Chara shivered at the look on Galla's face.

"Then we will all be on our way back to Rome, and most probably the arena."

Trophimus swallowed hard. "Then I'd suggest we not be caught."

Decimus frowned. "And what of Chara?"

Galla sucked in a breath, pressing his lips tightly together. "That is something

I need to talk to you and Chara about alone. But before I do, are we all agreed so far?"

His look went from person to person, pausing lastly on Caleb. Slowly the Jew nodded his head.

"Good. Then I need the three of you to go to the supply hold and help with the unloading."

Chara watched uneasily as the three others left the room. This was sounding more ominous by the minute. She swallowed apprehensively as Galla fixed his gaze upon her. He seemed hesitant to speak.

"Well?" Decimus prodded impatiently.

"I think the two of you need to marry." Galla dropped his bombshell and waited for a response. He hadn't long to wait.

"Are you out of your mind?" Decimus's fists clenched and unclenched at his sides.

Chara merely stared at Galla as though he had grown horns. His lips twitched. If the situation were not so serious, the looks on their faces would have been amusing.

"Before you take my head off, listen to me. The others will be leaving us soon. Eventually they should be able to find passage to wherever they wish to go. That will leave the three of us. You, Decimus, will have your letter of manumission, as we agreed. But what of Chara?"

"I will do the same for her," Decimus told him impatiently. "I will hardly keep her as my slave. She will be free, just as the others will be."

"So she will be a free woman alone in a foreign land. Or she can continue to accompany me, traveling with a group of soldiers. What then? What does that make her?"

Decimus felt his anger begin to rise. "Don't even suggest it."

"Would the two of you stop talking about me as though I weren't present? It's out of the question, anyway."

"Chara, it can be no other way. We have no choice," Galla remonstrated softly.

"I refuse," she told him adamantly.

"As do I."

Galla stared from one to the other. "Let me see if I can make it plainer. This is going to be a long, hard trip over a great distance. At times Chara will be the only woman within many miles. Now, if my men think her my slave, they may leave her alone for a time. But eventually this could cause difficulties. For her to sleep in my tent could cause. . .problems. They will think I should. . .share." He cleared his throat uncomfortably.

Chara stared at him uncomprehendingly, but Galla could see the dawning realization on Decimus's face.

"In any event," Galla continued, "she would have no privacy. I usually share my tents with my captains."

"Oh." Chara's tiny voice was the only sound for many minutes.

"I would marry you myself," Galla told her softly, "but Roman centurions are forbidden to marry."

Decimus and Chara exchanged looks briefly before they both quickly turned their eyes away.

"It's really the only way," Galla told them. "Unless, as I told Thomas, you want to risk six people's lives."

Chara dropped her head, her blond hair dropping down to conceal her face. "I can't."

Decimus raised his face to the ceiling, his teeth clenched.

Sighing, Galla turned to Decimus. "Let me talk to her alone for a minute, would you?"

Decimus glanced at Chara. Nodding his head briefly, he went to the door, turning back when Galla called him. "If Chara agrees, do you?"

Decimus looked briefly at Chara. He jerked his head in the affirmative and exited the room.

Before Galla could open his mouth, Chara attacked him with her words. "It will do you no good to *talk* to me, Galla. You could talk to me until the moon turned blue, and my answer would still be the same."

"Chara."

She leaped from the bunk, her hands curling at her sides. She turned to him. "No! I won't marry a man who doesn't love me."

Galla noticed she hadn't mentioned not loving Decimus. He was hopeful that he could win her to his way of thinking. And he didn't have much time.

"He does love you, only he doesn't know it yet."

Chara's eyes widened, her hands slowly uncurling at her sides. "I don't believe you," she whispered.

"I think you do. I don't know why you're fighting it. It's obvious to everyone that he cares for you."

"Oh yes," she told him derisively. "He handles his responsibilities well. He takes care of me as well as he would a horse."

"Were you his responsibility on that auction block?"

Chara dropped back onto the bunk. "That was different. He felt pity for me." She glared into his eyes. "And if he allows this marriage, it will be for the same reason."

Galla sighed. "What about you?"

"What about me?"

"Are you willing to let five men die and yourself, as well? Do you think it's any easier for the others to play the part of slaves when they are so close to freedom?"

"That's different," she argued. "Their situation is temporary. Marriage is permanent."

"So is death." Galla didn't mean to be cruel or to make her feel guilty, but as a trained soldier, he knew that sometimes one had to sacrifice oneself to save many. More was at stake here than their six lives.

Chara buried her head in her hands. "Oh, Galla! You're beginning to make sense, in an awful kind of way."

"Chara, listen to me. Decimus loves you; that I can tell. You love him; that I can tell, also. So where would be the harm?"

Chara threw back her head, closing her eyes. "What if you're wrong?"

"I'm not. Trust me."

Was what Galla said possible? Could Decimus actually have some feelings for her? She gave a wry smile. "I once told Decimus that I would trust you with my life. It seems I have to make good my words."

Galla returned her smile, then reached out a hand and stroked a curled finger gently down her cheek. "You won't be sorry."

Decimus stood beside Chara, his face drawn and white. Chara stood as she usually did, her golden hair a veil that hid her true feelings. The priest of the temple of Zeus chanted words and watched as the two exchanged grain wafers. After chanting a few more words, he stepped to the side. Another priest used a pot of ink, registering their names on the prepared document with his stylus. Galla paid the priest, taking the rolled document from his hand, and the three of them left the temple.

Married. The word echoed around and around in Chara's head. And by a pagan priest. All her life she had dreamed of what her wedding day would be like, and her dreams were nothing like the reality.

A tear trickled down her cheek. She prayed to God that this was not a horrible mistake. Looking at Decimus, she realized that he looked no happier than she. Did he really love her as Galla had suggested? She had wagered her whole life on one man's assurances. Her life and Decimus's.

Holding out her left hand, she stared at the ring that Decimus had purchased for her. A golden ring, the symbol of continuity, placed on the finger nearest her heart. She closed her eyes. One thing was certain: She loved Decimus. Now she had only to make sure that he loved her.

Decimus's voice broke the quiet that had shrouded them since they had left the temple. "Will there be any problem with the soldiers?"

Galla shook his head. "No. It's permitted for two slaves to marry as long as they have permission. Fortunately you made their acceptance of the act easier because of the disturbance you made on the ship." He shrugged. "They will merely think I tired of her and gave her to you."

Decimus felt his face burn with anger. He had felt like killing the soldier with his bare hands for suggesting that he and Chara were doing something inappropriate.

Now, the thought of the soldiers' assumption about Galla and Chara filled him with rage.

They walked slowly back to the inn where they had booked accommodations. Decimus thought of the document of manumission inside his pouch. It nestled safely next to the other document that declared him married. One scroll gave him his freedom; another took it away.

He sighed but refused to look at Chara. He had noticed the tear winding its way down her cheek, and his stomach had coiled tightly within him. He wanted to comfort her but didn't dare.

Opening the door to their room, Decimus allowed Chara to precede him inside. He hesitated on the threshold.

Galla came up behind him. "I'm going to the baths," he told them, looking from one to the other.

Decimus seized on the opportunity. "I'll come with you."

Galla raised his eyebrows but refrained from comment. *Let the two of them work this out for themselves.* He entered the room, going to his pack and taking out a clean tunic.

"Will you be all right by yourself?" he asked Chara quietly. She was looking at the floor, but she nodded her head slightly. He hesitated a moment before turning and leaving the room. Decimus followed closely on his heels.

Chara dropped on the bed and began to cry, deep, racking sobs. So much had happened to her since her mother had died, and now here she was, in a strange city on her wedding day, alone.

Thoughts whirled around in her head, giving her no peace. Where did she go from here? What was to become of her now? The words of Jesus came to her mind. *"Come to me, all you who are weary and burdened, and I will give you rest."* Closing her eyes, she did just that. Slowly her prayers brought the peace she was seeking. No matter what happened, God was with her. Exhausted, she slept.

Galla sat cross-legged on the pool floor, scraping his skin with the strigil and shaking the water off onto the mosaic tiles. Decimus sat beside him, his strong legs dangling in the cool water. He knew that Galla had something he wanted to say, but for some reason, he was keeping his silence.

"You may as well say it," Decimus told him at last.

Galla looked at him innocently. "Say what?"

"Whatever it is that is causing you to turn blue from choking it back," Decimus told him, aggravated.

Laughing, Galla continued to scrape his skin. "If I'm turning blue, it's from the water in the *frigidarium*."

"I think not," Decimus disagreed softly.

Galla regarded Decimus with veiled eyes. The Briton had changed much over the last few weeks. He had a maturity about him now that rested easily upon his shoulders. He was no longer the boy Galla had originally thought him.

"Do you love Chara?" Galla finally asked. He watched Decimus's brows instantly draw down in a frown.

"Why are you asking?"

"She's a special lady. I don't want to see her hurt."

Decimus glared at Galla, but the older man was unaffected. A few angry looks wouldn't frighten him, especially when he wanted to make sure someone he cared about would not be hurt.

"It's no concern of yours," Decimus finally told him.

"I disagree. I happen to love Chara, too. I want to see her happy."

The sparkle in Decimus's eyes intensified. "What do you mean you love her?"

"You know what I mean, so don't pretend you don't. She's like a sister to me. If not for you, I might have tried to make it otherwise, but I knew with you around that I stood no chance. She loves you."

Decimus sighed, lying back against the marble tiles. He closed his eyes as though that would ward off any other thoughts. "I know."

The admission surprised Galla. "You *know* she loves you? Then where's the problem?"

Decimus lifted his legs from the water and got quickly to his feet. "The problem lies within me. I'm not sure I love her. Not that way. I care for her, yes, but. . ."

"There's someone else?"

Decimus sighed. "There was. I thought I loved her, too, but the feelings. . . I don't know anymore."

"I see." Galla studied him a moment, then rose to his feet to stand beside him. He wasn't sure just what to say. How could he reassure Decimus that what he felt was real, when in actuality Galla didn't know? Only Decimus knew what was in his own mind.

They walked to the changing rooms, retrieving their tunics from the shelves and donning them. Decimus followed Galla into the street. Although his body felt rejuvenated, his mind was still in a shambles.

The sun was setting as they threaded their way through the streets to the inn. Decimus felt guilty when he realized that Chara might have wished to go to the baths, too. Instead, she had deferred to his wish to be away from her.

When they reached the room, Galla began to gather his things together. Decimus watched him, alarmed. "What are you doing?"

Raising his brows, Galla continued what he was doing. "I'm clearing out. I'll stay with the troops."

Chara came to her feet, twisting her hands together in front of her. "That's not necessary."

"I think it is."

Decimus and Chara exchanged glances. Decimus felt the heat rise to his own face as he watched the color flow into Chara's. He turned to Galla. "It's really not necessary for you to leave. I mean, on the trip north there will be little privacy."

"Exactly," Galla agreed. "You need some time alone *now*." He went to the door and opened it. Giving one last look at the couple, he left.

Chara and Decimus stood facing each other, eyes going everywhere but toward each other.

"Are you hungry?" Decimus wanted to know.

Chara shook her head. "Not really."

"Well, I am. How about if we go downstairs and get a meal?"

Chara shrugged. "If you want to."

Anything to prolong the time when they would retire, Decimus decided. He followed Chara down the stairs into the main room below. Already a crowd was beginning to congregate. Feeling eyes upon them, Decimus decided that maybe this had not been a good idea after all.

The proprietor showed them to a table set back in a corner, and Decimus breathed a sigh of relief. A few moments later, the man returned with a flask of wine and a platter of meats, cheeses, and fruits.

Chara picked up a piece of cheese and began to nibble. Slowly her appetite returned to her. She had not eaten since the meal at breakfast, of which she had consumed little.

Decimus poured himself a drink and one for Chara. The liquid slid coolly down his dry throat. He watched as Chara sipped at her own drink. Everything she did spoke of daintiness and refinement. Where had she learned such things?

"Tell me about your family."

Surprised, Chara looked up. "What do you wish to know?"

"You told me of your mother in Galilee, but what happened to her later? How did she get to Gaul?"

Chara smiled, her eyes taking on a faraway look. "The family who owned her treated her as a daughter, not as a slave. She was free to go anywhere she chose. My father was a merchant on his way back to Gaul from Syria when he saw my mother at the watering well. When he saw her, he fell in love with her. The family she was with gave her her freedom and their blessings. They were sad to see her go but joyful that she had found such happiness. I was twelve when my father died."

She paused, her brow furrowing in a frown. "She was a wonderful mother, and she taught me everything she could about being a lady. When my father died, something died within her. She was never the same." She stopped picking the meat from the chicken leg she was holding. "My stepfather married her a year later. She was a beautiful woman, and though many men wanted her, she chose him. Probably, I think, because he was wealthy and she thought he would look after us." Chara's voice softened. "I think he drank so much because he knew my mother didn't love him. He never said anything, but he knew all the same."

Decimus regretted asking, especially since he knew how the story ended.

The room was becoming more crowded. Crude language filtered the spaces around them, making Decimus wince. Color flooded Chara's cheeks as she heard some of the ribald jokes and coarse laughter.

"Are you finished with your meal?"

Chara nodded, rising to her feet. They made their way toward the stairs. Decimus gritted his teeth as he noticed the men in the room look their way. He heard their sly laughter, and he felt like shouting to the whole crazy place that they were legally married.

When they reached the room, Chara breathed a sigh of relief. If she had had to remain downstairs one moment longer, she thought she would have screamed.

Decimus stood leaning with his back against the door, watching Chara drift about the room. She picked up a garment, folding it and laying it across the room's only chair. Decimus's eyes flicked to the bed, and he swallowed hard.

Going over, he began to pull blankets from the bed. Chara stared at him in surprise. He went back to the door, laying the coverings on the floor. When Chara continued to stare at him, he shrugged his shoulders. "I thought it might be safer for me to sleep here. You can have the bed. That way if anyone tries to enter, I will know about it." The excuse sounded lame, even to his own ears.

Chara was relieved, but piqued at the same time. Would she ever understand this man? Sighing, she began to prepare herself for bed. She could feel Decimus's eyes on her as she began to comb out her hair with her fingers. Deciding that she could go to the baths in the morning when few others would be around, she lay down in her clothes. Within moments, she was fast asleep.

Decimus watched as Chara's breathing became even. Finally his own breathing slowed its erratic pace. He shook his head slightly. Getting up, he crossed to where Chara lay sleeping. He watched her for a long rime, awed that she belonged to him. Not as a slave but as a wife. Fear like none he had ever known before filled his entire being. He didn't know *how* to be a husband. He wasn't sure he wanted to know.

He went back and lay down on his cold pallet. Lifting his eyes to the ceiling, he began to pray. *Lord, help me to know what to do. Help me to do what's right.* Glancing again at Chara's sleeping form, he added, *Lord, help me to love this woman.*

Chapter 7

Decimus lifted Chara to the back of the huge roan gelding. Climbing up behind her, he settled himself firmly in the saddle, wrapping one arm securely around her waist. Memories of riding with Diana in the hills around Ephesus floated through his mind. His job had been to protect her and see that she came to no harm. He felt the same responsibility now.

Instead of traversing the distance through Gaul to the Loire River by foot, Galla had decided to mount the troops. Since the journey could be covered more swiftly by mount, he felt the expense was justified, and there would be the added benefit of using the horses later, if necessary, for battle.

Galla glanced swiftly about him, checking to see that all were accounted for. Thomas, Trophimus, and Caleb, each driving a wagon full of trade goods, gave him a quick nod of acknowledgment.

Captain Caltupa approached from the front of the column.

"We're ready, Centurion."

Looking around once more, Galla nodded his head and mounted his own horse. "Let's go," he told them, moving forward to the front of the entourage. Decimus and Chara would follow at the rear with the wagons, along with several of the soldiers.

As they moved forward through the city, the sun was suddenly hidden behind clouds that were steadily thickening in the sky. A mist of rain began to fall, causing Chara to shiver. Decimus felt her body begin to tremble.

"Are you cold?"

Although the weather was still somewhat warm, the wetness cooled the temperatures considerably, a precursor of the winter to come.

Chara shook her head. "No." She looked quickly about her at the countryside of her birth and shivered again. "I just hope the weather is not an omen of things to come."

Decimus was surprised at her morbid turn of thoughts. Noticing the direction of her gaze, he thought he understood. "You needn't be afraid of your stepbrother. He has no control over your life now."

They picked their way along the cobbled road as the rain increased in tempo. Before long they were soaked. Decimus tried to shield Chara as much as possible, but the moisture crept everywhere, filling every available space.

When Chara spoke, her voice seemed to come from a long distance. Decimus realized that she was speaking more to herself than to him.

"I never thought I would see my homeland again," she told him softly. "And now, here I am, back where I started from. I used to think that Franco was the closest thing to Satan that a person could be, but that was before I knew about Nero. I now realize that with Franco, it was just jealousy. I don't think he meant me any *real* harm."

Decimus shifted slightly in the saddle, refraining from comment. Surely her stepbrother knew what atrocities were perpetrated upon slaves, especially female ones.

"I can forgive him more easily now," Chara told him. "For if not for him, I never would have met you."

Decimus swallowed hard. There it was again, that complete trust in him. That faith that he was what was meant for her life. Her belief in him made him want to stand a little straighter, be a little stronger. He wanted to live up to her ideals, but he was afraid that he couldn't.

Before long they reached a thick copse of woods. The road continued through it, winding its way among the thick shrubs and trees. The rain fell softer here, and the column suddenly came to a stop.

A young soldier came riding toward them. "Centurion Galla says we are to stop here for a short spell. If you have any needs to attend to, do it quickly."

Decimus quickly dismounted, tying the reins to a small tree. Reaching up, he lifted Chara from the saddle and lowered her to the ground.

"I have a leather cloak in my pack that will help keep the rain off you," he told her, digging to find the article he was looking for. "You need to change out of that wet tunic."

Nodding, Chara rummaged around until she found a suitable change of clothes. Clutching the tunic to her chest, she looked hesitantly around her. Seeing her predicament, Decimus rolled the cloak into a ball, tucking it under his own tunic. He took Chara by the hand and led her a short distance into the woods until he found a large tree that shielded her from the others.

"Change quickly," he told her, "or someone might come looking for us."

While Chara was changing behind the tree, Decimus availed himself of the opportunity to quickly change his own garments. He pulled the leather cloak he had purchased for himself around him, thankful for the fur lining. The temperatures were dropping rapidly, and he was beginning to wonder if winter was going to come early to this part of the world. He certainly hoped not, because they still had a long way to travel.

Chara emerged from behind the tree, her bright blue tunic making her look for all the world like a small bird in the huge forest. Decimus handed her her own cloak and waited impassively while she secured it around her shoulders.

"Better?" he asked.

She smiled then, and Decimus felt his heart give a leap.

"Much."

They quickly made their way back to the others, who were already mounting up. Decimus once again lifted Chara to the saddle and positioned himself behind her. He had purchased Chara her own mount, but for now it was being used to carry supplies. Decimus smiled slightly. No matter. He was rather enjoying the arrangement.

The road continued through the forest for many miles. Decimus had never seen so many trees in his life, and although they provided protection from the elements, they also made him leery. Shadows seemed to move through the interior of the trees, and Decimus once thought he saw a pair of glowing yellow eyes.

Before long, the road widened out and the trees began to thin, ending as abruptly as they had begun. The road led down into a green valley, and although the rain hit them with greater force, Decimus was glad to be free of the forest.

Dusk was falling when Galla called a halt for the night. Everyone began to quickly ready their shelters. Chara tried to help Decimus and Caleb, but she was more in the way than anything else. Shrugging, she abandoned the effort, going instead to sit on a rock near a stream of water.

Trophimus was already there watering the horses. He smiled when she reached him.

"I have muscles that ache that I didn't even know I had."

Chara smiled in sympathy. "I can agree with that, although I think perhaps a wagon seat might be a little more comfortable than a horse."

Decimus found them arguing good-naturedly with each other about the advantages of traveling on horseback versus in a wagon seat. One eyebrow cocked upward, and he smiled.

"What, Trophimus, you think yourself ill used?"

Trophimus grinned back at him unabashedly. "I would gladly trade places with you."

Decimus's smile dimmed somewhat. "Perhaps. But I am not inclined to grant you that opportunity." He turned to Chara. "Do you think you can fix us a meal? Thomas will help you."

"Of course," she told him testily. She was aggravated that he continued to see her as little more than a child. What did he think, that she was useless? He might be surprised at what she could do.

Two pairs of male eyes followed her progress, the angry sway of her hips speaking to them more clearly than any words. Decimus turned to find Trophimus hiding a grin. He cocked an eyebrow at the young Roman, shrugging his shoulders. "What did I say?"

Trophimus turned quickly away, picking up a water bag and hefting it over his shoulder. "Don't ask me. She's *your* wife."

Decimus sat down on the rock Chara had so recently vacated. Women were so unpredictable.

Galla joined him, arching an eyebrow in inquiry. "Something bothering you?"

Reaching down, Decimus picked up a stick and began to draw circles in the sand. Water dripped down his nose and into a puddle at his feet.

"You're going to catch your death out here," Galla told him impatiently. "Come back to camp and get into some dry things."

Only then did Decimus realize that he had left his fur-lined cloak in the tent Caleb and he had erected for their group. Lifting his head, he stared hard into Galla's curious eyes. "I didn't sleep in the same bed with her last night."

Something flickered in Galla's own dark gaze before he pressed his lips tightly together. "Well, I'm afraid you had better here. If you leave an opening for these soldiers, you'll have to accept the consequences." He stopped, letting his words sink in. "She's your *wife*. I'd suggest you treat her like one so that she is afforded the respect she deserves."

Decimus rose to his feet, angry that Galla should so chastise him. Slowly the anger faded, and he realized that Galla only meant the best for both Chara and himself. Galla slapped him on the back.

"Come on. I'm hungry."

They walked back to camp in silence, although it was a congenial one. There would be much they would go through together in the future, Decimus realized, and they would have no one but each other to depend on.

Chara watched Decimus and Galla coming and rose to prepare them a plate. Soldiers traveling long distances depended on dried fruits and nuts, and that was what they ate for the most part. However, one young soldier had availed himself of the opportunity to practice his bow shooting and had brought down a young stag in the forest. The meat had been distributed around, and the soldier was strutting around the fire as he received congratulations from the others. Chara couldn't help but smile at the young lad's cockiness.

Decimus took a seat beside Chara, while Galla sat across from them. Lines of fatigue were etched around his mouth, and Chara decided that there was something troubling his mind.

"What is bothering you, Galla?" she asked him softly.

He looked at her a moment before his lips finally turned up in a smile. "Nothing that you can help me with," he told her finally. "Just soldier things."

She would have asked him more, but Caleb rose to his feet. "I don't know about the rest of you, but I'm ready for bed."

Thomas rose, also. "I'm all for that. How about you, Trophimus?"

Trophimus lifted his plate for their inspection. "I'm more hungry than tired. I have to finish eating first."

Chara leaned her hands toward the fire, trying to get as close as possible.

The rain had stopped at last, but with darkness, the cold intensified, tiny crystals of ice forming on every wet surface. Even in her fur-lined cloak, she was chilled.

Galla left to join his men, and Decimus and Trophimus continued to talk. Their soft murmuring voices soon lulled Chara into a state of semiwakefulness, and her head began nodding forward. She didn't realize the voices around her had stopped until she felt herself lifted into strong arms. She heard Trophimus's voice as though in a dream.

"She must be exhausted."

Chara felt herself carried into the tent and laid gently on a mat. She felt bereft when Decimus's warm arms left her. A moment later, she felt a fur blanket draped over her. Shivering, she pulled it close against her, huddling into a ball. Before long, her deep breathing told Decimus she was sound asleep.

He watched her several minutes, a soft smile curving his lips. She reminded him of a child, her lashes feathered against her smooth cheeks. The smile slowly faded. She hadn't *felt* like a child in his arms. She had felt warm, and a shiver of yearning ran through him.

Shaking his head, he left the tent to rejoin Trophimus. They talked a long time about many things. Until then, Decimus hadn't really seen the young Roman as anything more than part of their entourage. Watching the boy, Decimus realized how homesick he must be. No matter how decadent Rome had been, it was still his home, the only one he had ever known.

Trophimus finally rose to his feet, stretching his arms above his head. "Well, I hate to leave you out here all alone, but I'm tired. I'll see you in the morning."

Decimus watched as the tent swallowed him. He turned his eyes back to the fire, continuing to gaze at it for a long time. Galla's words kept echoing through his mind. Rising slowly to his feet, he made his way toward the tent.

He crossed to where Chara lay curled asleep. Lifting the cover gently, he crawled in beside her. He lay tense, his hands behind his head, listening to the sound of her breathing. Suddenly she rolled over, throwing one arm across his chest and her knee across his legs. His breathing almost stopped.

For several minutes he lay tensely waiting for her to move. Realizing she wasn't going to, he exhaled slowly. Carefully he moved one arm around her, pulling her tighter against him. She smiled in her sleep, cuddling closer. Decimus gritted his teeth. He began to count in his head. Finally his body began to relax and exhaustion took over, his eyes closing in sleep.

When Chara awoke in the morning, she found the tent empty. Noises from outside indicated that the others were preparing to leave. Rising quickly to her feet, she stumbled outside.

Decimus was strapping a pack on one of the horses. He glanced quickly at her, then away. "You better hurry and get something to eat. Galla wants to leave within the hour."

"Why didn't you wake me?" she asked, hurrying to his side. She tried to help him lace the bundles to the horse, but he pushed her gently away.

"I told you to get something to eat. Then you can pick up the bed furs."

Hurt, she hurried to obey. Decimus had refused to even look at her. What was the matter with him this morning?

She entered the tent and began to gather up the furs they had used to sleep on. Suddenly she stopped. Scanning the interior, she realized that there were only four beds. Frowning, she counted again. No, there was no mistake.

Sudden color flooded her cheeks as she realized that what she had thought was a dream must have been reality. She thought she had dreamed that Decimus had held her close, but it must have been true. Pressing her hands against her hot cheeks, she began to gather up the furs.

She couldn't look him in the face when she handed him the furs, one at a time, for him to pack on the wagons. Instead, she concentrated on the circles of frosty air forming in front of her mouth. She shivered, pulling her cape closer against her.

Decimus went with her into the woods while she answered nature's call. He kept his back to her, always on the lookout. When they returned to camp, Galla was waiting for them.

"Good morning," he called. "Are you almost ready to leave?"

Decimus helped Chara into the saddle. He nodded at Galla. "We're ready."

"Good. I hope to make better progress today. The rain slowed us down some yesterday, but it looks like today will be fair weather."

"How far do you think we can travel?" Decimus wanted to know, scanning the blue sky overhead. It boded well for their journey.

"I hope to make the first Roman station by nightfall. We can exchange horses there, and the soldiers can sleep in the garrison. There should be an inn, as well."

Decimus lowered his voice. "What of Caleb, Trophimus, and Thomas? Surely there will be no way to escape from there."

"No. It would be better if they wait until we are farther along the road. Too many soldiers patrol these roads, but the farther north we get, the fewer soldiers there will be."

Caleb walked up in time to hear the last part of their conversation. "The farther north we get, the harder it will be for me to return to Judea," he told them angrily.

Galla shook his head. "Longer, maybe, but not harder. It will actually be easier the closer we get to the Loire River. From there you could easily purchase your fare on a ship that would take you around Iberia and back to the Great Sea."

"Perhaps you're right."

Both Galla and Decimus could tell that the Jew still didn't trust the Roman fully. He had much reason to distrust, so Galla didn't hold it against him.

They finished loading their gear while Chara watched from astride her mount. The sun was beginning to warm her enough that she took off her fur wrap, rolled it into a ball, and put it in front of her.

Decimus climbed on behind her, taking up the reins. Clicking his tongue, he urged the horse forward, moving into position behind Caleb's wagon.

Chara marveled at the well-tended roads that were the hallmark of the Roman Empire. With such roads, they were able to move troops easily from one section of the empire to another, thus preventing uprisings from occurring in the various sections of their land.

The Roman war machine was well equipped, well trained, and lethal. Even this small band of troops rode with style, their imperial helmets glistening in the morning sun. Chara shivered. God was the only thing that could stop Rome now.

Galla watched his troops and felt saddened. Loyal, robust, faithful, they would die for Rome, only Rome would not care. Caught up in its own debauchery, its own pleasures, the empire was greedily devouring everything that came into its path. How long before it devoured itself?

Turning his head, he could see Chara and Decimus far behind. He smiled slightly, seeing the contented smile on Chara's face as she leaned back against her husband. Decimus, on the other had, was not smiling at all. Galla frowned, wondering what was going through his mind.

Galla would have been surprised if he could have read Decimus's thoughts. He was beginning to like this being married bit. The one thing that bothered him was the fact that the farther they moved north, the closer he was taking Chara into danger. He had no idea what to expect when they reached Britannia. It had been years since he had been there, and his memories were foggy. He had no definite livelihood there, no security to offer her.

He could dimly remember a midsummer's night, a huge fire, and priests dressed in robes. Why was it that thought stood out so clearly in his mind? When he tried to remember more, his thoughts shied away and his mind went blank.

The sun rose higher in the sky, its rays warming the air around them until they began to perspire. The extremes in temperature were uncomfortable, and he wondered if they were typical of Gaul.

Unlike yesterday, no forest offered them shade today from the intense rays of the sun. Just when Decimus thought he could stand the heat no longer, a gentle breeze sprang up, blowing against his face. Chara leaned into it, closing her eyes with a smile.

A sudden disturbance behind them caused Decimus to swing around. He could hear angry voices and cursing, and the caravan came to a sudden halt.

Galla quickly made his way to the rear. "What's going on here?"

One of the soldiers who had been traveling rear guard came forward. "It's the wagons, Centurion. Two of them have broken an axle."

Galla quickly dismounted, making his way past the guards who were standing around complaining of the heat. As he passed, they snapped to attention.

Caleb stood beside his wagon, scratching his head. Thomas leaned against the other wagon, shrugging his shoulders when Galla approached. Each wagon was loaded to the maximum. It would take hours to unload and fix them.

Decimus came up behind Galla. "What are you going to do?"

Galla caught a glimmer in Caleb's eyes before Caleb turned away to study the broken axle. Without taking his eyes from the Jew, Galla answered Decimus. "The last mile marker showed us to be about four miles from the station." He paused, taking note that the sun was sinking rapidly.

The captain made his way to Galla's side, snapping a salute. "What do you wish us to do, Centurion?"

Galla sighed. "Take the troops to the garrison." He turned to Decimus. "You take Chara and go with them. There will be an inn to stay at. I'll stay with the wagons, along with my slaves and a couple of the soldiers. We should be fine until morning." Turning back to the captain, he told him, "First thing in the morning, bring replacement wagons. Have the smith come with you, and he can repair these wagons and return them to the garrison."

Caltupa looked uncomfortable. "Centurion, would it not be better for me to remain with the wagons?"

"These supplies are my responsibility, Captain. You have your orders."

Galla and Decimus exchanged glances before Galla quickly turned away, giving orders for the unloading of the wagons.

Decimus went back to where Chara was waiting patiently on their horse. "What's worng?" she asked.

"Two of the wagons have broken down. They'll have to remain here until tomorrow. We're going on with the other wagons and the rest of the troops."

He climbed up behind her, taking the reins from her hand.

"What of Galla and the others?" she wanted to know.

Decimus looked over her head, clicking his tongue at the horse. Slowly they moved forward. "They're staying with the wagons until tomorrow."

Chara frowned, glancing behind her. Something didn't seem quite right, but she couldn't decide what it was. Looking up at Decimus, she found his expression closed and unreadable.

The captain picked up the pace in order to reach the garrison before nightfall. The last rays of the sun were setting behind the hills when they pulled to a stop in the courtyard of an inn.

"I'll leave you here," the captain informed him. "But don't try to run away. I'll leave word with the proprietor to keep an eye on you. Do you understand?"

Decimus understood all too well. And although he was not particularly fond of inns, he would welcome a respite from the soldiers' company.

He lifted Chara down from the horse, and she leaned against him until her legs strengthened beneath her. Dark circles around her eyes bespoke her fatigue.

Taking her by the hand, he led her to a table in the corner of the inn. Glancing around, he noticed very few customers, and those were mainly soldiers who had wanted a change from the garrison. Their interest quickened when they noticed Chara. Decimus was reluctant to leave her, but he had to stable the horse.

"I'll be right back," he told her. "When the proprietor comes, order us something to eat."

Although many eyes followed her movements, the soldiers kept a respectful distance. Decimus returned, hurrying them through their meal. This time when they retired to their room, they did not quibble over who would sleep where. When Chara closed her eyes that night, she was snuggled safely in her husband's arms.

Chapter 8

Decimus watched Chara ambling along in front of the wagon he was driving. She rode a horse well. He caught the eye of Caltupa and almost smiled at the man's menacing glower. After all, he had reason to scowl. During the night, Thomas and Caleb had disappeared, slipped away when no one was looking. Decimus grinned. Even Galla had been unaware of their disappearance until morning.

Captain Caltupa had wanted to organize a search immediately, but Galla had forestalled him, telling him that getting the supplies and men to Britannia was more important than the disappearance of two slaves.

Decimus had been surprised when Trophimus had driven his wagon into the compound behind the others. He hadn't had time to talk to the young Roman, but he was curious as to his reasons for staying. Had he not been able to slip away with the others? Surely Caleb would have waited for him, though everyone knew that the Jew had no love for Romans.

Chara turned and caught his eye, and her smile lit up her face. How was it that he had considered her rather plain in the beginning? She had beauty much like that of young Sara, the kind of beauty that seemed to come from within. Hadn't the apostle Peter said something to that effect?

Decimus felt butterflies tumbling about inside him. How long could he continue to sleep with his wife and do nothing besides hold her gently? Every time he held her close, he felt himself drawn perilously near to holding her tighter, pressing his lips to hers, and. . . He frowned, considering the consequences.

If Chara were to become pregnant. . . The thought terrified him. He had no idea what would happen over the next several months, and he wasn't about to take such a risk. Very possibly not one of them would come out of this alive. He could remember little of his life as a boy, but the stories circulating around the empire did nothing to calm his fears. Did the Druids truly offer human sacrifices to their gods? What kind of reception would they give to someone trying to teach them of another God, one who didn't desire sacrifices at all?

But was that really true? Didn't the Lord want His people to give their whole lives to Him? Even to the point of facing lions in an arena of Rome? There was no greater sacrifice than the one Antipus and Agrippina had made.

They traveled without incident the remainder of the day. The sun spilled its rays warmly across the verdant hillsides. Rolling, undulating hills met the eye wherever one turned. The scent of pine from the forests in the distance drifted to them on the cooling breeze.

Decimus noted that they were passing another mile marker. Every ten miles or so, one could find another station where soldiers could refresh their horses or stay for the night. According to his calculations, this made the ninth marker. He sighed, wondering if Galla would choose to press on. Since they had only come nine miles, he decided that Galla would most likely choose to continue.

They passed one small village and then another. Everywhere they went, they were greeted with hostility. Fear and hatred emanated from the eyes of the people they passed.

Galla called a halt when the sun was high in the sky, for they had reached a small stream and needed the time to water the horses. Decimus helped Chara to the ground, keeping one arm protectively around her as his eyes skimmed the nearby forest. Deciding that nothing was in the vicinity, he walked with her into the woods. Keeping his back to her, he watched the others mingling about.

When Chara rejoined Decimus, he was sitting on a boulder next to the stream, allowing the cool water to run over his bare feet. He smiled up at her, taking her hand and pulling her down beside him.

"Try it," he told her. "It's refreshing."

Feeling like a child again, she slid her sandals from her feet and plunged them into the cold water. Squealing, she quickly pulled them back.

"It's like ice!"

Decimus grinned. "That's because it comes from the mountains."

Glancing up, Decimus noticed that Caltupa wasn't far away. The man's constant vigil was beginning to wear on Decimus's not-so-good humor.

Noticing the direction of her husband's fierce gaze, Chara turned her head. She turned back to the spring, cupping her hands and letting the water run through her fingers.

"Did you know that Caleb and Thomas were going to leave last night?" she whispered.

Decimus focused his attention on his wife, trying to forget the other man's presence. "I thought they might. It was no accident that *both* their axles broke."

"I wondered." Her eyes met his. "But why didn't Trophimus go with them?"

Decimus shrugged. "I haven't talked to him yet. I don't know."

A shadow blocked out the sun. "Time to leave."

Rising slowly to his feet, Decimus gave the man glare for glare, his muscles rippling as he clenched his fists at his sides. Chara moved quickly to place herself between them, taking Decimus by the hand.

"We were just coming, Captain."

Decimus was aggravated that the man followed so closely behind. Grinning wryly, he realized that it hadn't taken him long to appreciate his freedom. How long he would have to suffer the company of the soldiers, he didn't know; but one thing was for sure: He hoped he never knew the bonds of slavery again.

Decimus lifted Chara back onto her horse, helping her adjust herself to the saddle. Laying a hand against the mare's shoulder, he smiled up at Chara. "You ride a horse well."

She smiled. "My father taught me when I was a child. I have missed it."

"What other skills have you that I know nothing about?"

Chara arched a supercilious brow. "Only time will tell."

For some unknown reason, this only served to make Decimus uncomfortable. The smile fled from his face, and turning, he made his way back to his wagon, climbing aboard. Chara had already started to move forward when he clicked to his horses to begin the journey.

When they reached the station that evening, Galla chose to remain at the inn instead of the garrison.

"If I don't, I have no doubt that Caltupa will. He seems obsessed with making sure no other slaves escape." Galla grinned wryly as he loosened his saddle. "He already doubts my expertise in handling the matter."

The captain was obviously reluctant to leave and return to the garrison. Only direct orders had made him submit.

"He seems to have developed a personal vendetta against me," Decimus told Galla quietly, hoping that Chara wouldn't hear.

"I noticed." Galla studied the man beside him but could see no evidence of fear. "I wouldn't let it worry you. As long as you're considered my property, there's not much he can do about it."

Chara was waiting for them, a platter of meats, fruits, vegetables, and cheeses on the table in front of her. A serving girl brought them drinks and then left them alone.

"Back to the beginning," Galla told them, shaking his head. "It seems we are fated to spend our nights together."

Decimus realized what he was trying to say. If Galla didn't remain with them, Caltupa most assuredly would. He shrugged. "No problem. As you said, we have done so before."

Galla picked up a knife and began drawing circles on the wooden platter. "By tomorrow we should reach the Loire River. We'll take the river west to the Narrow Sea that separates Britannia from Gaul."

"More travel by sea?" Chara questioned, less than enthusiastically.

Galla nodded. "It should take us only a few weeks altogether."

A group of soldiers noisily seated themselves at the table next to them. They noticed Galla and quickly rose to their fee, snapping a salute.

"Centurion! We didn't see you."

Decimus had no doubt that was because their eyes had been on Chara. She flushed, the color making her lovelier.

Galla nodded his head, and the soldiers resumed their seats. Although the men were talking among themselves, the wine they continued to consume loosened their tongues considerably. Their strident voices could be heard clearly around the room.

"I hear we're going to mount another counterattack in Britannia," one soldier slurred. "I'd have thought we taught them a lesson seven years back when we slaughtered Queen Boudicca's forces." He gave a coarse laugh. "No matter. I won't mind another chance at wiping out the likes of the Druids."

Galla noticed heads turned their way. Many in the room were not soldiers, but civilians from nearby towns and provinces. As far as he knew, the counterattack in Britannia was still a secret. More than likely, the drunken soldier was guessing, but his mouth could very well cost lives.

Galla rose quickly to his feet, striding to the table beside him. "On your feet, Soldier."

The man stared up at him in confusion, his stupefied expression giving him a comical appearance. Slowly recognition dawned, and he struggled to his feet. Swaying, he snapped a salute that landed somewhere near his right arm.

Another soldier, less drunk, rose from his seat. Galla glared at him angrily. "Take your comrade back to the garrison. Now!" He glanced around at the others. "All of you! Back to the garrison."

Grumbling, they got to their feet and started for the door. Galla returned to his seat, his eyes still on the door.

Decimus studied the Roman and began to have serious misgivings. How much of Galla's heart was truly Roman, and exactly how much could he be counted on? Decimus decided he would have to watch more closely in the future.

The town of Lugdunum was much like any other town they had passed thus far, only larger. Here were more of the civilizing influences of the empire. Since it was the largest town near the Loire River, there was much trade and commerce here. The streets were thronged with people going about their daily business.

Galla smiled in appreciation when he noticed that this city boasted a public bath. "I know where I intend to spend the evening," he told them cheerily.

Decimus smiled. "I could stand to use the facilities myself." He turned to Chara. "How about you?"

Chara readily agreed. Tomorrow would find them on board ship again, and it would likely be days before they saw land. They all agreed that food could wait, so after renting a room at an inn, they headed for the baths.

Unlike most of the public baths in Rome and Ephesus, these baths had separate facilities for men and women. Chara sighed with relief. The Romans would no doubt think these people too provincial, but Chara appreciated their modesty.

Later, feeling refreshed, they sat down to a hot meal at the inn. Chara felt her stomach rumble, her nose twitching at the smell of the roasted chicken placed before them. She dipped her bread in a bowl of gravy, licking her fingers as she consumed the delicious food.

The noise in the inn was growing as the evening progressed. Remembering past nights, Decimus knew there would be little sleep for him. He was always amazed that Chara could sleep so peacefully with all the noise around. The ruckus would finally abate sometime after midnight when the inn was closed for the night.

They made their way to their room, Galla holding the small oil lamp used to light the passage. Decimus followed him into the room, carrying their fur rugs. Experience had taught them that tiny uninvited guests usually resided in the bedding provided by the inns.

Chara seated herself on the only chair available, smiling slightly as her fingers traced the graffiti etched on the walls. *Arestes loves Portia,* read one. Did Portia love poor Arestes, Chara wondered, or had Arestes merely dreamed of his loved one? Were they married? Some of the scratched messages left Chara blushing. She decided to refrain from reading any others.

Decimus had positioned their bed as far from the door as possible, but Chara noticed that Galla placed his pallet directly in front of the portal. She wondered if they were expecting any trouble.

Even though the din from below penetrated through the floor, Chara was asleep almost as soon as her head found its position on Decimus's shoulder. He pulled her closer, smiling down at her innocent features.

As quiet descended for the night, Decimus found himself able to think. The woman he held so securely in his arms was a part of his life now, no matter what happened. His heart was hopelessly entwined with hers. As he did every night, he prayed for their safety. Was he jumping from the coals into the fire? Only God knew, and He wasn't telling.

Chara watched the sailors and the captain preparing their sacrifice before the ship was about to sail. She shuddered at the cries of the lamb as it struggled ineffectively against its captors. She turned and fled to the other end of the ship.

Stevedores carried amphorae of wine and olive oil in a never-ending procession below deck. Grain would be poured directly into the hold, and the amphorae's pointed ends shoved deeply into the grain. The amphorae would be stacked in tiers as high as the hold itself.

Chara marveled at the size of the ship they would be sailing on. One hundred eighty feet from end to end. Enough space for all the supplies they had brought from Rome plus the trade goods from Gaul to Britannia. For this trip, she and Decimus would be sleeping on deck, as would Galla. All available space was being used to store the goods for Britannia.

Trophimus joined her at the rails, his eyes sparkling merrily. One thing could be said for Trophimus: He enjoyed life. Smiling, she leaned back against the rails. "Why didn't you go with the others?"

He wrinkled his nose, watching the sky above. Finally he shrugged his shoulders. "I'm not sure. Something told me to stay with you and Decimus." His look was penetrating. "Does that make sense to you?"

A dark cloud of foreboding momentarily darkened her happiness. She laid a hand on his arm. "Trophimus, you could be free to do anything you please, yet you remained with us. I don't know what voice made you do what you did, but I know I'm glad. I would miss you."

He smiled into her soft brown eyes, a mirror image of his own.

Chara returned his smile, realizing that he was a very handsome boy. She wondered what the future held in store for him. She had noticed women look his way at every town they passed. He would have no hard time finding himself a wife. She felt a decidedly motherly instinct where he was concerned.

Decimus and Galla joined them.

"Are we going to sail soon?" Chara asked them.

Galla smiled wryly. "It took a few more denarii than I expected, but it looks like we'll be heading out soon. We need to be on our way quickly so that we are not still at sea when the first storms of winter set in." He turned toward the deck. "We had better find ourselves a spot, before all the good spots are taken."

Sailors scurried to carry out their business. Chara watched them with interest. Each time she had sailed, she had been impressed with the sailors and their expertise. They scrambled about the ship like busy little ants.

At last, the huge ship's sails filled with wind. The boat creaked and swayed, tossed gently by the river. Chara stood with Decimus at the rail, watching the lights of the port city fade into the distance. The sun was setting in an awesome display of radiant reds and oranges.

"Red sky at night, sailors' delight," Decimus told her, putting an arm around her shoulders. Chara snuggled into his embrace, as much for the need to be close to him as the need for warmth.

Darkness descended, and the stars appeared in all their brilliance. The inky black sky seemed alive with the glow of a million simmering lights. The moon rose round and orange above the horizon.

They stood a long time marveling at God's universe. How could a person witness such sights and be immune to the Almighty's presence? Surely sailors should be closer to God than anyone, if they would only listen for His voice.

Watching Decimus's face in the moonlight, Chara wondered what he was thinking. Was he thinking about their unusual marriage? Was he regretting it? She considered asking, but she was afraid she wouldn't like the answer.

She knew he desired her. She could tell from his reactions when he held her in his arms, but he never made any move to make their relationship into a real marriage.

"What are you thinking?" she ventured.

His eyes flickered briefly before he looked down. "I was just wondering what I will find at the end of this journey." He leaned his forearms against the rails and stared pensively out at the dark waters. Chara felt chilled when he moved away. "Will I find any of my family? I fear my parents are both dead, though I do not know for certain. But is my sister still alive? Would I know her if I saw her? I don't even know where to begin."

"You could begin by praying. Asking for God's guidance."

"I have."

"Then trust Him to show you the way. He'll never forsake you."

Decimus smiled, lifting one blond brow. The breeze blew a lock of hair across his forehead, and Chara was tempted to reach up and push it back for him. What would he think of such a loving gesture?

"I'm beginning to realize that more and more. Every time I think some catastrophe has just about ruined my life, it turns into a blessing."

Chara smiled softly in return. "I have found the same to be true."

Decimus pushed away from the rails, taking Chara by the hand. "Come. It's time to retire for the night, before our spot is taken away."

They settled themselves on the furs beside Galla and Trophimus. Caltupa had relaxed his guard, obviously no longer concerned with the slaves' escape.

Galla was describing Britannia to Trophimus. Although he had never seen his homeland, he knew it well from his father's descriptions. One of the younger soldiers was listening closely to everything he said. Leaning up on one elbow, he fixed Galla with a fearful gaze.

"I hear they offer human sacrifices to their gods," he told them, a slight quaver in his voice. Chara felt sorry for the lad, knowing that he couldn't be much older than she was. His youth and inexperience could cost him his young life.

"We don't know whether that is true or not, Phlebius," Galla remonstrated. "Those are only rumors that have been circulated. No one knows much of Britannia. Even I know only what I have been told."

Phlebius shivered. "Imagine sacrificing *humans* to a god. That's despicable!"

"Is it any different from sacrificing humans for the enjoyment of a mob and calling it entertainment?" Chara asked him softly. "What difference if people are sacrificed to Nero, or some unknown god?"

Decimus tensed beside her, expecting a violent reaction. Instead, the young man looked at her uncomprehendingly a moment before he realized the import of her words. His eyes flickered away, and Decimus could have sworn that he saw guilt written across his features. The boy turned away, rolling over on his mat.

Galla and Trophimus smiled at Chara before they, too, settled down for the night.

Relaxing back against his own furs, Decimus pulled Chara down into his arms. She curled against him, mumbling into his chest.

"What did you say?"

"I said, I'm sorry."

Decimus was surprised. "You have nothing to be sorry for. What you said was true. And who knows what seeds you may have just planted."

" 'I planted the seed, Apollos watered it, but God made it grow,' " she quoted softly. "That's what the apostle Paul wrote in one of his letters to the church at Corinth. I will have to pray that God sends someone to water my seed."

Decimus gazed at the stars above. The pagans believed their lives and destinies were governed by those pinpricks of light. He was glad he knew that the Maker of the stars controlled his life. And he thanked God with all his heart for bringing this woman into his life.

Chapter 9

The weather held for the first three days, though the nights were growing colder the farther they climbed in latitude. The first morning after they left the river behind and entered into the sea, ominous dark clouds began to appear in the northwest. The captain watched them for a long time.

Chara, huddled in her furs, lifted worried eyes to her husband. "Are we in for a storm?"

Decimus glanced down at his shivering wife. If a storm did come, everyone and everything aboard this ship would be soaked within a short period of time. Already Chara's teeth chattered with the cold and damp, and Decimus was beginning to fear that she would become ill.

"It looks that way. Hopefully we can outrun it."

But the storm approached them with incredible speed. As the clouds rolled low over the horizon, the wind began to gain in intensity, causing the sea to heave with its fury.

Chara stared in surprise as the sailors, one by one, began to cut their fingernails and throw them over the ship's rails. When that failed to calm the sea, they started snipping off locks of their hair and doing the same. Regardless of their superstitious entreaties, the storm grew in strength.

Water sprayed over the deck as the ship's bow rose, then crashed into the hollow of the waves. With each plunge of the ship, Chara was thrown mercilessly about on the deck. She noticed that the men were not having the same problem, save Trophimus. Each man seemed to be made from stone as they rolled with the pitch of the ship.

The ship's captain made his way to their side. "We're in for it," he yelled above the increasing wail of the wind. "Take the woman below deck to my quarters, then come back. I'll need every hand on board to help us ride out this gale."

Although it was the middle of the day, it seemed more like dusk, the sun hidden behind the thick mass of clouds. Decimus helped Chara to her feet, holding her tightly against his side. They slipped and slid toward the galley entrance. Before going below, Chara saw the men scampering about ship, trying to tie everything down. Galla and his soldiers were spreading out to make themselves of use wherever they were needed.

Decimus pushed Chara into the captain's cabin. "Stay here. Whatever you do, don't come on deck unless I tell you to." He could see the fear in her eyes.

Reaching out, he pulled her into his arms, kissing the top of her head. "We'll be fine. Remember what you keep telling the rest of us: God is with us."

Releasing her, he strode back up the stairs, taking them two at a time. Clinging to the doorjamb, Chara watched him go. When he was out of sight, she closed the door and stumbled across to the captain's bunk. It was nailed down at least, and she clung to it like an anchor as the ship rocked from side to side.

Her fingers grew numb from gripping the wooden bed frame, and she began to shake as the temperature plunged. Her teeth chattered furiously, both from the cold and from fear.

Time passed slowly. Would the storm never end? Chara prayed zealously, hoping the storm would soon spend its energy.

At last, she heard feet in the passageway outside the door. Stumbling across the room, she opened the door. Trophimus was in the corridor, unlashing several ropes from their positions on the walls. He glanced her way briefly.

"What's happening?" Chara yelled above the noise of the storm. Water rushed down the stairs from the open door above, and Chara jumped back, squealing as the cold water soaked her feet.

"It doesn't look good," he yelled back. "We may have to start unloading the cargo to save the ship. You need to. . ."

He stopped as they heard a sound above their heads. A strange creaking sound was followed by a loud crash as one of the masts from topside crashed through the deck and below.

Chara screamed, leaping to safety. Water plunged through the gaping hole left above her, quickly filling the corridor to a depth of several inches.

Trophimus flung himself across the corridor to Chara's side. "Are you all right?"

At her nod, he handed her the ropes in his hands. "Here, take these ropes to Decimus. I have to try and stop the water from coming in. Whatever you do, though, don't go out on the deck. Just hand the rope to someone close to the door."

Chara took the ropes, holding back another scream as more water rushed into the passageway. She struggled to the gangway, clinging to it as she made her way to the top. The door at the top was hanging on its hinges. Water rushed across the deck and down the gangway. Chara clung more tightly to it, not giving an inch.

At the doorway, Chara searched for a familiar face. Everywhere men struggled with the elements. Sailors fought alongside legionnaires, all fighting for their lives.

She finally spotted Decimus a few yards away. He was binding amphorae to the masts with ropes. She yelled, but the wind was so fierce it threw her words back at her. Clinging to the gangway with one hand, she began to frantically motion with the ropes in her other. Her arms began to ache with the effort.

The ship plunged into another trough, and waves crashed over the side, knocking Decimus from his feet. Chara screamed. Throwing the ropes down, she tried desperately to reach him as he was swept toward the side of the ship.

The mighty ship rose high in the air, then plunged and slammed itself against the water. Chara was thrown off her feet, knocked about like a straw doll. Waves rushed over the sides, pulling at her as they were sucked back to the ocean from whence they came.

Chara managed to lunge for the edge of the gangway, but her grip was tenuous. She clutched frantically with both hands, her fingers digging into the wood posts. She yelled for Decimus, but she knew he could not hear her. Closing her eyes, she prayed for his safety.

Oh, Lord God, she prayed fervently, *save me! Save us all!*

When the second wave came, Chara's slight strength was no match for it. She was ripped from the gangway, her body hurtling toward the side of the ship. She just managed to grab hold of a piece of rope that was holding an amphora of oil before the ship rose again on the waves.

What had happened to Decimus? Clinging tightly to the rope with both hands, Chara prayed for help. Through eyes filled with saltwater, she saw Decimus pulling himself to his feet. His clothes clung to his body. With one hand, he pushed his drenched hair from his eyes.

Then Chara noticed what she hadn't seen before. A rope was tied to Decimus's waist, securely holding him to the ship's mast. *Thank God!*

Trophimus reached the top of the gangway just in time to see Chara's precarious hold on the rope give way. She slid quickly to the ship's bulwark, her body plastered momentarily to the wood.

Decimus glanced up in time to see Trophimus standing in the stairway, a look of horror upon his face. His eyes flew in the direction the young Roman was looking, and the color suddenly drained from his face.

"Chara!"

Both men lunged toward her at the same time. Decimus was brought up short by the rope around his waist. Clawing frantically at the knot, he watched helplessly as Trophimus was knocked from his feet. A huge wave sucked him toward Chara. Still, he couldn't reach them. If only he had a few more feet of rope.

Trophimus grabbed Chara around the waist, holding tightly as the ship dipped again. They were again plastered to the bulwark. Trophimus knew he had only one chance to save Chara's life. As the ship lifted again, he heaved Chara with all his might toward Decimus.

Decimus had only enough time to grab her tunic before the ship lunged again. Clinging tightly to her garment, they both watched helplessly as Trophimus was slowly sucked over the side of the ship.

"No!"

Chara's scream echoed around the ship, rising above the whine of the wind. Decimus didn't know if the moans he was hearing were coming from his wife or the bansheelike winds.

He managed to get them below, helping Chara to the bunk. Although she clung to him tightly, she stared at him with vacant eyes. Picking her up, he gently lowered her to the bunk.

There was no time to change her clothes. He had to get back topside. He knew he shouldn't leave her, but he had no choice. Teeth chattering, he covered her with a fur blanket, kissed her cold lips, and returned to help fight the storm.

Chara must have slept, for when she awoke, fingers of light were piercing the darkness of the cabin. Disoriented, she lifted herself on one elbow, wondering momentarily where she was. Then the events of the night before came crashing down on her like the waves that had pummeled the ship. Moaning, she lay back down, her body racked with sobs.

First Antipus and Agrippina. Now Trophimus. *Dear God! Why? Why?* She remembered Trophimus saying that he felt led to stay with her and Decimus. Had that been God's plan? That Trophimus would lay down his life for hers? She sobbed harder. Dear, dear Trophimus.

Galla and Decimus found Chara buried beneath a damp fur, crying as though her very heart were breaking. Decimus felt his own heart squeeze tightly within him. What could he do to comfort her? He hadn't been much use when the others had died, so what could he say now?

Deciding that words were useless, he took her in his arms and held her tightly. His eyes found Galla's, and there was sympathy there.

"You better stay with her. My men and I will help the captain repair the ship." He nodded at Chara. "She needs you more."

Decimus pulled Chara with him as he lay back against the bunk. She was no longer sobbing, but her body was tight with tension. He began to stroke her hair gently, murmuring soft words of encouragement. Eventually he could feel her begin to relax. She lifted her eyes to his, the ravages of her tears plain upon her face.

"It was my fault!"

Decimus stiffened in surprise. "What?"

"I didn't know that you were in no danger. I didn't see the rope around your waist. When I saw you being washed to the side. . ." She buried her face against his chest. "I didn't listen to you or to Trophimus. I went out on the deck."

He was humbled to know that she loved him that much. He sighed, pulling her closer. "It wasn't your fault. It wasn't anyone's fault. It just happened."

"Oh, God!" she moaned, wishing the Lord would take away the picture of Trophimus's face as he was plunging over the side.

Decimus knew that nothing but time would take away the memories. "He saved your life, my love, and he did it because he loved you. Remember that. Think on that."

Chara clung to him more tightly. What if she lost Decimus? It seemed that everyone she loved died. *Dear God, please don't let anything happen to Decimus. Please!*

As Decimus continued to hold her, the hours he had spent fighting the sea began to take their toll. His body relaxed, and soon his breathing told Chara that he was fast asleep. She sighed, snuggling closer. Whatever happened, they still had each other.

It took several days to repair the ship. The mast that had plunged through the deck was split in two and had to be roped together.

The sun shone brightly, a mocking reminder of what they had endured. Many supplies had been washed overboard, but the captain felt they had enough to make it to Britannia without touching those of Rome.

Since temperatures had dropped with the storm and were slow to increase, the captain thought it best if the soldiers, crew, and others made their sleeping quarters in the storage hold. Quarters would be cramped, but a lot better than freezing or becoming sick.

Decimus worried about Chara. She was lethargic, her eyes dulled with pain. He hadn't realized how much she loved the young Roman. A twinge of jealousy twisted his insides, but he immediately felt ashamed of himself. What right had he to complain when he withheld his own love from her?

Even now, she leaned against the masthead, huddled in her fur blanket, staring morosely out to sea. Decimus had been unable to reach her with his comfort. He didn't know what else to do.

He watched as Galla approached her, dropping to a squatting position. Decimus could see the soldier talking, but Chara continued to stare ahead. Finally something Galla said seemed to penetrate the fog of her grief. Turning her face to him, she shook her head at whatever he had said. They talked for some time before Galla reached out and cupped her cheek with his hand, then rose to his feet.

Decimus watched as Galla crossed the deck, drawing up beside him. His eyes went beyond the Roman to where Chara sat, a look of peace on her face for the first time in days.

"What did you say to her?"

Galla shrugged. "I merely reminded her that Trophimus did exactly what the Lord had done for us. He gave his life for someone he loved." His eyes went over Decimus before he turned, leaning on the bulwark. "I also reminded her that she was trying to do the same thing. I asked her if she would have wanted you to feel guilty if she had died trying to help you."

"She very well could have!" Decimus choked, his heart thudding at the possibility.

"But she didn't. Have you told her that you love her?"

Decimus shook his head, not bothering to deny it. "No. There doesn't seem to be a right time."

"There almost wasn't *any* time," Galla told him roughly. "What if she had been washed overboard?"

Decimus felt his heart sink. Even the thought of it nearly drove him mad.

Galla squeezed his shoulder. "Don't wait *too* long, my friend. There may never be a *right* time, but there also could very well be *no* time."

Decimus watched him walk away, making his way toward the captain. His eyes went back to Chara. She was sitting there, trying to soak in what little sunshine she could, her eyes closed, her head thrown back. Decimus clutched the bulwark tighter. He stood a long time thus. Sighing, he turned and went below.

Chara opened her eyes and watched Decimus leave, her heart heavy within her. If only she could believe Galla when he told her that Decimus loved her. But Decimus, though he was gentle and kind, was definitely not loving. He had comforted her as he would have comforted a child.

She sighed, watching the gulls flying overhead. A good omen, the sailors said. But not for Trophimus. Galla was right, she knew. Trophimus wouldn't have wanted her to feel guilty at his loss, but still it was hard.

Trophimus had given his life for her, and Jesus had, too. If she felt guilty because of Trophimus, how much more should she feel guilty because of her Lord? Jesus would have died for her had she been the only human being on earth. What had He done to deserve to die? The same as Trophimus. He loved her more than His own life.

Trophimus would forgive her, just as her Lord had. Jesus didn't want her to feel guilty; He wanted her to feel *loved*. She bowed her head, giving her burden over to her Master.

The remainder of their voyage was uneventful. The sea's peaceful serenity mirrored Chara's. Once she had given her guilt over to God, peace had come.

The sun shone weakly on the surface of the water, giving it a glassy appearance. Chara watched as schools of fish rose to the surface, flying along through the water as though racing the big ship. She laughed aloud at the thought, wishing them well in their endeavor.

Decimus, coming upon her at that moment, smiled at her laughter. It seemed as if it had been such a long time since he had heard it. He leaned against the bulwark, looking at her seriously. "It's good to hear you laugh."

She didn't turn to him but seemed to be contemplating something in the distance. "You know, the farther we get from Rome, the lighter my heart feels."

Decimus frowned. The closer they got to Britannia, the more uneasy he became. "Are we ever truly free from Rome?" He didn't really expect an answer.

When she turned to him, the look in her eyes sent chills racing down his spine. Her look was distant, as though seeing into the future. "I feel like we are on the edge of destiny, and that you and I will have a part in changing that destiny."

"What do you mean?"

"We have the opportunity to preach the Word to a people who have never heard it before," she mused. "At least not that we know of."

Biting his lip, Decimus took her hands into his. Hers were like ice, and he began to absently rub them between his own. "That may be a whole lot more dangerous than anything we have experienced thus far."

"Perhaps," she answered softly. "But you can only lose your life once. Jesus died for me; I will gladly do the same for Him."

Decimus pushed back from the bulwark. He didn't want to frighten her, but Britannia was far from the civilization she knew. Its people still lived in tribes, and from the accounts he had heard, they were far fiercer than anything the Romans had introduced. He knew that the wilds of Gaul were very similar to Britannia—but Chara had lived in a city, surrounded by civilization. She had never been exposed to the Druids' religion, and he wondered if she would be able to even comprehend the cruelty of human sacrifice.

Remembering the blood-soaked sands in the arenas of Rome, he decided that, on second thought, perhaps the Britons and Romans were more alike than he had at first thought. At least the Britons were fighting for their lives, their homes. They didn't kill on a whim. Not from what he remembered, which honestly was not much. But Chara was strong, he knew, stronger than he sometimes thought; certainly her faith in God was even sturdier than his own, and with that behind her, perhaps she would be able to withstand anything.

Chara smiled, reaching up a hand and gently cupping his cheek. "You needn't fear for me, Decimus. And no matter what happens, I wish to be right by your side."

Decimus shook his head, an answering smile appearing on his face. "Galla might have something to say about that."

"Galla is not my husband, nor is he my master. Only you are both."

"No, my love, I am not your master. You and I share the same Master." He pulled her into his arms, enfolding her in his warm embrace. "We will serve Him together, come what may."

They stood watching as the sun began to dip below the horizon. Before long, the moon replaced the sun's light with that of its own bright orb, its reflection sending a shimmering path across the water to the ship.

Chara wanted the moment to last forever, but eventually the cold drove them inside. Decimus helped her prepare a pallet as far from the others as possible. Chara lay down, one eyebrow winging upward as Decimus turned to leave.

"Are you not coming to bed?"

Decimus shook his head. "No. Galla and I have much to discuss. According to the captain, we should reach the shores of Britannia by morning."

"What do you think we'll find there?"

He would have reassured her if he could. The problem was, he couldn't. He had no idea how Galla would extricate them from the company they seemed to find themselves in. Decimus had no desire to spend any more time with Caltupa than was absolutely necessary.

"I guess we'll find out when we get there."

Decimus crossed to where Galla awaited him. They seated themselves far away from the others, lowering their voices so as not to be heard.

"We should reach the southern coast of Britannia tomorrow," Galla told Decimus. "Caltupa will probably tell me what orders he received when we reach there. As of yet, I have no idea what has been planned. Caltupa has been very close-mouthed. I assume his orders were to wait until we reached Britannia and he heard the reports from Rome's spies."

Decimus leaned back against the rough planks of the ship. "Chara certainly can't march into Britannia with your troops. What can we do?"

Galla expelled his breath slowly. "I don't know. I hadn't planned on having Roman company on this trip."

"What will you do if your orders are to lead Caltupa and his men against the Britons?"

Galla shook his head. "Let's not borrow trouble. I don't think that will happen."

"What if it turns into a full-scale war?" The thought had Decimus's stomach roiling. How could the people of Britannia withstand another siege by the Roman war machine? Soldiers who had fought here told humorous stories of farmers who went to battle against the seasoned Roman troops with nothing but long, slashing swords and no armor. They depended upon their speed to try and outmaneuver the Roman troops. Many men had died, impaled by Roman javelins.

Galla's voice dropped even lower. "My concern is not whether I will be forced to go into battle with the troops. I am in a dilemma as to what to do about you and Chara."

Decimus glanced at his wife curled against the ship's timber. Her chest rose and fell softly, assuring him that she was fast asleep. "She's been through a lot," he told Galla softly.

Nodding, Galla got to his feet. "And now, my friend, it is time for us to sleep as well, for on the morrow I believe we will have a lot more to go through." Reaching down, Galla helped Decimus to his feet. "I take it you still have not found the right time?"

Irritated, Decimus shook his head. Galla watched him a full minute before turning and without a word striding to his sleeping mat in the corner.

Decimus crawled beneath the fur with Chara, for the first time aware that his teeth were chattering. In her sleep, Chara turned and curled herself against him. Slowly his teeth stopped chattering. As warmth spread through him, he closed his eyes and began to pray. His petitions were short and to the point. Within minutes, he was fast asleep.

Chapter 10

Centurion."

Galla looked up at the man standing next to him as he lowered the rope he was holding to the deck beside him. Caltupa's face was rigid, his features betraying nothing of his thoughts. He certainly hadn't taken long to make his presence known. The ship had docked only moments before.

"You have orders for me, Captain?"

"Aye, Centurion."

Galla rose to his full height, which was several inches taller than the captain. His eyes betrayed nothing of the trepidation that was inching its way along his midsection.

Caltupa held out a long leather cylinder, and Galla took it. His eyebrows flew upward as he recognized the seal. Caesar's.

Several things ran through Galla's mind, not least of which was whether Captain Caltupa was aware of what was in the document. Since both the container and the scroll were sealed, Galla felt fairly certain that the contents were something which he would not care to deal with.

His eyes met Caltupa's. "You know what this document contains?"

"No, my lord. I was told merely that if anything happened to you on the way here that I was to burn the pouch and its contents. Unopened."

"I see." Galla absently tapped the pouch against his hand. "I'll read this in the captain's quarters."

As he turned to leave, Caltupa put a restraining hand on his arm. "My orders are to wait for you to read the discharge and then to burn it."

Galla was surprised, his curiosity growing. "Very well, come with me then." Galla opened the scroll after they were safely in the captain's cabin. His eyes grew wide, the color disappearing from his ruddy face. Slowly his eyes met Caltupa's. The captain stared at him impassively.

"You know nothing of what's in this discharge? You are certain?"

The captain snapped to attention, slapping a salute. "On my honor, Centurion. I have not read the parchment. As you can see, the seal was intact."

Galla nodded slowly. He handed the scroll to the captain. "Carry out your orders then."

With Galla watching, the captain strode across the small room and placed the parchment in the burning brazier. As the flames licked at the paper, Galla watched, mesmerized. Thoughts were swirling swiftly through his mind, and he was trying to sort them into order.

"Centurion, I was told that you would have orders for me."

Galla sighed. "Your orders are to head north, as far as Londinium. You, the troops, and the supplies. You are to meet up with several other contingents awaiting your arrival."

"And you?"

"I will not be going with you."

Caltupa's eyes narrowed, but he said nothing. He hadn't seen the scroll; therefore, he knew nothing of the orders it contained. The only thing he knew for certain was that he didn't trust the centurion. He couldn't say why exactly; it was just a feeling he had. For one thing, he treated his slaves more like friends than servants. It didn't make sense to him, but he knew better than to argue. If the centurion was lying, he would find out once he reached Londinium, and *if* he was lying, then may the gods help him, Caltupa would not hesitate to track him down and have him crucified.

Galla turned and left the scowling captain standing alone in the center of the room.

Decimus finished tying the furs into a bundle, securing the knot tightly. Chara sat on the deck surrounded by piles and packs. She lifted worried eyes to her husband.

"What do you think will happen now?"

Decimus shrugged. "We'll have to wait and see what Galla's orders are. Whatever happens, God is with us." He wasn't nearly as confident as he led Chara to believe. If Galla had to lead an expedition into Britannia, Decimus knew they would have to part company. He would have to take Chara and flee. Glancing around at the ship's crew hurrying to and fro, he decided that wouldn't be too hard to accomplish.

He frowned as Galla strode across the deck toward them, his face a study in contradictions. His forehead was creased in a frown, yet there was a small smile on his face.

"You have your orders?" Decimus asked.

Galla nodded. "Yes, and with them an answer to prayer."

Chara stood up and came to their side. They waited for Galla to continue, curious as to how orders from Rome could be an answer to anyone's prayers.

Galla lowered his voice. "My orders are to proceed north and locate my grandfather's tribe. Nero knows that my grandfather was an influential man. I'm supposed to try and convince them to ally themselves with Rome against the other tribes."

Decimus glowered. "How is this an answer to prayer? Tribe betraying tribe?"

Grinning, Galla reached down and started lifting packs from the deck. "I'm supposed to go alone. Caltupa is to proceed to Londinium to meet up with other Roman troops that are waiting there."

"And what of us?" Chara asked the question Decimus was thinking.

Galla straightened. "You'll come with me, of course."

Chara frowned. "But you just said that you were to go alone."

Suddenly comprehending the turn of their thoughts, Galla laughed. "I'm sorry. I meant no other troops will attend me. Only my slaves."

Decimus sighed with relief. He began to help Galla lift their packs and followed him down the plank to the dock.

"Wait here," Galla told them. "I'll see about our horses."

Before long, the ship was unloaded, and Galla had their things removed from the others. "Fortunately we bought these horses with our own money, or we would be walking. As it is, I had to pry them from Caltupa."

"What do we do now?" Decimus asked, lifting Chara to her horse.

"I had intended to stay in town, but I think it best if we put some distance between us and this fair city."

Chara looked around curiously. "Why?"

"It seems that hostility toward Romans is growing. Since Queen Boudicca of the Iceni tribe was killed several years ago and her daughters raped, a few of her followers have mounted another effort against the Romans. They are trying to rout any and every Roman in Britannia. They are even killing anyone considered to be a Roman sympathizer."

Chara paled. "But what has that to do with staying in the city?"

"Local tribes have been burning cities they think are necessary to the Romans." Galla smiled wryly. "Obviously this city would be a great target."

"But couldn't we stay the night? Chara is tired. It's been a long voyage."

Galla shook his head. "No, I think not. One of the dock managers sympathetic to Rome tells me that there are rumors of a raiding party in the vicinity."

"All the more reason to stay here," Decimus told him.

Again Galla shook his head. "If they come, it will be for one purpose. We can't take that chance. I think it would be safer farther inland."

"And if we meet them on the road?"

Galla smiled. "I have thought of that. Come, we have much to do."

Later, Chara studied Galla on his lead horse. He was an impressive man in the uniform of the Roman soldier, but he was equally impressive in the warrior uniform of the southern tribesmen. His yellow brown tunic, or *pais*, as the Britons called it, hung midway between his thighs and his knees. A broadsword was affixed to his waist on a belt, tucking the pais in and giving it a fitted appearance.

The one piece of attire that seemed to give both Galla and Decimus some problems was the *llawdyr*, wrapped closely around their thighs and legs. Chara grinned as she noticed Decimus shift again in his saddle. Obviously the pants took some getting used to.

Galla's *sagum* was draped around his shoulders, providing warmth from the autumn chill. Although Galla's was checkered, the predominant color being red, Decimus had chosen one of sky blue, dyed from the woad plant.

The thought crossed Chara's mind that she would have been more comfortable in the same garb, but since this was men's clothing, and warriors' at that, she had settled for a long woolen pais. She was still enthralled with the checkered pattern of the material. Blues, yellows, reds, and oranges vied for prominence in the garment. The colors were somewhat loud, so she had chosen a brown sagum to go with it. The mantle was made from thick sheep's wool, and she snuggled deeply into its folds.

As they traveled, the sun began to move toward its zenith, though the rays were tepid at best. Chara felt herself beginning to nod in the saddle. Jerking herself upright, she concentrated on the steam coming from her horse's nostrils. The steady *clop*, *clop* of the horses' hooves, however, began to lull her to sleep again.

Decimus heard a soft *thud* behind him. Turning, his heart lurched into his throat at the sight of Chara lying beneath the hooves of her mount. Fortunately the beast was so well trained that it remained absolutely immobile.

"Galla!"

Decimus didn't wait for an answer. Flinging himself from his horse, he rushed to Chara's side. She was sitting up, rubbing her hip.

"Are you hurt?"

Shaking her head, Chara started to rise. "I don't think so. Only my pride." When she tried to stand, she fell back to her knees with a cry of pain.

Decimus was on his knees in an instant, lifting her foot. Gently he tried to turn it. At Chara's soft gasp, he stopped.

"What happened?" Galla bent over them, watching Decimus lower Chara's foot gently to the ground.

"Chara has hurt her ankle. I don't think anything is broken. It looks like a bad sprain, though."

Already Chara's foot was beginning to turn slightly blue. Decimus reached down and lifted her into his arms. As gently as possible, he settled her back on her horse, but no matter how gentle he was, he could tell she was in excruciating pain.

"More than your foot is hurt."

"I think perhaps you are right," she answered him softly, her lips beginning to tremble.

Galla turned around slowly, surveying the countryside around them. "Wait here," he told them.

They watched as Galla was swallowed up by the forest. Decimus took a fur and spread it on the ground.

"Come," he told Chara, reaching his arms for her. "You'll be more comfortable lying down."

Chara slid carefully into his arms, wincing at the pain that ran through her body. More than likely, she was just very bruised. How heavenly it would be to soak in a hot bath and then go to sleep.

Decimus carefully put her on the fur, then sat down beside her. "Are you sure you're all right?"

"I think so."

As Decimus had predicted, it did feel better to lie down, and before long, Chara drifted off to sleep. Decimus kept a sharp lookout. He was beginning to worry at Galla's absence. What was taking him so long?

Decimus finally spotted Galla returning. Decimus grinned. If not for the hair, Galla could easily be mistaken for a Briton. Although most Britons had conformed to the style of the Romans, many were returning to the longer hairstyle of earlier tribesmen. Decimus suspected it was more as a way of throwing off any Roman influence than because it was more preferred.

Galla knelt beside Chara, his eyes softening as he watched her sleep. "How is she?"

"She doesn't complain, but I think she's pretty bruised."

Galla rose to his feet. "Let her sleep awhile. I've found a cave through the trees and slightly up that hill there." Decimus followed his pointing finger. "There's a place where we can keep the horses, too. As you can see, it's pretty well hidden from the road."

"What then?"

"I think Chara will need to rest a few days, give her body time to heal." Galla paused, staring off into the distance. "You'll be safe there for a while. I'll leave provisions with you, and there's a stream nearby where you can get water."

Decimus rose quickly to his feet. "What do you intend to do?"

"I'm going to investigate the countryside."

"What? Are you out of your mind? What if something happens to you? What do we do then? How will we even know?"

Galla smiled wryly. "Calm down. If I'm not back in three days. . ."

Decimus's eyes flashed fire. "What? What should I do then?"

Galla took a moment to answer. When he did, his eyes were serious. "You must go on."

Decimus shoved his hands back through his hair, expelling his breath angrily. "This is crazy. We should stick together."

"Decimus." Galla's quiet voice stopped Decimus from pacing like an angry lion. "Look to the north. Feel the air."

A thin, dark line was spread across the horizon, and although it was still afternoon, the temperature was beginning to drop.

"A storm?"

Galla shook his head. "More than a storm. The beginning of winter. When this storm passes, winter will set in with a vengeance. We can't stay in a cave. We have to find a village or town."

"But if you get caught out in that. . ."

"That's why I said three days. I'm predicting the storm won't start for at least three days. I hope to be back by then."

Realizing they could do nothing else, Decimus sighed. "Very well, but I don't like it."

"That makes two of us."

Decimus bent to gather Chara in his arms. Her eyes opened briefly, then flickered closed again.

"I hope she stays asleep," Decimus told Galla. "She won't feel the pain that way."

Galla nodded. "The cave is not far. Do you think you can carry her?"

Decimus smiled down into Chara's sleeping face. "She weighs little more than a feather."

By the time they reached the cave, Decimus had altered his opinion. Although Chara was light, after two miles she became a weight in his arms. Finally they reached the cave, and Decimus breathed a sigh of relief. He followed Galla inside and saw why he had taken so long to return. A stack of wood lay at the back of the cave near a dark tunnel that led farther into the cavern.

Galla spread the furs on the floor, making a pallet for Decimus to lay Chara on. When he put her down, she opened her eyes. Blinking up at him sleepily, she smiled. "Is it morning?"

Galla and Decimus burst into laughter. At Chara's puzzled look, Galla turned to go outside. "I'll bring in the rest of the things. You explain to our sleeping beauty here what we've decided."

Chara didn't like their plan, but neither was she in any position to argue. Every time she tried to move, pain sliced through her body. Finally she lay back and stared up at the ceiling of the cave.

Decimus had already started a fire, and the flames caused fingers of light to swirl eerily on the rock walls. Chara watched their dancing patterns as she listened to Decimus and Galla finalizing their plans. She prayed for Galla and his safety.

When Galla knelt beside her, she smiled slightly at his worried expression. She took one of his hands in her own. "I'll be fine," she told him reassuringly. "It's you I'm concerned about."

He grinned. "I'm not the one inclined to fall off horses."

She wrinkled her nose at him. "No, you're the one who would drive others until *they* did."

Galla stopped smiling. "Chara, I am so sorry. You are right. If not for my pigheadedness, none of this would have happened."

"No!" Chara tried to rise. Crying out in pain, she slid back to the furs. "I was only teasing. Please don't feel that it was your fault!"

"She's right," Decimus told him. "We could have refused to agree with you, but we thought you were right. Don't start second-guessing yourself now."

Galla didn't look convinced.

"Remember, Galla," Chara told him. "Everything that has happened so far and continues to happen in the future is according to God's will. You reminded me of that when Trophimus died."

He touched her cheek briefly, a wry smile twisting his lips. Rising to his feet, he turned to Decimus. "Take care of our girl. You should have time to tell her something."

Decimus frowned, his eyes sending messages to the Roman that made Galla grin. He lifted a small pack and threw it over his shoulders, then fixed Decimus with a steely eye. "Remember, three days."

Decimus watched Galla wind his way down the hill. He looked back once and waved; then he was gone from sight. Decimus felt a powerful sense of loss and realized that he had come to depend on the soldier. Looking to the north, he saw that the ominous dark line was still there. He hoped Galla was right about it not reaching their location for three days. He offered up a prayer for Galla's safety, then returned to the cave.

Chara lay as he had left her, staring up at the ceiling of the cave. She turned her head when he entered.

"What did Galla mean when he said you could tell me something?"

Decimus shrugged. "Who knows what that crazy Roman has on his mind?" He put more wood on the fire, refusing to look in Chara's direction. Although she knew he was keeping something back, she didn't press him. He would tell her whatever was on his mind when he thought it necessary.

Although the temperature had dropped to freezing, their shelter was relatively warm. Chara would have preferred less smoke, but she was thankful not to be spending the night in a tent.

Darkness descended quickly, another sure sign of winter. Decimus rummaged through their supplies to get them a meal. He brought Chara hers and helped her sit up, propping her against the wall.

She flinched, but she didn't cry out. Every bone in her body felt as if it were bruised, but she knew she would probably be a lot sorer tomorrow.

When they settled down for the night, Decimus was careful to stay close enough to share his warmth but far enough away not to hurt her. Chara missed the security of his arms around her. Her last waking thought was of Galla.

Galla paused beside a stream, dipping his hands in and drinking thirstily. He scanned the forest around him, listening for sounds of life. None were present. He frowned. There should be forest sounds: birds, frogs, something.

The hair on the back of his neck prickled in warning. Turning, he had no time to draw his sword before something smashed against his head.

Chapter 11

Galla awakened slowly, his head throbbing. Moaning, he tried to open his eyes, but they were too heavy, as though a bronze weight were holding them down.

He tried to remember what had happened, but his mind was still fuzzy. He lay still, letting consciousness slowly return to him. As he lay there, he became aware of whispered voices in the room. They were speaking the language his father and grandfather had taught him as a child.

"Why did you have to bring him here?"

Although the words were whispered and low, Galla could tell that the voice was that of a woman. An angry woman at that.

"What could I do, Mother? I couldn't leave him there to die!"

The owner of the second voice was obviously young. A boy. If he was the one who had struck the blow, Rome would do well to have such in their legions.

A long silence was followed by a soft sigh. "I suppose not. But Cadvan, only you would have the audacity to try to kill someone and then bring him home for me to take care of."

Galla opened his eyes. Slowly his vision came into focus. The first thing he noticed was that they were in a cave, but one that was much more homelike than the one where he had left Decimus and Chara. Obviously someone had taken pains to make this a home.

Turning his head in the direction of the voices, he noticed a young boy, about thirteen or fourteen, standing before a woman, his head bent. He was tall, his skin dark, his hair as black as the midnight sky. He was a handsome lad.

The woman was so opposite him in looks that Galla could only stare. She was tall for a woman, but her skin was as creamy as ivory, her hair yellow and as pale as the moonlight. She was neither young nor old. She seemed close to Galla's age, but her face wore the look of having seen much of life.

Feeling eyes on her, she turned to Galla. Her ice blue eyes were cold, distant. She came across the room and looked down at him lying on the mat.

"So, you're awake."

Galla tried to rise but found himself unable. Looking down, he saw he was tied with ropes. He looked to the woman for an explanation. Instead, she turned and went back to her son.

"Did you make sure you left no tracks to follow?"

"I made sure. Not even Cadwaladyr could track me this time."

The woman smiled at the pride in her son's voice, her eyes softening. "Go now. Make sure he was alone." Lifting a quiver of arrows and a bow from beside the entrance to the cave, she handed them to the boy. "Cadvan, deer would be nice for supper."

The boy's chest swelled with pride at her confidence in him. Nodding, he turned and left.

The woman returned to Galla, fixing him with a cold gaze. "What is your name, and what tribe are you from?"

Galla was hesitant to answer her, but he knew he couldn't lie. "My name is Galla. I am from the Trinovantes."

If anything, her eyes grew colder. Galla almost shivered under their intense look. "Where am I?" he ventured to ask.

The woman studied him for a long time, and Galla took the time to study her in return. She was a beautiful woman. Never had he seen hair such a color. Even Chara's was a much brighter blond. This woman's was almost silver.

"I'll ask the questions," she informed him, and Galla felt himself bristle at the woman's arrogance. He might be trussed up like a pheasant, but he knew ways to free himself. He smiled slightly as he considered the look on his captor's face if he should choose to do so right now, though he needed time to regain his strength.

The woman watched him silently. Her heart skipped a beat when she saw his eyes darken, a slow smile spreading across his face. She felt a thrill of fear for the first time in years. He looked so much like. . .

Her mind shied away from such futile thoughts. Reaching down, she gave the ropes a tug to check their security. Satisfied, she leaned back. "Why is a Trinovante traveling alone through Cantiaci land?"

Again Galla hesitated. A voice seemed to whisper in his mind to tell the woman the truth. Still. . .

"I am looking for the Trinovantes. I have just arrived from Rome."

She jerked back as though he had struck her, her eyes going wide. "You're a *Roman*!" She almost hissed the words.

Galla nodded. The motion sent a wrenching pain slicing through his head. Closing his eyes tightly, he fought the bile rising in his throat. He gritted his teeth until the nausea slowly subsided.

When he opened his eyes again, the woman was gone.

Decimus looked up at the sky for what must have been the hundredth time. The storm was moving closer, but Galla had been right. Two days had passed, and the storm was still a good distance away. He turned and went back to where Chara was sitting on the furs.

"Still no sign of Galla?"

Decimus shook his head. "No, but he said three days, so I don't really expect him back before tomorrow." He sat down next to her. "How are you feeling?"

She smiled slightly. "My ankle still hurts, but the rest of me seems to be healing. I'm just a little stiff."

Positioning himself behind her, Decimus began to gently knead her shoulders. Chara dropped her head forward, closing her eyes.

"That feels good," she murmured.

For a moment, Decimus's hands stilled, then he started rubbing again. Swallowing hard, he soon realized that this was a big mistake. The very smell of her stirred his senses. Abruptly he stood and walked back to the entrance of the cave.

Chara stared at him, mystified. What had she done now? Every time she thought they were growing closer, Decimus pulled himself away. What was he so afraid of? She frowned. Perhaps he knew that she loved him and he wanted to make certain she understood that he didn't feel the same way. Did his heart belong to another? In the beginning she had thought so, but now. . .now she wasn't so sure.

He had called her "my love" for some time now, ever since they were married, but she knew that had been for the soldiers' benefit. How did he really feel about her? If only she could really be his love. If only he would look at her with eyes of love when he said it. Lately the words had become just a habit with him.

Getting up, she slowly made her way to his side. Laying her hand on his arm, she felt him tense.

"What is it, Decimus? Did I do something wrong?"

He didn't look at her for a long time. Finally he sighed. Turning to her, he looked deep into her eyes. That was his first mistake. The second was not looking away when he had the chance. Now it was too late. He was hypnotized by the luminous glow emanating from the depths of her soft brown eyes.

"Chara. . ." Whatever he had been about to say was lost to the moment. Bending forward, he pressed his lips to hers.

Chara reached up, curling her arms about his neck, pressing herself closer. Decimus wrapped his arms about her slender body, pulling her tightly into his embrace. He pulled back for a moment, staring intently into her eyes. The soft light of love answered the question he had been about to ask. Still, he had time to turn back.

A fire began to burn within him, slowly affecting his reason. Seeing his hesitation, Chara pulled his head back down to hers. "Please, Decimus," she whispered against his lips.

Lifting her into his arms, Decimus made his way back to the furs. He laid her against them, then joined her on their softness. There was no turning back now.

Galla watched the opening to the cave for a long while. Finally the woman returned.

"Is there a reason I'm being held prisoner?" Galla asked.

She ignored him. Going about her business, she fed more wood to the brazier she used for light. Galla watched her as she pulled a basket of woolen yarn over to a loom and began to weave.

"My lady," he said softly, "could you not tell me what crime I have committed? Could you not at least tell me your name?"

He watched her shoulders slump; her fingers stilled their movement, but still she didn't turn around. After what seemed a long while, her voice came quietly across the room. "My name is Eudemia."

Galla frowned. Where had he heard that name before? It was an elusive memory, one that hovered on the edge of his consciousness.

"I mean you no harm," he continued softly.

"Romans mean nothing else," she spit at him.

Galla tried again. "It is true I am a Roman, but my father was Trinovante, as was my grandfather."

She turned on her stool. "That endears you to me no more than being a Roman."

Curious, Galla studied the woman. "Do you not belong to one of the tribes?"

Her lip curled derisively. "I claim no tribe." She turned back and began weaving again.

Galla glanced around him. It was hard to believe that this was a cave, so homelike had she made it. But why did she live in a cave?

"Do you and your son live alone here?"

"You certainly are a pushy-nosed one." He could hear the amusement in her voice.

Galla thought about it. Yes, he supposed he was inquisitive, but the woman intrigued him. Why would a beautiful woman live alone with her son in a cave? And why did she say she claimed no tribe? He didn't miss the fact that she had said she didn't *claim* one, not that she didn't belong to one. Sometimes it helped to surprise an answer from someone, so Galla decided to put his thoughts into a question.

"Why would a beautiful woman choose to live alone in a cave? Have you no family?"

She glared at him angrily. "Don't call me beautiful."

Surprised, Galla decided not to answer her. Instead, she got up from the stool and came to him. She knelt down beside him, her look intense.

"What are you doing here, Roman?"

For some reason, Galla felt he could trust her. He paused only a moment before he told her his story. The only part he left out was about Chara and Decimus. Better that she not know of their whereabouts. If anyone was going to die, let it be him.

When he finished, her lips curled derisively. "And you expect me to believe that a *Roman* has come all the way to Britannia to tell others about a *Jewish* God."

"He is not a Jewish God. He is everyone's God."

"So you say." Getting up, she went back to her work, her back once more to him. "I have no time for gods. Nor do I have any desire to worship any."

Galla lay there a long time, trying to decide what to do next. Eudemia turned on her stool. "What does your God ask in the way of sacrifices?"

Galla's eyebrows flew up. He took his time before answering, realizing that this was no idle question. "He asks for no sacrifices, only your life."

Her eyes widened. "You must give up your life? I'm surprised anyone would choose to serve such a God." She continued to regard him curiously. "How old must you be before you surrender your life?"

Frowning, Galla tried to reason out her thinking. "Any age is permissible. Even the young can believe."

Her eyes grew cold again. "Young as in my son's age?"

Galla had no idea what had caused such an abrupt change in the woman's demeanor. "I know boys his age who choose to serve God. Girls, too."

"And you? How old have you decided to be before you give your life to this God of yours?" she snarled.

Galla was really confused now. "I have already given my life to my Lord," he answered softly.

Her eyes went slowly over him, returning to his face. Her eyebrows rose slowly upward. "You seem in perfect health for a dead man."

Suddenly comprehending the turn of her thoughts, Galla smiled slightly. "When I say 'give my life to the Lord,' I mean I will serve Him all the days of my life. I would die for Him if necessary, but He does not require human sacrifices, because His own Son was sacrificed for all."

Puzzled, she came back and knelt beside him again. "His Son was sacrificed? If He were God, how could He allow this?"

Galla pressed his lips together. How could he make her understand? Deciding that it would be best to start at the beginning, Galla unfolded the Lord's plan of salvation to her.

When he finished, Eudemia was staring over his head, lost in thought. She could not comprehend such love. Give her son to save another? No, it was beyond her imagination.

Cadvan came through the entrance, a young fallow deer slung over his shoulder. He looked at his mother sitting so close to the man and frowned.

"Is something wrong, Mother?"

She rose gracefully to her feet. "No, son." Tears formed in her eyes as she watched her boy. Galla's words were fresh in her mind. Going to her son's side, she hugged him tightly.

He pulled back slightly, puzzled. "Mother?"

Smiling, she stroked a hand down his cheek. "Sorry. Dress the meat, will you?"

"What about him?" Cadvan shrugged his shoulders in Galla's direction.

"I don't know yet. Go dress the meat."

When the boy left the cave, Eudemia turned to Galla. "You have an unusual God. Maybe you could tell me more about Him sometime."

"If you would free me, perhaps I could help with your work."

She glowered at him. "I didn't say I believed you. No, Roman, I am still unsure what to do about you."

Cadvan came back into the cave. "There's a winter storm approaching. I'd say two days away."

He handed his mother the meat, and she took it to a table and began cutting it into chunks. "Get me some vegetables to go with this."

Galla watched the two as they prepared their meal and went about preparing for the night. What was to become of him? More than that, what day was this? His thoughts on Chara and Decimus, Galla began to wiggle the ropes. He had to get back.

Eudemia brought him a bowl of stew. Kneeling down beside him, she began to feed it into his mouth a little at a time. Galla chewed slowly, all the while watching the woman. Where had he seen eyes like that before? There was something vaguely familiar about Eudemia. And what of her son? His coloring was more the coloring of the Mediterranean region than of Britannia. What was their story? He was more than a little curious.

"You need to rest tonight. Tomorrow we'll decide what's to be done about you."

Cadvan came and stood beside her. "I'm sorry, Mother. I wasn't thinking. At first I meant to kill him, but. . ."

Reaching up, Eudemia took his hand in hers, rubbing it against her cheek. "Don't be sorry, my son. You are not a killer. I am proud of you."

He frowned at her. "But what if he is from Cadwaladyr?"

Galla glanced from one to the other. "Is Cadwaladyr another tribe?"

Eudemia grinned. "He probably wishes it were so. His own tribe. Yes, I could see Cadwaladyr strutting to such a tune."

"I know nothing of this Cadwaladyr," Galla told them. "I am only here to try and find my father's tribe."

"Perhaps," Eudemia agreed. "But for now, let us get some sleep." She rose and went to snuff out the oil pots. Darkness filled the cave, save for the light from the brazier. The cave was still comfortably warm, and Galla noticed the furs covering the entrance to keep out the cold.

That was a good idea. He hoped Decimus would think to do the same.

Decimus leaned over Chara, stroking the hair from her face with his fingers. She smiled dreamily up at him.

"What are you thinking?" he asked her softly.

She answered him just as softly. "How much I love you."

Frowning, Decimus sat up, turning his back to her. Chara began to run her fingers lightly over the scars on his bare skin, and he shuddered.

"What is wrong, Decimus? Have I displeased you?"

Decimus shoved his hands back forcefully through his unruly gold locks. Had she displeased him? Never! In her innocence, she had pleased him more than he could have imagined. She was soft and gentle, loving and kind. Expelling his breath harshly, he threw himself back against the furs. He rubbed his face with his hands.

"What if you get pregnant, Chara?"

She frowned down at him. "You don't wish to have children?" The thought had never occurred to her, and it hurt her now. She loved children and had hoped for a big family.

Reaching up, he pulled her down onto his chest. His hand slid around her neck, and he began to stroke her silky skin. Chara felt her heart begin to pound.

"My love," he told her. "It's not having the children, it's having the children *here*."

Chara suddenly sobered. She had given no thought whatever to their circumstances. She smiled ruefully. She thought mainly with her heart. So sure was she of Decimus's protection, so secure was she in his ability to care for her, she had given no thought to an uncertain future.

As Decimus continued to stroke his fingers down her back, Chara's eyes became liquid pools.

"Don't look at me like that," Decimus warned her huskily.

She lay on his chest, propping her cheeks on her balled fists. "I love you, Decimus, for now and for always. And I believe God will take care of us."

"Like Trophimus?"

Chara frowned. "Are you beginning to doubt? Trophimus is in God's hands. No power on earth can take him away from the love of God. Just as no power on earth can separate *us* from Him." She placed her hands on the ground on either side of his head. "Someday, someone may separate us from each other, but they can never separate us from God. Satan is trying to weed you out, beloved. Don't let him do it."

Decimus wrapped his arms around her waist, smiling into her serious eyes. "So wise for someone so young. You are beautiful."

She flushed hotly and would have pulled away, but Decimus held her firmly.

"You *are* beautiful, inside and out. I thank God for you every day. I love you, Chara. I think I have from the moment I laid eyes on you."

Tears welled in her eyes at the unexpected admission. One spilled over and dripped down her cheek. Decimus watched her, not sure what had made her cry. Suddenly he felt very uncertain.

"I didn't mean to make you cry."

She smiled then. "Tears of joy. I never thought any man would say such things to me. Oh, Decimus, I love you, too."

She bent to kiss him on the mouth. He rolled over, taking her with him. Neither one heard the wind begin to howl outside. Neither one noticed when the fire died down. Neither one noticed when darkness descended.

Chapter 12

Decimus knelt beside the stream, filling the goatskin flask with icy water. His mind was not on what he was doing. Three days had passed, and they still had seen no sign of Galla. Decimus had no idea what he would do if Galla didn't return. Although Chara's foot had healed to a point where she could limp on it, she still couldn't travel far.

Suddenly his arms were seized in an ironlike grip from behind. He was pulled back from the stream and spun around. Two men held him fast in their tight grip, his arms twisted behind his back. He struggled a moment but then realized he couldn't possibly outfight them.

Another man stood towering above him, his long brown hair flowing just past his shoulders. Brown eyes stared coldly into his own.

"Where are you from, and what are you doing here?" the man demanded in the language of Decimus's boyhood.

Decimus's mind began to churn frantically. He had to keep them away from the cave and Chara. When he tried again to jerk loose, he was lifted slightly from his feet. Hanging suspended in the air, he felt like a limp rag doll. These men had incredible strength.

"Answer me, or I'll slay you where you stand."

"My name is Decimus. I'm here seeking news of my tribe."

The giant fixed him with a dubious glance. "And what tribe might that be?"

"I am Cantiaci," he told them and had the satisfaction of seeing their faces change. Only the giant remained unfazed.

"And where have you been that you need to seek news now of your tribe?" he wanted to know.

Decimus was hesitant to tell them anything. In the end, he decided to tell them a partial truth. "I have recently arrived from Rome where I was a slave." He glanced to the hill behind him, hoping that Chara wouldn't come looking for him.

"My name is Cadwaladyr, from the Trinovante tribe." The giant nodded to his men. "Release him."

They flung Decimus down, but he managed to keep his balance and stay up on his feet. His hands clenched at his sides. Now was not the time to try to induce a battle. He was hopelessly outnumbered, if not by numbers, then definitely by sheer strength.

Cadwaladyr stood, arms folded across his chest, obviously awaiting an explanation. He was an imposing figure in his warrior garb. The temperature was below freezing, yet the man wore only a pair of *llawdyr* and a *bryean* vest. The wool was treated with vinegar, Decimus knew, in a way that supposedly rendered the material so strong it could repel even a sword. His arms were bare, yet he gave no sign of feeling the cold.

"I have returned to Britannia seeking news of my family," Decimus told them truthfully. "I was taken prisoner by Roman soldiers almost twelve years ago. The last sight I had of my family was my father lying in a pool of blood, my mother across his chest, and my sister. . .my sister being passed from one Roman soldier to another."

Something flashed briefly in Cadwaladyr's eyes, but it was hidden instantly. "What were their names?"

"My father was Lucid; my mother, Gamina; my sister, Eudemia."

"Eudemia!"

The startled exclamation from the man on his right brought both Decimus's and Cadwaladyr's eyes to him. One look from Cadwaladyr and the other man closed his lips tightly.

Decimus turned back to Cadwaladyr. "You know her?"

Cadwaladyr shrugged. "Perhaps. Many girls have that name. Come, we will take you back to our village. Perhaps Der-wydd can help you."

Before Decimus could decide on his next move, a piercing scream rent the air. Shoving Cadwaladyr aside, Decimus hurriedly climbed the hill behind him. The other three men were close on his heels.

Scrambling over the top, Decimus flung himself through the entrance to the cave, coming up short when he saw two men, one standing on each side of his wife. Before he could react, he was grabbed roughly from behind, finding himself once again a prisoner.

Cadwaladyr moved past him into the cave. He went quickly to Chara's side, jerking the sagum from her head.

Gritting his teeth, Decimus continued to struggle against the men who held him fast. "Leave her alone!"

Cadwaladyr studied Chara for a moment. Suddenly he smiled. "Many pardons, my lady. I thought you were someone else." He turned to Decimus, one dark brow arching. "We heard that there was a woman and her son living in a cave somewhere in the vicinity. We thought perhaps she was the one."

"She's my wife!"

Blinking, Cadwaladyr finally nodded to his men. They released him, and Decimus went quickly to Chara, taking her in his arms. He could feel her trembling as he whispered in Latin what Cadwaladyr had said.

"I know," she said softly. "This language is very similar to that which I grew up speaking in Gaul. I can't catch everything—but enough to be afraid."

Meanwhile, Cadwaladyr was studying the cave and its contents. Apparently he was satisfied with what he saw.

"You stayed here to avoid the storm?"

Decimus nodded.

"Wise move. But our village will be safer. Gather your things and come with us."

Although the words were gently said, Decimus had no doubt that an order was behind them. The five men waited while they gathered their things. Decimus put out the fire but left the wood. Perhaps Galla was on his way back even now. How could Decimus let him know what had happened?

"We need to hurry, Cadwaladyr. The storm is almost upon us."

Cadwaladyr was watching Decimus. "Bring their horses round."

Chara stayed close to her husband, her heart thudding with fear. What was to become of them now? And where, oh where, was Galla?

Galla watched Eudemia as she worked around the cave. She was an industrious woman, her hands never idle for a moment.

Two days had gone by since he had entered their world. His head no longer pounded as it had, but a scab had formed on the laceration across his temple. The sore itself throbbed continually.

Eudemia had decided that he was not a threat, so she had released him. The only problem was that the winter storm had hit with a vengeance. He could not go out in the elements, or he would be lost within minutes and dead a short time later.

The wind howled angrily outside their shelter. Galla felt the same violence roiling within himself. He was almost mad with worry over Decimus and Chara.

Had they stayed at the cave even after he hadn't returned in the appointed time? They had enough provisions. Hopefully Decimus had thought to bring the horses inside.

Cadvan sat silently in a corner, sharpening his knife with a stone. Periodically he would look up and catch Galla's eyes on him. Frowning, he would turn himself slightly away.

"Is there anything I can do?" Galla questioned.

Eudemia looked at him in surprise. She thought for a moment before shaking her head. "Not that I can think of."

"Perhaps he would like to help me fix the feathers to my arrows," Cadvan suggested.

Galla smiled at the boy. "I can do that."

Cadvan brought the feathers and long sticks that he had already prepared. He laid several sharpened stones next to them. They were well done, but Galla lifted curious eyes to his. "You have no iron or bronze?"

Without looking up, the boy answered him, "No."

Shrugging, Galla began to affix the feathers with swift, deft movements. The boy watched him, his eyes growing wide. Still, he said nothing.

Galla began to tell him stories, not of Rome and her conquests, but from scriptures. Cadvan sat listening, enthralled.

Before long, Eudemia joined them, a ball of yarn in her hands. She began twisting the yarn into lengths, the whole time listening intently to everything he said.

She looked up at one point. "The Druids have a story similar to the one you just told. What did you call the man?"

"Noah," Galla answered.

She nodded her head. "Much of what you have said the Druids say, also."

"Probably," Galla agreed. "Since God created the whole earth and everything in it, people are bound to have similar stories. Although the people wandered to different places on the earth after the Tower of Babel, they still had the same beginnings."

She stared into Galla's eyes, and for the first time, Galla noticed a softness there. "Funny how people can get things so turned around."

"Tell me of the Roman gods," Cadvan demanded. "Especially Mars."

Eudemia rose swiftly to her feet. "Enough. Enough about gods and their capriciousness. Go to the other cavern and bring back some wine."

Her son looked disappointed, but he obeyed. Galla watched him go, then turned to his mother. "You have a fine son."

She smiled. "Thank you. I think so."

"But there is one thing I must correct you on." She waited for him to continue. "My God is not capricious. He is unchanging, and His love is eternal."

She hesitated as though she wished to say something, but then she turned away. Galla watched her go back to her loom and begin weaving the threads in and out.

Cadvan came back with the wine. He placed the amphora on the table and then came back to help Galla with the arrows.

"You do this well," Galla told him. "Did your father teach you?"

The sudden silence in the room made Galla look up. Eudemia was frozen as though she were a statue. The boy looked from his mother back to Galla. "No. My father died before I was born."

"I'm sorry." Feeling uncomfortable, Galla hurried to change the subject. "How long have you lived here?"

Again Galla got the impression he was treading on thin ice. Not knowing what to say, he lapsed into silence.

"We've lived here since before Cadvan was born," Eudemia finally told him.

Galla decided retreat was in order. Leaning forward, he showed the boy how to better affix the arrows to give them more buoyancy. Cadvan smiled his appreciation.

The storm continued for three days. Cadvan seemed to follow Galla's every move. He was there whenever Galla returned from outside, he was there when Galla explored the cave, he was there when Galla helped prepare the meals.

Eudemia didn't miss the fact that her son had become enamored with the Roman. She smiled ruefully. No matter how hard she tried, some things only a man could provide.

"The snow is beginning to lessen," Galla told them, watching the swirling layers of whiteness. Dropping the fur curtain, he turned back to the room.

Eudemia nodded. "It should stop by tomorrow."

For some reason, Galla felt reluctant to leave, but he knew he must. Almost a week had passed since he had left Chara and Decimus.

That evening when they sat down to their meal, Galla told them about his two friends. Eudemia was surprised. "What did you say his name was?"

"Decimus."

She looked down, her lip beginning to tremble. He saw such pain in her eyes that Galla felt moved to comfort her.

"What is it?" he whispered.

She shook her head slightly. "I had a younger brother by that name."

"What happened to him?"

Suddenly she looked up, glaring into his eyes. "The Romans took him. I doubt he's still alive. Most likely he was sent to the galleys."

Galla felt the color leave his face. Could it be possible? Could Eudemia's brother and Decimus be one and the same? The resemblance was there, and hadn't Decimus mentioned the name *Eudemia*? What a streak of fate that would be. But stay. Fate? There was no such thing. Had God arranged this all along? And if so, what else had He planned?

Galla bit his lip in indecision. Should he tell Eudemia his suspicions, or would that get her hopes up too high? Finally he decided to confide in her.

That night when they lay down, Galla knew he would never get to sleep. He lay staring up at the flickering shadows caused by the fire from the brazier.

"Galla?"

Galla turned toward the soft voice. Eudemia rose from her mat and came to sit next to him. She looked down, her hair falling forward to conceal her cheeks. She looked so much like Chara in one of her shy moods that Galla almost reached out to touch her.

"There is something I need to tell you," she told him softly, glancing at her son to make sure he was asleep. His even breathing told her it was safe to continue.

Looking back at the ground, she started to talk to him, so softly he had to strain to hear her. Finally he moved closer, watching her face in the semidarkness.

"Twelve years ago, Romans attacked our village. They killed my mother and father, took away my brother, and. . ." She stopped. When she continued, he heard tears in her voice. "The soldiers, they. . .they. . ."

Suddenly Galla understood. He took her hand into his. Hers was like ice. "I understand."

Nodding, she continued. "I became pregnant. When my tribesmen found out, they decided. . . The Druids thought my child would make a perfect sacrifice."

Galla's eyes went wide. It was true then. The Druids did offer human sacrifices.

Eudemia looked into his face, her eyes burning intensely. "He may not have been born of love, but he is a part of me. I told them no." She grimaced. "Cadwaladyr wanted me for his wife, but he refused to have a 'Roman brat' for a son. He plotted with the Druids. My best friend, Brianna, heard them talking and came to tell me." She gripped his hand tightly as she continued to remember. "I ran away. Cadwaladyr tracked me, but winter was setting in. Miraculously I found this cave. It's so well hidden that it's hard to spot unless you are right up on it. Cadwaladyr had to return to the village because heavy snows came. This part of Britannia usually has mild winters, but for the last twelve years, the winters have been hard and cold. Another miracle, for it has made it harder for us to be found."

Privately Galla agreed that God's hand had been miraculously on Eudemia's life.

"Cadwaladyr has never stopped looking for me. I'm not sure why." Galla could have told her. "But anyway, he's never been able to find me. Once or twice when I was away hunting, he has almost caught up with me. But each time I was able to evade him and get back to this cave safely."

She looked at him again. "You asked Cadvan who taught him to set arrows. I did."

Galla was surprised. "And who taught you?"

She was quiet for a long time. "Decimus."

When Decimus and Chara rode into the village, several people hurried out to meet them. Men, women, and children stood gawking at the visitors. One young boy ran to the other end of the village.

Chara was captivated by the dwellings. They were round, and instead of tiles on the roofs, these were thatched.

The young boy returned, followed by an elderly man in white robes. Decimus felt the tension coil tightly within him. The man was a priest, and from the look of him, the Druid high priest, or archdruid as they called him.

His white robes flowed around him, cinched at the waist by a girdle of gold encasing a blue crystal. A gold tiara rested on his white locks, and round his forehead he wore the sacred mistletoe.

Decimus remembered now. The ring on the old man's hand was the chain ring of divination. Around his neck was the *Jodhain Morain*, or breastplate of judgment. Supposedly it had the power to squeeze the neck of anyone uttering a false judgment. Since Decimus doubted that was true, he certainly hoped he wasn't called upon to challenge the man's word.

"Der-wydd, we have visitors." Cadwaladyr dismounted, handing the reins of his horse to one of his men.

The Druid looked from Decimus to Chara and back to Decimus. There seemed to be a flicker of recognition in his eyes, but he waited for an explanation.

Cadwaladyr moved closer to the priest, with his hand indicating Decimus. "The man claims to be of your tribe. He has come searching for news of his family."

The Druid glanced sideways at Cadwaladyr but immediately turned his attention back to Decimus. "I see. What is your family?"

"His sister's name is Eudemia." Cadwaladyr frowned at the young man who spoke.

"Indeed. And your father and mother?"

"My father's name was Lucid. My mother, Gamina." Decimus felt a deep pain in his chest as he accepted at last what he had always suspected. "I think they are both dead."

Sucking in a breath, the Druid motioned for everyone to step aside. Nodding his head at Cadwaladyr, the Druid indicated that Decimus and Chara were to follow him.

Decimus felt Cadwaladyr close on his heels as though to prevent any chance of escape. The hair prickled on the nape of his neck. He felt more trapped than he had sitting in that warehouse in Rome. The Druid stopped beside one of the larger houses in the village. Motioning them inside, he followed and closed the door.

The main room had little furniture. Cubicles in the plaster walls held numerous scrolls. A brazier was lit, giving light to the semidark room.

The Druid seated himself on one of the couches, indicating that Decimus and Chara should sit across from him. When they were seated, Decimus became aware that Cadwaladyr was still in the room. He could feel the man's eyes on his back.

"We know of your family," the old Druid stated.

Excitement gleamed in Decimus's eyes as he leaned forward. "Are they still alive?"

The old man shook his head, his eyes grave. "Lucid and Gamina were killed by the Romans. As we feared you had been." His face softened. "I remember you from your youth," he told Decimus. "You were impatient and headstrong even then."

Decimus tried to remember, but he seemed to have a mental block. No picture would come. The regalia he could remember, the man he could not. He shut his eyes for a moment, letting his acceptance of his parents' deaths wash over him.

The Druid looked at Cadwaladyr. "Perhaps you remember Cadwaladyr?"

Decimus turned back to the other man, studying him with narrowed eyes. Slowly he shook his head. "Should I?"

"Well, perhaps not," the Druid answered. "It was a long time ago, and you were but a boy. Cadwaladyr and others from his tribe fought with us against the Romans—but our forces were not enough."

"And my sister? What of Eudemia?"

Cadwaladyr stepped forward. "She is alive."

Decimus came to his feet. "Where is she?"

Shaking his head, the old Druid shrugged his shoulders. "We don't know. After she became pregnant, she ran off into the hills to hide. No one could find her."

Sinking back to the couch, Decimus was barely aware of Chara taking his hand. "Then she's probably dead. No woman could survive out there alone. Especially if she was with child."

"She is alive," Cadwaladyr insisted. "We haven't been able to find her, but we have found evidence over the years of places she has been."

Decimus stared at the man, his mind beginning to question the man's integrity. "You make it sound as if she doesn't want to be found."

"She doesn't."

Decimus looked from Cadwaladyr to the old Druid. "What's going on here? You're not telling me something."

The two exchanged glances. Finally the old man sighed. "You are right. There is more, but you won't like it."

The Druid told Decimus how at the time these things had happened, he had been far away attending a judgment in another village. He explained to Decimus how the other Druids had planned to sacrifice Eudemia's child to the gods, hoping to gain support in their fight against the Romans since the child was part Roman.

Chara listened carefully, growing accustomed to the strange dialect and accent. She was appalled at their callousness regarding a child. A baby at that. Unconsciously, her hand went to her stomach. Decimus was right. This was no place to raise a child.

Decimus glared at Cadwaladyr, his hands clenching and unclenching at his sides. The man's veiled eyes stared impassively back at him.

"I'm not proud of my part in this," he told Decimus. "Der-wydd told us that the gods would judge us harshly for our acts. He made us see our error. I have tried to make amends, but I have not been able to find her."

Decimus remembered the times he had gone with his sister out into the hills, while their father taught them to hunt and track. Their father had been the finest tracker in all of the countryside, and he had taught Decimus and his sister well. No wonder they had never been able to find her. If she chose not to be found, he had no doubt that they wouldn't find her.

"You've tried to find her for twelve years?"

Surprisingly Cadwaladyr blushed. "Your sister is a remarkable woman."

"Aye, she is that," the old Druid agreed. "Perhaps you can join us in helping to track her down. Then we can lay all of this to rest once and for all."

Rising to his feet, Der-wydd smiled at Chara. "You must have a place to stay." Turning back to Decimus, he touched him on the shoulder. "Your father's house still stands. We have cared for it, just in case your sister did return to us someday. Cadwaladyr will show you the way."

When Decimus stepped across the threshold of his old house, memories came swarming back to greet him. Everything was much as he remembered, except he could tell several repairs had been made to the house. Cadwaladyr told Decimus how they had found the house partially burned by the Romans when they returned that fateful day.

"I'll leave you now. Someone from the village will bring you food."

Decimus watched him go, wondering if he had made a mistake in trusting these people. Chara came up and slid an arm around his waist. He smiled down at her.

"So much has happened," she told him softly.

"My mind is in total confusion," he agreed. "Somewhere out there is my sister. I wonder if her child lived."

Chara stared pensively at the surrounding hills. Darkness was beginning to fall, and winter had set in with a surety. "I don't know, but out there somewhere is Galla, also. I pray to God he's all right and that he will be able to find us."

Chapter 13

Cadvan looked up from the floor of the cave where he was kneeling. The light from the entrance showed clearly the tension on his face.

"There were six men—one smaller than the others—and a woman." His hand stroked one of the footprints. "This man is very large."

Eudemia blew out her breath in a sigh. "Cadwaladyr."

The boy nodded. "I believe so."

Alarmed, Galla began to search the cave. There had been no evidence of anything untoward from the outside, but the snow had covered everything to a depth of several inches.

"You won't find them here," Cadvan told him. Galla looked at the boy, once more aware of how old he seemed for his age.

"How do you know?"

"There was a struggle. Here." He pointed to a spot on the floor, and Galla noticed what he had missed before. The dirt was disturbed in a violent manner, obviously from a scuffle.

"All the footprints lead out," Eudemia agreed. "Whatever happened, they seem to have gone willingly."

Galla stared helplessly around. No tracks were left outside to follow. What was he to do now?

"They are probably traveling to the village," Cadvan suggested.

Galla's face seemed etched in granite, his eyes becoming the color of iron in their intensity. "Then that's where I must go."

Eudemia felt her heart drop. What did this one Roman think he could do against a whole tribe? He would be killed. Her eyes grew wide as she realized she didn't want to see this happen. She didn't even want him to leave.

Cadvan went to the entrance of the cave and studied the sky. "I think that will have to wait," he told Galla.

Galla was already shaking his head. "I haven't time to lose. I have to try and help my friends."

Shrugging, Cadvan turned back of the cave. "It will be hard to help them if you are dead."

"Cadvan!"

"It's true, Mother. Another storm is about to hit. It doesn't look as though it will be as strong as the first, but it will still be a killer for anyone unfortunate enough to be stuck out in it." He looked at Galla. "We have barely enough time to get back to our own cave."

"How far to the village?" Galla wanted to know, still unconvinced.

Eudemia answered him. "About half a day's ride north."

Galla continued to study the terrain outside the cave. The other two waited for his answer. Galla's first instinct was to try for the village, but he realized that would be foolish. Sighing, he glanced at the others. "Let's go back to your cave. As soon as the storm passes, I will set out to find them."

When the snow began it fell lightly at first, but it rapidly turned into a full blizzard. Galla shook his head. This was not the weather his father had described when he had told him of Britannia. Galla had always heard that the winters were mild and the summers cool, but the snow that fell now was as cold and heavy as that which he'd seen high in the mountains north of Rome. He began to fret at his enforced inactivity. He should be trying to find Decimus and Chara.

Six men and one woman. Cadvan's words kept coming back to haunt him. One woman alone with all of those men. Galla swallowed the knot that formed in his throat. His eyes took on a feral gleam. If anything happened to Chara *or* Decimus. . . He shook his head to free himself of such thinking. Where had such murderous thoughts come from? Decimus and Chara were in God's hands, just as they had been all along.

He jumped when Eudemia laid a hand on his arm. "Your thoughts are far from pleasant. You are worried about your friends." It was more a statement than a question.

Nodding his head, he smiled slightly. "You are right, my thoughts *were* far from pleasant. I'm afraid they were far from *Christlike,* also."

"Your God doesn't approve of killing?"

Galla thought before answering. "My God doesn't approve of *murder*."

Eudemia frowned. "Is there a difference?"

Sighing, Galla sat down on his pallet. "I think so. The scriptures tell us that David was a man after God's own heart, yet he killed hundreds of men and was responsible for thousands of other deaths."

"Even women and children?"

"I'm afraid so."

Glaring, Eudemia threw herself down beside him. "This doesn't make sense. Why make war on children?"

Galla stared intently into her icy blue eyes. "Why offer them as sacrifices? Why make them slaves? Why leave them on rocks to die?"

With each question, Eudemia watched Galla's face become more and more savage. He had a heart for children, this one. He would make a fine father. Sensing his reluctance to discuss the subject, still she pressed on. She had to know.

"So it is all right for soldiers to kill?"

Instead of answering her question, Galla began to tell her a story. "Several years ago, my father met a man who had been to see Jesus' cousin. The cousin's name was John, but everyone called him 'the Baptizer.' This soldier asked John what he had to do to be in accord with God's will."

Curious, Eudemia's eyes roved over Galla's solemn features. "And he told him not to kill?"

Galla shook his head. "No. He told him not to extort money from the people or accuse people falsely, to be content with his pay."

"But to make war on children!"

"War is bad anytime," he told her. "But sometimes it is necessary."

Unexpectedly Galla smiled as he watched Eudemia's animated features. She was so passionate about everything! Her heart was so full of love and gentleness, and she cared about life. All life. She hadn't even held it against him that he was a despised Roman.

She was so hungry for God's peace, yet she didn't even realize she was. Galla tried to explain again about God's gift of salvation. He could tell that she didn't understand but she wanted to. She continued asking him questions long into the night.

Cadvan had stopped listening to them long ago. His deep, even breathing told them that he was fast asleep. Eudemia rose and went to him, pulling the furs securely around him. Her love flowed out of her eyes as she stroked the boy's cheek.

Galla felt a lump in his throat as he watched her. She had so much love to give. How could her people have treated her so cruelly?

She came back and sat down across from him again. She looked him in the eye, and suddenly, to Galla, the cave seemed terribly warm. Before, her eyes had been icy blue. Now they were the warm tranquil blue of the Mediterranean. He felt himself hypnotized by their iridescence, the lights flickering in their depths.

"Tell me more of your God," she demanded softly, and Galla did so, unaware of what he was really saying. The words came, but his thoughts were not with them. His thoughts were focused on the pair of soft lips smiling so closely to his own. He had only to move a fraction. . . .

"Galla."

Her soft entreaty sent a warm fire racing through him. He tried to keep his self-control, but it was a lost cause. Leaning forward, he closed the distance between them.

She responded to his kiss with a fervor that surprised him. As her arms wound their way around his neck, he felt his defenses beginning to crumble. Pulling her to him, he intensified their kiss.

Keep yourself pure. Where had the thought come from? Galla felt his ardor beginning to cool. Pulling away slightly, he stared down into Eudemia's face. She watched him, puzzled at his resistance.

Galla pushed her gently away. "Go to bed, Eudemia." His voice was harsh to his own ears. God had once again saved him from his own weak nature.

Miffed, Eudemia rose quickly to her feet. Without looking at him, she went to her pallet and lay down.

Galla stared up at the ceiling. He had every nook and cranny memorized by now, knew where every shadow was, every hole. He sighed. This was going to be a long night.

Chara smiled at the woman standing before her. Although she was not beautiful, her features were pleasant. Her blue eyes held a softness that bespoke of a gentleness within.

"Tell me, Brianna, what is everyone doing?"

The young woman smiled back at her. "We are getting ready for Samhain. The boys will climb the oak trees to find mistletoe, then the girls will weave it into headpieces. Everyone will gather oak, our sacred wood, to be burned in a huge bonfire. You will see. We must each find a rock, also."

The smile fled from Chara's face. Samhain? Was this some kind of pagan rite?

"What is the purpose of the rocks?" she wanted to know.

Brianna continued to empty her baskets of their contents. For days now the people of the village had supplied them with food. Although Decimus could pay for the goods, he was as yet unwilling to do so. He told her that he wasn't sure these people would have much use for coins, so instead Chara traded with them.

"Everyone will write their names on a rock and then later throw them into the bonfire. If the rocks are still there in the morning, all is well. If your rock is gone. . ."

"Yes?"

"If the rock with your name on it is gone, then you will die sometime in the coming year."

Chara shivered at her casual reference to death. She watched the woman gather her things together in preparation for leaving. She couldn't be so very old, yet there was a sadness about her that never seemed to go away.

Was it the fact that she was in love with Cadwaladyr, but he didn't return that love? The man barely registered Brianna's existence. But that didn't stop Brianna from following the giant with her eyes, her love shining through.

Impulsively Chara laid a hand on the girl's arm. "Brianna, have you ever heard of Jesus Christ?"

She shook her head, smiling into Chara's face. Chara wanted to seize the moment and speak of Christ to the woman, but something held her back.

"Never mind," she finally told her and watched as the girl left the house.

Chara went to the window and saw Brianna heading down the hill in the direction of the village, picking up loose oak branches she found along the way.

Chara shook her head. This place was so far from Rome, yet its religion was much the same. Only, Romans didn't offer human sacrifices to their gods, except for the gladiators, of course. She saw Brianna stop to talk with Decimus as he rounded the bend and came into sight. He laughed at something she said, and Chara felt the first stirrings of jealousy. These were his people, and she was an outsider.

Decimus came in the door, laying his mantle across a stool. He briskly rubbed his hands together before the fire. "Cadwaladyr says that after tomorrow we can go search for Galla."

"Why after tomorrow?"

"No one will travel tomorrow. It's a feast day. Everyone will be celebrating, or feeling the effects thereof."

Chara placed a bowl of stew on the table for him, its steam curling invitingly into the air. "Sit down and eat." Seating herself across from him, she frowned at him. "Brianna was telling me something about this Samhain celebration."

Decimus began hungrily devouring the food. In between bites, he managed to tell her more of their superstitious beliefs.

"So they believe this Samhain, this god of the dead, allows the souls of the dead to return for this one night?"

He nodded. "Before the end of the day, Der-wydd will come and tell us to put out our fire. Then we will relight it from the bonfire they will build."

Chara rose from her seat, taking the empty bowls from the table. "And what of the sacrifices?"

Decimus's brow furrowed in thought. "I'm not sure there will be any. I don't understand this festival myself."

"And will we be required to participate in it?"

Decimus's frown deepened. "Of course not. Their gods are not our God. Why ask such a thing?"

Chara shrugged. "Just the way Brianna spoke. She seemed to assume we would be a part of the celebration."

Sighing heavily, Decimus got up from his seat and took Chara in his arms. "Let's worry about that when the time comes."

She clung to him, closing her eyes. "Oh, Decimus, these people are so. . .so *pagan*."

"So were we at one time," he told her. Chara shook her head, and Decimus remembered that she had been raised as a Christian. He smiled. "Sometimes I forget how pure you are."

She flushed with color. Decimus found her enchanting, a mixture of innocence and desire. Even now her eyes spoke clearly to him. Before he could take advantage of the situation, a pounding shook the door.

Opening the portal, Decimus found himself face-to-face with Der-wydd. "It is time to put out your hearth fire and come to the ceremony of the Samhain."

Decimus hesitated. Did watching the ceremony mean he was participating in it? He thought not, and he wanted to understand these people. How could he ever hope to reach them otherwise?

They followed Der-wydd as he headed back down the hill to the village, his long white robes taking on the colors of the sunset. The evening sun reflected brightly off his golden tiara. For a man his age, he was still spry.

Decimus and Chara continued to the village while Der-wydd continued on his journey to the other villagers. Already a huge pile of wood was gathered at the end of the village. Many were already in the midst of celebrating the coming of a new year. Strong beer, the favored drink of these people, was flowing freely from person to person.

Chara shrank closer to Decimus's side. These festivities reminded her of the stories her mother had told her of Moses, when the people had built the golden calf as he was talking to God on the mountain.

A young girl screamed as she was lifted over the shoulder of a burly young man. Grinning, he spun her around and around, finally falling in a heap in the soft snow. Bodies entwined, they laughed uproariously.

Frowning down at his wife, Decimus took her hand safely and securely within his own. Maybe coming to the celebration hadn't been a good idea after all.

Darkness descended, but the revelry continued. Cheers went up from the gathered crowd as Der-wydd lit the now huge stack of wood. Louder and louder rose the voices of the people. Soon Decimus realized that they were chanting, their bodies swaying back and forth. Their movements and their singsong voices soon had him in a semihypnotized state. Shaking his head to free himself of the effects, he glanced down at Chara to see how she was affected. Her eyes were closed and her lips were moving.

Grinning, he felt a curious pride that nothing seemed to affect her relationship with her God. Come what may, she would hold her own.

The fire was beginning to die down yet was still bright enough to allow a bright halo of light far down the streets of the village. Some of the older people were making their way to their houses, torches from the bonfire lighting their way. Only the youngest remained, and most of them were so drunk on the strong brew they craved that Decimus doubted they could see to find their way home. As people left, they threw their rocks into the fire, hoping that they would still be there come morning.

Cadwaladyr was making his way toward them, only slightly staggering. As he reached them, he held out his hands. In the curve of each palm rested a rock, one with Chara's name and the other with Decimus's.

Chara frowned, not realizing that the rock was meant for her. *Strange,*

Decimus thought, *that I can still recognize my name written in the Celtic language.*

Cadwaladyr bowed low before Chara, stumbling slightly. Decimus sucked in his breath, moving to place himself between them. If the big giant were to fall on Chara, he would surely crush the life from her.

"For you, my lady."

Chara slowly reached out a hand. Looking up into Cadwaladyr's face, she realized that this was a test. Since the rock held no symbolic significance for her, she turned and threw it into the fire. When she turned back to Cadwaladyr, his eyebrows were raised slightly.

"May the gods not choose your rock," he told her.

Decimus hid a grin behind his fingers. Cadwaladyr looked as though he were disappointed. Had he hoped that they would defy the gods?

A disturbance at the other end of the fire brought their attention elsewhere. A young man was close to the fire, swaying back and forth. In one hand, he held a small squirrel, swinging it over his head. In his other, he held a gleaming knife. In one quick movement, he slit the squirrel's throat.

Chara gasped, burying her head in Decimus's arm. Decimus watched in fascination as the boy drained the blood from the animal and then threw it into the fire. Cheers rose from the onlookers as they spurred him on. Again they took up their chant, their bodies swaying to the rhythm.

Decimus put his arm around his wife and turned to Cadwaladyr. "My wife has had enough. I'll take her home now."

Cadwaladyr grinned, aware of their real reason for leaving. "Aren't you going to stay for the reading of the bones? I will be throwing in my own sacrifice so that Der-wydd can tell me my destiny."

Before Decimus could answer, a woman's voice spoke eerily from the darkness beyond the fire. "You needn't wait for the readings, Cadwaladyr. *I* can tell you your destiny."

An uncanny silence descended on the whole group. Squinting his eyes to see better, Cadwaladyr strained to see the owner of the voice. A shadow moved from the darkness and into the light. Cadwaladyr gasped as the woman became visible.

"Eudemia!"

Chapter 14

Galla stared over Eudemia's head at the giant standing before the roaring fire. Although Galla knew he himself was big, standing at least six feet, this man would tower over him by at least six more inches.

Never had he seen a man sober up as fast as this one did. His eyes never left Eudemia, as though he believed himself to be hallucinating. For a moment Eudemia returned his stare, her own eyes challenging, before she looked to his side.

Decimus stood beside the giant, his look of wonder telling Galla better than words could have that Decimus recognized his sister. They stood contemplating each other several moments before Eudemia let out a cry, running into her brother's arms.

Galla's searching gaze found Chara, puzzled and uncertain beside her husband. In all the time they had known Decimus, he had rarely shown any emotion. Now his face was wet with his tears.

Chara spotted Galla and was instantly running across the darkness, throwing herself at him. "You're alive! Thank God, you're alive!"

Squeezing her tightly, Galla felt his own eyes brimming with tears. "I thought I would never see you two again."

Looking over her shoulder, Galla's eyes met Decimus's. They smiled at each other, and Galla pulled Chara with him to their side.

Forgetting everything, they laughed and hugged, content to be together again. A shadow looming over them brought them to sudden silence.

Cadwaladyr stood towering over them, his dark eyes unblinking. Slowly his gaze roved over Eudemia. Instead of cringing away, she pulled herself to her full height, which, compared to Chara's, was considerable.

"So tell me my destiny," he growled.

Shaking her head, she glared up at him. "There will be only one destiny for you if you continue to hunt me and my son. Several times we could have struck you dead, yet we did not. But I have had enough now."

She pulled a leather girdle from inside her sagum and handed it to the big man. His eyes went wide.

"Where did you get this?"

"I took it from your horse last spring when you camped near my home."

His admiring look didn't please Galla at all. There were things here he didn't understand, but he was determined to find out about them.

Most of the crowd of people had dispersed at Eudemia's sudden appearance, their eyes filled with terror. He didn't know that according to their superstitions, the dead were supposed to walk the earth this night. Nor could he know that they believed Eudemia to have been one of those freed by Samhain, their god of the dead.

Decimus spoke up. "Let's go to Der-wydd. He must know that Eudemia has returned."

Cadwaladyr nodded once, his eyes never leaving Eudemia's face. Galla felt himself beginning to bristle at the man's constant attention.

Der-wydd explained the story to Eudemia the same way he had explained it to Decimus. There was a kindness in the old man that caused Decimus to doubt his involvement with the happenings of that time so many years ago.

But if he was not a part of it, where were the other Druids who were? There had been no sign of other Druids in the vicinity, not even a young bard in training.

Decimus learned that he had a nephew. They decided that Cadwaladyr, Galla, and Eudemia would leave at first light to fetch Cadvan. An undercurrent of tension flowed between the big man and Eudemia, as though they still had unfinished business between them.

For now, Decimus felt at peace. He had found his people and was reunited with his sister. Soon his nephew would join them and they would be a family. Life was good. God was good.

When Cadvan joined them, he soon fit in with the community. The other boys were impressed with his hunting and tracking skills. He shared with them the new way Galla had showed him to affix feathers to the arrows, and they made sport seeing whose arrows could go the farthest.

One day Chara was returning from the village when she spotted Eudemia and Cadwaladyr arguing on the path. Neither noticed her, and she stopped, afraid to go on. So heated was their argument that Chara had no trouble hearing what was being said.

"You were promised to me long ago, Eudemia. You belong to me."

Shoving a forefinger into the big man's chest, Eudemia punctuated her words with sharp, angry thrusts. "Never will I belong to you! You would have killed my son! Given half a chance, you would have killed me for defying you."

"That's not true," he argued. "That's why I left my people, my home to come and wed you."

"Bah! Your thirst for blood brought you here. You wanted to kill *Romans*!"

Chara shoved her hands hard against her ears, yet still their voices reached her clearly.

"It's that Roman you came back with, isn't it? You prefer a Roman dog to me, one of your own people."

Eudemia's eyes glowed like blue ice as she stared angrily into Cadwaladyr's. Turning, she strode away from the big man, heading for the house. He caught up with her in two strides. Gripping her by the arms, he pulled her forcefully against his chest.

"You will be my wife, or no one's. I have the right, and if necessary, I will challenge the Roman to a fight."

Eudemia's face paled. "He would not fight you. He does not want me."

Cadwaladyr threw back his head, his brown eyes gleaming like polished bronze. "He wants you, all right. I see how he looks at you." Shoving her away, he turned on his heels. "Remember what I said."

He stopped when he reached Chara's side, his eyes narrowing. "You have something to say, woman?"

Chara watched him silently, her eyes never leaving his. He was the one who first looked away. Without saying anything, Chara followed Eudemia to the house.

After that, Chara noticed Cadwaladyr watching Eudemia whenever he was near. Wherever she happened to be, he was there, also. Eudemia ignored him although Chara knew she was aware of him.

Chara shared her concerns with Decimus, telling him about the conversation she overheard. After much consideration, she decided not to tell him about Cadwaladyr's threat to Galla.

Decimus started watching his sister more carefully. Whatever Cadwaladyr's plans, Decimus had no doubt that Eudemia could handle the man; however, he wanted to head off any trouble before it occurred.

Although Decimus and Eudemia has assured Galla that there was plenty of room in their home, he had chosen to build himself a small one of his own, closer to the village. Chara thought it might have something to do with the fact that due to Cadvan's hero worship of the Roman, the other boys followed him, also. She noticed that he took every opportunity to share stories of Jesus with them, and though they didn't show much interest, neither did they turn away.

For the first time in weeks, Galla had joined them for the evening meal. He smiled as Eudemia laid his plate on the table in front of him. She in turn blushed a rosy red.

Decimus was not unaware of his sister's attraction to Galla. He watched them to see if there was any sign of a returned affection. Although he loved the Roman, he loved his sister more, and he didn't wish to see her hurt.

Galla pulled the meat from the bones of the quail he was eating, dipping it in the broth. Decimus sensed he had something on his mind.

"I'll be leaving in a few days to go north to Trinovante country."

Slowly he looked up, finding four pairs of eyes riveted to his face.

"It's time for me to find my own people and fulfill my duties."

"You aren't really going to try to turn the Trinovante against the other tribes," Decimus argued.

"That is not my intention," Galla returned quietly. "You have found your family; now I have a yearning to see my own." Although that was partly true, Galla hid his real reason for leaving.

"But, Galla," Cadvan wailed. "You said you would teach me to fight like the Romans."

Eudemia said nothing. Suddenly her appetite was gone. Had Cadwaladyr threatened Galla? Was he fleeing because he was a coward? Or did he realize how she felt about him and he wanted to get as far away as possible?

"We'll miss you," Chara told him softly, and Galla returned her smile.

"As I will you. All of you," he told them, his eyes fixing on Eudemia.

Cadvan flung himself away from the table, running to the ladder that led to the house's loft. They could hear his sobs through the ceiling. Galla swallowed hard, rising to his feet. He started to go to the boy but stopped himself. It was better this way. Gritting his teeth, he turned to the others.

"I have to leave now." Without looking at them, he gathered his sagum and his bow that he carried with him. "I'll talk to you tomorrow."

After he left, Eudemia hurriedly rose to her feet. "I'll get some wood for the fire."

Both Chara and Decimus refrained from comment on the full stack of wood in the corner.

Eudemia hurried after Galla, calling him urgently. He turned when he heard her voice, waiting for her to reach him. She stopped in front of him, her eyes liquid in the moonlight.

"You have to leave?" she asked him, biting her lip to keep it from trembling.

Galla heaved a sigh, reaching out a hand to stroke down her cheek. "Yes."

"Why?"

Frowning, he turned to study the trees that grew beside the path. "I told you why. I have an assignment to fulfill."

"And will you return?"

He was so quiet that Eudemia thought he wasn't going to answer. "Galla?"

"I don't know. I have no reason to. Decimus can do here what needs to be done, and I can go elsewhere. Together we can cover more territory with the Word."

She shook her head angrily. "I don't know what you're talking about. I only know I want you to stay."

Galla's insides twisted at the tears in her voice. He didn't want to hurt her, but he couldn't stay. He didn't trust himself. She was a nonbeliever, and as such, he couldn't contemplate a future with her.

He closed his eyes. On the other hand, he couldn't contemplate a future without her, either. He had finally admitted to himself that he loved her. And Cadvan. The boy was so eager, so bright. So easy to love.

Determined to make him see, Eudemia put her arms around his neck, pulling his head down to hers. She kissed him fully on the lips. Galla could taste the salt from her tears.

Throwing pride to the wind, she begged him softly, "Please stay. Please don't go. I love you."

Her words immediately filled him with joy, but just as quickly the pain followed. He wasn't pretending when he said he had a job to finish. He had sworn to serve Rome's army, and he would keep his vow. He had sworn to serve his God, and he would keep that promise, also.

Taking her hands from his neck, he folded them in front of her. His eyes watched her intently. "I have to go."

"It's Cadwaladyr, isn't it? He's frightened you away!"

Galla frowned. "What are you talking about? Cadwaladyr has nothing to do with this."

She continued to cry. "No matter what you say, no matter what you do, I *won't* marry him."

Galla felt himself go cold inside. Gripping her arms, he shook her slightly. "What are you saying? Who said anything about marrying Cadwaladyr?"

Eudemia told him of the promise between her parents and Cadwaladyr's. A hope of uniting the two tribes with a marriage between two noble houses.

Releasing her, Galla shoved one hand back through his dark hair, glaring at the sky. The bright moon cast light over the terrain around them, causing everything to be highlighted by dark shadows.

Regardless of his feelings, he had to go. Nothing had changed. He still had a job to do, and Eudemia was still a nonbeliever.

Taking her face between his palms, Galla softly kissed her lips. "I love you, Eudemia. But I have to go. I can't marry you. There are reasons, but most of them you probably wouldn't understand."

Seeing the hope die in her eyes was almost more than he could bear. Turning, he quickly retreated down the hill. Eudemia watched him go, tears coursing a path down her cheeks.

He had said he loved her, and her heart flowed with joy. She would go to him tomorrow. No matter what his reasons, she would try again.

The next day, Galla was gone. Eudemia had found the hut where he lived empty.

His absence affected nearly everyone. Decimus missed the Roman more than he thought possible. He had grown to love him like a brother, and he missed his wise counsel. Chara cried for her friend, but more than that, she prayed for him. Hopefully he would be able to send them word wherever he went.

There was one person who missed Galla for a different reason. Brianna had hoped the Roman would marry Eudemia, and then in turn she hoped that Cadwaladyr would notice her.

Life went on in the village. The inhabitants came to realize that Chara and Decimus served a different God, but although they were curious, they didn't feel intimidated. They couldn't believe that anyone as loving and kind as Chara could be a threat to their lives.

Brianna brought bread to the house one day while Decimus and Eudemia were out hunting with Cadvan. Brianna exchanged bread for some of the salt Chara had brought with them. Today Brianna didn't immediately rush off as she usually did. Instead, she began fiddling with Chara's sewing that was sitting on the table.

"Did you wish to speak with me, Brianna?" Chara asked her.

The other woman sat down at the table, twisting her hands in her lap. "I. . .I wanted to hear about this God you serve."

Joyfully Chara told her all that she knew about God, and she shared what she had been taught from the apostles' writings.

Brianna sighed. "It would be nice to be loved like that. I have noticed that you and Decimus aren't fearful like the rest of us. You don't fear the dark, or the storms, or even death."

Chara smiled wryly. "We're all afraid of something." She then told Brianna about her life, her trip through captivity, her marriage to Decimus.

Brianna's face was filled with awe. "Your God has truly taken care of you. Could He. . .could He love *me* that much, do you think?"

Taking her hand, Chara told her, "He already does."

Later, Chara watched Brianna walking down the path that led to the village. Whatever was on the girl's heart seemed to weigh down her steps.

That night Chara shared the happy news of Brianna's search for the one true God. Decimus smiled, his eyes roving her joyful countenance.

"I have seen fruit from some of the seeds we have planted, also. Illtud and some of the others are beginning to realize that their fears are what make them weak. I have told them that perfect love drives out fear." He grinned. "It's been several months, but already many of the people are beginning to question the old ways."

Feeling a sense of unease, Chara frowned. "What of Der-wydd? How will he take the proselytizing of his people?"

Decimus sat down on the couch, pulling her down with him. "You know, I think he doesn't mind. I'm not sure why—maybe it's an answer to prayer—but Der-wydd seems relieved that many of his people no longer request sacrifices to tell their futures or plan their lives."

"And what of Cadwaladyr?"

He shrugged. "Cadwaladyr has left the village. He has followed Galla back to the Trinovantes, though I'm not sure why."

Chara looked alarmed. "Will he try to hurt Galla?"

Decimus pressed his lips together. "I don't know, but I'm betting Galla can take care of himself. Remember, he has God on his side."

Bending his head, Decimus began to nibble on Chara's neck. Giggling, she pulled away. "Cadvan might come."

Decimus slowly shook his head, his blue eyes gleaming. "He is staying the night with a friend. They want to start early on a hunt."

As he bent to her again, she pushed him away. "Eudemia might come."

Again he slowly shook his head. "She plans to go with Cadvan in the morning, so she has decided to stay with Kolin's family, also." He raised an eyebrow. "Any more objections?"

Shaking her head, she grinned, nibbling his chin. "None, my love."

Isolated as they were from the other tribes, news took weeks—sometimes months—to reach their village. One day, a rider rode in from the outside and informed them that Nero was dead. A ripple of voices could be heard from the gathered crowd. No one knew what this would mean for Britannia.

"How did he die?" Decimus asked, pulling Chara close to his side.

"Committed suicide," the rider told them. "His army turned against him."

"Who is in charge now?"

"General Galba. You know of him?" he asked Decimus.

Decimus nodded his head. "He's an old man, but I heard he was a wise general. God only knows how he'll be as Caesar."

On their way home, Chara commented softly to her husband, "It's hard to believe he's dead."

Decimus shook his head. "What a wasted life. I would not want to be Nero when he stands before God's throne."

Remembering Agrippina and Antipus, Chara agreed. Then she cupped her abdomen with her hands and smiled. The first green fingers of spring were beginning to shoot their way up through the thawing ground. Geese flew over, hinting at an early spring. All around, life was blooming—and soon another life would spring forth. Chara's face took on a glow that soon had the village women talking.

Chara was a favorite among the village people. She was so shy and sweet that she attracted people like bees to honey. Everywhere she went, she tried to help the people who most needed it. Sometimes she gave food, sometimes she helped with housework, sometimes she cared for children so a tired mother had some time to rest. Because of her help, many were willing to listen when she talked to them of her God, which she did tirelessly.

Decimus smiled as he watched his wife. His sister, too, had succumbed to her charm. As Chara's pregnancy progressed, so did Eudemia's mothering.

He had to admit, though, his own heart was filled with dread for the pain he knew Chara would have to bear. He continually prayed that God would keep her safe.

The trees were in full bloom and summer was full upon them when Galla rode into the village. Heads turned as he walked his horse through the village and headed it up the hill without stopping.

Eudemia saw him coming before anyone else. Throwing down the rag she was using to wipe the table, she ran outside and met him as his horse came to a stop.

"Galla."

He slid from his horse. He stood there a long time, his hands curling and uncurling at his sides.

Decimus came running from the fields behind the house where he was tending the crops. Throwing his arms around Galla, he hugged him hard. "We've missed you, you old horse. Come on in, come on in."

Galla followed him inside, intensely aware of Eudemia only three steps behind him.

"Chara!" Decimus bellowed. "Come see!"

Chara hurried from the back of the house, her brows lifting in surprise. Her eyes sparkled with delight as she threw her arms around Galla's neck.

He smiled wryly, noticing her gently rounded stomach. "You seem to have grown a bit since I last saw you."

Blushing, she threw him a pretend pout. "What a thing to say to a woman. Are you becoming a barbarian, Galla?"

He grinned fully. "I always have been."

The news Galla brought them was not good. "I foresee much bloodshed," he told them, his face grim.

"And what of you, did you accomplish what you set out to do?"

Although Chara asked the question, Galla was watching Eudemia. "I resigned my commission in the army. I know General Galba, so I'm confident my resignation will be accepted."

"Did you find your people?"

He nodded at Decimus. "Cadwaladyr caught up with me and led me home."

Eudemia frowned. "Where is Cadwaladyr?"

Galla sighed heavily. "He decided to stay with the Trinovantes for the time being. They are arming themselves for battle, and it seems they will be the first to attack."

Eudemia's soft voice penetrated the silence that followed his words. "And then we will follow."

Shrugging, Galla got to his feet. "Maybe. Maybe not. Let's not borrow trouble. God has worked miracles before. No matter what happens, my trust is in the Lord."

Decimus rose to his feet, also. "We have some good news for you, my friend."

Galla looked at Chara. "So I see."

Chara blushed. "Not *that* good news." Turning, she took Eudemia's hand. "Eudemia has accepted Christ as her Savior. She and Cadvan both."

Since Eudemia was looking down, she didn't see the joy that filled Galla's eyes. "I'm pleased," he said softly. The tone of his voice brought Eudemia's eyes flying to his.

Exchanging glances, Decimus and Chara excused themselves. Galla watched them walk away. When he turned back to Eudemia, she had already turned from him.

Taking her by the arms, he turned her back to face him. She looked in his eyes, and her breath caught in her throat. Such love shone from their dark brown depths that tears sprang to her eyes.

"I need to explain," he told her softly.

She shook her head. "No. Chara explained it to me. You could not marry an unbeliever."

He nodded. "That is so, but as a centurion in Rome's army, I was forbidden to marry, also."

She looked in his eyes, her own full of questions.

"If you still love me, Eudemia, I would like you to marry me."

A slow smile spread across her face. Her eyes began to glow, and Galla pulled her close. Burying his face in her hair, he thanked God for all He had done. What the apostle Paul had said was true. Everything had worked together for their good.

Cadvan burst through the door, halting on the threshold. His eyes rapidly searched the room, landing at last on Galla. With a cry, he threw himself into Galla's arms.

Eudemia smiled, tears misting her eyes. Looking up, she caught Galla's tender look. A knot formed in her throat. Nodding her head, she smiled.

"We'll be glad to marry you, Galla."

Epilogue

The Romans first invaded Britannia in 55 BC, and they conquered Gaul the same year. The Celts lived on both sides of the English Channel, and Druidism was practiced in Gaul as well as Britannia. The Romans especially hated the Druids and tried to eliminate them; the Druids, however, continued to keep a hold on the people for almost two hundred years.

Although the Romans tried to annihilate the Druids and their religion, no amount of force could accomplish this. What the Roman army with all their might was not able to achieve, a carpenter from Galilee did.

As Christianity spread slowly through the region, many of the polytheistic religions died. Christians fleeing the persecution of Rome headed for Britannia where Rome's army was not as powerful. As they flowed over the countryside, God's love went with them.

This story transpires from AD 67 through AD 68. After Nero died, Rome had a difficult time. Over the next thirty years, they had six caesars, which caused much chaos in the empire. Troops were recalled from the outer regions of the empire to reinforce and protect Rome's emperor.

Although Rome eventually conquered all of Britannia, only God could conquer the Druids.

My Enemy, My Love

I would like to dedicate this book to my minister, Kenneth Hoover.
His sermons have inspired many of the thoughts in my books,
and his knowledge of the Bible has helped me more times than I can number.
I am especially thankful for his help on this book and for his willingness
to help me portray the early church as accurately as possible.

Chapter 1

The city of Jerusalem gleamed whitely in the bright afternoon sun, its huge walls resplendent among the verdant hillsides. It nestled among valleys—the Kidron to the east, the Hinnom to the west.

Two young men approaching the magnificent city paused in their journey to marvel at the grandeur. One young man shifted the lamb he carried in his arms, his dark eyes growing large with wonder.

"Look, Barak. The City of David!" The words were not much more than a whisper of awe.

His friend smiled slightly, his teeth showing briefly through his short, dark beard. "Your first pilgrimage to the holy city. Is it as grand as you had imagined?"

"More so. Never could I have imagined such a wonderful place, not even in my dreams."

Barak reached to take the lamb from his friend's tired arms. "Believe me, Adonijah, it is not all so wonderful."

Adonijah turned to Barak in surprise. "You sound as though you are disappointed. Or maybe *offended* would be a better word."

They resumed their walk. "Neither, and both." Barak shook his head in disgust. "Who would have thought that the City of David would harbor such a motley crew of people. Romans, Egyptians, Greeks. They even offer sacrifices at our holy temple."

"But, Barak. It has been this way for many years. You have lived among it all of your life. What makes you so offended by it now?" Adonijah turned a puzzled frown on his companion, his own short beard reflecting the sheen of the bright sunlight and turning it from brunette to a dark almond.

Barak sighed heavily. "I don't know. I think I'm just disgusted with everything right now." He couldn't begin to explain his restlessness when he didn't understand it himself.

As they approached the city gate, the crowd increased until it was hard to move more than a few feet at a time. Amid the babble of accents and foreign tongues, and under the vigilant, watchful eyes of Roman soldiers, the two were funneled through the gate to be swallowed up by the crowd.

The sun beat hotly on the raucous crowd of people milling among the streets. Everywhere, merchants loudly hawked their wares, purchasers haggled over prices, and people shouted and teased with each other.

The streets of Jerusalem were as crowded as the roads along the way, and everywhere the citizenry mixed in a kaleidoscope of sights and sounds.

To speak, one had to shout above the noise. Adonijah addressed himself to Barak, his loud voice causing the other to flinch. "What makes you so dissatisfied with life, my friend? How can you be bored among such marvels?"

Barak sighed as Adonijah stopped at yet another merchant's stall. At this rate, they would never reach the temple to offer their sacrifice.

Adonijah lifted a jeweled necklace from the table and held it up for Barak's inspection. "How about this for Miriam?" The lapis lazuli stones glinted brightly—almost as brightly as the merchant's eyes as he haggled with Adonijah in hopes of a quick sale.

At the closed look on Barak's face, Adonijah lost his smile. It took only a moment for him to assess the situation. "Ah. It is not life you are dissatisfied with, is it, but this marriage to Miriam?" He placed the necklace back on the table, his gaze sweeping briefly over the man who was closer to him than any brother could have been. Barak was strong. Handsome. He could have his choice of women.

At the same time, Miriam was beautiful beyond comparison. Why would his friend deign a marriage to one such as she, especially since it would unite two already close families?

"Let's move on. We want to be among the first to offer our sacrifice, or it will be late when we get back to the others," Barak suggested.

Barak knew his friend wasn't fooled, but he had no desire to speak of something so personal with him. These thoughts and feelings were things he had to deal with himself.

Jerusalem was a buzzing hive of activity on any day, but during Passover, its streets were choked with pilgrims, as well as its normal workmen, tradesmen, slaves, and other citizenry. The two men pushed themselves forward past the Antonia. Helmeted soldiers moved among the garrison, their wary gazes following the crowds of people.

They finally reached the colonnaded portico around the Court of Gentiles. Barak made his way to the money changers to exchange some of his coins for Tyrian shekels, the only coins acceptable for temple offerings.

As he waited his turn, he gazed around him at the crowds of people. Anger rose inside him at the array of obvious Gentiles. Even Roman generals were known to offer sacrifices here for their victories in battle. Thank Jehovah they could not go beyond this court. The temple was defiled enough by their mere presence.

A glint of gold caught his attention, and he found himself watching two young women across the street. One was a dark beauty, her excitement making her eyes glow with an almost feverish pitch. The other was just as dark, her long hair hanging below her waist, and she was without adornment save the sparkling gold Star of David hanging from her neck that had first caught Barak's attention.

For a moment, Barak found himself intrigued. It was unusual to see a woman nowadays who wore so little jewelry. Even the girl standing next to her was covered from head to foot with gleaming bracelets, ankle chains, necklaces, and hair combs.

The star proclaimed the girl's Hebrew heritage, but Barak knew it was a rare thing for women to sport such a trinket. Her face was perfect of feature, but plain compared to that of her lively friend.

When the girl turned, her hazel eyes meshed with his own, and Barak realized that, although the girl wore a Jewish symbol, she had obvious Gentile blood. A Samaritan, no doubt! His own eyes grew cold with anger; the girl studied him a moment longer before turning away.

"Do you know them?"

Pulled from his thoughts, Barak turned back to his friend. "No. No, I don't know them."

Adonijah's own gaze was riveted to the flashing-eyed beauty. "Have you ever seen such beauty? Even Miriam would find it a hard contest to win, and I thought I had never seen anyone as beautiful as she."

One dark eyebrow rose as Barak contemplated the two. "They're Samaritans, I think."

Adonijah's look turned from one of admiration to one of disgust. "Samaritans! And they are headed for our holy temple."

The two girls were indeed making their way across the street toward the Court of Gentiles.

A loud commotion from the other end of the street caused them to pause, and as Barak watched, an out-of-control chariot came careening down the street.

People screamed as they moved quickly out of the way, leaping and jumping like frightened frogs.

The two girls had moved swiftly to the side when they saw what was happening, but at the last moment, a little child moved into the street intent on reaching his mother on the opposite side. Unaware of the danger to himself, he toddled right into the path of the oncoming chariot.

Barak sucked in a sharp breath, but before he could react, the Samaritan girl ran into the street, snatched the child into her arms, and threw him to a man on the other side of the street. There was no way she could make it back to her side of the street. The horses from the chariot were only feet away.

Moving like lightning, Barak ran toward her, diving. Almost as though time had slowed down, Barak felt himself leave the ground, wrap his arms around the woman, and roll with her to the other side of the street.

Seconds later, the wind from the rushing chariot brushed across their inert forms. Barak shoved the girl's face hard into his chest, ducking his head at the same time, as he waited for the wheels to go by.

For a moment, all sound ceased, and then in the next instant, it rushed back upon them. People were running toward them, wildly gesticulating.

Barak slowly released the woman from his crushing grip, lifting himself up and away on his forearms until he could look down into her eyes. She lifted her head from his chest, her hazel eyes wide with wonder.

It seemed a long time they lay thus, searching each other's eyes, but it was only seconds later that the crowd reached them.

Several men helped Barak to his feet, brushing him down and praising God for his heroic deed, but Barak was trying to reach the girl to see if she was unharmed. For the time being, he had forgotten that she was a Samaritan.

Adonijah joined the crowd ringing the two. His face deathly white, he insistently questioned Barak about his well-being while trying to maintain his hold on the struggling lamb.

"I am well," Barak assured everyone around him.

He felt a light touch on his arm and turned to find the woman he had just saved staring solemnly up at him. "Thank you," she told him, her voice quivering. "I know that is inadequate, but I thank you anyway."

The frightening experience had turned her eyes from an almost brown to a shimmering green. It was this that brought home to Barak again that she was a Samaritan.

Nodding his head briefly, he turned to leave. What made him turn his head at the last moment he was unsure of, but as he did so, he saw the girl place a hand to her forehead and begin to reel giddily as she tried to walk away. The next moment, she was pitching forward, and Barak leaped to catch her.

Lifting her in his strong arms, he called for assistance. The girl's friend touched his arm, her eyes wide with fright.

"This way," she told him, indicating that he should follow.

By rights, he should just leave the woman here for someone else to deal with, but he knew he could not do that. Turning to Adonijah, he directed him to take the lamb to the temple for the sacrifice. "I will return as soon as I am able."

Adonijah was less than pleased. Never before had he been to the temple to offer sacrifice, and he was unsure just what was expected of him. Still, it was obvious that Barak expected to be obeyed. Besides, if they missed the sacrifice, they would also miss Passover. Nodding, he turned to do as he was told, and he began pushing his way through the slowly dispersing crowd of people.

Barak had a hard time keeping up with the girl he was following. His sandals slapped against the pavement stones, and with each step the girl was leading him farther from the temple. The crowd surged around him on all sides, and if some looked at him with astonishment, he chose to ignore them.

A moan reached him from the girl in his arms, and he found himself once again staring into the most unusual eyes he had ever seen. Her head lolled back against his arm, and when she spoke, he had to lean closer to hear.

"Where are you taking me?"

Barak's lip curled wryly. "I have no idea."

Before she had a chance to say more, the girl ahead of him turned and passed through the gates of the Upper City. Barak grew more uncomfortable as they passed large villas and tree-lined streets. The crowd had thinned as they entered this area where the wealthy lived.

"Put me down. I can walk now."

Ignoring her, Barak continued on, holding the girl firmly against her ineffectively weak struggles. He knew if he put her down, she would most likely find herself face forward on the ground. As she continued to strain against his hold, he was sorely tempted to do as she wished. The thought that he was even *touching* a Samaritan was enough to make him shake his head with disgust.

"Be still," he commanded, and it had the effect of bringing the girl to instant submission. Surprised, he glanced down at her again only to find himself pierced by fiery darts of anger shooting from incensed eyes.

Spoiled was the word that came to his mind.

The sun burned against his back, and beads of sweat began to form on his brow. Although the girl was light, she was becoming a leaden weight in his arms as they traveled. He was just beginning to think that he would indeed have to put her down, when the girl ahead stopped and opened a large iron gate leading into a courtyard of one of the larger villas.

Barak followed her through the gate and was instantly engulfed by the coolness of the shade trees lining the path to the door. Sighing with relief, he shifted the girl in his arms. He looked down at her again and found her attention on the house as they approached. Except for that one time, she had refrained from speech.

Before he reached the steps leading to the colonnaded entryway, the door was flung open and two men came down the steps.

The older man was overweight and puffed his way to Barak's side, while the younger man, dark and of obvious Arab distinction, ambled down the steps in his wake.

"Anna! Anna, what has happened?"

The older man's scruffy white eyebrows almost disappeared under his turban, his hands flailing about in agitation.

"Put her down." Although the Arab spoke with authority, Barak was unmoved. His chin set with instant stubbornness. There was no way he would allow an Arab to command him.

As the Arab drew closer, Barak felt the girl in his arms shrink against him and realized that she was afraid of the dark man. And with good reason, it would seem.

The Arab's small eyes glittered strangely as they went from the girl to Barak.

"Uncle," the other girl intervened. "Anna was almost run over by a chariot in the marketplace. This young man saved her life at great peril to his own."

Surprised, the old man faced Barak. "My son. How can I ever repay you?"

Slowly Barak allowed Anna to slide to her feet, but he kept a protective arm around her waist. The Arab was less than pleased. He moved to take Anna from Barak, but the girl twisted from his grasp and went to the old man instead. He wrapped her in beefy arms, cuddling her close.

"Father. I am all right now."

Again the old man's eyes sought out Barak. "What would you have as your reward?"

The Arab's sullen gaze wandered over Barak from head to toe. There was a strange animosity in his stare that took Barak by surprise. "You're a Jew, are you not?"

There was no disguising the sneer in the Arab's voice. Barak pulled himself up to his full height and froze the man with his look. Turning to the older man, he addressed himself to him. "I seek no reward. What I did, I would have done for anyone." He turned to leave, but the girl reached out, placing a detaining hand on his forearm.

"What is your name?"

Surprised, Barak glanced from her to where her hand lightly rested on his arm. With slow deliberateness, he pulled from her touch, giving her a speaking glance.

Her father nodded. "Yes. We would have a name to place on you."

For a minute, Barak thought of refusing. It was the small smile on the lips of the Arab that changed his mind. "I am Barak, son of Ephraim."

The old man smiled. "A fine Jewish name. I am Tirinus, of Sychar. And this is my daughter, Anna, and her cousin, Pisgah." He turned to the Arab. "This is a business associate of mine, Amman."

Amman moved forward, his look intentionally insulting. "And Anna's betrothed."

Anna's head snapped up, her mouth open in instant denial, but her father spoke first. "Well, not yet. But if everything goes well, soon that will be true."

The fact that Anna seemed less than enthusiastic about the situation, even frightened by it, bothered Barak for some unknown reason. His look went to each member of the group before settling once again on Anna.

"If you will excuse me now, I must return to the temple."

Ripping a huge ruby ring from his finger, Tirinus held it out to Barak. "Please. Take this as a memento of our sincerest thanks."

Barak's hands remained firmly at his sides. "I think not. Offer your thanks to Jehovah. Good day."

He turned on his heels and left them standing there. Four pairs of eyes watched him disappear through the gate and back into the street, one pair glittering with malevolence.

—

With something akin to panic, Anna watched the young Jew leave. She knew Amman's eyes were staring at her, and her skin crawled at the thought of having him touch her.

"Anna, Anna. The boy was right! Thank the Lord that He protected you today." Her father placed a loving arm around her and one around Pisgah, unthinkingly omitting Amman from their company.

The Arab followed them inside, his dark gaze moving from one to the other. Anna could feel his eyes on her back and shivered.

"Father, I am still a little shaky. I would like to go to my room now."

Tirinus became instantly concerned. "Of course, my dear. Amman was hoping to have your company, but I am sure he understands."

Amman smiled knowingly at Anna. Yes, she could see that he understood all too well.

"Rest assured," he told her, "I wish you all health. I will still be here when you have recovered." There was a threat in his voice that was missed by all save Anna. Amman's eyes promised retribution for her rejection of him.

Somehow Anna had to find a way to dissuade her father from making this marriage contract.

Pisgah followed Anna to her room. "Wait until Mother hears about this," she told her cousin. "Wasn't that the most romantic rescue you have ever seen?" She rolled her eyes, clutching her hands over her heart melodramatically. She dropped to the bed, sighing.

Anna refrained from comment.

"He was so handsome and brave."

Anna rolled her own eyes, exasperated at her cousin's continued romanticizing.

"And Amman was jealous," she crooned. "Oh, Anna. To think, you have two men fighting over you!"

"For goodness' sake, Pisgah. They were hardly *fighting* over me. Didn't you see the Jew's face when he realized I was from Sychar? He knows I'm a Samaritan."

Pisgah took instant offense. "What right has a Jew to condemn us?"

Anna shook her head, taking off her tunic and laying it on the foot of the bed. "It is the same old bias." She stared dreamily out the window. "But he was handsome."

Pisgah giggled. "Don't let Amman hear you say that."

Turning on her cousin, Anna clutched the girl's arm. "Don't you dare tell him!"

Surprised at the vehemence, Pisgah grew serious. "I would not. Besides, Amman has eyes only for you; surely you know that."

Anna kept her thoughts to herself. Amman had eyes only for her father's money, but no one would believe her if she told them so. Father thought the sun rose and set on Amman, and Pisgah thought him the most handsome man she had ever seen. Only Anna herself seemed to recognize the evilness of the man.

The light within her own soul rejected the darkness it saw in his, but since Father was not of the Way, he wouldn't understand. And although Pisgah's mother, Father's sister, was a child of Christ, Pisgah herself was not.

Jerusalem did that to some. Although it was a holy city, it had all the attractions of any large city. Pisgah saw no need of a Savior when she had the world at her feet. Both Anna and her aunt had agonized over it for some time.

"You don't wish to marry Amman, do you, Anna?"

The confusion on her cousin's face was amusing. Although seventeen, only two years her cousin's senior, Anna felt immeasurably older. Pisgah was like a little child, her curiosity making her reach out to grasp everything in her path. Anna feared for her soul.

"No, Pisgah, I do not." She wanted to add that she would as soon marry a serpent but resisted the impulse.

Anna poured some water from the pitcher into the basin on her washstand and began rinsing her face and hands, the cool water refreshing after the heat and dust of the city. It had been Pisgah's idea to go to the temple today. She had wanted to see the crowd of Passover pilgrims, and although Anna had felt it a bad idea, she had succumbed to her cousin's pleading.

"I don't see why not," Pisgah argued, returning to their earlier conversation. "He is so handsome! And when he looks at you, it takes my breath away."

It took Anna's breath away, too, but for an entirely different reason.

Anna pulled a clean tunic from the chest by her bed. The silky material draped becomingly over her full figure. Although Anna knew she had no looks to speak of, her figure was not displeasing. Still, she had no desire to have a man seek her out for such a reason.

She turned to her cousin. "Pisgah, I would like to take a nap. I am tired."

Instantly contrite, Pisgah got quickly to her feet. "I'm sorry, Anna. You must be devastated by your experience this afternoon. I will leave you now."

After her cousin departed, Anna crawled between her silken sheets. She cupped one hand under her cheek and stared out the opened window to the balcony beyond. A soft, warm breeze drifted over her, and she felt herself relax. Her thoughts were not on her cousin, nor even Amman. Instead, they focused on a strong young Jew who had looked at her as though she were some loathsome thing. The thought shouldn't bother her, but it did.

When she had first noticed Barak across the street, she had seen the way he was studying her. For the first time in her life, Anna had felt an instant attraction to a man, and her breathing had quickened at his dark-eyed scrutiny.

Only when his eyes lifted to hers had she seen the light of interest change to one of scorn. Many times had she encountered such contempt, but it had never bothered her. Until now. A lone tear trickled from the corner of her eye, coursing a path along her cheek.

Barak strode along the crowded streets of Jerusalem, oblivious to the crush of people. He frowned as he thought of the girl he had just left behind. Her eyes had been almost pleading, reminding him of the lamb he had brought for the temple only this afternoon.

He gritted his teeth. This was ridiculous, thinking about a Samaritan woman. It was bad enough that she was a Samaritan, but she was betrothed to that Arab! Was she insane? Being a Samaritan, it wouldn't surprise him.

Still, she had seemed genuinely afraid of the man. He could still feel her body curl into his when the Arab approached. Samaritan or no, he had felt instantly protective. Even now the thought of her warmth against him was hard to dislodge from his mind.

Adonijah would think him insane if he knew. Frankly he was beginning to think so himself. Perhaps the heat from the sun had affected his reasoning.

Those strange eyes! They shifted from brown to green. He had never seen anything like them. Only someone of mixed blood could have such eyes, because those of pure Jewish descent had only brown.

He made his way toward the Court of Gentiles, through the inner courts to the courtyard of women. Here the crowd thinned somewhat because it was forbidden to outsiders. The sign posted on the wall warned of punishment by death for any outsider who entered.

Barak continued up the fifteen curved steps that led to the Nicanor Gate in the west wall until he reached the Court of Israelites. Here the crowd was even thinner, for no women were allowed at this point.

Searching the crowd, Barak tried to locate Adonijah among the milling throng. The air grew heavy with the mixed scents of blood, incense, and charred animal fat. Cattle, goats, sheep, and doves added to the cacophony of sound.

Barak could see the barefooted priests across the stone pavement in the Court of Priests, their tired faces speaking of long hours among the slaughter.

Adonijah was making his way toward him among the crowd, and Barak was relieved to see that his sacrifice had already been made. They could take the meat and return to their families in plenty of time to observe the Passover feast.

The waning of the sun told Barak that sunset was not far away, and when the sun set, Passover would begin. His family was waiting for him outside the Jerusalem walls on the Mount of Olives.

For a brief moment, his searching gaze wandered toward the Upper City. Disgusted with himself, he turned with Adonijah and headed for the gate leading out of the city.

Chapter 2

Amman dropped the bag of coins on the table, sliding into a seat across from two rough-looking cutthroats. His dark eyes studied both men thoroughly until each man began to squirm under his perusal. All around, the boisterous crowd from the inn was lifting its voice in celebration.

"Here is the money. You know what to do?"

Both men nodded, the bolder of the two reaching for the bag. When Amman's hand came down across the money bag, the other man lifted his one good eye slowly until it encountered the Arab's. The patch where his other eye had been at one time gave him a sinister appearance, yet still the man swallowed hard when faced with the Arab's menacing glower.

"Don't fail me, Kasim. If you do, there will be nowhere for you to hide from me."

Kasim leaned back in his chair, giving back stare for stare. He turned to his companion. "What do you say, Uzzah? Should we accept this gentleman's *kind* offer?"

Uzzah glanced uneasily from one to the other, shrugging his shoulders. Kasim knew the cowardly fool would follow him wherever he led. He turned back to Amman.

"I'm curious, Amman. Why should you need to abduct the girl when you are going to marry her?"

The Arab's eyes darkened even further. There was no way he would tell this ignorant heathen the true reason behind his sudden desperate act. Amman knew that Anna despised him, and being the darling of her father, it was quite possible that she would eventually cajole him into forgetting about their marriage. No contract had been made yet.

Seeing the chance for old Tirinus's fortune to slip through his fingers had made Amman seek out the two men across from him. He had had dealings with them before, and he knew them well. Kasim might seem bold, but underneath all of his bravado, he was a coward.

"It is of no concern to you. Just do as you have been instructed. Remember, don't seize the girl unless you are told to."

Kasim lifted a finger, flicking it against his forehead in salute. "As you wish."

Getting up, Amman crossed the crowded room of the inn and opened the door. He gave one final glare to the two men before he disappeared into the velvety darkness.

"But Father, I don't wish to marry Amman!"

Tirinus stared at his daughter, nonplussed. It had never occurred to him that she would decline such a fine offer of marriage.

"But Anna," he wheedled. "Amman is such a fine man. And he *loves* you."

Anna turned to her aunt for help. If anyone would understand, it would be Aunt Bithnia.

"I'm curious, Tirinus," the older woman interrupted. She reached languidly for a date on the tray by her side. "Why would you choose an Arab for Anna instead of one of our own kind?"

Tirinus spread his hands apart, confusedly turning from one to the other. "He came to me and asked. He told me how much he loved Anna and that he wished to make her his wife."

"And you accepted, just like that?"

The old man's brows drew down in a frown, color beginning to creep into his cheeks. His face was beginning to take on the ruddy hue of his tunic. "Amman is an old and trusted friend. Of course I considered it. I haven't yet given my pledge, if that is what you are suggesting." He turned to Anna, and she could see the stubborn glint that came into his eyes. "Besides, Anna will do as she is told."

Anna recognized the look and knew where this conversation was headed. If she didn't do something quickly, she would be bound and married by morning. Hastily she spread a smile across her face. "Of course I will, Father."

Suspiciously he glanced from his daughter to his sister. He didn't trust the two when they were so agreeable. Seeing nothing in their innocent faces, Tirinus relaxed back against his cushions. "Good."

Bithnia smiled at her brother placatingly. "Of course she will, Tirinus. She has always been a dutiful daughter. It just seems so soon. She hasn't had time to really enjoy her childhood."

"Childhood! She's seventeen years old already, almost past the age of marriage. Honestly, Bithnia. I sent her here for you to teach her the duties of being a wife and mother, and instead, you want her to remain a child."

Knowing her brother, Bithnia offered her final suggestion. "She is your only child. Would you wish her to leave you so soon?"

Anna turned pleading eyes to her father. "I only wish to make you happy, Father. I only thought that I would like to spend a little more time with Pisgah and Aunt Bithnia before I. . .before I have children of my own."

Bithnia knew that Anna's words had hit their mark, and she applauded silently when she saw her brother's face pale. His own wife had died giving birth to Anna, and Tirinus had loved his wife with a passion. He had never found another to take her place, though there had been many willing to try. Instead, he had lavished his only child with the love he would have given her mother.

Tirinus cleared his throat. "Well. . .I. . .don't see any reason why you shouldn't have some time to enjoy yourself. I will speak with Amman."

"Father," Anna pleaded once more. "If we are betrothed, it will mean that Amman has all the rights of a husband."

Scratching his head, Tirinus pursed his lips together. "You are quite right."

"Quite right about what?"

Everyone jumped. No one had heard the Arab enter the room. A swift glance at his face assured Anna that he had overheard most of their conversation, though for some reason he was choosing not to admit to it.

Tirinus cleared his throat again. "Anna was just mentioning that she wished to spend more time with her aunt and cousin. I have decided it is a reasonable request, so I am going to postpone your engagement." Tirinus glanced quickly at Amman and then hastily looked away. "If your feelings for Anna are as strong as you say, then I am sure they will withstand the wait."

Not a muscle moved in the Arab's face. His very stillness seemed an ominous threat. Anna felt her throat go dry when his dark gaze fastened upon her. Suddenly his face creased into a smile, and he bowed low to Tirinus.

"As you say, my feelings can withstand the wait." When he rose again, his onyx eyes glittered menacingly, and Anna shivered in spite of the heat from the brazier.

He came to her, bowing over her and lifting her hand to his face. As his lips fastened upon her, Anna was hard pressed not to jerk herself away with revulsion. His dark beard and thin mustache tickled her skin as though a worm were crawling over it.

Anna and Bithnia exchanged looks. Tirinus, however, was smiling at Amman with relief. "You do not mind, my friend?"

Amman turned back to him. "Of course, I am disappointed, but her reasons are sound. Shall we set a date then when we will agree to consummate the arrangement?"

Anna's eyes flew to her father. He was nodding his head. "That is a sensible idea. Shall we say. . .next Passover?"

Again Amman went still. His fathomless eyes went slowly over Anna, taking in everything about her appearance. The bright blue of her tunic added a soft luster to her face, which flooded with color at Amman's steady scrutiny.

"A long time to wait, but I agree."

Weak with relief, Anna turned to her aunt. "You don't mind me staying with you that long, Aunt Bithnia?"

"Not at all, child. Pisgah will be pleased."

Bithnia was studying Amman, a slight frown marring her features. Unaware of her regard, Amman was in turn watching Anna.

Rising quickly to her feet, Anna told them, "I will tell Pisgah."

"A moment," her father commanded, and Anna stopped on the threshold.

"Yes, Father?"

"Amman and I will be returning to Sychar in the morning. I will wish you good-bye now."

Anna crossed the room to his side. She really did love her father and missed him when he was gone. She resented that she would have to be away from him again for such a long time because of Amman.

Leaning down, she kissed his cheek softly. "Take care. I love you."

Hurriedly she left the room before she lost her composure and began to cry. She made her way quickly up the stairs, turning when she reached the landing. She knew what she would find when she looked down. She could feel his evil eyes watching her even from that distance.

When her eyes met Amman's, she knew she would pay dearly for having thwarted him.

Twilight came, and with it the beginning of Passover. Barak glanced around the Seder table at those gathered there. Adonijah was to his left, Uncle Simon to his right, and his mother next to Uncle Simon. Miriam and her father were also among those present, and Barak could feel the Jewish girl's gaze upon him.

Since Barak's father had died several years before, Uncle Simon was the next in line as head of their family. Although Barak was considered a man at the age of twenty and five, he was still unmarried, so it fell to his nearest male relative to arrange a match. Barak and his mother lived alone and were quite content to do so, but Uncle Simon took his guardianship quite seriously.

Uncle Simon handed round the Paschal Lamb, matzah bread, endives, and chicory. He picked up the Haggadah and began to read. As always, Barak lost himself in the scriptures.

As the meal progressed, wine was passed around along with Barak's favorite fruit, mulberries. Uncle Simon again read from the scriptures. Unlike many of Barak's teachers, Uncle Simon always made the story come alive. Barak glanced briefly around the table to see if the others felt the same. It would seem so. Even little Josiah, Uncle Simon's youngest son, sat enthralled. Only Miriam's eyes were focused elsewhere.

Barak felt his impatience rise. The girl made her feelings all too apparent. He supposed he should feel flattered, and maybe in a way he did, but these discussions with Uncle Simon about setting a date for marriage to the girl were beginning to wear on his nerves.

She was, as Adonijah had said, a very beautiful girl. Her dark hair hung past her thighs, its sheen enhanced by the oil she used to keep it soft. Her brown eyes were dark and luminous, her bone structure perfect. Even her skin shimmered in the reflected glow of the torchlight, giving her a radiant appearance. She wore a bold red tunic that secretly Barak considered inappropriate, but Ahaz, her father, looked with nothing but favor upon his only child.

Adonijah glanced up, catching his look. A slight smile tipped up the corners of his mouth, and Barak felt himself color hotly. After denying a desire to be married, his friend had caught him gaping at the girl.

Still, it was Adonijah who loved Miriam, and if for no other reason than that, Barak could not bring himself to agree to a marriage. Adonijah had been his best friend since the boy had come to their home as an orphan with no family. Father had thought it a good idea since the Lord had seen fit to close Mother's womb and they had never had another child. The fieldwork was hard and required many hands, and Adonijah had been willing and eager. He quickly became a part of their family.

Every time Barak and Father had come to Jerusalem, Adonijah had had to stay behind to care for the crops and later to care for Mother. He never complained, but Barak knew Adonijah longed to see the great city.

Since Barak's home was many miles to the northwest, the trips to Jerusalem had been few and far between. During one of their trips, Mother had developed a raging fever, and when they had returned, they found her recovered from the fever but permanently paralyzed. This meant that someone needed to be with her at all times, and when it was necessary for Barak and his father to be away for various reasons, that job had fallen to Adonijah.

Barak smiled across at his mother, so caught up in the Exodus story. It was good to have her here with them. Uncle Simon had arranged for her to come, along with Miriam and her father—his way of showing Barak that they were all family, no doubt.

Both Uncle Simon and Miriam's father were wealthy men, and both thought a marriage between Barak and Miriam an excellent idea. That Miriam was agreeable to the idea only added to their anticipation. That Barak was not, they refused to consider.

The only thing that had kept his uncle from making the marriage contract had been Mother. She remembered the great love of her life, even though he had been dead some years now. To be in the same room with them was to feel the air alive with the fire of their love. Barak wanted that for himself, and his feelings for Miriam were nowhere close to being that intense. Mother understood and pleaded with Uncle Simon not to contract the marriage.

He had bowed to her wishes, but as Barak grew older and there was no sign of a desire to marry and have children, Uncle Simon's patience was growing thin. He felt it imperative that Barak have a son to pass on his name.

When Miriam was in a particularly flirtatious mood, Barak found his mind wandering into forbidden paths, and he considered what marriage to her would be like. Even now, her eyes were sending clear messages to him. Although he had never touched the girl, it was not for lack of opportunity.

For a moment, a pair of hazel eyes filled his mind with their vision. Barak sat up straighter, pushing the thought aside. To think of a Samaritan on this most holy of days was tantamount to sacrilege.

The meal finally came to a close, and Barak rose to his feet, intent on helping his mother to her tent. It would be seven more days before the celebration of Passover would end and they would return home. He hoped his mother could withstand such a lengthy stay.

Lifting his mother gently into his arms, he paused by the open door of the tent.

"We will see you in the morning," he told the room at large.

Miriam came quickly to her feet. "I will help you."

Without sounding ungracious, he had no way to refuse. Nodding his head, he turned and left the tent, Miriam close on his heels.

Barak left Miriam inside with his mother. Knowing it would take some time to prepare for the night, he quickly made his way from the tent and through the olive trees. He headed for a spot he had noticed earlier.

A large rock sat in the middle of a circle of the ancient trees. Barak sat down upon it, his eyes raised heavenward. A soft peace stole into his heart, and he relaxed for the first time in days.

The majesty of the gnarled old trees dwindled beneath the splendor of a million shimmering lights peering at him from above. He felt a longing to know better the one who had created such a beautiful universe.

In olden times, Jehovah had spoken directly to the heads of the households. Barak wondered for the hundredth time what it would have been like to hear the voice of God.

The Torah spoke of God walking in the garden with Adam and Eve. How was it possible to walk among the living God and still remain alive? Even Moses had hidden his face from the awesome majesty of that great being.

Why did God not speak to them now? The stars twinkled reassuringly back at him from the dark night sky. Incredible to think that each one had been given a name by Jehovah Himself.

Rustling in the brush alerted him to someone's presence, and it wouldn't take him more than one guess to figure out whose.

Miriam crossed the glade and sat down beside him. Instantly, Barak felt the peace of the preceding moment flee.

When she spoke, her voice was sultry. Evocative.

"I have been searching for you. Father is busy discussing something with Uncle Simon."

Barak tensed. "What are they discussing?"

She shrugged, her tinkle of laughter grating on Barak's nerves.

"Not our marriage, if that is what concerns you."

Glancing her way, Barak caught the shimmer of her liquid brown eyes. She leaned closer, and Barak could smell the scent of myrrh as it drifted to him on the slight breeze. His heart began to pound, and his palms grew clammy, not from desire but from fear.

It amazed him that Miriam could reduce him to such a state, but he knew that she held his future in the palms of her small hands. And she knew it, too. It was there in her eyes.

The blood of his warring ancestors flowed freely through his veins, and he reined in his suffocating panic. He would not give in to such anxiety.

"Had you not better return to the others?" he asked her quietly.

She leaned closer until the breath from her mouth fanned gently across his cheeks. "It is not my desire to do so."

Barak's eyes grew hard. For a Jewish girl to be so wanton was beyond the bounds of propriety. Still, Miriam was an only child and spoiled in the bargain. *Her father should really put a rein on her.*

Inexplicably he thought of the Samaritan girl. He had thought her spoiled also, but she was nothing like Miriam. Whereas Miriam's eyes shone with passion, Anna's eyes had reflected only her innocence.

Barak was unsure just what would have happened had not Adonijah chosen that moment to come looking for him. His friend's look went from one to the other.

"Your uncle Simon wishes to see you."

Relieved, Barak rose quickly to his feet. "I am coming."

Miriam was not pleased with the interruption. She threw Adonijah a beguiling smile and patted the rock next to her. "Come and keep me company, Adonijah, until Barak returns."

Sensing trouble, Adonijah smiled diffidently. "I cannot. Barak's uncle wishes my presence, as well."

Throwing them both a pout, Miriam got to her feet and followed them reluctantly from the trees. Uncle Simon was waiting at the opening to his tent.

"Both of you, come inside." He smiled at Miriam, and she returned the favor. Even Miriam would not dare enter where she knew she was not bidden. She waved lightly, going to the tent shared by the women.

Barak and Adonijah made themselves comfortable on the rugs scattered on the ground. Lifting inquiring eyes to his uncle, Barak waited for him to make his wishes known.

Uncle Simon's look passed from one young man to the other. What he saw pleased him much. Both were fine to look at, strong of body from their work in the fields, handsome by the Lord's design. Miriam was not the only one interested in his nephew, nor for that matter, young Adonijah. He would have no trouble making them both a fine match.

A frown puckered the old man's forehead. Barak was being most difficult about this matter with Miriam. Why he was balking at the marriage, Simon couldn't understand. The girl was a sultry beauty and would be a pleasure to spend the long nights with. If she were a bit older and he were a bit younger, he would seek a match for himself.

But that was not what he had brought the young men here to hear. Clearing his throat, he sat down across from them.

"I know that you two were looking forward to spending some time in the city, but something has come up that demands my attention. Mine and Ahaz's."

Barak lifted a brow at the mention of Miriam's father. For some reason, he felt his insides grow cold.

"What I am saying is that I need one of you to stay with Tamar."

Relieved, Barak leaned back against the throw pillows. "I will stay with Mother. That is no problem. Adonijah has been longing to spend some time in the city, and I would be glad for him to go. He can purchase the things we need for the return trip."

"Good." Simon sighed with relief. "Then that is taken care of. Miriam will be staying with you, of course."

Adonijah could sense that Barak was loath to agree to such a thing. His eyes twinkled with mischief. "Perhaps it would be best for you to go, Barak," he told them in what he hoped was a suitably regretful voice. "I am not certain that I would get what we need. You have a better working knowledge of the fields than I."

Barak threw his friend a grateful look. "Perhaps you are right."

Simon regarded them suspiciously but refrained from comment. "Whichever. Ahaz and I will be leaving early to try and avoid the crowd."

"Where will you go, Uncle?"

Without looking at them, Simon opened the tent flap. "We have to make arrangements for tomorrow's fire sacrifice, and we wish to speak with the temple priests about a contract." He left them gaping at his retreating back.

Chapter 3

Barak wandered among the streets of Jerusalem, careful to stay within the mile boundary prescribed by Jewish law for Passover. Although the streets were still bustling with activity, they were much less dense than the day before. Most of the Jewish community would be staying within their own homes or visiting with one another since it was forbidden to do any work during this time.

Still, there was much to see among the rousing babble of pagan voices. This holy time held no special significance for other than Jew.

Briefly Barak wondered about the Samaritan woman. For her to be here in Jerusalem was odd, for the Samaritans held Mt. Gerizim as their sacred place of worship instead of the City of David. Surely she should be at Shechem to celebrate Passover.

Barak had no place in mind to go, but he found himself outside the temple walls gazing up at the magnificent structure that Herod had built. Uncle Simon and Ahaz were somewhere among the throng of people going to and fro, and Barak had a pretty good idea of why they were there.

They had left the encampment shortly after first light, and Barak had followed soon after, not sure exactly what he was going to do with himself but equally sure he couldn't remain in camp with Miriam.

He had looked forward to this trip to Jerusalem, anxious and excited to show his friend something of the great city. He felt a slight pang of remorse, realizing that it should have been him, Barak, attending to his own mother and not Adonijah.

Still, Adonijah seemed to understand. Barak felt the noose of marriage tightening about his neck, inch by inch. He frowned heavily. Marriage to Miriam was not something he would desire, but he knew he would obey Uncle Simon's dictates.

But would he ever feel the great love his parents had known? Somehow he doubted it. More likely he would wonder if his wife were being faithful to him.

He stopped to watch an Arab merchant with a little monkey on his shoulder. The little creature was drawing quite a crowd with its antics. One tiny, hairy paw snaked out, quickly grabbing a turban off a man who had gotten a little too close.

The man howled in anger, but the crowd's laughter encouraged the little monkey to place the turban on his own head. Leaping off his master's shoulder, the creature began to run around the merchant's table.

The chase was on, and there was instant pandemonium. Barak found himself forgetting his own troubles as he was caught up in the laughter around him and the antics of the little monkey.

The monkey's master chased his pet, the turbanless man close behind. When the monkey disappeared down an alley, Barak decided maybe it was time to help. He paused but a moment, trying to decide if this would constitute work or not. Shrugging his shoulders, he offered his apologies to Jehovah in advance if he was, indeed, breaking Passover law.

The crowd that had formed huddled around the mouth of the alley, but no one except Barak offered any assistance. After climbing to the top of a canvas awning, the diminutive monkey gazed down at them with its beady little eyes, the turban perched on his head giving him a comical appearance. It took the Arab merchant but a moment to coax the beast down, all the while offering apologies to the man beside him, who jammed his turban back onto his head and strode away.

Chuckling, Barak was about to turn back to the market street when he noticed a familiar figure enter the alley from the opposite direction. So intent was the man on his destination, he failed to notice Barak standing only twenty feet away.

There was something so furtive, so ominous about the way the Arab moved that Barak slowly drifted toward where the man had disappeared. Barak knew he had no reason to snoop on Amman's business, but something drove him forward until he was outside the door to an apartment that opened onto the alley.

He could hear voices from within, but they were muted by the closed door. Noticing a window just a short piece from the door, Barak moved closer and was finally able to distinguish what was being said.

"The time has come."

Barak recognized the lazy drawl of Amman's voice.

"You want us to abduct the girl?"

The second voice was unknown to Barak. He tried to see into the room, but at this angle it was impossible.

"That is correct. Her father and I will be leaving momentarily, which will keep any suspicion from me. We shall be returning to Sychar. You can reach me there."

"Where would you have us take the girl?"

There was silence for several seconds. "I will leave that to you. I'm sure, Kasim, you will know just what to do."

Barak felt himself go cold. Were these brigands talking about the Samaritan girl, Anna?

There was a sneer in Kasim's voice. "I take it the girl was unwilling."

When he answered, Amman's voice was laced with anger. "She has convinced her father to wait until next Passover before making the contract for our marriage."

"But that is only a year, Amman. If you are assured of the marriage and Tirinus's fortune, why abduct the girl?"

Barak could hear the reluctance in Kasim's voice.

"I need the money *now*! Now listen to me. I will be with Tirinus when you send word of the ransom. Tirinus would pay any amount for that foolish girl, but ask only for the amount I have told you. Remember, I will be with Tirinus when he receives the note."

There was a threat in the words that was hard to miss.

Barak could hear someone moving toward the door. He slipped hastily back to the street, barely rounding the corner before the door opened and Amman moved out. "Don't fail me, Kasim," Amman ordered menacingly.

Barak watched him disappear around the other end of the alley. A moment later, two other men exited the building. They came Barak's way. As they rounded the corner, Barak leaned nonchalantly against the building and watched them as they passed him.

The smaller of the two men turned to his companion. "Kasim, what will we do? I don't like this. I don't like it at all." There was no denying that Kasim's partner was hesitant about the act they were about to commit.

"Listen to me," Kasim hissed. "You know that Amman is a powerful man. He has eyes and ears all throughout Jerusalem. Be assured, Uzzah, if we fail him, they will find us in some alley somewhere with a knife in our backs."

Uzzah's face paled considerably. Although they kept their voices low, Barak had no trouble hearing their whispered comments. He continued to watch them, their heads close together as they wandered down the street.

Now what to do. He couldn't go and warn the girl's father because no doubt Amman would be with him. Perhaps he could go to the girl herself, but it was possible that Amman would still be at Tirinus's house. And if what Kasim had said was true, it was quite possible that if he asked for help he would find himself instead in the enemy's camp.

Aggravated with himself, he took a moment to question as to his reasons for interfering in the first place. They were Samaritans, for goodness' sake. They deserved whatever they received for having profaned the name of the great Jehovah!

Despite his reasoning, Barak found himself following Kasim and his cohort. If he could keep an eye on the two, perhaps he could keep tragedy from striking. Although he had no sure plan, he was confident that he could find a way to warn the girl. But that was all he would do. Let her father take care of his own.

He drifted along in the wake of the two, carefully avoiding their searching glances as they looked around them. When they stopped just outside the walls to the Upper City, Barak stopped also, moving to a position where he could keep an eye on them.

Kasim pulled a torn tunic from inside his other tunic and dropped it over his head. Bending to the street, he lifted a handful of dirt and began rubbing it on his face and arms.

His partner also pulled some rags from his tunic and wrapped them around his leg until it looked as if he were a cripple.

Kasim handed his partner a plate, and both men settled themselves near the wall. It looked for all the world as though they were two beggars, one blind and one lame, merely begging alms on the street.

Before long, Tirinus and Amman came down the street. The older man paused beside the two beggars and gave them each a coin. Reluctantly Amman followed suit. The look on the faces of the two brigands was amusing as Tirinus and Amman walked away. If they had any conscience whatsoever, they would feel guilty right about now; but it would seem if they did have one, it was buried deep inside them, because they pocketed the coins and continued their stance.

How long he stood there Barak didn't know, but the sun was high in the sky and his stomach began to rumble with hunger. Perspiration clung to his skin, and even in the shade, it was extremely hot.

He was just beginning to wonder why he was bothering when he noticed a woman moving toward them. The glint of the sun off her necklace bespoke of her identity long before Barak could make out the features of her face. Her tread was graceful and sure, and as she came closer, Barak could see the slight smile tilting her lips.

The two across the street were watching her intently as she came nearer. They shifted their positions ever so slightly.

Launching himself off the tree where he leaned, Barak moved to intercept the young woman. As he drew closer, Anna glanced up, her eyes going wide in surprise.

Before she had a chance to speak, Barak took her by the arm. Out of the corner of his eye, he noticed the other two had risen to their feet.

"My lady." Barak almost choked on the title. "Your father sent me to see you safely to the market."

It wasn't a lie exactly. Surely it was the Lord who had led him to that alley this morning, and even Samaritans claimed Abraham as their father.

Anna's mouth had dropped open at his announcement. Now she lifted puzzled, searching eyes to his face.

Barak squeezed her arm ever so slightly, his glance flicking to the side. The confusion never left her face, but she was obedient to Barak's urging as he pulled her forward.

A look behind told Barak that they were being followed. He lowered his voice until it was a mere whisper.

"Those two men are not beggars. I will explain as soon as I get you out of here."

Barak had presumed that the two would give up their chase when the market came into view, but they showed no signs of doing anything of the kind. He took them on a meandering course, thinking that he could shake them in the crowds, but no matter how hard he tried, Barak couldn't lose them. Finally he pulled Anna into the Court of Gentiles and mingled with the crowds gathered there. He saw Kasim and Uzzah follow, but the crowds were so thick that the two couldn't locate Barak and Anna immediately.

Barak watched the two as they moved among the people, searching.

"What is happening?"

His look focused on Anna mere seconds before returning to their pursuers.

"Shh. I'll tell you later. Just do as I say."

Anna's lips set mutinously. "I won't do anything you say or go any farther with you until I know what is going on."

Angrily Barak jerked his head toward Kasim. "Do you see those two men?"

She scrutinized the people coming and going before she finally caught sight of Kasim. Her eyes went wide. "The beggars. They followed us?" she questioned, studying the two from the concealment of the group of pilgrims gathered around the rabbi.

"They intend to abduct you."

Her mouth dropped open, and she turned puzzled eyes to Barak. "That's ridiculous! How do they even know who I am? And why should they wish to kidnap me? And how do you know such a thing?"

Ignoring her for the moment, Barak saw the two men slip to the entrance and take up guard.

"Thunder! Now we will never get by them!"

Anna jerked her arm from his punishing grip. "Barak. Tell me what is going on!" she demanded, rubbing the spot where she knew bruises would appear by morning. She knew Barak had no idea that he was hurting her. His attention had been solely on the two beggars.

"Stay here," he hissed. She watched him as he slipped away to get a closer look at the two. His dark beard was attractive against his swarthy skin, and although he looked much like any of the other Jews surrounding the area, his size distinguished him from others. It was no wonder the two beggars had not accosted him when he took her from their presence, at least if what he had said was true. It would take someone of stronger character than those two appeared to have to tangle with such a muscular specimen of manhood.

Barak returned to her side. "Come with me."

They wandered around the swarming, chattering people until they were not far from the gate. Barak opened his mouth to say something, when suddenly two other men appeared at Kasim's side. They whispered together furiously, Kasim gesticulating madly.

Anna drew in her breath sharply, and Barak turned to her, lifting one brow in question.

"That's Micah. He is a servant in my aunt's house."

Barak's lips pulled down into a frown. He looked around at the large group of people, thinking. Finally he spotted someone he knew, and an idea began to form in his mind.

"Stay here," he told Anna again. "And stay out of sight."

She watched him slip unobtrusively among the crowd until he was at the side of a young man. They greeted each other warmly, clasping forearms. Barak began talking quickly, and the other young man's eyes went to the ragtag group at the gate. Even from that distance, Anna could see the young man's eyes darken. Nodding his head, he moved toward the group while Barak returned to her side.

"Come on."

"Where are we going? What are you going to do?" she asked as he pulled her hurriedly along.

"Just do as I tell you, okay?"

She wanted to argue, but she bit her lip firmly instead. Why she should trust this Jew when he so obviously despised her was something she couldn't fathom. Still, trust him she did, even though she had known Micah far longer. It was hard to believe that her aunt's servant meant any harm to her.

They were hidden behind a group of people who were about to exit the temple area. As they drew closer to the gate, Anna noticed the young Jew Barak had been speaking with move closer to the beggars. His eyes briefly met Barak's, and at a nod the young Jew began to berate Kasim in a loud, angry voice.

Immediately people began turning their way, and Anna could see Kasim and his friends draw closer together as they began to argue back with the Jew. The opening this interchange had created allowed Barak the time he needed to slip through the gate unnoticed.

He quickly put distance between them and those at the temple, hurrying them along the still crowded streets. Finally Anna could stand it no longer. Jerking her arm from his grasp, she turned suspicious eyes to her would-be rescuer.

Her face wrinkled in confusion. "I don't understand any of this."

Barak sighed, rubbing a hand around to the back of his neck in agitation. "Look. It has to do with Amman. But we can't stop now for me to explain it all."

At the name of the Arab, Anna's face went pale. "What about Amman?"

"I overheard him plotting with those two beggars in the market. From what I can tell, he's paying those two to abduct you. He needs your father's money, and since you obviously decided not to marry him, he determined to get it another way."

"You heard him say this?"

"I did."

He studied her a long time before turning away. It was obvious that she didn't altogether trust him, and in reality she had no reason to do so. Even now Barak wondered what had come over him.

As he turned from her, Anna could see the same puzzlement she was feeling mirrored in Barak's eyes. She laid a hand gently against his, and seemingly of its own volition, his own hand turned and curled around hers for a moment before he dropped her fingers as though they had burned him.

"Thank you again," she told him softly. "Twice you have saved my life."

He turned back to her, and she could tell he was angry. "I haven't saved you yet. You need to decide whether you wish my help or not."

It was obvious that he wanted nothing to do with her. She should just turn and walk away. Hurt, she turned from him, looking back the way they had come. "Can't we return to my aunt's villa? My aunt will take care of me."

"Amman is an evil man," he told her seriously. "I would not trust your aunt's ability to care for you against someone such as he. It might be safer for all of you, your aunt and cousin, as well, if you don't return there."

Anna felt her stomach tighten. Surely her aunt and Pisgah would come to no harm. Surely Amman's power didn't extend that far. Still, there was always that chance. She had heard stories of Amman through others, but her father had called them preposterous lies. Anna believed every one of them.

"What can we do?"

Barak turned to face her. "I have an idea, but you will have to trust me."

Anna sighed, her shoulders drooping. There was too much happening too fast, and she was unable to think clearly. Her eyes lifted to his in bewilderment, but she could read nothing in his face. It was as though it was carved of granite.

"What would you have me do?"

She saw his shoulders relax. "Come with me."

Barak led her among the winding streets until he reached a poorer section of the city. He was almost sure Kasim wouldn't follow them here. He would probably expect Anna to return to the villa.

Anna trailed him to an abandoned house. Barak glanced furtively behind them until he was sure they were not being followed. Quickly he slipped to the back of the house.

"I will hide you here until I can return for you. Give me time, but know that I will return."

Anna shivered as she peered into the unused cistern he indicated. The walls were still sturdy but beginning to crumble around the edges. "In there?"

He nodded, awaiting her decision. Again their eyes met. Could she really trust him? The hatred of the Jewish people toward the Samaritans was well defined. Had been for years. Still, there was something in his eyes that spoke to her soul. Anna was the first to look away. "As you wish."

Barak helped her into the small well. "No one will bother you here. This was my uncle Simon's house many years ago. He still owns it, but he never comes here, so it is considered abandoned. You will be safe until I return."

His head disappeared before she could respond. Crossing her arms, she began rubbing them, although it was far from cold. It suddenly occurred to her that since Barak was a Jew, he might well have plotted this whole thing. Jews had been killing Samaritans for many years now, and vice versa. But their war was not her war. She wanted only to live in peace. Groaning, she dropped to the ground. "Oh, Jesus. Master. Help me."

When Barak returned to the marketplace, he could find no sign of Kasim. He made his way through the gate into the Court of Gentiles and found Bashan waiting for him.

"You were able to get away with the girl?"

Barak had neglected to inform his friend that Anna was a Samaritan, or more than likely, he would have had the same reaction as Barak had to begin with. Even now it was incredible to him how his opinion had been altering as he tried to help the girl.

"I did. Where are the others?"

Nodding his head, Barak followed the direction of Bashan's gaze. Micah and the other one who had come with him were mingling among the crowd. There was no sign of Kasim.

"Where is the Arab?"

Bashan grinned. "He was forced to flee when the crowd turned on him."

"What did you say that caused such a reaction?"

The grin spread, and brown eyes sparkled. "I accused his friend of leprosy and trying to hide it beneath his rags. He made haste to remove the rags, but when the people saw that he wasn't really a cripple, they became even more angry. Never have I seen two men move so fast."

Barak clutched his friend's shoulder. "Thank you, my friend. Now I will see what I can do to help the girl."

"Do you need any more help? Is there someone we should tell?"

Barak shook his head. "No, leave it to me. But if you would, keep an eye on those two. I will return this way soon to see what they are doing."

Barak left the temple area and made his way quickly toward the Upper City. He didn't understand what drove him on, but a voice inside his head kept spurring him forward. For some reason, he had to help Anna.

When he reached the walls of the Upper City, there was no sign of Kasim. Barak made his way to the gate of Tirinus's house or, according to Anna, her aunt's.

He peeked in the gate and saw the boy Micah pacing in the courtyard. Jerking back, Barak quickly turned and hurried away before he could be seen.

Now what? Who on earth could he go to for help? How far did the Arab's influence extend?

He needed to hurry. He couldn't leave the girl in the cistern long. He hated to leave her there in the first place, but he knew that except for Kasim and his friend, no one knew who he was. He could move more easily on his own.

Forget going to Uncle Simon for help. He would take one look at the girl and know that she was a Samaritan, and then all the heavens would break open. No, far better for him to do this on his own.

As he was passing the Antonia fortress, Barak spotted Kasim among a group of soldiers. They were listening to him intently, nodding as he handed each man a coin. Barak leaned back against the wall, trying to decide his next move. There was no telling what arrangements the Arab had made with the Roman guards. He would have to move carefully.

Hastening back the way he came, he dodged among the throngs of people still on the streets. As he flew along, he was devising a plan, but he would have to enlist his mother's assistance. He only hoped that she would understand, because he knew that Uncle Simon would not.

The sun was growing lax in the sky as he finally reached his destination. Dusk was fast approaching, and the first day of Passover was nearing an end. The others would expect him to return soon for the evening meal. His stomach rumbled loudly at the thought, and he realized that he hadn't eaten since early morning.

He crossed to the well, leaned over the side, and peered into the darkness. The well was completely empty.

Chapter 4

As Anna watched Barak disappear, she felt a terrible sense of dread. What if he didn't return? She felt abandoned, much like this old well.

She offered up a prayer for her own safety and the safety of those of her aunt's house. Then, while she was at it, she offered one for Barak, as well. If Amman ever found out about the young Jew, there was no telling what might happen.

Drawing her knees up to her chest, she wrapped her arms around them and buried her head in her tunic. Aunt Bithnia would be appalled if she could see Anna now, her tunic torn and dirty.

Sniffing back tears, Anna berated herself for leaving her aunt's house without an escort. Pisgah had come down with some stomach ailment, and now Anna wondered if that might have been deliberate. Her eyes grew dark with suppressed fury when she thought of her young cousin in so much pain, knowing that it could have been planned so that she, Anna, would go to the marketplace on her own.

She remembered now that Micah had offered to go with her. Shivering at the thought of what might have happened if she hadn't slipped out unobserved, she threw back her head and glared at the sky overhead.

"Protect them, Lord. Your power is greater than Amman's."

How long she sat there among the coolness of the cistern, she had no idea, but she was beginning to grow alarmed. The sun was descending rapidly, and the well was growing colder by the minute. She shivered. Had something happened to Barak? Maybe this had been a plan after all between him and Amman.

No, she could not believe that. His eyes were too open, too honest. It just couldn't be. But then again, she would have said the same of Micah.

For a moment, she grew still as she thought she heard the sound of voices close beside her. Listening carefully, she strained to hear any sound of human occupation. The only sounds that drifted back to her were the shrill calls of the kites as they circled overhead.

Before long she did, indeed, hear voices. From the sound of them, there were two men close by. She couldn't discern what they were saying, only the sound of their voices.

She didn't realize that she was holding her breath until the voices grew fainter, and she let it out in a rush. She had been hoping that it was Barak, and now that she knew it was not, the tears began to come. Rubbing at them angrily, she picked up a rock from beside her and threw it against the cistern wall. A shower of rock and dirt rained down upon her, and she covered her head with her arms.

"Foolish well," she cried.

A moment later, two bearded faces peered over the sides of the well. Alarmed, Anna could only stare openmouthed as a large man frowned down at her. He looked to be in his late fifties, but he had the build of a much younger man.

The man beside him was slightly younger, his brown hair graying at the temples. Both men tried to peer past the gloom to get a good look at her.

"What are you about, woman? Come out of there."

Realizing there was nothing else she could do, Anna got to her feet and allowed the men to lift her out.

"Do you know her, Simon?" the younger man asked.

"I have never seen her before in my life, Ahaz." Turning back to the girl, he studied her thoroughly. His eyes missed little in their inspection, and his voice gentled.

"You wear the Star of David. You are a Jew. How come you to be here?"

Anna wondered how to explain her presence. She cast about in her mind for some explanation that would seem feasible.

Simon studied the girl, her head down-bent. It was obvious that she was not destitute. Although her tunic was torn and ragged, it was of fine quality. He frowned again. Something was not right here. And how had the girl gotten into the cistern in the first place?

Anna knew that if she lifted her eyes these men would know at once that she was a Samaritan. Her necklace proclaimed her Hebrew heritage; but she was not a Jew, and these men would know it. Just as Barak had.

She realized that wearing her necklace brought her trouble with the Jewish community, but it was a favorite of hers given to her by her father many years ago. Now she regretted the desire to wear it among the crowds of Jerusalem.

Although her father was a Samaritan, he was not held in high esteem by the leaders of Sychar. They considered themselves God's chosen people, but they forgot how in times past they had prostituted themselves with Gentiles of captivity. When Sargon the Second deported most of the Jews living in Samaria, Gentile captives were brought in to settle the region. Anna had no doubt that that was where her unusual eye coloring had come from. The Jews of Jerusalem despised the Samaritans, and the feeling was surely mutual.

But her father was a merchant, and a wealthy one at that, and he had learned over the years to recognize people as people and not nationalities. He showed no discrimination among any of the people he served. Amman was evidence of that. Her father would buy and trade with any who chose to do so. She was proud of him for this.

"Girl?"

The brusque question brought her back to the present.

"I am sorry, sir. I wanted only to be alone for a time. I did not know there was anyone living here."

Simon cleared his throat and studied the down-bent head. "It is of no matter. You were right; there is no one who lives here now. However, my friend here was thinking of buying it as a wedding present for his daughter. Tell me, would a woman find favor in such a house?"

Surprised that he would ask her opinion, Anna flicked a glance around her from under lowered lids.

The house seemed sturdy, yet it was dilapidated from lack of use. It would take time to fix it up to be habitable, but it could be done. She wondered if the woman in question would like to do such.

"It. . .it seems adequate."

The only reason Simon had asked the girl such a question in the first place was to try and relieve her of the fear he could sense as she trembled before him. But her hesitation over the property intrigued him. Would a woman such as Miriam find favor among such surroundings?

"You would like such a house?"

Anna didn't know how to answer him. If she was marrying a man she loved, she could enjoy living here with him and together fixing it up to be a home. The place was much larger than many others in the area, even if it was in a poor section of town.

Since her father was a wealthy man, Anna knew she wouldn't have to consider such a dwelling, but she would gladly give up all of her father's wealth if she could be allowed to marry someone she truly loved. She would be more than glad to live here.

"I cannot speak for your friend's daughter, but I can find no fault with this place."

Ahaz spoke for the first time. "I agree, Simon, though I would much rather find her a place among the Upper City."

Simon shook his head slowly. "Barak would never agree to that."

The name instantly caught Anna's attention. *Barak.* Surely there were at least a hundred Jews by that name, but hadn't Barak said that this place belonged to his uncle Simon?

"Leave that to Miriam. She will change his mind."

Anna's head jerked up at the suggestive tone. Before she could think to avert her gaze, Simon glanced back at her. Never had Anna seen a man's eyes grow so cold. Even Barak had looked nothing like this.

"You are a Samaritan," he snarled, and Ahaz turned on her.

"A Samaritan?" When Anna didn't deny it, he drew himself up with haughty disdain. "Be gone from here, woman. Go back to your idol-worshiping, infidel brethren."

Anna felt the heat creep into her cheeks, her eyes growing dark with anger. She wanted to argue, to berate these men for their attitudes, but at the look on their faces, she truly feared for her life. Quickly she turned and walked away, refusing to look back.

She hadn't gone very far when she stopped. Placing a shaking hand on her forehead, she tried to think what to do.

Barak would return and find her gone. Taking a deep breath, she straightened her shoulders. She would go back to Aunt Bithnia. Since Barak hadn't returned, she began to believe that he had played a malevolent prank on her. Well, if he had wanted to frighten her, he had certainly succeeded.

She made it as far as the Hasmonaean Palace before she realized that she was being followed. Her thoughts had been in turmoil over Barak and his deception. The sadness she felt at knowing that he was betrothed she chose not to think about. It was silly to give more credence to her feelings than they deserved.

Feeling as though she were being watched, she turned to look behind her. There, not thirty feet away, was the man who was with Micah at the temple this morning. She let her gaze pass over him as though she didn't recognize him. It was not far to the gate leading into the Upper City, but if Micah truly was involved in something sinister, she couldn't take a chance on going back to Aunt Bithnia's.

Biting her lip in indecision, she debated going home or trying to lose her tracker among the alleys and streets here. A crowd of laughing women heading for the Pool of Siloam briefly hid Anna from the eyes of her pursuer. Taking the opportunity, she ducked behind them and darted into a nearby alley.

Her headlong flight took her in and out among the houses between the gate that led to the temple and the road that would lead to Bethlehem. She had no idea where she was going; her only purpose was to escape from her stalker.

She could see the main street as she passed another alleyway. She froze, her heart pounding in sudden fear. The man named Kasim had joined the other, and both were searching and asking questions of the people nearby.

Before long they headed toward the alley where she was hiding. Sucking in a frightened sob, she turned to retrace her steps. She darted in and out of alleys and doorways, always dodging her pursuers by less than a few steps. It occurred to her that if anyone saw her they might very well think her a lunatic, with her hair disheveled and her tunic torn and dirty.

She knew she hadn't been spotted by the men as of yet, but it was only a matter of time. She began to see enemies everywhere she turned and realized her panic was making her paranoid.

Her legs began to ache, and her mind grew weary. She began tripping over her own feet. Once, she landed on her hands and knees, and for a moment, she thought she could not go on. But only for a moment. Setting her lips stubbornly, she got to her feet and struggled on.

When she came to the end of the alley she was hiding in, she looked across from her and saw Kasim only a street away. His one dark eye met hers, a slow smile of triumph lighting his features. He started in her direction only to be stopped as a caravan of camels came between them.

Anna took the opportunity afforded her and hurried back in the direction she had just traversed. As she was passing a doorway, a strong arm snaked out, pulling her into a small, dark landing of an apartment building. She opened her mouth to scream, but a hand was shoved roughly against her mouth, a man's body effectively pinning her to the wall. The door slammed behind them.

"Shh. Be quiet, it's only me."

Recognizing the voice, Anna went still. *Barak.* Her heart stopped and then thundered on again. How had he come to be here? Relieved, she leaned against him, her legs trembling so much they barely supported her.

Barak released her mouth but kept her pinned firmly to the wall, his body acting as a shield against anyone who might enter the building after them. They could hear pounding footsteps outside, and after several moments of silence, Barak released her and moved away.

"Let's wait here until we are sure they're gone."

All of the confusing thoughts about this Jew came back to her with a vengeance. "You didn't return like you said you would."

She couldn't see his face in the dark, but she felt him move. His voice was filled with aggravation. "I did return, but you weren't there. Why did you leave?"

Anna was able to keep the hurt from her own voice but not the anger. "Your uncle ordered me to leave."

He moved closer, and Anna could see his face in a pinprick of light coming through a hole in the wall. "Uncle Simon? What was he doing there? He hasn't been to that house in years!"

"He was negotiating a sale to a friend of his. It would seem his daughter is about to be married and he wanted to buy her a house."

Barak went so still that Anna thought the others had returned, and her heart began to pound. She sighed with relief when he asked her, "What did they say?"

"Your uncle seems to think that you will not like living in the Upper City, but his friend thinks that Miriam will be able to persuade you."

Breathing out harshly, Barak jerked a hand through his dark hair, tumbling it into disorder. "By all the prophets! I knew he was thinking this."

For the moment, Barak seemed to have forgotten Anna. She allowed him time to think but grew impatient as the moments ticked by.

"Can we leave now?"

"What? Oh, yes."

He moved to the door, opening it quietly and peeking outside. There was no sign of either Kasim or any of the others. Barak glanced uneasily at the lengthening shadows. It was almost sundown. What was he to do? He couldn't take Anna back to Uncle Simon's camp, and he couldn't leave her here. From what he had seen of Kasim's activities, he didn't think it would be prudent to return her to her aunt's villa, either.

"I have to get you out of the city."

"Out of the city! Are you demented? And then what? If I go home to my aunt, she can contact the authorities."

Barak closed the door of the apartment landing behind them, his gaze searching the streets around them. "I saw Kasim talking to the Roman guards today. Money exchanged hands, but I have no idea what story Kasim might have told them. I'm not certain who to trust."

Barak took her arm and led them toward the Golden Gate. He had to reach the Mount of Olives and see his mother, while at the same time avoiding Uncle Simon. But what to do with Anna?

"I need to find someplace that it would be safe to leave you until I can speak with your aunt."

She stopped shortly, bringing herself around to face him. "Why are you doing this? Why are you trying to help me? You don't even know me."

Barak was drawn into the depths of those intriguing eyes. Was it any wonder that the Jewish people had intermarried with heathen women if they all had such hypnotic power in their eyes? Giving himself a mental shake, he turned her around and continued walking. He really had no answer as to his reasons for wanting to help this Samaritan.

"I wouldn't wish harm to come to any human being," he finally told her.

Barak could hear the anger in her voice when she challenged him. "Since when have Jews seen Samaritans as *human*?"

In the beginning, he had felt the same about this woman. Somehow his feelings were evolving, and he no longer saw her in the same way. Feeling slightly guilty, Barak ignored her question. "Is there anywhere I can take you that would be safe?"

She thought for a moment, and suddenly her face was lit by a smile. "I have a friend. He will let me stay with him."

For a moment, Barak felt a slight twinge of something akin to jealousy. Appalled at such a reaction, he only nodded brusquely. "Tell me where."

Anna guided him through the lower section of Jerusalem. At the end of each street, Barak would stop and search the area carefully before proceeding farther. Before long they found themselves in front of a small house, its walls and roof clean and white against its more austere and dilapidated neighbors. Someone had taken the time to plant poppies and mustard, and the bright red and yellow added a note of cheer to the otherwise drab surroundings.

When Anna knocked at the door, it was flung open, and a large, burly man with wild gray hair stepped across the threshold. His smile spread across his face in a dazzling display of white.

"Anna!" Poking his head back inside the door, he bellowed, "Leah! Come see! Anna has come to see us."

Turning back to Anna, he reached for her, giving her a bear hug. Barak watched bemused, and with an unusual sense of relief as another woman came to the door and then flung herself at Anna.

Anna embraced the older woman. Tears shimmered in both pairs of eyes.

"Anna, Anna! What brings you here?" Leah's wrinkled face studied the younger woman carefully. She could see the fear radiating from those brown-flecked green eyes.

The smile fell from Anna's face. She glanced hesitantly at Barak before she informed them softly of her predicament.

Barak saw the old man's face grow livid with rage. "Amman!" He spit on the earth. "I knew there was evil in that man. I would like to wring his scrawny neck!"

Leah placed a placating hand upon her husband's back. "Now, Sentius. That will not help Anna." She took Anna by the arm. "Come inside, my dear, and bring your friend with you."

Both Sentius and Leah looked at Barak questioningly.

"His name is Barak."

Noticing the color flood the young girl's face, husband and wife exchanged looks.

"Welcome," Sentius told Barak.

Although Leah was a Jewish name, Sentius was not. Barak wondered if this couple was from Samaria, also. His thoughts were confirmed when Sentius told him, "We have known Anna since she was a child."

Barak felt his skin crawl as though it were alive. That he was defiled was beyond question. He would have to bathe at the purification pool in the temple before partaking of tonight's fire offering. Still, this couple radiated joy and hospitality, and it was hard to see them as anything other than ally.

After Anna explained her whole story, Sentius and Leah were quick to offer her shelter for as long as necessary.

"I will go to her aunt and explain the situation and see what she has to say," Barak told them, already moving toward the door. "I will return as soon as possible."

"Wait."

Barak lifted a brow as he waited for Anna to cross the room to his side. "Take this."

She unfastened the golden necklace from her throat and handed it to Barak. "If my aunt has any questions, show her this."

Clutching the star in his hand, Barak gazed again into Anna's candid eyes.

Once again he felt that strange stirring deep within. Turning, he left her as quickly as his legs would allow. When he felt the sun upon his face again, Barak breathed deeply.

These people were kind and helpful, yet old prejudices were hard to overcome. Not that he particularly wanted to overcome them. Every Jew knew that Samaritans rejected most of the Holy Scriptures. The only books they believed in were the writings of Moses. How could they not believe the prophets of old, the psalms of King David, the wisdom of King Solomon? What foolishness. Hadn't the prophets been vindicated by their fulfilled prophecies?

After carefully searching the courtyard of Bithnia's villa and ascertaining that Micah was nowhere in sight, Barak opened the gate in the wall and walked swiftly to the door. The cool breeze from the shade trees was a welcome relief after his long walk in the fading sun.

A servant answered his summons, and Barak asked to speak with the mistress of the villa, all the while hoping not to be seen by any who might be working in league with Amman. Bithnia hurried to the door, her agitation evident by the twisting of her hands in her garment.

"Yes?"

Barak glanced quickly around. "May I speak with you in private?"

He was taken aback by the sudden terror in her eyes. She studied him briefly before turning and leading the way to a large peristyle. Her bottom lip quivered as she waited for him to speak.

"I bring you news of Anna."

Closing her eyes tightly, Bithnia dropped to the garden bench behind her. "I knew it," she whispered.

Frowning, Barak told her, "I don't understand."

"How much more do you want?"

Thoroughly confused, Barak tried to make reason of her question. "I still don't understand."

She glared up at him angrily. "When the other man brought the note this afternoon, I knew it wouldn't be long before the demands were increased. What is it you want now?"

Taking a deep breath, Barak shook his head. "Someone sent you a ransom note?"

Perplexed, she lifted an impotent hand, waving it back and forth. "You are not the one who has taken her?"

Barak smiled slightly. He seated himself beside her on the bench. "Well, yes, but I only bring you word that Anna is safe and with friends. But there is at least one in your house who is working with the perpetrators, and perhaps others, as well."

She jerked her head up in surprise. "Who?"

"His name is Micah."

Mouth forming into a perfect O, she began to shake her head in the negative. "I don't believe you. Micah has been with me many years. He and Anna have been friends almost as long. I can't believe he would do such a thing! Why would you tell me such a preposterous lie?"

Barak slowly uncurled his palm and held his hand out to the woman. Her eyes went wide at the star nestled among Barak's rough palm. When she lifted her gaze to his, her eyes held none of the terror from before, but instead a wary kind of acceptance.

"You say she is well?"

He nodded. "She is with a man named Sentius and his wife."

"Praise God!" Her shoulders slumped with relief. "I forgot that Sentius still lives in Jerusalem."

She seemed to forget his presence as she pondered the information he had just given her. Suddenly she turned to him in horror.

"Oh, no! I have already sent word to Tirinus. I didn't know what else to do, but I'm not sure what this news will do to him. He hasn't been well."

Barak felt brief sympathy for the old Samaritan. Even in the short time he had seen the other man, it was obvious how much he adored his daughter. If they shared a love such as Barak shared with his own mother, he knew what pain the other would suffer.

"Anna wondered if her cousin's ailment might have been premeditated. Is the girl well?"

Such fury darkened Bithnia's eyes that Barak unconsciously moved backward. He had once seen a mother bear protect her cub, and seeing this woman now reminded him very much of that she-bear.

"If I find this to be true, I will have Micah flogged until the skin on his back runs red with his own blood!"

Barak's eyebrows flew upward at such vehemence. It was the same tone Uncle Simon used when speaking of these people and their country. It left him vaguely unsettled.

"Your daughter, is she well?"

Slowly the anger drained from her visage. She nodded unhappily. "She is well, but very weak. We thought it was something she ate."

"It is possible, but beginning to seem unlikely. Micah offered to escort Anna to the market this morning. I have no idea how she managed to elude him."

Bithnia grinned. "When Anna wants to be alone, nothing can stop her."

"What would you have us do? Do you wish for her to stay with Sentius?"

Bithnia gnawed her lower lip. "I am not certain." Placing a hand to her forehead, she closed her eyes and sighed. "What do you think I should do?"

When he spoke, there was hesitation in his voice. "Perhaps it would be best if she went to her father, if she could be gotten out of the city undetected. I'm fairly certain that Kasim and his brigands will continue searching the city here. Perhaps she could reach him before he gets the message you sent."

Bithnia's eyes began to glow, and a slow smile curled her lips. "Your idea has merit. I could give you all the money you will need to make the journey."

Surprised, Barak quickly got to his feet, shaking his head. "I did not suggest that *I* would take her. I thought perhaps Sentius."

The smile slid slowly from her face. "You would not take her?"

Old feelings of hatred struggled with newer feelings of—what? What exactly was he feeling right now? The desire to protect the girl, the equally strong desire to leave her alone.

"I have never set foot in Samaria, nor do I intend to." If he offended her, so be it. He had done more for these infidels than he had originally planned.

She turned away from him and moved to the archway leading into the villa, her shoulders slumped with despair. "Will you send Sentius to me?"

Feeling as though he were lower than an Egyptian asp, Barak agreed. He was so preoccupied with his guilty thoughts, he failed to see the figure slip out the gate behind him.

Chapter 5

Barak stared somberly at the flickering flames of the fire. In Uncle Simon's tent, Uncle Simon would be giving thanks for the evening meal. For the most part, it would consist of unleavened bread and fresh fruit, no lamb having been left over from Passover night. Barak didn't care much one way or another. His lack of hunger came from the tightness of his stomach as he thought about Sentius leading Anna to Sychar.

Adonijah dropped down beside him, both men watching the small campfire, each busy with his own thoughts. A gentle breeze lifted the hair slightly from Barak's forehead, where it lay curled against his dark skin. Finally Adonijah turned to his friend.

"Your uncle only wants to see you happy."

Barak snorted. It would seem his private life was not so private after all.

"My uncle is only concerned with me having children, so all that my father owned will pass down for generations to come."

Perplexed, Adonijah lifted one dark brow. "Is this not the desire of all men? You needn't sound so unhappy about it. Perhaps you and Miriam will sire the future Messiah."

Barak picked up a stick and angrily snapped it in two. "Of course I want to have children, but there's plenty of time." He smiled without humor. "Remember Father Abraham."

Adonijah didn't return his smile. "Remember Japhez."

Both men settled into a melancholy mood, reflecting on their friend who had been killed only the week before when a millstone had fallen on him, crushing him to death.

"Has your uncle told you that he has made marriage arrangements?" Adonijah asked.

Barak shook his head. "No." He glanced suspiciously at his friend. "Has he said any such thing to you?"

"No. It was more a conversation I overheard between him and Ahaz. Nothing definite. Only I did hear them say something about where the two of you would live after you were married."

Shoving his forehead into the palms of his hands, Barak gritted his teeth. Adonijah studied his down-bent head.

"Truly, Barak, I don't see why you aren't excited about having Miriam for a wife. I know you want to marry for love, but surely that will come in time. She's a wonderful woman."

Barak turned his head slightly, lifting a dubious brow. It would seem that love made one blind. Still, he would not contradict his friend. It was obvious that Adonijah was besotted with Miriam, yet he was such an honorable man he would never do anything to jeopardize Barak's future. What would it do to his friend if Barak *did* eventually marry the girl? He hated to think of causing Adonijah such grief, yet he was beginning to see no way out.

"Perhaps," he finally answered, sighing. "But for now, I think I will go and talk with Mother before she lies down for the night." He got to his feet, patting Adonijah on the shoulder as he passed by. "Good night, my friend."

His mother was busy preparing her clothes for the night when Barak sought admittance to her tent. She smiled widely at her son.

"Come in, Barak. Sit down. Tell me about your visit in the great city today."

Barak joined his mother on the cushions. He lay back and breathed out softly through his lips. It hadn't occurred to him before just how tired he was.

"There's not much to tell. I just wandered around on my own for a while, and then I met some people and visited with them."

"Other Jews?"

Not wishing to worry her with his afternoon's escapades, he began to tell her instead about the little monkey at the market. She laughed lightly.

"I can just see it, with its little turban."

"The turban's owner was not so amused."

Tamar made a sound with her lips. "He obviously had no sense of humor."

When Barak spoke again, his mother was surprised at the turn of his thoughts. He lay back with closed eyes.

"Mother, tell me about when you met Father. When you were first married." He sat up, wrapping his arms around his knees. There was something so intense in his eyes that his mother searched his face with the probing eyes of a concerned parent.

"What do you wish to know?"

"Anything. Everything. Did you love each other from the moment you met?"

Tamar laughed, shaking her head. "No, my son. I couldn't stand the sight of him. And he thought me a naive child. I hated the way he talked to me as though I were nothing but an infant."

Barak was too surprised to speak. His parents had loved each other, of that he was sure. You could see it in their every look, feel the power of it whenever you came near. Others had often commented on it.

"You didn't marry for love?"

Tamar's eyes took on a faraway look. There was a small smile on her face as she remembered back to the first days of her courtship and marriage.

"No. Our fathers arranged it. I cried and pleaded, but to no avail. They were adamant."

She looked at Barak. Such thoughts as love were unusual coming from a man. Marriage was a means to an end for most. She should have known it would be different with her son. He had the body of a warrior but the heart of a poet. Much like King David.

"I grew to love him. After we were married, I began to see the qualities I had missed before. My eyes were clouded by my anger and averseness to the marriage. It took time, but your father and I found that it was indeed Jehovah's will."

Were these sudden questions of love brought on by Simon's talk of marriage to Miriam? She scrutinized her son carefully, trying to read into his questions.

"Miriam is a beautiful woman," she told him guardedly.

Barak sighed heavily. "Mother, I do not wish to marry Miriam."

"Not right now?"

He shook his head. "Not ever. Let Uncle Simon arrange a marriage between Adonijah and Miriam. Adonijah would be thrilled; though truth to tell, I would wish differently for him."

Tamar was quiet for several moments. When she spoke again, there was regret in her voice. "Simon has already decided. He and Ahaz both. I don't think there's a way to dissuade them."

Barak unfolded his legs and climbed swiftly to his feet. He brushed a hand through his hair in vexation. "Can you do *nothing* to stop them?"

Looking up at her son, Tamar wondered just what she could say. Placing a hand gently on Barak's leg, she worried her bottom lip with her teeth.

"Barak, I don't know what to tell you. I had no idea that you felt so strongly about this." She paused. "Is there another woman you would choose?"

For a moment, images of Anna's serene face and glowing eyes filtered into his mind. The way her lips had parted slightly as she had studied him had set his heart to pounding. Such a provocative, yet innocent gesture. He shook his head to free it of such disturbing images.

"No. There is no other, but that doesn't mean I should marry in haste."

"Barak, you are twenty-five years old. It is time you settled down and had a family."

"I have you," he told her softly.

Her mother-heart thrilled at the sound of such love in his voice. How many men truly loved their mothers as much? How had she been so blessed? What could she say to such a statement?

"I will talk with Simon," she told him quietly.

He nodded. There was really nothing more he could say.

Adonijah's voice reached them from outside the tent. "Barak. Someone is here to see you."

Tamar and Barak exchanged looks. "I will see who it is." Thinking that it might very well be Miriam, or Ahaz on her behalf, Barak bent and kissed his mother on the forehead. "This might take awhile. I will wish you good night now."

But it was not either of the two. When Barak opened the tent flap, he found Leah standing outside. Her face was extremely pale, her large, dark eyes filled with distress. She twisted the belt on her robe in agitation.

"May I speak with you?"

His eyes swept the area around, but there was no sign of Sentius. Something was seriously wrong. His eyes locked with Leah's, and he could read the message there. For some reason, she wished him to remain silent.

Uncle Simon came from his tent and joined the group. His heavy brows drew down into a scowl. "Who is this woman?"

"A friend," Barak told him but would say no more. "You wished to speak with me?"

The flickering light of the fire added planes and hollows to Leah's cheeks, giving her an otherworld appearance. Barak heard Adonijah's indrawn breath behind him. He didn't miss the hesitation as Leah glanced quickly at the people around her.

"May we speak in private?"

Concern was beginning to tie his stomach into a knot. Regardless of what he disclaimed, he hadn't been able to get Anna off his mind all day.

He lifted a torch from its holder and nodded. "Lead the way."

Barak could feel the eyes of the others on his back as Leah led him toward the thicket of olive trees beyond their camp. She didn't stop even when they were clear of the sight of the others, but continued instead farther into the mammoth trees.

Suddenly she stopped, and Barak could see a figure beyond her. Waiting. Lifting the torch to push back the darkness, his heart began to beat faster as he recognized the young woman.

"Anna." His look sought an explanation from Leah.

"I would ask a favor of you. I know it is much to ask and you have no reason to grant it, but I am pleading with you to take Anna safely to Sychar."

Surprised, his look went from one to the other. Anna moved slowly toward them, and in the light from the torch, he could see traces of tears on her dusty cheeks.

"Where is Sentius?"

A soft sob escaped from the older woman, and she began twisting her hands together.

"They came to the house." She stopped, unable to continue.

Growing more anxious by the moment, Barak demanded impatiently, "Who came?" although he thought he already knew.

"Kasim and the others," Anna told him softly.

Puzzled, Barak shrugged his shoulders, his hands spreading apart. "I don't understand. What of Sentius?"

Anna glanced once at Leah, her eyes dropping to the ground before rising to meet Barak's.

"Sentius had just come back from seeing Aunt Bithnia. He had a bag of gold in his hands, enough to see us safely on our journey. No more had he arrived than we heard the neighbor's donkey sounding an alarm. When Sentius looked out the window, he could see several men moving around the house."

She stopped, swallowing hard.

"And?"

"Sentius shoved the money bag into Leah's hands and told us to run out the back way."

She stopped again, and Leah took up the story.

"Micah was waiting at the back entrance. For a moment, I thought he would let us pass, but then he reached for Anna."

Both women seemed reluctant to continue. Apprehensively Barak asked them, "How did you manage to elude him?"

The two women exchanged glances. Anna dropped her eyes, and Leah squared her shoulders. "Anna grabbed a water jug beside the door and smacked Micah across the head."

For the first time, Barak noticed the blood on Anna's tunic. His eyes went wide.

"Did you kill him?" he asked incredulously.

"I don't know." Anna's voice was little more than a trembling whisper.

Barak didn't know whether to be impressed or revolted. How had such a little thing managed such a crushing blow? Maybe there was more strength in her character than he had at first supposed.

"And what of Sentius?"

"We don't know," Leah whispered. "I must go back and see. But Anna needs to be gotten away from Jerusalem. If they know that I have returned, they will think Anna is hiding somewhere in the city, maybe at her aunt's house. They will take time searching for her there."

Leah held out the bag of coins to Barak. "Please take her to safety."

Barak did nothing toward taking the bag. His eyes went from the coins to each woman in turn. He didn't know what to do.

Anna told the other woman, "I don't wish to leave until I know if Sentius is well."

"You must. Your father will receive word soon, and there is no telling what that will do to his health. Think, Anna. We can't chance you being caught by those brigands."

It was a light scolding, but it brought Anna to instant submissiveness. Leah was right. She had to think of others, but right now her mind was too clouded to think clearly at all.

Barak was in a dilemma. He knew he had to help the girl, though every ounce of training he had had as a Jew forbade it. He wavered back and forth, finally turning his back on Leah's pleading eyes.

Before he could decide, Adonijah stepped from the trees, bringing the light of a torch with him. His look went around the circle of expectant faces before coming to rest on Barak.

"Your mother was concerned. She sent me to see if everything was all right."

Adonijah's look fixed on Anna, studying her in puzzlement. He knew he had seen that face before, but where? A picture came to his mind of two girls standing across from the temple gates, and the sudden remembrance brought a swift frown to his face.

"The Samaritan." His voice was laced with disgust. "What do you want here?"

In that instant, Barak knew what he had to do.

"Adonijah, I must go on a journey. I need your help, but I want your word that you will say nothing to anyone."

Adonijah's eyes narrowed with suspicion. "Has it to do with these two women?"

Barak nodded, watching his friend closely. "Yes."

"You will explain it to me in time, I know." His voice was heavy with doubt.

"I will, but I cannot take the time now."

Adonijah stared silently at the small group. The look that passed between the two men spoke of trust and acceptance.

"I must go and speak with Mother. Please stay here until I return. If anyone comes, hide the two women."

Barak passed his friend swiftly, going back to the camp. He found his mother alone and waiting for him.

"Mother, I must leave on a journey. I will not be able to return before Passover is finished, so I will meet you at home."

Tamar became alarmed. "What are you saying? Where must you go? Does this have something to do with the woman who came to see you?"

Realizing that his mother had heard Leah's voice from outside, Barak tried to think of a way to explain. He cleared his throat, his voice gruff. "I think it better that you not know. Uncle Simon would not understand."

"Barak—"

"Trust me, Mother. It's very important. I will explain it to you when I return."

"Can you tell me nothing? Not even where you are going on this journey?"

Barak sighed. He knew she wouldn't understand, but he had never kept things hidden from his mother. "I must journey to Sychar."

"Sychar! In Samaria!"

He stood there before her, a man yet still her baby. Tamar couldn't begin to sort her thoughts in time. Barak was already heading for the tent entrance.

"Wait! Barak, you can't just leave in the middle of the night. Where will you go? What will you do?"

He stared back at her steadily. "I will trust Jehovah. You must, too."

"But Samaria! Barak, if they know you are a Jew, they will likely kill you! Why must you go?"

Barak crossed quickly to her side and, bending, kissed her on her cheek. Without another word, he left her.

Anna studied the young Jew, who was making a point of not looking at her. His dislike was obvious.

Leah paced to and fro, awaiting Barak's return. Anna knew that her friend was in a hurry to return to her home to seek news of her husband.

All three jumped at the slight rustling of leaves, but then Barak came into view and they relaxed. His look passed over each of them before he presented himself to Leah. Without saying anything, he held out his hand.

Looking relieved, Leah placed the money pouch in his outstretched palm. She fell on her knees before him. "Thank you. Thank you."

Growling slightly, Barak lifted her to her feet. "Where can I take her for the night? We can't begin our journey at night. We wouldn't get three miles before being beset by robbers."

"Sentius had news of a caravan traveling to Nazareth. They will pass through Sychar on their way. You will find them camped on the far side of the city, beside the road that leads to Nazareth."

Adonijah had remained quiet throughout this exchange, but now he stepped forward. "You are going to Sychar? Barak, that is insane."

Barak closed his eyes, taking a deep breath. When he opened them again, his gaze focused unwaveringly on Adonijah. "I know. I can't explain now. I have told Mother that I will explain when I return."

Anna waited without saying anything. Her feelings were in chaos right now. She wanted desperately to find out if Sentius was all right, but she knew Leah was right—that she needed to be on her way. Still, it rankled that she was dependent upon a man who held such contempt for her and her country. As she dwelt on these feelings, her ire began to rise. Finally she spoke.

"I don't need your help. I will go on my own."

Leah stared at her in surprise, the young Jew gazed at her with no expression in his eyes at all, and Barak chose to ignore her. To Anna, this was the straw that broke the camel's back. She marched across the space between them and tried to jerk the money bag from Barak's tightly closed fist. It was no use.

"Don't be a foolish child," he told her in aggravation. "I will see you safely to

Sychar, and that is the end of it."

Leah's soft voice quelled the anger rising in Anna. "Please, Anna. I can't worry about you now, too."

Anna's shoulders slumped with defeat. Leah was right again. She turned to the older woman. "You will get word to me about Sentius?"

"I will."

They could hear someone moving toward them through the trees. Adonijah lifted himself from the tree where he was leaning. His look met Barak's.

"Miriam. I will lead her away. Jehovah be with you, my friend."

He quickly left them, and they could hear his voice not far beyond in the trees. Barak held his breath until they could hear the two moving away. He turned to Anna.

"Let's be on our way."

The two women hugged, tears shining in both pairs of eyes. Together Barak and Anna watched Leah quickly disappear among the trees.

Barak and Anna made their way in total silence to where the caravan was situated just beyond Jerusalem's western walls.

Already, many in the caravan had retired for the night in preparation for the long and tiring journey on the morrow. Still, others were gathered around their campfires chatting and laughing. A mood of revelry permeated the atmosphere, and Anna realized that it was probably due to the fact that these people had traveled far and were close to their journey's end. She, on the other hand, was just beginning hers.

Still, Sychar was only about thirty miles from Jerusalem, so it would take them less than three days to reach their destination.

Night had spread its dark fingers to the farthest corners of this camp, yet the interior was bright with the lights of many small fires and torches. The caravan seemed small, yet it would swell in the morning when others from Jerusalem would add their company to this small group. It was much safer to travel in the comradeship of others.

Barak touched her lightly. "Wait here. I will see if I can find the caravan commander and make arrangements."

Anna was reluctant to be left alone, but she remained obediently where Barak had left her. It took some time before Barak returned to her, a short, rotund man following in his footsteps.

When the man smiled, his mouth sported a multitude of missing teeth.

"Welcome." He bowed low before Anna. "Your servant has told me of your problem, and we will gladly make room for you among one of the tents of our women. Please come this way."

Anna stopped beside Barak. "What of you?"

"He will find room among the other servants. Do not worry."

Bothered by the caravan commander's statement, Anna opened her mouth to protest. She snapped it shut tightly when Barak shook his head at her, his dark eyes warning her to be careful of her speech. Turning, she followed the commander without further comment.

"My name is Azuba, mistress. If I can be of assistance, please let one of the servants know." Bowing, he left her standing beside a large tent where a series of giggles could be heard as the women within prepared for the night.

What had Barak told the man, anyway, to cause such an attitude of servitude? She would ask him tomorrow, but for now she would take advantage of this opportunity for rest. Though her mind was filled with worries, her body was craving respite from any further physical exertion.

Feeling shy, she was relieved to find that the other women of the tent were ready to welcome her among them. They even provided clothing for her night's rest, for which Anna was thankful. The silky material slid softly over her as she moved about the tent, giving her morale a much-needed boost.

When she lay down that night, all of the thoughts she had been holding at bay suddenly crowded in upon her. She closed her eyes, wondering how Sentius was and, for that matter, whether Leah had arrived safely within the city's walls. She prayed fervently for all of them, even Barak's family, who, she supposed, would be anxious about his sudden departure.

Had it only been ten hours since she had left the villa? It seemed a lifetime. If anyone would have told her this morning that she would be on the road to Sychar with a man who obviously despised her, she would have laughed. But this was no laughing matter.

What would happen to her father when he received Aunt Bithnia's message? She prayed to Jehovah that he was stronger of health than Aunt Bithnia believed.

That night she had a dream. A man stood before her, His clothing sparkling like white snow. She couldn't see His face, but when He held out His hands to her, she could see scars in the palms of His hands. His words shivered through her intensely, though softly spoken.

"You must teach him about Me."

Before Anna could ask His meaning, He disappeared.

Barak lay on the rough mat with his hands crossed behind his head, staring up at the twinkling stars above him. He couldn't remember a time when he had done anything so impetuous. He had always been a thinker. A planner.

He closed his eyes, hoping that sleep would come. It was no use. His mind was so active it would never allow him to sleep. Giving in to the inevitable, he allowed his thoughts free rein.

The thing that bothered him most was the fact that despite his resolve, he felt something for the Samaritan girl. What exactly, he wasn't certain, but there was something powerfully alluring about her. Her extraordinary eyes held such peace that he felt himself drawn into their compelling depths.

And what of Miriam? He still didn't know if he was betrothed or not, probably because he was afraid to stay around and find out. He closed his eyes and sighed. Could two women be more different than Anna and Miriam? How was it that being near Anna sent his pulse pounding when he should feel nothing but disgust, and whenever Miriam came close, he felt nothing but aggravation?

His eyes popped back open when the man nearest him shifted on his mat. A loud snore followed, and Barak grinned slightly. Already the murmurs of irritation drifted across to Barak from others trying to sleep.

The smile left Barak's face as he remembered his mother's face when he had left her. For years now, he had been the one to care for her. He didn't take his responsibility lightly, and it bothered him more than a little that he had had to leave her in Adonijah's care.

How long this journey would take he was not certain, but he felt uneasy as he contemplated the task ahead. He would be doing well if he could manage to refrain from arguing with the girl at every opportunity. It was either that or fall under her tantalizing spell. No woman had ever touched him as this one had. Jaw clenched tightly, he contemplated the stories he had heard of Samaritan women. A tick formed in his cheek. He would *not* let that happen to him.

The last sound he heard was a dove cooing softly as it settled among the trees.

Chapter 6

The bright morning sun warmed Barak as he walked along beside the *carpentum* he had rented for Anna. The two-wheeled cart would serve dual purposes. It would save Anna from having to walk among the dust being scattered by the plodding camels, and it would also help to keep her from prying eyes as long as she kept the drapes pulled.

The low-lying hills to the east were already turning a flourishing green. A carpet of red, green, purple, and white spread across the hills on both sides, giving the area an energetic feeling of life.

Walking along the hot, broad valley floor, Barak could almost imagine himself returning to his own home in Jotapata. Spring was upon the land, and it felt good to be alive. He yearned to be home in his own fields, the freshly turned soil sliding silkily through his fingers. There was nothing he would rather be than a farmer.

As the morning progressed, so did the intensity of the heat from the sun. Before long, Anna pushed back the drape of the carpentum and peered out. "I would like to walk."

"I don't think that's a good idea."

Sighing, she gave him an indignant glare. "I think it is. It's hot in here."

Barak studied her flushed face, dewy from perspiration. Perhaps she was right; they were now several miles from Jerusalem. Stopping the two horses, he helped Anna from the cart.

She took a moment to look all around her, and a broad smile lit her face. "How beautiful! I must say, it didn't look like this when we traveled this way last year. There was nothing but dirt and dried thistles everywhere you looked."

Clucking to the horses, Barak began moving forward again. "And it will look that way again in just a few months. We're fortunate to be traveling in the spring."

Anna agreed, walking amicably beside her rather taciturn escort. She couldn't help but notice how well he handled the horses. He had a feel for them that transcended mere ability.

"You have horses of your own?"

Surprised, he flicked her a swift glance. "No, but we have many oxen. There is very little difference, I think."

"Tell me about yourself," she coaxed.

He shrugged. "There is nothing much to tell. I am a farmer from Jotapata.

Our family can trace our ancestry back to Adam."

Anna was aware of the slight, but she chose to ignore it. Many Jews thought themselves superior because of their pure heritage. While it was true that not many Samaritans could trace their lineage back as far as Barak claimed, it didn't make them less of a people in God's eyes.

Deciding not to respond to the challenge in his tone, Anna instead studied the hills to her left rather than look at her companion. "You are breaking Passover law to help me," she told him softly.

Barak was breaking *all* the unwritten Jewish laws by helping a Samaritan anyway, regardless of Passover. He shrugged. What was done, was done.

"It is no matter."

"I think, perhaps, for someone like you it is. You don't strike me as the kind of person to flagrantly defy God's law."

He gave her a look of haughty disdain. "What do you know of God's law when you only have the Torah? Your people deny the writings of the prophets and kings, and you speak to me of Jewish law? And what of you? Are you not breaking *Samaritan* law by being in Jerusalem on Passover instead of on Mount Gerizim?"

She was surprised by his vehemence, although she probably shouldn't have been. "I have never denied being a Samaritan by birth, but that does not make me one in faith."

Stunned, he turned to her, but she kept her face averted as they continued to walk along.

"You are not Samaritan?"

"Only by birth."

He frowned. "Then are you Jewish?"

Anna licked dry lips, knowing that she was suddenly on slippery ground. "I accept the writings of the kings and the prophets," she answered hesitantly.

Anna could see Barak trying to assimilate what she was saying and what she was not saying. It would be far better to change the subject.

"What will you do when we reach Samaria?" she asked him.

Reluctantly he discontinued their previous conversation. Perhaps he sensed that there were things better left unsaid, things that would only cause more dissension between them.

"I will take you to the home of your father."

The glittering determination in his brown eyes turned them to a polished bronze. Anna had no doubts that he would do just that and that nothing on this earth would stop him.

"And if we happen upon Amman?"

The light in his eyes deepened. "Leave that to me." His look passed over her briefly before he once again focused his attention on the horses. "Anna," he told her, "I will do all in my power to see that nothing happens to you."

She wanted to again ask him why, but she was too afraid of the answer she would receive. There was something in his eyes when he looked at her that made her breath catch in her throat. She was too inexperienced in the ways of men to understand the feelings this Jew aroused in her.

They traveled in silence for several miles. Anna's throat soon became parched from swallowing what seemed to be fields of dust. Still, she refused to say anything, because she knew that if she did, Barak would more than likely insist she return to the carpentum.

Before long, Barak reached into the cart and lifted out a water flask. Opening it, he first handed it to Anna.

Smiling her appreciation, she took a hearty swallow, swishing some of the warm liquid around in her mouth to relieve it of the sand clinging to her teeth. She handed the flask back to Barak, and he did the same.

Up ahead, carrion birds could be seen circling an area to their right. Anna shivered as she realized what the huge birds meant. Barak's serious face turned her way.

"It is time for you to return to the carpentum, I think."

Anna made no demure as Barak lifted her into the cart. His hands remained at her waist as his eyes were caught by hers. A long look passed between them until Barak was brought to his senses by the man following behind him, shouting for Barak to move forward.

Barak dropped the curtains into place on the cart, not so much for Anna's protection from prying eyes, but more for her protection from a sight that he was sure would be quite grisly.

As they passed the area, a couple of men lifted a body from the ground and wrapped it carefully in a blanket. No doubt a lone traveler had defied the odds and received his reward. These hills were notorious for hiding thieves and murderers. Someone would return with the body to Jerusalem.

The caravan commander had told them they would be stopping at a caravansary in Lebanoh for the night. This pleased Barak. The safe walls of a caravansary would be a welcome relief to him after having witnessed such a sight.

They were about halfway to their destination when Azuba called for a halt to water the animals at a small wadi still full from the winter rains. Anna climbed from the cart unassisted and made her way to the watering hole.

She was unused to walking over the rough terrain, and already her ankles sported blisters from her previous trek. She took off her sandals and scooped up handfuls of water to pour over her burning feet. She sighed with pleasure at the blessed relief.

Barak joined her, leading the two cart horses. He smiled slightly at her euphoric expression.

"Feel good?"

"Mmm."

She watched Barak go farther upstream to refill the water flask. Kneeling, he filled the bag and then plunged his own head beneath the cool water. He came up shaking droplets in every direction, the sheen from the water droplets adding a silver tint to his dark hair and beard.

He returned to her and held out a hand. Placing her small hand in his larger one, Barak lifted her easily to her feet.

Taking the horses by the reins, he led the way back to the cart. Already others were preparing to leave. There was, in reality, no need to make such a stop, but the water had looked refreshing, and Azuba had wisely decided to save his own supplies.

Barak drew back the curtains so that Anna could climb into the carpentum. After that last encounter, he would not touch the girl again. His pulse had accelerated to such an extent that he had found it suddenly hard to breathe. He motioned her into the cart, but Anna remained where she was standing, her hands folded behind her back. "I wish to walk again."

Barak raised his eyes heavenward, sighing. *Why me, Lord? I know this is not a good idea.* Still, he wouldn't like being stuffed into a cart all day, either.

"As you wish."

He could only hope their conversation wouldn't end up in some kind of argument. Perhaps she would remain silent as before. This hope was not to be realized.

"Barak, what do you think the Messiah will be like?"

"What?" Such a question was totally unexpected.

"The Messiah. When He comes, what do you think He will be like?"

"He will be a king who will rule on the throne of David. He will set our people free as Moses did long ago."

"And do the scriptures say that He will be a king?"

Barak tried to curb his impatience. After all, she was but a woman.

"The scriptures say He will rule on the throne of David. I have just said that."

Anna wrinkled her forehead, her face twisted with intense concentration. "And does ruling always mean being king?"

Suspiciously he studied her averted face. He had the oddest feeling that the woman was deliberately leading this conversation. "What else could it mean?"

She tapped her lip thoughtfully with a finger, and Barak found himself mesmerized by the innocently alluring gesture.

"Well, my father *rules* our house."

"That's true, but it is something quite different. The Messiah will free His people. Only a ruler can do that."

"Moses was not a king. Did he not free the Jews?"

Although her voice was completely innocent, Barak suspected these questions were more than idle curiosity, and he had no idea what it was that was putting him suddenly on the defensive.

Anna returned her gaze to the road. "What exactly do the scriptures say about the Messiah?"

"What I have told you."

"And that is all?"

Barak stopped suddenly, taking Anna by the arm and turning her to face him. His eyes narrowed warily. "Why are you asking these questions about the Messiah? What do you wish to know?"

She met his look boldly. "The Samaritans have only the prophecies of Moses. I understand there are more. Do you know them?"

Unwilling to admit his ignorance, Barak shrugged. "Some."

"Well, what do you know?"

The horses with the cart had gone on without them. Barak hurried to catch up. When he looked back, he noticed Anna limping after him. His brows drew down into a frown. Without a word, he lifted her into the cart, and walking by its side, he drew the sandal from her foot.

The blisters had burst, and dirt clung to the wetness. If something wasn't done soon, infection would set in.

"Why didn't you tell me?" Barak's eyes met Anna's. He set her foot gently among the cushions.

"I thought nothing of it," she told him breathlessly, sucking in her lip.

"I'll be right back."

Anna watched his retreating back, her breathing just now returning to normal. His hands had been so gentle, even with the rough calluses of his palms. She blew out a breath and lay back among the cushions, knowing that the horses would continue without Barak's assistance.

The Jew's presence was unsettling, to say the least. She had known from the moment she had set eyes on him that their lives were bound to entwine. It was an uncanny premonition on her part. She had never had such feelings before.

Her main problem was keeping her head in his presence. That he was handsome was undeniable. That he was strong was obvious. That he was a Jew was awkward.

She wanted to reach out to him with the love of Christ, but if there was one thing Jews hated more than Samaritans, it was Christians. Jews believed Christians to be polytheistic, saying they worshiped more than one God. It was impossible for them to understand that God, Jesus, and the Holy Spirit were one, yet separate. Sometimes it was hard for her to understand, as well. Her mind boggled at the implications.

If she could only get Barak to understand Jesus' fulfillment of the scriptures. She would try to get him to remember more, for there was a wealth of prophecy concerning Him among the Jewish scriptures. Unfortunately the same could not be said of the Samaritans. Believing only in the writings of Moses, they eliminated much of what it would take to see Jesus' trial, crucifixion, and resurrection as the fulfillment of God's plan for mankind.

Barak returned carrying a small amphora. He continued to walk alongside the cart as he ministered to Anna.

First he used some of the water to wash her blisters clean. Periodically her foot would jerk and she would wince.

"I'm sorry, but we need to make sure the lesions are clean before I pack them with salt."

Biting her lip, she nodded for him to continue. After cleaning the sores as thoroughly as possible, he opened the small amphora.

"This is going to hurt."

"Go ahead."

Her hands turned white where they clenched the cushions, but she made no sound. There were tears swimming in her eyes when he finished. Barak felt her pain as his own. Salt in an open wound was no laughing matter.

"That should keep the infection away," he told her, replacing the stopper on the flask. He lifted the curtains to allow the air to circulate. "You will ride from now on," he told her implacably.

Pivoting on his heels, he went to the front of the cart to walk with the plodding horses. Anna smiled slightly. That was certainly an effective way to keep from answering theological questions. She wondered just how much Barak really knew of the scriptures.

Leaning back, she fell into dreaming of Barak as a child learning among the priests and scribes. Probably he was a little imp, if the man was any indication.

The sun was low to the horizon when they entered the outskirts of Lebanoh. Although the caravansary was not large, it was adequate for the needs of this small caravan. They entered the courtyard through the single gate, and all members of the party scattered round the courtyard until the last traveler was through. The innkeeper shut the gate behind them, and Barak breathed a sigh of relief.

Since Anna's aunt had given them money enough to cover their expenses, Barak made use of the coins now to procure Anna a room on the upper balcony, away from the noise and stench.

He found her in the cart, her veil pressed tightly against her nose.

Barak grinned. "I know. The smell is almost unbearable."

"Almost!"

Smiling, he lifted her into his arms and carried her up the steps to the small enclosure used as rooms for the more affluent. This caravansary didn't provide beds or bedding, so Barak retrieved some of the pillows and coverings from the cart. He could feel Anna watching him as he arranged a pallet for her to sleep on.

Rising to his feet, he turned to her. "You'll be safe here for the night. I'll sleep in the courtyard with the cart and horses." He turned to leave. "I'll bring you something to eat."

When he left, he dropped the mat that covered the front opening on to the balcony to afford Anna some privacy.

Anna could hear others moving about in the apartments around her preparing for the night. The noise in the courtyard would grow progressively louder as the evening advanced. She was thankful that Barak had procured her a room here. Hopefully he would be able to get some sleep among all the rabble below.

He returned carrying a tray. The smell of the roasted chicken made Anna's mouth water. She hadn't realized just how hungry she was.

She looked up at Barak. "Will you join me?"

He hesitated.

"Please. I don't wish to eat alone."

One eyebrow lifted, and the smoky light from the brazier gave him a somewhat arrogant appearance. Nodding, he seated himself across from her. Anna noticed that there was nothing on the tray that would violate Passover precepts.

As they consumed their meal, they talked of trivialities. Barak told Anna of his home in Jotapata, and she in turn told him of Sychar. Both were careful to keep away from incendiary subjects. Only when Anna asked about Miriam did Barak grow tense.

"She is the daughter of my uncle's neighbor and good friend. They have wished to see a marriage between us since we were children."

"Is she beautiful?"

Barak's eyes met hers, roaming slowly over her features. Embarrassed, Anna dipped her head and lifted some unleavened bread from the tray. She knew she could not compare in beauty to most women, so why had she invited the possibility of criticism?

"Yes, she is quite beautiful." His voice was so soft, Anna glanced at him in surprise.

Barak's look was intense as he studied Anna, causing her heart to catch in her throat. "But as far as I am aware, we are not yet betrothed. Thankfully my mother has had some influence on Uncle Simon. She knows that I wish to marry for. . .love."

It was so unusual for a man to speak of love in such a way that Anna was taken aback. She could think of nothing to say. The silence between them grew long and uncomfortable.

Dropping his napkin to the tray, Barak rose to his feet. "I must see to the animals." He paused by the door, unexpectedly reluctant to leave. Anna sat in the glow from the brazier, oblivious to the enticing picture she made. For a moment, he was tempted to cross the room and place a kiss on those inviting lips. How could a woman be so innocent yet look so tempting? Shaking his head, he turned away. "Good night."

Anna could hear him move along the balcony until he entered the stairway leading to the courtyard. Only then did she release her breath.

Kasim glared at the man standing before him. He slid his knife slowly from its scabbard.

"I should kill you where you stand, Micah. How did she manage to elude you?"

Micah shrugged, the sweat beading across his forehead and soaking the bandage wound turban-style around his head.

"She hit me when I wasn't looking. The old one was with her."

Kasim rose from his seat and came menacingly across the room. He drew up in front of Micah. "Do you know what this means? Amman will have me dropped in a wadi somewhere. So help me, Micah, you had better find the girl."

"We have searched all of Jerusalem. Even our people on the street know nothing of her whereabouts."

"And the old couple?"

Micah lifted a dubious brow. "You shouldn't have hurt him, Kasim. Sentius has many friends, and they aren't particularly happy with you right now. While we are trying to find the girl, they are trying to find us."

Kasim's eyes narrowed. "Let them come. I can deal with a few old Jews. *You* find the girl. Understand?"

Micah held his hands out helplessly at his sides. "I don't know where else to look."

Kasim stared off into space for a moment. A sudden gleam came to his eyes. "If they are not to be found in Jerusalem, then perhaps we had better broaden our search."

Perplexed, Micah could only stare.

"There was a caravan that left yesterday, traveling north. It should pass through Sychar. Perhaps our little bird has managed to find accommodations among that group."

"They will be halfway to Sychar by now," Micah stated skeptically.

Kasim's glittering eyes fixed upon the young Jew, making him swallow hard. It had not occurred to Micah until now just what dangerous men he had managed to ally himself with. In the beginning, he had thought they would help in the rebellion against Rome. They had promised weapons and support, but now Micah realized these were notorious killers bent on their own selfish ambitions.

"Take some men and find out," Kasim ordered. His voice lowered to a hiss. "And don't let me see your face without the girl's. Do you understand?"

Micah understood all too well. Nodding, he spun on his heels and left.

Kasim watched the young man leave, his thoughts in a turmoil. It never did one any good to seek help outside one's own kind. He would much prefer dealing with cutthroats and thieves than these Jewish zealots.

Even now these men were quietly supplying themselves with weapons in hopes of stirring a revolt against Rome.

They were all fools. Rome would squash them like flies. Kasim shook his head. *Better to take care of yourself than to worry about others.*

When Micah returned with the girl, he would have to do something about that young man. Although he and Amman had made much profit from these insane zealots, it was time to sever ties. It would not do to have Roman authority come down on their heads.

Chapter 7

Anna was growing weary of riding in the carpentum. She much preferred the cool breezes blowing down from the surrounding hills. The road wound unendingly ahead, inclining ever so slightly upward.

Growing more petulant by the mile, Anna pushed her lips out in a childish pout. This day would see the end of their journey, and still she had been unable to converse with Barak. He was stubbornly avoiding her as much as possible.

Flinging herself back among the cushions, she stared up at the roof of the cart. She hadn't imagined that look in his eyes last night. Even from across the room, her blood had pounded in response.

Whatever was happening between them was disturbing, to say the least. Anna wanted so much to be able to act with Barak the way any young woman would with the man she had chosen. But then, their relationship was hardly normal. A Jew and a Samaritan. What was worse, a Jew and a Christian.

What would Barak say if he knew? Anna shivered at the thought. She could just imagine how cold those eyes would become. She couldn't bear the thought of that happening, but she knew it was bound to, sooner or later. If only they had more time so that she could help him to see that Samaritans, or Christians for that matter, were only normal people.

Funny. It had never bothered her before if others knew she was of the Way. What then made the difference?

Sighing, she closed her eyes. She knew what made the difference. She was far too attracted to Barak, and from the look in his eyes last night, he was not indifferent to her.

But then there was Miriam. Anna squinched her eyes tighter, biting the knuckle of her finger. She didn't want to think of the beautiful young Jewess, for when she did, she realized how ludicrous it was to think that Barak could feel anything for Anna herself.

Still, there had been *something* in his eyes that had spoken to her deepest inner feelings. She found herself responding to him in a way she had never responded to any other.

Barak lifted back the material surrounding the cart. His eyes met hers briefly before he reached for her foot.

"I found some aloe. I imagine the sores are throbbing today."

He was certainly right about that, but they were as nothing compared to the throbbing of her own heart in his presence. It aggravated her to be so vulnerable.

Barak gently removed the strips of cloth from her ankles and cautiously removed the salt that was still caked around them. He snapped the aloe and spread the liquid from the stems on the sores.

Anna clenched her teeth as a burning pain shot through her foot. Before long, it began to ease and then cease altogether.

Blowing out through pursed lips, Anna's eyes met Barak's. There was awareness there, and Anna caught her breath sharply as she returned his look.

Barak fought with a curious mixture of longing and enmity. Old prejudices were hard to surmount. Dropping his gaze, he wound fresh strips of linen around Anna's feet. He stood back, intent on putting as much distance between them as he could, but Anna stopped him with a touch on his arm.

"Could you not walk beside the cart and keep me company?"

One dark eyebrow lifted upward, and Anna's cheeks flushed a rosy hue. She refused to be discouraged by that look.

"Barak," she told him softly, "I'm lonely in here."

Although every instinct told him to flee, he fell into step alongside the cart. He kept his attention focused on the horses, however.

Anna licked suddenly dry lips. Now that she had started, how should she continue?

"We were talking about the Messiah yesterday," she finally said.

Barak rolled his eyes heavenward. "If I remember correctly, *you* were the one talking about the Messiah."

Unperturbed, she agreed. "I was hoping you would share some of the scriptures concerning Him."

Deciding to be honest, he told her, "Actually, I know very little of the scriptures about Him. Uncle Simon has joined with others who are studying them very thoroughly, but it seems that I am always busy with something else."

"I remember one," she told him. "It says, 'He will proclaim peace to the nations. His rule will extend from sea to sea and from the River to the ends of the earth.'"

Barak looked at her in surprise. "The prophet Zechariah said that."

Anna's voice was soft with feeling. "Yes. I know."

Barak's narrow-eyed look scrutinized her thoroughly. "How come you to know the words of Zechariah? Are you truly a Jew?"

She ignored the last part of his question. "I have studied with some friends. They taught me much about the words of God."

Barak's face settled into tight lines. "These friends were men, no doubt."

She chose to ignore him again, asking a question instead. "If He will proclaim peace to the nations, does this mean to the Gentiles, too?"

He gave her such a dark look, Anna had to turn away.

"The prophet speaks of the Jewish nations."

Anna shook her head. "That doesn't make sense. The Jews are twelve tribes but one nation."

"That shows how little you know of Jewish history. Even in Rehoboam's time, the Jews became two nations, Israel and Judah."

"But the prophet also says that His rule will extend to the ends of the earth."

Barak's eyes glittered strangely when they fixed on her. "So says the prophet, and one day the Messiah will make this happen. The Jews will once again be the mightiest nation on earth."

Anna felt she was losing this argument. She had meant to help Barak see the fulfillment of scripture in Jesus, for truly His words brought peace as the prophet had foretold.

It would take more than one scripture for Barak to see the connection, but she was reluctant to say any more. She felt inadequate to the task. Still, she had to try.

"But King David himself said, 'Your ways may be known on earth, your salvation among all nations.'"

Anna could feel Barak's eyes on her, though she refused to turn his way. He was quiet for so long that she hesitantly peeped at him from the sides of her eyes. He was studying her as though she were an insect among his fields of grain.

Barak wanted to reach across the cart and shake the woman. What was she trying to say? Should even pagans and infidels be given atonement by Jehovah? He thought not. But perhaps for all her denial, she *was* a Samaritan and, being part Gentile, wished the Lord's forgiveness for her own idolatry.

"Tell me," he questioned sardonically. "Are there other scriptures you know?"

Anna blushed, turning her face away from his sarcastic examination. Oh yes, she knew many scriptures, but the most important information she could give him was not in the Torah.

"You are angry."

Barak sighed heavily. She was right, but exactly what was it that was making him so? Perhaps it was the thought of a *woman* knowing so much of the scriptures. Or perhaps it was the fact that *this* woman seemed to know more of the scriptures than he did. More likely, it was knowing that for Anna to know so much, her friends would surely have to have been male.

Recognizing the feeling for what it was, Barak grew angrier thinking of his jealousy over such a woman. He barely knew the girl, after all.

"I'm sorry."

Anna's apology was so soft, he scarcely heard her. Shaking himself from his irate mood, he shrugged his shoulders.

"You have no need to apologize. You were only asking a question. It is good that you seek news of the Messiah."

Sighing with relief, Anna changed the subject. "We will soon reach Jacob's Well."

Barak glanced ahead, nodding his head in affirmation. "Another five miles, I should say."

"It will be good to be home," Anna sighed softly.

Mount Gerizim came into view, rising upward in all its majestic glory. It was covered with a shadow of green and grew larger as they approached.

"Your holy mountain," Barak told her, and for once there was not ridicule in his voice. David had chosen Jerusalem as his sacred sight, but the Samaritans believed that Jehovah had chosen this mountain as His holy place. They believed this mountain to be the tallest in the world, closer to Jehovah than any other. In their own way, the Samaritans were as zealous in their beliefs as the Jews.

Barak frowned. Still, they rejected the full scriptures and were lax in their obedience to them. They didn't respect the sacred days as fully as they should.

Guilt washed through him. Did he? Here he was, for the first time in his life, visiting a country most Jews would go miles out of their way to avoid. Not only that, but he was doing it during the most sacred week of Passover.

Barak glanced heavenward, fully expecting to be struck down by a bolt of lightning. None came.

"Barak?"

Anna's soft voice brought his reflections to an abrupt halt. He felt himself tense. When he turned her way, his face was closed, empty of all emotion.

"Yes?"

"Are you Sadducee or Pharisee?"

His look passed over her and returned to the road. "I am a Pharisee."

"How is it that the two can worship together in harmony? Both serve on the same councils, the same Sanhedrin. How is this possible?"

"We worship the same God. Their interpretation of the scriptures is a little faulty," he told her impatiently. He was not used to women discussing such things with him. For some reason, it bothered him.

As Mount Gerizim drew closer, Anna knew she didn't have much time. She was afraid to continue, because as intelligent as Barak was, it wouldn't take him long to put things together and come to the right conclusion.

"Have you ever heard of a man named Saul of Tarsus?"

Barak's lips thinned with displeasure. "I've heard of him. I believe he calls himself 'Paul' now and follows the way of the infidel." He shook his head sadly. "He was a brilliant man, although his words were more powerful than the man himself."

The look he threw her was suddenly full of misgiving. "How do you know of Saul?"

"I have heard the elders speak of him, even in Samaria. He says that the Lord came to him when he was on the road to Damascus. . . ."

"I have heard the story," he interrupted. "The Lord whom he claims came to him was a crucified carpenter from Galilee. A man they call Jesus. They claim this man was the Son of God." He gave an incredulous snort. "Imagine believing such a thing. Our God is so powerful that He could defeat all the armies of the Israelites and make them the most powerful nation on earth, and they believe He would just allow them to kill His Son? And in such a way?"

"The Jews are no longer the most powerful nation on earth," she reminded him, and he turned on her a look full of annoyance. She shrugged her shoulders lightly. "Things are not the way they were in Father Abraham's time. If they were, the Jews would not be scattered about the earth."

"It comes from disobedience."

"Yet we offer sacrifices every year for the removal of our transgressions. Somehow it doesn't seem to work."

The perspiration increased on Barak's face, and he wasn't sure if it was from the increasing intensity of the sun or this woman's conversation. For the first time in his life, he felt his faith waver. Pressing his lips tightly together, he told her, "I need to see to the horses. Azuba has found another wadi to water the caravan."

"Barak. . ."

He had already gone from sight. Anna leaned back, feeling as though she had just fought a major battle with an enemy. As in a way, she had. Keeping someone from seeing the truth, or even listening to it, was Satan's best defense against the Christian faith.

She could not stop now. She had to make Barak see that he needed to search the scriptures and compare them to the man known as the Christ. If only he would do that, she knew he had the mind and the heart to believe.

Anna began praying fervently that God would give her the words, the wisdom, and the opportunity. Why it was so important to her, she didn't know. But it was.

Barak led the horses to the wadi and allowed them to drink. He tried to turn his thoughts away from the things Anna had just told him, but they refused to be swayed.

Little things from the scriptures were returning to him now.

" 'I desire mercy, not sacrifice.' "

Words from the prophet Hosea. If mercy was what Jehovah wanted, then how did this fit in with the Jewish idea of a battle to free the people?

"The sacrifices of God are a broken spirit; a broken and contrite heart."

Barak shoved his palms hard against his forehead, closing his eyes and trying to eliminate the thoughts from his head. They refused to be budged. It was almost as though now that a crack had been found, they were spilling forth until he felt for sure the dam would break.

"To do what is right and just is more acceptable to the Lord than sacrifice."

Raising his eyes heavenward, Barak beseeched the Lord. "What then do You want from me?" he whispered.

There was no answer, only the gentle sighing of the wind as it brushed faintly through the trees surrounding the wadi.

Others began to trickle back toward the caravan, ready to leave, but Barak lingered longer, hoping to hear the voice of the Lord. If he listened hard enough, would Jehovah speak to him as He had spoken to others in the past?

He sighed in frustration, knowing this would not happen.

When he returned to the carpentum, he fastened the horses into their harnesses. He was reluctant to be with Anna, yet he found himself making his way toward the cart.

She was reclining among the cushions, a distant look in her eyes as she studied the nearby mountain. The look she fixed upon him held such sadness that he wanted to reach out and comfort her.

"Beneath that mountain lies Jacob's Well and the end of our destination."

Barak felt himself go cold. He had refused to let himself think about the end of this journey, because he knew it would be the end for Anna and himself. She knew it, too. He could see it in her eyes. He should be glad to be free of the woman, but instead, he was filled with dread and misgivings.

He turned away. "As you said, it will be good for you to be home."

Everyone was in line and ready to leave, but still the caravan remained where it was. Barak frowned. "I will go see what is holding us up."

When he returned, his face was set in immobile lines. "There are some problems with a few of the camels. Azuba says that we will leave in about two hours."

Barak wasn't sure whether he was relieved or not. Two more hours with Anna. But to what end? The time he spent with her only made these new feelings grow stronger. He needed to get away as quickly as possible.

Anna slipped her legs over the side of the cart.

"What are you doing?" Barak asked in consternation.

She gave him a puzzled glance. "I wish to sit in the shade of the trees near the wadi."

Sighing in exasperation, Barak lifted her effortlessly into his arms and strode with her to the spot where he had been before. He set her on a boulder near the stream. The air was cool, the breeze heavenly.

"I can walk, you know. The sores have healed well." She smiled, and Barak felt his heart give a strong thump.

"It's peaceful here," she told him when he didn't answer.

He looked everywhere but at Anna, and she felt growing confusion over his attitude. Although he had never been other than reserved, he now was aloof to the point of coldness. She was unsure just what to say to return them to their earlier amiability.

She lifted the shawl from her shoulders and shook it out, allowing the breeze to blow through her hair. She closed her eyes, leaning her head back in the enjoyment of the moment.

Suddenly she laughed.

"What do you find amusing?" Barak wanted to know, his ire increasing as he watched her graceful movements and felt himself helplessly caught up in the maelstrom of feeling she invoked in him.

She opened her eyes slowly, the smile still on her face. "Oh, I don't know. It just feels good to be alive."

Barak needed to get away. *Now.*

"I'll get us something to eat," he told her and exited before she could object.

Anna watched his retreating back, a frown forming on her face. Was he avoiding being alone with her? Had her questions perhaps opened a hole in his defenses? She knew that there was too little time to really help him believe, but she also knew that the Word of God would not come back empty. Better to leave things in the Lord's hands and just allow herself to be His vessel.

Yet hadn't he overcome some of his silly prejudices against the Samaritans in helping her? Perhaps God would open a way for her to do the same where his hatred of Christians was concerned. Although she hadn't mentioned the Christian faith, she knew without a doubt that Barak would abhor any connection with it. He was so purely Jewish.

He returned with some fruit and water. Together they ate in silence—hers, reluctant; his, unyielding.

Anna saw him tense when she opened her mouth to speak. "Will you return to Jerusalem for *Shavuot*?"

She saw him relax. "I think not. That Uncle Simon was able to arrange this journey to Jerusalem was a miracle in itself." His eyes met hers. "Will you return to Jerusalem?"

She looked away. "I am uncertain. I don't know what will happen when Father finds out about Amman's treachery. I'm certain he will have him arrested, but the Lord only knows where it will go from there."

"He will want to keep you close to him for safety's sake until he can be sure."

"Most likely," she agreed, turning back to him. "And what of you?"

He shrugged, his eyes fixed on the cool water. Picking up a stone, he spun it into the wadi's depths. "I will farm."

Anna wanted to ask about Miriam, but she didn't feel it her place to do so. She lifted her shawl, shaking it free of dirt and leaves. A stray breeze caught it and flung it from her fingers.

She reached for it at the same time as Barak, their hands colliding among its soft folds. When Barak lifted his eyes to hers, his face was mere inches from her own. The tension between them crackled like a burning fire. They stayed thus a long moment before Barak lifted one large hand, wrapping it around the back of Anna's neck.

Anna closed her eyes, inviting his kiss. For an instant, she thought he would refuse, but suddenly his lips were on hers, and she gave herself to him freely.

The hair from his beard tickled her face, but in a tantalizing way. Anna kept her hands still, afraid that if she so much as touched him, he would retreat from this moment.

When he lifted his lips slowly from hers, she wanted so much to pull him back. She knew their time was limited, and she knew that if she wasn't in love with him already, she was at least halfway there. There was so little time left.

His eyes glittered like polished bronze, and she felt herself drawn into their depths. But suddenly she saw them grow cold, and he immediately released her.

Without a word, he lifted her from the rock and returned her to the carpentum. After he settled her among the cushions, he left.

Anna raised a trembling hand to her lips, closing her eyes as tears came unbidden. In her own selfish desire for pleasure, had she severed any hope of communication between them? Would he even allow her to speak to him now, or would he studiously avoid her as he had in the past? *Please, Lord, give me another chance.*

Before long, the caravan began moving forward, but Barak didn't return to his place by the cart. Sighing with frustration, Anna leaned back against the cushions and intensified her prayers.

What seemed only moments later, the caravan halted beside Jacob's Well. From here part of the caravan would move on to Ginae, the other part to Scythopolis. Here is where Barak and Anna would leave the caravan.

Barak returned the carpentum to Azuba, who bowed, thanking Anna politely for her presence with his caravan. Anna offered her thanks in return.

Anna and Barak watched the caravan disappear from sight. Sighing heavily, Barak turned to her. "Can you walk now?"

She nodded, unable to speak. The tears were still in her throat.

As they passed Jacob's Well, Anna stopped, sliding her hand slowly over the stone structure. Her eyes took on a glow.

"You are a Christian, aren't you?"

Shocked, she turned to him in surprise. "How did you know?"

He rubbed a hand behind his neck, blowing out through clenched teeth. "I should have figured it out sooner. How could I be so stupid?"

She felt he was talking more to himself than her. "Barak. . ."

"No!" He straightened. "Don't tell me any of your heathenish nonsense."

Pressing her lips tightly together, she turned back to the well. "The Messiah talked to my aunt here several years ago."

"What?"

"It's true," she told him, her eyes imploring him to believe.

"Bithnia?"

Anna shook her head. "No. My father's other sister. She died some time ago."

Barak stared at her, unable to say anything. His mind was reeling with chaotic thoughts, but eventually one stood out from the others.

"You speak blasphemy."

She turned her face away and sighed. "Speaking the truth is not blasphemy."

She truly believed what she said. Bothered by her steadfast denial, Barak asked her, "What makes you believe this man was the Messiah?"

"He was a prophet. He knew everything she had ever done in her life."

"That information wouldn't be hard to find out from anyone who knew her. There have been others before who claimed to be the Messiah, practicing their tricks and deceit."

"This man was different."

"In what way?"

Anna sat on the well and looked clearly into Barak's eyes. "He offered her life, not death." She moved her hand in a circle. "He told her that it wasn't important *where* you worshiped, but *how*. He said that true worshippers will worship in spirit and in truth."

The silence hung between them.

"He wishes to share God's love with *all* people," she told him softly.

Everything he had ever been taught rose up in defense of his faith. He glared at Anna, remembering again how the Israelites of old had succumbed to the beliefs of the people in this land. Intermarriage had made them weak. And he was no better. His senses swam whenever this woman was close to him. Had she managed to put some kind of spell on him that bound his thoughts to her?

Such was the way of the pagans of old. But he would not let them have his mind nor his soul. His voice was biting when next he spoke.

"I will hear no more of your blasphemy. If you speak of this again, so help me, I will leave you here for whatever brigand comes this way!"

Chapter 8

Anna followed the broad, rigid back of the man before her. His silence was unrelenting, and she began to despair of him ever saying another thing to her.

"Barak?"

He threw her a brief dark look and continued on.

"I was only going to say that my home is that way."

His eyes followed her pointing finger. Switching directions, he continued to lead the way in silence.

The green hills of home surrounded Anna like a welcoming embrace. She sighed, realizing for the first time just how much she had missed her home and her father.

The flax bloomed in sky blue profusion along the hillsides. It would be used to make the linen that was a mainstay of Sychar's economy. Everywhere spring covered the land in radiant beauty.

When they drew within sight of the small town, Anna grew uncomfortable. Most of the people here knew her. She needed to make her way home without anyone seeing her and possibly getting word to Amman before she could reach her father.

"Wait."

Barak turned to her impatiently. "What?"

She was not looking at him, but beyond him to where several children were playing beside the nearest house. As yet, they were still undetected.

"I must go another way," she told him, turning and heading back the way they had just come.

He caught up with her quickly, taking her by the arm and pulling her to a stop. "Where are you going?"

"There is an unused path that leads around the village to my father's house on the other side. It would be better than going through the town."

Barak glanced behind them and then fell reluctantly into step beside Anna. She led the way through the thick brush blooming on the hillsides. A seldom-used path could barely be seen through the greenery.

"Tell me," Barak asked finally. "What do the Samaritans think of your religion?"

Relieved that he had been the one to open the conversation, Anna told him, "Many in this village are Christians. After speaking with Jesus, my aunt returned to the town and told others about Him. Many of the people went with her to see for themselves, and many believed because they trusted my aunt's words."

Barak snorted. "They took the word of a woman on so important a matter?"

Anna stopped, turning and facing him with anger blazing in her eyes. "She was respected by many in the town, even though. . .even though. . ."

"Even though what?"

"Nothing."

Anna started forward again, but Barak took her by the arm to stop her. His hold was gentle but inexorable.

"Even though what?"

"It's not important." Her eyes met his doubtfully. "Jesus stayed in this town for two days. Many believed in Him after listening to Him and seeing the miraculous things He could do."

"I heard He was a magician."

Anna shook her head. "Not a magician. The Son of God."

Barak's eyes hardened. Pushing past her, he began to lead the way along the path.

"It's true," Anna insisted. "He fulfilled all the prophecies. You have only to search for the truth yourself."

He turned on her. "Be silent, woman."

"Barak. . ."

"Enough!" he thundered, and the forcefulness of his voice scattered a dove from the branch of an olive tree. "Your people are well-known to accept any and every god that comes their way. The Jews are not so foolish!"

"There are many Jews who believe in Him. Even the great Saul of Tarsus who once killed Jews for their belief in the Way was turned. Only the power of God could have swayed such a man."

Barak glared at her in impotent fury. He remembered Saul. He remembered when a man named Stephen had been stoned for blasphemy for trying to spread such a cult. Anna deserved the same thing, and it could happen to her, as well as any other. His blood went cold at the thought.

"Saul was run out of Jerusalem just a few years ago, and you expect me to accept that there are Jews who believe what he said?"

"Christians are persecuted everywhere. Jesus warned us that this would be so."

Her tears were his undoing. Without stopping to consider the consequences, he pulled her close, sighing heavily. "Oh, Anna. Anna. How can you believe such a thing? You are intelligent beyond most women. If you know so much of the scriptures, how can you let yourself be persuaded by such teachings?"

She pulled back from him, the tears running freely down her face. "Oh, Barak. Why can't you see?" She closed her eyes. "Please, Lord, don't let him harden his heart."

Anna didn't care if he heard her prayer or not. She was desperate to make him understand.

His large hands came up to frame her face, and he brought his own within inches of hers. His eyes glittered with some unnamed emotion. "I don't want to love you," he told her fiercely. "I *can't* love you."

His lips closed over hers, and Anna clung to him. When Anna's arms slid round his waist, he jerked away, dropping his hands to his sides and slowly backing away from her. There was a strange yearning in his eyes that Anna's heart responded to. Pivoting on his heels, he left her standing there as he retraced their path.

She watched his back disappear from sight. Dropping to her knees, she began to cry.

Barak strode down the hill not once looking back. His thoughts and emotions were waging war within his mind and his heart.

Search the scriptures! As though *she* could teach him anything about them. He had been raised on the scriptures from birth.

Hands clenching into fists at his sides, his spirit continued its battle.

Even if he could believe, there was no future for him in it. Like many, he would lose everything if he embraced such a philosophy. His mother. His uncle. Adonijah. Miriam. A sudden smile tilted his lips. Well, maybe not everything would be so bad.

He hadn't reached the first mile marker before remorse began to overcome him. He should never have left her alone. Anything could happen to her, even that close to her home. *Especially* that close to her home.

He stopped in his tracks. Amman was in Sychar, and there was no telling how many people he might have working for him. They might get to Anna before she could get to her father.

He had made a promise to God that he would deliver the girl safely into her father's care or die trying. His own emotions had gotten in the way, and now he had broken that vow. Full of regret, he turned quickly and headed back.

The more he thought of Anna's danger, the quicker his steps, until he rounded a corner and came upon three men. They were close to his own age, and they were obviously headed for the olive groves. The tools used to trim the trees dangled languidly from their fingers. Until they noticed Barak.

An instant change came over the three men, and Barak knew he was in serious trouble. It was almost impossible to tell a Samaritan from any other unless you were in the country itself, but everyone knew the mark of a Jew. The patterns used in their cloth proclaimed their Hebrew heritage, as did Barak's overcoat.

Slowly the three moved to encircle Barak.

"You're a Jew."

He was the larger of the three and the obvious leader. He almost spat the words as he hurled an insult.

Barak grew strangely calm, his adrenaline beginning to pump through his veins in an ever-quickening movement. He could either run or fight, and he had not been taught to do the former.

"I know who *I* am. Who are you?"

The leader moved closer. "I'm one of those Samaritan dogs you despise so much. What brings you to our distasteful part of the country, not that it makes any difference?"

Barak's eyes went from one to the other, assessing. Although he was broad and muscular from working in the fields, the same could also be said of these three. They were fine specimens of manhood, even if they were Samaritans.

"I am here on business," he told them, the tone of his voice letting them know that he would divulge no more.

These three were aching for a fight, and at any other time, Barak would have been willing to oblige. But not now. He needed to get back to Anna.

"Your business will have to wait. You have business with us instead."

"I am not looking for a fight."

Another man snickered. "Well, we are."

The third man glared at Barak. "Let's rid the earth of one more foul Jew. The less of them, the safer *our* people will be."

"I have heard that Samaritans were cowards who attacked the unsuspecting. It would seem I heard correctly."

Even from a distance Barak could hear the leader's breathing increase, and he realized his rash words had doomed him to a battle there was no way he could win. He was outnumbered, for one thing. When he saw one man reach for a rock, he knew he was outweaponed, also. He only had time to duck the rock before the three were upon him.

Barak fought valiantly, but when a huge rock connected with his head, he went down. Stars swam in circles before his eyes momentarily.

Jehovah, help me!

Darkness closed in, mercifully bringing unconsciousness.

How long Anna knelt there, she had no idea. Mixed with her tears were fervent prayers. There were no words in her mind, only thoughts and feelings, but she knew God would understand.

She climbed wearily to her feet. Barak had left her. At first she couldn't believe it, but then she realized it was true. He wasn't coming back.

His passionate declaration had left her shaken. Vulnerable. He was fighting his feelings for her as much as she was fighting hers for him.

No. That wasn't true, either, because in all honesty, Anna knew she hadn't fought very hard at all.

She turned to head for home, but something stopped her. She should go after Barak and tell him of her feelings.

Shaking her head, she started on. What good would that do? It would only serve to destroy her pride, of which at the moment she had very little left.

A small voice seemed to whisper in her mind. *Pride goes before destruction.*

An odd premonition sent a shiver of chills throughout her entire being. She stopped, wrapping her arms around herself and shaking with some unknown dread.

A moment more and she was hurrying after Barak. In her mind, she believed herself foolish for her flight of fancy, but her heart drove her on. She had to be sure.

The farther down the road she went, the more she became convinced she was being ridiculous in her thinking. Her feet began to ache as her sandals rubbed against the partially healed sores.

For the first time in days, she gave no thought to her own predicament. *Lord, I know You'll protect me. Please protect Barak, too.*

She was almost a mile from the path that led to her village when she slowed, her breath coming in hurried gasps. She could see far ahead down the road, and there was no sign of Barak. His rapid stride would have taken him much farther, and she had no hope of catching him.

It had been absurd to think that he needed her. Probably her own foolish longings had inspired her thinking in such a rash way.

Stopping to catch her breath, Anna moved to the side of the road and sat gingerly on a large rock. Lifting one foot, she noticed that the sores were open and bleeding again. Sighing, she dropped her foot, her gaze once more lifting to the azure sky.

Help me, Lord, to know Your will. Help me to die to myself and live only for You. I love You, Yahweh.

Anna looked about on the land of her birth, the land that she loved. She knew in her heart that she would give it up in an instant to follow the man whom she now knew she loved. But not without the Christ. Never without her Lord.

How was it possible for love to come so quickly? Were her feelings mere infatuation with a strong, handsome man who had shown her the attention she had never received before? She shook her head. It couldn't be. These feelings had drawn her to him before she had ever met him. She had seen him in the temple courtyard, and suddenly her world had changed.

All of a sudden, she felt an affinity for the Jacob her well was named for. He had loved Rachel on sight, too. Their situation was much different from hers, however.

Her melancholy thoughts were brought to an abrupt halt by a piece of material caught on a bush across from her. Getting swiftly to her feet, she went and lifted it from the branch, recognizing the pattern from Barak's coat.

So, he had come this way. But how long ago? She lifted a hand to block the sun shining in her eyes. For as far as the eye could see, there was no one in sight. Nothing seemed to be moving.

It was only as her eyes dropped to the ground that she noticed the bare foot peeking out from behind the bushes.

Gasping, she pushed her way through the brush, ignoring the barbs tearing at her own dress. What she saw made her draw back in horror.

Pressing the back of her hand against her mouth, Anna stifled a cry. A man lay covered in blood from head to foot. His clothes hung tattered against his body.

She could see now where he had been dragged from the road and dumped in the bushes to die.

Almost afraid, but determined to know, she knelt beside him and gently turned him over. A small cry escaped her.

"Barak!"

She felt for a pulse and found it weakly beating. "Lord," she begged. "Don't let him die!"

Bruises covered his body, and a large gash at the side of his head continued to bleed. Tearing off her belt, she wound it around his head to stem the flow of blood.

She had to get help, but she didn't want to leave him. She struggled with indecision.

"Oh, what do I do?"

Realizing that he was well hidden from any others passing that way, she made her decision and got quickly to her feet.

"I'll be back," she told him, knowing that he couldn't hear her. The promise was more for herself than for him.

Anna ran back the way she had come until she found the house where the children still played outside. They drew back from her as she approached, for truly she looked demented and her tunic was splotched with blood.

Taking a calming breath, she held her hand out slowly. "Shimei, it's Anna."

The young boy's mouth dropped open, his eyes widening. His little sister pulled close against his side.

"Shimei, I need help. Would you please go for my father? Tell him that Anna needs him."

Nodding, the boy turned to obey.

"Wait." He turned back to her. "Tell only my father, no one else. Understand?"

He nodded again.

"Hurry then. I will be about a mile back down the road."

Anna waited to see the boy on his way before turning to his sister.

"Sarah, go and tell your mother that Shimei is giving a message to my father. Okay?"

"Okay, Anna." The little girl hurried inside to deliver her message, and Anna flew back the way she had come. She prayed the whole way, petitioning the Lord on Barak's behalf and pleading that her father would be home to receive the message.

She found the spot easily and bent once again over Barak. His stillness frightened her. Her hands floated over him like a butterfly reluctant to settle. There was hardly a place on his body that was not marked in some way.

Who could have done this to him? She remembered the purse of money that Bithnia had given him. In his anger, he had forgotten to give it to her.

She searched and found the purse still intact. Puzzled, she tried to fathom the reason for such an attack if not for robbery.

Snatches of conversation between her father and others came back to her now. Enmity between the Samaritans and Jews was escalating. Only a few months ago, some Samaritans had killed a party of Jews on their way to Jerusalem.

"Jesus," she pleaded. "Help me to show them Your love. Let the fighting stop."

In what could only have been a short time but had seemed an eternity, Anna could hear horses galloping toward her. She lifted herself from her position on the ground and stood waiting until her father came into sight, followed by several other men on horses.

Anna recognized some of her father's servants, and Amman was with them. His eyes met Anna's, and she realized in that instant he knew that she knew everything. She could see his fear, but she had no thoughts for him just now. She would handle that situation later.

Tirinus threw himself from his horse, wrapping his arms tightly around his daughter.

"Anna! Can it be?" He pulled back and looked into her face, framing it with his beefy palms. "I received a message from your aunt only hours ago that you had been abducted and were being held for ransom." He frowned. "Is your aunt playing some kind of sick jest?"

Anna pulled from his arms. "I'll explain later. Right now Barak needs help."

"Barak?"

He followed her to the bushes, sucking in breath at the sight of the bloodied young man. "Dear Jehovah."

In moments, Tirinus had everyone organized. He had a cart brought from the town, and they lifted Barak gently into it. Anna refused to leave his side.

Tirinus's eyebrows lifted in question, his glance meeting Amman's. The Arab shrugged, his eyes narrowing as he watched Anna gently stroke the dark hair back from Barak's bloodied forehead.

When they returned to her father's villa, Anna helped the men take Barak to one of the guest rooms. She turned to the nearest servant.

"Ajah, go for the healer. Quickly."

Tirinus came to stand beside her. "Now suppose you tell me what this is all about. How do you come to be here with this young man when I left you, I thought, safely in Jerusalem?"

Anna turned blazing eyes to her father. "It's Amman's doing. He wanted your money *now*, not in a year. If he couldn't have it one way, he would get it another."

Tirinus's eyes narrowed. "What are you saying? Amman has been as worried about you as I. We were getting ready to come to Jerusalem when Shimei came tearing to the door."

Rising to her feet, Anna laid her hand on her father's forearm. "Father, Amman arranged for me to be abducted and held for ransom. He is a ruthless man. If not for Barak, I would be only God knows where." Her eyes softened when she looked at the young man lying on the bed. "The Lord sent him to me when I needed someone most."

Tirinus lifted a skeptical brow. "He doesn't look much like an angel."

"He does to me."

Her voice was so tender, Tirinus jerked his look back to her. Anna was kneeling next to the bed, carefully washing blood from Barak's face.

Anna could feel her father's rage mounting as he watched her, but she was uncertain of its intended victim until he bellowed for one of his most trusted bodyguards.

Emnon was a giant of a man, a Philistine her father had hired many years ago. His look went from daughter to father.

"Bring me Amman."

The fire in Tirinus's eyes provoked a response in his servant. Bowing, he left to do as he was bidden.

"Anna, are you certain about this?"

There was no questioning the sincerity of the eyes she turned his way. "I am positive, Father."

Tirinus shook his head. "I don't understand. Why didn't Bithnia tell me?"

"When she sent the message, she didn't know. Micah was in on it, too."

Dropping to a seat behind him, Tirinus could only stare uncomprehendingly. "Not Micah."

"I know, Father," she told him softly. "I felt the same."

Tirinus's eyes went to Barak. "And how does he enter into this?"

"It's a long story."

The look he fixed on his daughter made her swallow hard. "I have plenty of time," he told her.

Anna began at the beginning, leaving out only the kisses she had shared with Barak and the strange attraction they seemed to feel for each other.

Her father listened intently, his face going white, his eyes growing colder as the story progressed. Fearing for his health, she tried to minimize much of what had happened, but she knew he could tell more from what she didn't say than from what she did.

She was unaware of what she told her father merely by the looks she bestowed on the young Jew. He frowned.

Tirinus wondered why a Jew would go to so much effort for a Samaritan. Troubled, he studied the young man. That his daughter had fixed her affections on him was beyond doubt.

And what of Amman? His eyes darkened in anger. If what Anna had said was true, and he had no reason to doubt her, on his life he would see the Arab stoned to death.

The healer came soft footed into the room. His dark eyes took in the scene as he moved across the room to the still figure on the bed.

Anna got up to allow him better access, but she didn't stray far from Barak's side.

After a moment, Tirinus asked him, "How is he, Sibbecai? Will he live?"

Sibbecai lifted himself from his inspection of the inert figure. "He has lost a lot of blood. Many people die from less injuries than he has, but then I have also seen others more serious who survive." He crossed to Tirinus, wiping the blood from his hands on the towel the servant provided. "Still, he is strong."

Anna agreed, and to see such strength diminished brought tears to her eyes. She reclaimed her position by the bed.

Sibbecai began mixing a potion, which he then brought to Anna. "See if you can get some down his throat. Not too much, or he might choke."

"What's it for?"

"It will help to keep fever away." He then began mixing together some ingredients to make a salve for Barak's wounds. "After the wounds have been cleaned, put this on them. It will stop the flow of blood and help to stay infection."

Anna took it from him, adding her thanks.

"I will return tomorrow if you need me. There's not much I can do. It's up to this young man now."

Tirinus walked with him to the door. Emnon reached the portal at the same time.

"Amman has disappeared."

Chapter 9

Anna tended to Barak's wounds throughout the day and long into the night. He seemed no worse, but then neither did he seem any better.

Emnon entered the room and took up a position near the door, his burly arms crossed against his chest. His huge sword glinted menacingly at his side.

Always before, Anna had resented her father's protectiveness. Now she was grateful. Knowing she didn't have to watch her back allowed her to concentrate fully on Barak.

A servant came in and lighted the lamps. Already the sun was sinking below the horizon, and the light from the lamps cast eerie shadows around the room.

Anna leaned forward. "Barak, can you hear me?"

There was no answer, and her heart sank. She had been praying all day, and she would continue throughout the night if need be.

A girl brought her a tray of food, but Anna shook her head. "Take it away, Beniah. I don't want anything."

The girl looked distressed. "Your father insists, my lady."

"Tell him that I will fast for tonight. I will eat something tomorrow."

Beniah watched her mistress's fingers graze ever so slightly across the forehead of the stranger. "I will tell him."

Anna should have known that that wouldn't be the end of it. Her father strode into the room and drew up beside her.

"What's this I hear? You will make yourself ill if you don't eat."

Sighing, Anna glanced up at him. "Not for one night, Father. Just for one night, I wish to fast and pray."

His smile was gentle. "You think to influence Jehovah that way?"

She smiled in return. "It can't hurt. I want the Lord to know how serious I am, that my prayers are not just a fleeting thought."

Tirinus studied the man on the bed. He could see no change, and for the first time, he realized just what it would do to his daughter if the young man were to die. Annoyed, he wondered how this whole thing would turn out.

"I don't wish you to leave the villa without Emnon. We are still searching for Amman."

Anna had no intention of leaving the villa until Barak returned to health, if God would so will it, but she didn't say this to her father.

"I understand."

Tirinus left her, and Anna went back to her vigil. She talked to Barak softly, hoping that he could hear her. She smiled slightly. The things she said to him she could never say if he were awake. He would walk off and leave her.

She told him of Christ's virgin birth, of a woman named Elizabeth who bore the prophesied "Elijah" who would come ahead of the Messiah. She quoted him scriptures that she had been taught by other believers that showed the way of the Lord's salvation.

"Oh, Barak," she pleaded softly. "Please believe me."

And so she continued on through the night talking to Barak, talking to God. When her eyes grew heavy, she got up and splashed water on her face. She was determined to stay awake all night. Sleep could come when she was assured of Barak's safety. She covered him with her prayers as she covered him with the silk sheet.

Before the night was half over, Emnon was replaced by her father's second favorite bodyguard. Cleopas wasn't nearly as large as Emnon, but he made up for in tenacity what he lacked in size. He and Anna had been friends for a long time.

Sometime toward morning, Anna could detect a change in Barak's breathing. It no longer sounded as ragged as before, and she praised God. Feeling his forehead, she could tell that there was still no fever.

Fingers of morning light penetrated the closed shutters, brightening the room. Tirinus found Anna exactly as he had left her.

"Bed for you," he commanded, and Anna recognized the inflexible quality of his voice. "Beniah will sit with the young man while you sleep. We will call you if there is any change."

Anna rose reluctantly to her feet. She frowned at her father, and he read her thoughts correctly.

"You needn't fear; there has been no sign of Amman. He is probably halfway to Jerusalem by now, if he knows what's good for him. Still, Emnon or Cleopas will be with you at all times."

Cleopas followed Anna from the room and took his place as guard just outside her bedroom door. Anna partially closed the curtains around her bed and lay down. Sleep was a long time coming. Instead, her thoughts were in the other room, her prayers heaven bound.

Her room was spacious, airy, and cool. At one time she had thrilled over such material things as much as her father did now. But then Jesus had come into her life and shown her a different kind of love. A different way. All the riches in the world couldn't compare with what she would one day receive in heaven.

She rolled to her back, laying a forearm across her forehead. If only she could make Barak believe. She respected his unyielding belief in the faith of his forefathers, but she hoped that he could be persuaded to search for the truth. *If* he lived that long.

A prayer to that effect was the last thing on her mind when she finally drifted off to sleep.

When Anna awakened, she could tell by the shadows in her room that afternoon was well on the wane. Her stomach rumbled, reminding her of her self-imposed fast.

Climbing from the bed, she made her way across the room to her dressing alcove. She freshened herself with the water in the basin. Dropping her torn and dirty tunic to the floor, she chose another of bright blue, the color of the flax blossoms she had noticed earlier.

She chose to leave the sandals off her feet and padded barefoot along the landing to the room where Barak was still being watched over.

This time her father brought the tray of food. "Eat," he commanded, and she knew better than to disobey.

He sat down beside her while she consumed the food with relish. There was a sparkle in her eyes.

"He looks better, don't you think? There's more color in his face."

Tirinus let his gaze pass over Barak dubiously. The only color he could see was black-and-blue.

"I'm sure you are right," he agreed, loath to disappoint her. "Anna, we need to talk."

"What about?"

"About your inappropriate feelings for this young man." There was a harshness in his voice she had never heard before.

She raised surprised eyes to his face. "Why inappropriate?"

He noted that she didn't deny having any feelings for the Jew.

"Anna. His people hate our people. There can be nothing but heartache for you in this matter."

"You would rather I fix my affections on someone like Amman?" she asked angrily.

Tirinus had the grace to blush.

"That this young man was willing to help you is a miracle in itself, but to think that there could ever be anything between you is foolish."

Anna turned her gaze back to Barak. His face was so swollen it was almost unrecognizable, but to her he was beautiful.

"There is already something between us. I don't know how to explain it, but it's there. We both have tried to fight it, but it's. . .it's there."

Tirinus shook his head. "It's not like you to be so foolish. Would you wish Barak to give up everything for you? He would have to, you know, because his family would never accept you even if he did."

"With God, all things are possible."

He sighed. "You and that confounded faith of yours. Your aunt was a silly woman. How she could manage to persuade so many people is beyond me."

"Father, she talked with the Messiah. He told her how to find eternal life."

Tirinus fastened his look on Barak. "And have you told *him* about it?"

Anna hesitated. "Yes."

"Ah."

Leaning back in his chair, Tirinus studied his daughter's averted face. "So, he rejected you, did he?"

Anna got to her feet, taking the bowl of water and throwing its contents from the balcony to the yard below. She poured more fresh water from the pitcher and began changing the compresses on Barak's forehead. Although he had no fever, the cool water would help to comfort his body.

Tirinus watched her a moment before rising to his feet. "I will leave you to play healer. I only hope you know what you're doing."

Days passed into a week, and still Barak resisted all efforts to awaken him.

Sibbecai came and went periodically. His only reaction to the news was that Barak had suffered severe internal injuries and his body was concentrating on healing those first.

Anna was far from satisfied with these answers.

Three days later, Bithnia arrived. She and Tirinus locked themselves into a room for several hours. Normally Anna would have been dying of curiosity, but as it was, she hardly gave it a thought.

Bithnia came into the room, her eyes focused on her niece.

"You've lost weight."

Anna smiled slightly. "What brings you here, Aunt Bithnia?"

The look on her aunt's face told Anna that something was wrong. "What is it?"

"Micah was found dead in a wadi between here and Jerusalem a few days ago. Kasim was arrested for the crime. It seems that Kasim was helping to finance a Jewish sect of zealots who hoped to overthrow Rome, and Micah was one of them."

Anna shook her head sadly. "Poor Micah."

Bithnia pursed her lips. "Bad company." She glanced at Barak before fixing her steady regard on Anna. "Your father has talked to me."

Twisting her mouth wryly, Anna shrugged her shoulders.

"Anna," Bithnia told her softly. "He is not of our faith."

"Aunt Bithnia, God has placed this love for Barak in my heart, and only God can remove it. If it is His will, then who am I to deny it?"

There was no mistaking the warning in her aunt's voice. "Don't try to use the Lord to justify your own feelings."

Ashamed, Anna dropped her eyes.

"Your father wants you to return to Jerusalem." She glanced again at Barak. "But he knows you won't leave just now."

"He's right."

Bithnia nodded. "I understand. When the time comes, let me know, and I'll come for you." She kissed Anna's cheek and went out.

Perhaps it was awful of her to think it, but at least two of her would-be abductors were out of the way.

Suddenly she felt a great loss for the friend Micah had been. Now he was lost for eternity. She should have done more to reach him, but even her own father rejected the faith. She sighed. So far, she had done nothing toward leading *anyone* to Jesus, and she felt a great regret that this was so. She longed to be as impassioned as the apostles.

Gentle Micah a zealot! It was hard to imagine. Had his zeal for his cause driven him to deny the friendship they had shared for years? At first she was hurt by the thought, then awed. Micah's was the same kind of fervor she should have for Jesus, but whereas Micah would give up all for his crusade, Anna had given up nothing.

Nothing save Barak, a little voice seemed to whisper.

A stirring from the bed brought her quickly to Barak's side. He moved his head slightly, moaning in pain.

"Quickly, Emnon. Send someone for Sibbecai."

Anna knelt beside him, stroking her fingers across his forehead. His eyes opened slowly and stared uncomprehendingly into hers. Those blank brown eyes brought a quick frown to Anna's face.

"Barak?"

"Who are you?" he croaked, and Anna felt her heart go still.

Before she could answer, Sibbecai came into the room and came to stand beside them. Anna rose to her feet.

"He doesn't know me," she told the healer hollowly.

Sibbecai moved her aside so he could examine his patient. "Who are you?" he asked as he lifted Barak's eyelids to look inside.

Barak frowned at him. "I. . .I don't know."

Straightening, Sibbecai turned to Anna. "It's to be expected. He had a savage blow to his head. More than one from the looks of it."

"Will he. . .will he ever remember?"

Sibbecai shook his head. "Only time will tell. Maybe. Maybe not."

Tirinus came into the room, followed by Bithnia. "What's going on?"

"Barak's awake."

There was little joy in Anna's voice. Her father glanced at her quickly before turning his gaze on Barak. "What's wrong?"

"What happened to me?" Even after a week, Barak's face was still swollen, and his voice came out obscured by the twisting of his lips.

Sibbecai told them about Barak's memory loss. Bithnia went and put her arm around Anna, hugging her close. They waited for someone to say something.

Barak tried to rise, but Sibbecai pushed him back against the cushions. "You're alive, young man, and if you want to stay that way, then be still." He checked Barak's injuries further, asking a few questions. It was clear his memory loss was only partial. He could remember some things, but others eluded him.

Anna explained to Barak what had transpired on the road, leaving out his reasons for being there. She was saddened when he looked at her without recognition.

He lay back against the cushions, staring at the ceiling. Before long his eyelids drifted closed.

Giving a tired sigh, Anna settled herself beside him. Sibbecai patted her shoulder.

"At least he is alive, and that is something to praise Jehovah for, huh?"

Anna nodded.

"If it's God's will that he remembers, he will," the healer told her. "Leave it in His hands."

"All things work for the good. . . ." she murmured.

"What?"

"Nothing."

Anna watched everyone leave, her father and Sibbecai deep in discussion. Aunt Bithnia turned back at the door to give her a reassuring smile before she closed the door behind her.

For the next several days, Barak wakened for gradually longer periods of time. Anna refused to allow anyone else to tend to him except when her father insisted she get some much-needed sleep.

Each day brought improvement in his health, but his mind still refused to remember. Anna fretted over him until one day he took her by the wrist, grinning.

"You act like a wife." It was more a question than a statement.

Anna's cheeks bloomed with color. She shook her head, and he released her. "No. I'm. . .I'm just a friend," she stammered.

"My family?"

"You have family in Jotapata."

A slight frown puckered his brow. "I. . .I can't remember." The eyes he lifted to her were full of frustration.

"I know. It must be hard for you, but Sibbecai says there are signs that your memory loss is not permanent."

His eyes studied her face. She could see him trying to remember, and she added her will to his.

"The bruises are fading," she told him happily, "but the broken ribs will take much longer. You're fortunate that there was no serious injury to you inside."

Anna took the tray the servant brought her and prepared to feed him. His eyes darkened in irritation. Struggling to sit up, he told her, "I can feed myself."

She put her arm around his shoulders, trying to help him into a sitting position. They worked for some time before they had him adjusted to his satisfaction.

Anna turned a smiling face to his, only inches from her own. His eyes narrowed when she hastily moved away.

Barak took the tray from her, studying her face as he did so. He hadn't been mistaken. Anna's breathing had quickened, and her pupils had darkened perceptibly. His own pulse had jumped in response.

There was something going on here that he couldn't understand, and wouldn't understand, until he got back his memory. Something to do with Anna and himself. What made her so nervous when she was near him?

Anna watched anxiously as he slowly consumed his food. Periodically he would raise his eyes to hers, and she could see the questions there. She began to fidget with her tunic, twisting and untwisting the material. She couldn't bring herself to meet his eyes again.

"My family in Jotapata. Is there a way to get a message to them?"

Surprised, she told him, "I can send someone with your message."

"Are they expecting me?"

Anna dropped her eyes. "I believe they were expecting you home a few days ago."

He leaned back against the pillows. "Send the message, if you will."

Anna took a deep breath. It was only right that she send the message and relieve his family of worry, but if she did, would they come for him angry that he was among Samaritans? Would it cause more trouble?

Jesus had once told a story of a Samaritan helping a Jew. This was the same situation in reverse, except that in Jesus' story the two were strangers. Barak and Anna were not.

When Barak was ready to lie down again, Anna helped him as gently as possible. He winced in pain, but he didn't complain.

She leaned over to fix the covers, and he wrapped one large hand around the back of her neck and drew her close. The intensity of his dark eyes made her almost afraid.

"What am I to you?" he whispered.

She almost blurted, "Only everything." Instead, she answered him softly in return. "Someday your memory will return. We will discuss it then."

He held her captive with his eyes for a long moment, finally dropping his hand and turning away. "I look forward to that day."

As do I, she thought. But when that day came, would he walk away from her again, before she had a chance to explain anything?

Several days later, Anna was helping Barak to get up from the bed for the first time since his attack. She giggled as she tried to hold up his immense body with her own frail strength.

He smiled in return. "This is like a dove trying to hold up a bear."

She hid a grin. "And lately you've been acting like one, too."

Suddenly serious, he took her by the shoulders, searching her eyes with his own. "I have been. I'm sorry."

Barak recalled how he had snapped at her only that morning for trying to help him remember things from his past. He was frustrated that after so much time he still could not remember. Little things were beginning to come back to him, like knowing the month and the season, but not the important things like family and friends.

"I understand," she told him. "I try to think what it would be like for me, but my mind boggles at such a thought. Just know that you are welcome here for as long as you need to stay."

Barak let go of her and moved to the open window. A gentle breeze fluttered the drapes, the warm sun lighting his face as he moved into it.

For a long time, he stood staring at the landscape from the balcony. His brows wrinkled in concentration as fragments from his past assaulted his mind. He turned back to Anna.

"I'm in Samaria," he said and frowned.

Anna swallowed the lump in her throat. More of his memory was coming back to him, and she grew afraid of what this would mean for her now.

His eyes raked over her as the frown increased. "There's something about you. . . ."

He didn't finish. His stare grew harder. Anna decided it was time to leave.

"I think you'd better rest for now. Supper will be served before long. I'll see you then."

For all his injuries, he beat her to the door. He held the door closed with one hand while reaching for her with the other. When his eyes connected with hers, there was the same awareness there that she had seen before, and Anna knew that his memory had returned with a vengeance.

"Anna."

She lifted her eyes to his fearfully, expecting to see the anger he so often exhibited. Instead, there was a wealth of tenderness in his look.

Anna sucked in a breath, hardly daring to breathe. "Barak. You remember."

He nodded slowly, his eyes roving her face. "I was coming back to you. Coming back to make sure you got to your father safely."

"I'm sorry," she told him, tears in her voice, and he knew to what she was referring.

"I meant what I said. I can't love you."

But they both knew it was already too late.

He kissed her gently on her lips before setting her away from him. Turning, he went back and lay on the bed. "Go away, Anna. Go away and don't come back."

She knew that if she didn't, Barak would find some way to leave. He would fight their love every step of the way, and his zeal was as powerful as Micah's. Her shoulders slumped wearily, knowing she hadn't the strength to defy him. Besides, she didn't want to make it any harder on him than it already was.

She closed the door softly behind her.

Barak stared at the closed door, gritting his teeth in frustration. He knew he was not well enough to travel, but he knew he couldn't stay here. Temptation was only a short distance away.

Yet if he tried to leave, he knew he would be dead before he got anywhere close to home. Probably he would be found by the cutthroats who lived among the hills, and they would finish the job those infernal Samaritans had begun.

How could he possibly be falling in love with a Samaritan, and a *Christian* one at that? Even the thought should make him ill, but somehow it didn't.

Jehovah, he prayed, *protect me from the evil one. Save me from my sin. Help me to stay faithful to You.*

A hazy memory flitted in and out of his mind like a sibilant whisper. What was it? He closed his eyes, trying to concentrate. Something about a virgin birth and a woman named Elizabeth. Something about the "Elijah" to come.

Scriptures. Scriptures he hadn't thought about in years. Was it possible the Messiah had really come? He shook his head angrily. Anna's Messiah died on a cross. Could the Messiah really be killed in such a way? Wasn't He going to lead His people out of bondage?

"He was despised and rejected by men, a man of sorrows, and familiar with suffering. Like one from whom men hide their faces he was despised, and we esteemed him not."

The prophecy from Isaiah hit him with stunning clarity. The Messiah would be rejected, not respected.

He shoved a hand hard against his forehead, trying to remember more. He had to remember more!

His head began to pound with the fury of a thousand storms. Moaning, he was unaware of Anna returning to the room.

He ground his teeth together as the pain in his head increased.

A cup was held to his lips, and he drank thirstily. Lying back against the pillows, he sighed when a cold cloth was pressed against his forehead.

Drowsy eyes lifted upward to meet worried hazel ones. "Don't leave me," he whispered, and for Anna, it was enough.

Chapter 10

For three days, Barak suffered excruciating headaches that left him weak and confused. On the fourth day, he awoke clear-eyed and free from pain.

Anna hovered close by, unsure of her reception but adamant in her refusal to leave his side.

Barak reached out a hand and gently stroked his fingers down her forearm. She swallowed hard at his tender look.

"How long have I been ill?"

"Three days," she told him, removing herself to a safe distance. She took the water basin she had used to frequently bathe his forehead and dumped the water from the balcony. Her insides were quivering with relief that the Lord had spared his life. For a time, even Sibbecai had thought that Barak might find his way to Sheol.

Barak noticed the dark circles under Anna's eyes. The pallor of her skin bespoke of fatigue.

"You stayed with me the whole time?"

Anna met his eyes briefly but turned quickly away. "Yes."

He reached out a hand to her, his voice compelling when he commanded softly, "Anna, come here."

Her stomach turned into a leaden weight. Reluctantly she moved across the room to his side.

Barak took her trembling hand in his own, tugging until she dropped to his side. There was remorse in his eyes.

"I'm sorry," he told her.

Anna's chin lifted a notch. "For what?"

"For telling you to go away and never come back. I was foolish."

"You were right," she answered heavily. "It would be best."

"For whom?"

There was a subtle change in his eyes as they studied her. Anna once more dropped her chin. "For both of us, I think."

He shook his head. "There is a reason Jehovah brought us together."

He lifted himself slowly to a sitting position, putting his head in his hands as the room began to reel giddily around him. Nausea clenched his stomach, and he swallowed hard to keep the bile from rising into his throat.

"You need to rest," Anna told him in alarm. "You are still not well."

"Well enough," he disagreed. "I need to make arrangements to leave. My mother will be frantic with worry."

"I sent her a message, as you suggested."

He glanced up quickly. "What did you say in it?"

"I told her that you had been attacked and that we were tending to you. I also told her that your beating was so severe it might be some time before you could return home."

His eyes smoldered with a strange light. "I can't stay."

Lips pressed tightly together, she got to her feet and went to a stool, where she lifted some garments and held them up for his inspection.

"These are for you. My father hopes that you will accept them with his thanks for your kindness in bringing me safely to Sychar."

Barak fought with his desire to refuse. For one thing, he didn't wish to hurt Anna any further, and for another, he knew that his other clothes had been rent beyond repair.

"Thank him for me."

Relieved, Anna smiled slightly. "I will do so."

They continued to stare at each other until Barak's mouth tipped into a lopsided grin. "If you will allow me, I will change. I must be on my way."

Anna's heart sank at the declaration but lifted slightly when she told him, "It is the Sabbath."

Barak frowned in annoyance. He turned his eyes away from her. "Then I will leave on the morrow."

"We just received a message today from your mother. She says that she is sending Adonijah to bring you home."

Barak's head whipped back to her, a slow smile lighting his face. "That is good. I will wait for him then."

Anna moved to the door, and Barak was once again struck by her grace. She moved like a nimble gazelle.

Her eyes met his briefly before she turned and exited the room, and Barak knew with certainty that she would not return.

"No, Anna."

Anna stared at her overprotective parent in frustration. "But, Father, I wish to worship with other believers."

He was already shaking his head. "You are not to leave this villa."

She sighed. "Even if Emnon or Cleopas comes with me?"

"No, and that's final."

Anna dropped her bread to her plate, her hunger suddenly vanishing. For a long time now, she had been looking forward to spending tomorrow, the Lord's Day, with others who followed the Way.

Although King Herod Agrippa had instituted a heavy persecution among the Jewish Christians, the numbers in Samaria were steadily growing. It was only one more thing to establish enmity among the people of the region.

Tirinus continued eating as though nothing were out of the ordinary. He was fully aware of his daughter's disapproval, and though he had given concessions in the past, he was not willing to do so now.

He felt her regard and grew uncomfortable under that look. He knew if he lifted his eyes to hers he would find nothing but censure there, and he had always been unable to stand firm under those expressive eyes.

"Why not ask the worshipers to come here," he finally acquiesced and heard her suck in her breath.

"You would allow this?"

He nodded, still without looking up. Anna squealed, throwing herself at her father and hugging him tightly.

"Thank you, Father."

Tirinus smiled to himself, shaking his head at his own weakness where his daughter was concerned. But at least the food no longer tasted like dust in his mouth.

Barak found Anna in the walled garden behind the villa. The ever-faithful Emnon wasn't far away. The two men eyed each other warily before the Philistine nodded his head ever so slightly and turned away.

Anna turned from where she knelt, lifting her face to his in surprise. Barak dropped down beside her, noticing the basket of flowers as he did so. One brow lifted in query.

"I wished some flowers for the triclinium," she told him, and he wondered at the color that suddenly flooded her cheeks.

Barak's eyes fixed on the Philistine. "He guards you well. I am much relieved."

"Why?"

The soft whisper sent the blood quickstepping through his veins. He turned and caught her look. "You know why."

Anna looked away. It was the closest he would come to admitting any feelings for her, and she knew it.

Barak lifted his face to the sun, reveling in its warmth. "It's a beautiful day."

"Yes," she agreed. "A beautiful Lord's Day."

"Lord's Day? *Every* day is the Lord's Day."

She smiled, continuing to cut flowers. "For Christians, it is the day we remember our Lord having risen from the dead. A time to worship."

She refused to look at him, but she sensed his displeasure. He said nothing.

"You are welcome to join us."

His voice was biting. "I think not."

She turned to him then, her eyes pleading. "I am not suggesting that you participate, but wouldn't you like to see for yourself if this religion is as vile as you believe it to be?"

"I have heard of the cannibalism among Christians, and the practice of brothers and sisters meeting together in incestuous and sinful ways."

Anna's eyes grew cold with fury. "That is a lie! We do no such thing!"

Barak couldn't believe it of this woman, either, but he was afraid to find out the truth. What if the stories were true? Would it cure him of this obsession he seemed to have with this one Samaritan? Or would it perhaps draw him further into their mystical, sordid practices? He needed to find out.

"Perhaps I *will* attend this meeting with you."

Mouth dropping open in surprise, Anna could only stare at him. What was on his mind now? Would he perhaps do as the apostle Paul had once done by reporting the Jewish believers to the authorities in Jerusalem? She grew fearful, and yet she knew that the Lord could use this opportunity to reach Barak as Anna never could.

Getting to her feet, she passed him to return to the villa. "You are welcome. We will meet in the triclinium for supper."

Barak watched her go, his insides heaving. Tonight he would know, one way or another.

Barak's eyes grew wide with surprise at the number of people gathered for the evening meal. There were wealthy, as well as poor. Elderly, as well as children. His look encompassed the entire crowd, coming to rest at last on Anna herself.

She was sitting close to a man, their heads nearly together as they discussed something. The man was not young, but neither was he old. He was probably around forty years of age and quite handsome. Anna's eyes were focused intently on the man as he continued to expound some point. Barak felt his insides twist with jealousy.

As though she could feel his look, she turned and caught sight of him hovering near the doorway. She said something to the man at her side and rose, quickly making her way to Barak's side.

"Welcome," she told him softly.

One brow quirked upward, but he refrained from comment.

"Come with me." Anna turned to make her way back to her seat, and Barak followed her, aware of several pairs of eyes on him. He met each look with a cold glare.

Anna introduced Barak to the man she had been speaking with. Dark eyes studied dark eyes as each man sized the other up. A slow smile began in the depths of Naboth's eyes and continued until it reached his lips.

"Welcome, Barak," he said, and Barak felt himself unsettled by the man's friendliness.

Naboth's eyes went back to Anna, and she gave him an imperceptible nod. The man rose to his feet in one graceful movement, and all eyes suddenly riveted on him. The room grew quiet with a hushed expectation.

"Brothers and sisters," he began, and Barak's attention was arrested by the title. His eyes went to Anna's, and she lifted her chin a notch. He could read the message in her eyes. *See, we are not involved in incest.*

As the man continued to speak, Barak found his mind caught by the strength of the man's message, his magnetic personality.

"We have come together to remember the Resurrection of our Lord Jesus," he told them. "It was on this day several years ago that Jesus Christ overcame death and rose not only in spirit, but in body, as well. Because of that victory, we all have the assurance of eternal life if we continue in the Lord's ways and live our lives as He commanded us to live."

He paused, and Barak felt himself holding his breath. This man spoke of a resurrection of the dead, and being a Pharisee, Barak had no problem in hearing the words of this message. The problem came with espousing this Jesus as Lord.

"Before we continue," Naboth went on, "let us give thanks to the Lord and ask His favor on this assembly."

As Naboth's voice rose in supplication, Barak felt a shiver of apprehension. Was he indeed committing an act of blasphemy?

Naboth ended his prayer with the words, "in Jesus' name," and suddenly the room grew loud with conversation. Barak glanced at Anna and found her watching him. Her eyes were, for once, unreadable.

When Naboth lifted his hands for attention, the room stilled again.

"Abner has some scripture he wishes to share with us."

A young man rose to his feet, and although his countenance was shy, his eyes were like fire.

"I have here a translation of the Hebrew scriptures from the prophet Isaiah. Let me read.

" 'It is too small a thing for you to be my servant to restore the tribes of Jacob and bring back those of Israel I have kept. I will also make you a light for the Gentiles, that you may bring my salvation to the ends of the earth.'

"This is what the Lord says—the Redeemer and Holy One of Israel—to him who was despised and abhorred by the nation, to the servant of rulers: 'Kings will see you and rise up, princes will see and bow down, because of the Lord, who is faithful, the Holy One of Israel, who has chosen you.' "

There was utter silence as the words seemed to echo with power throughout the room. Suddenly the silence was broken by a man's voice.

"Amen!"

Other voices followed.

"Praise God!"

"Thank You, Lord, for Your salvation to all."

The noise grew until the timbre of it threatened to rattle the walls. Naboth again rose to his feet, and the room grew quiet once more.

"Thank you, Abner," he told the young man, and Abner's cheeks flushed under his look. "Let us discuss this scripture. What do you think it means?"

One man rose to his feet. "It tells us that salvation will be given to all nations."

Another man rose. "Even kings and princes will bow before the Lord."

Barak listened as several others offered their opinion on the scriptures just read. For a long time, voices intermingled as people deliberated it among themselves. He turned to Anna.

"And what do you think?"

Before she could comment, Naboth once again took to the floor. "Brethren, before we partake of the Lord's Supper, are there any who need to confess their sins so that they might not receive it in an unworthy manner?"

For several seconds, there was no sound or movement in the room. Then slowly one man rose to his feet. He glanced briefly at another man across the room before turning to Naboth.

"I have sinned against my brother, Damon. He. . . I. . . I told the council that he was responsible for the death of one of my sheep. After hearing my story, they agreed and made him pay for the sheep. But then I found that it was not Damon's fault, but my oldest son's, who had left the sheep gate open." He stopped, unable to go on. He bowed his head. "I wish to ask forgiveness and make restitution."

Damon rose to his own feet, and without saying anything, he crossed to the speaker's side. The speaker stood with head bowed low until Damon wrapped burly arms around him, hugging him fiercely. "I, too, ask forgiveness. I have held a grudge this long while against Jezer. I ask his forgiveness, also. I wish no restitution. It *was* my cart that hit his lamb."

Under the law, Jezer was in the wrong. Barak marveled that Damon would accept no recompense. The two men sat down together, goodwill restored.

"Are there others?" Naboth inquired.

The people in the room looked about them, but no one else had anything to say.

"Good. Then let us give appreciation to our Lord for the sacrifice He made."

Barak wrinkled his nose in distaste, fairly certain that the stories of cannibalism he had heard were about to be revealed as truth. His look once again fastened on Anna, willing her not to be a part of this. She turned on him a look of innocence and hope.

"On the night the Lord was betrayed, He was partaking of the Passover supper with His disciples. He instituted a ceremony that we have come to recognize as a means of keeping His memory alive, just as He intended." Naboth took a loaf of bread and held it up for all to see. "Do this in My memory, He told His disciples, and giving thanks to God, He handed it to all. Let us do the same."

He lifted his eyes upward. "Father, thank You for this symbol of Your Son's body that was broken on the cross for our sins. Forgive us for making Him die."

He then took a piece of the bread and handed it to the man on his left. As the bread was passed around, each person took a piece, passing it on to the next.

When the bread reached Barak, he almost threw it into Anna's waiting hands. He rubbed his hands against his tunic as though to remove all traces of the offending symbol.

Anna took her piece and, together with everyone in the room, placed it in her mouth. They bowed their heads in reverence, and all was silent in the room.

Moments later, Naboth lifted the cup sitting in front of him. He held it high as he continued his prayer.

"Father, we thank You for this symbol that represents the blood of our Savior, Jesus Christ. Help us to never forget all that He did for us, and help us to take this symbol into the future for our children, and our children's children."

He handed the cup to the man beside him and sat down. This quiet ceremony was not as Barak had expected.

Once again, when the cup reached him, Barak quickly handed it to Anna. He watched her drink from the cup and hand it back to Naboth. Diffidently, not knowing what she would find, Anna's eyes met his.

She could see the confusion mirrored on Barak's face. Although he wasn't accepting, neither was he rejecting. He was clearly puzzled.

The rest of the meal continued without any more prayers or rites, but periodically someone would begin a hymn and others would take up the chorus. This was a time of happy fellowship, and Anna thrilled to be a part of it.

Naboth leaned across her and spoke to Barak. "Anna has told me that you are from Jotapata."

Barak nodded.

Undaunted by such a lack of response, Naboth continued. "We are thankful for your recovery. Anna asked us to pray for you. Praise God, our prayers were answered."

Color flooded Anna's cheeks, and she refused to meet Barak's look.

Barak motioned to the room. "A large gathering. Are there many of you in Samaria?"

Naboth followed his look, nodding. "Yes, many. The apostle Philip came to our country to tell us of God's love." His gaze went to Anna and softened. "I'm sure you know of Anna's aunt, as well. She spoke to the Messiah." He nodded across the room. "As did Jezer and Damon."

Barak slanted Naboth a dubious look. "The Messiah?"

"He has come, Barak," the older man told him with conviction. "There are so many scriptures that foretold of His coming, and they have all been fulfilled."

"All of them?"

Naboth observed his skeptical antagonist for a moment. He noticed Anna watching the young man with eyes speaking plainly of her love. He felt his own heart drop. Although Anna had said that Barak would not claim her, Naboth had his doubts. The yearning in the young Jew's eyes was obvious to anyone who cared to see, and Naboth certainly did. For some time now, he had considered speaking to Tirinus about having Anna as his wife. He had held back only because of his age.

Barak recognized a rival for Anna's affections, but he could do nothing about it. Soon he would be gone, and Anna would be just a memory. At least that's what he told himself. Better that she share her life with such a man as this one who shared her faith.

When Anna leaned toward him, her dark hair fell over his forearm, sliding silkily against his skin. The smell of the lotus blossom perfume she wore swirled around him until he began to feel lightheaded.

"Naboth has studied the scriptures thoroughly. He has also searched far and wide, questioning people about the man named Jesus." She smiled at Naboth. "It didn't take him long to conclude that Jesus was the Christ, the Anointed One."

Barak grew angry at the looks the two exchanged. They excluded him in a way that left him in no doubt that he was an outsider. Well, so be it. Let them have each other and their pagan religion.

Anna touched his hand, and suddenly all thoughts skittered around in his head into more confusion than he had felt before. Behind those incredible eyes there was such a strong belief in what she was saying. He was almost swayed. Almost.

"I would be glad to teach you," Naboth offered.

Naboth read Barak's look correctly. There was *nothing* the young Jew would wish to learn from a rival.

Anna glanced from one to the other hopefully, but Barak rose to his feet. "If you will excuse me, I need to get some rest."

Anna and Naboth watched him stride from the room, his very body oozing disapproval. Anna sighed, and Naboth turned back to her.

"Don't be so downhearted, little flower. He will come around."

Surprised, Anna stared at him in puzzlement. "How can you say that?"

Naboth's eyes studied the empty portal that Barak had disappeared through. "That was *me* several years ago. He will not stop until he ascertains the truth, one way or the other."

"But what if he decides that the Way is a lie?"

Naboth grinned at her. "How can he? You can't deny the truth."

"Others have," she disagreed, her eyes fixed firmly on the doorway.

"Trust in God, Anna. He has a purpose for Barak, or why would He bring the two of you together?"

"I hope you're right."

"I am. You'll see." He rose to his feet. "Brethren, before we depart, let us say the prayer our Lord taught us through his apostle Philip."

When he had everyone's attention, he began. " 'Our Father in heaven, hallowed be your name. . . .' "

As Anna followed along, she added fervently to the petition.

" 'Your will be done. . . .' " *Please, Lord, let it be Your will that Barak accept Your truth.*

"Forgive us our debts, as we also have forgiven our debtors." *Even Amman, Lord? All right, I will try.*

" 'And lead us not into temptation.' " *I am weak, Lord, where Barak is concerned. Help me fight my weakness.*

" 'But deliver us from the evil one.' " *Yes, Lord. Especially Amman.*

As the others rose to leave, Anna said her good-byes and accepted their thanks for opening her house to them. Her heart was strangely heavy as she watched them leave.

Chapter 11

Anna watched from the balcony window as Adonijah handed Barak a small package. They exchanged words, and then Barak moved from her sight as he reentered the villa.

Turning away from the window, she moved across her room and sat on her bed, her mind in confusion. Barak was leaving today. She had known the time would come, but she had hoped and prayed that she would have more time to reach him with the truth.

She prayed Naboth was correct in assuming that Barak would eventually find the Way, but her faith right now concerning Barak was rather weak. He had the stubbornness of a donkey, and for some reason, she doubted even the Lord could reach him.

Feeling guilty for such thoughts, Anna fell to her knees to ask forgiveness. She had to let go of these powerful feelings she had for Barak. Satan was using them to make her faith as gossamer as the web of the spider on the garden wall.

A firm knock on her door had her heart jumping into her throat.

"Come," she called, rising to her feet.

Emnon opened the door, moving aside so that Barak could enter. He started to follow the Jew inside, but Anna forestalled him.

"Wait outside, Emnon."

The Philistine did so but left the door partially open. Barak stood just inside the entry, his hands clenching and unclenching at his sides. His dark eyes swept over Anna briefly before capturing her gaze with his own.

"It is time for me to leave. Adonijah brought money to recompense your father for the care he has given me, but no amount of money can compensate you for the time you took to wait on me." He came closer. "I can never. . ."

"Don't say any more," she begged softly. "It was my pleasure to do so."

The silence between them lengthened. Finally Barak came to her, taking her face between his palms. He studied her features as though to impress them on his memory for all time.

Lowering his lips to hers, he kissed her gently, a kiss of good-bye. Only when he heard the catch in her throat did he wrap her tightly in his arms, his kiss deepening until Anna thought he would never let her go. She prayed that he wouldn't.

Keeping her enclosed within his arms, he pulled his lips from hers and buried his face in her neck. "Oh, Anna."

There was such torment in his voice. Quick tears sprang to Anna's eyes. She had to let him go.

She pulled from his arms, rubbing at the tears that ran down her cheeks. Turning her back on him, she told him quietly, "Go with God."

"May the Lord keep watch between you and me when we are away from each other."

The words of Moses hung in the air between them until she heard the door close softly behind him. She heard his retreating footsteps and with a small cry flew to the balcony.

Adonijah helped Barak into the cart. Although much of his strength had returned, he still had a long way to go before he would be healed completely.

The oxen snorted as Adonijah lifted the reins. Two men waited nearby on horseback and fell in behind the cart as it started forward.

Barak lifted his eyes and encountered Anna standing on her balcony, tears flowing unchecked down her face. His heart constricted within him. He wanted to go back, to take her in his arms and promise her his love for a lifetime, but he knew that could never be. She was a pagan. He owed his allegiance to Jehovah.

Adonijah turned and followed the direction of Barak's look. His lips set into a tight line, but he refrained from comment. Barak was a man full grown. He didn't need any advice from Adonijah. Still, he couldn't help asking, "You love the girl?"

Barak turned his gaze back to the road before them, a twitch working in his jaws.

"Be still, Adonijah."

Sighing, Adonijah did as he was told. It was going to be a long, silent trip to Jotapata.

Barak strode into the synagogue on the Sabbath and dropped to a seat beside Adonijah. He curled his arms around his upraised legs, placing his chin on his knees.

Adonijah studied his friend, noting the tired lines around his eyes. Barak rose before sunrise and worked in the fields long after sunset. He had no idea what his friend did in the fields when darkness came, and he wasn't about to ask. Barak would confide in him when, and if, he was ready.

The priest opened the Torah and looked for a scripture to read. His eyes caught Barak's, and he smiled. "Would you like to read for us today, Barak Benephraim?"

Barak swallowed hard. He had prayed for such an opportunity, but now he was reluctant. Chin setting with determination, he rose and moved to the priest's side.

"Where would you like to read?"

Barak glanced at the priest and then took the scroll and began to unroll it. As he unrolled one side, the priest rolled the other until they reached the section in Isaiah that Barak was looking for. Voice steady, he read the same scripture that Abner had read several weeks ago at Anna's.

The priest turned to him in surprise. Adonijah watched him with a knowing look. Others in the room began to murmur until the priest raised his hand for silence.

"The scripture speaks of salvation for the Gentiles, does it not?" Barak demanded.

Clearing his throat, the priest told him, "It is as you say. Even now, many have turned to the Jewish faith."

The room grew loud as others joined in the discussion. Unsatisfied with his answer, Barak took his seat beside Adonijah. A frown drew down his dark brows as he listened to the others argue among themselves over what the scripture entailed. Barak had not meant those who were proselytized. Is that what the scripture truly meant?

Adonijah's eyebrows disappeared among the hair curling over his forehead. "What did you hope to accomplish?"

Ignoring him, Barak rose to his feet. There was a fever raging inside him that refused to be restrained. "I would like to study the scriptures concerning the Messiah."

The room grew silent. One man frowned heavily at Barak. "Then join us tonight when we will do so. We have asked you in the past, but you have always been too busy. Now it is time to harvest the grain, and you suddenly wish to study the scriptures?"

Barak felt the hot color flood his face. What they said was true. Why now, of all times, did he feel compelled to seek news of the Messiah? In his heart, he knew. Anna had shaken his faith, and he needed to find the truth.

When he left the synagogue, Barak was in no better frame of mind than when he had first arrived. He moved aside as two women passed him, their arms laden with baskets.

Adonijah's look followed the two women. "Taking food to old Beker."

His thoughts elsewhere, Barak turned back to his friend. "What?"

Adonijah nodded to the two women making their way up the hill. "Sarah and Milcah. They are taking food to old Beker."

There was something in the way Adonijah said it that brought Barak to an abrupt halt. His look followed the two women as they disappeared out of sight over the hill.

"That's right. Beker is a Christian."

Adonijah shrugged. "The elders think he has lost his mind, or else they would have surely stoned him to death. That's why they have no objection to Sarah and Milcah tending to him."

Although Beker had been banished to a cave on the outskirts of the village, his daughters made sure that he lacked for nothing. They were devoted girls and couldn't be faulted for their loyalty, though they were often ridiculed by the other village women.

Without looking at Barak, Adonijah told him, "No one has more knowledge of the scriptures than Beker. Not even the priests."

Barak stared up the hill. "You may be right," he told Adonijah absently. He turned to face his friend, his eyes narrowing in suspicion.

"You seem to know an awful lot about old Beker."

Adonijah fixed his friend with a direct look. "Talk to him, Barak. Talk to him."

A message flashed from Adonijah's eyes, and Barak frowned, not certain that he knew what the younger man was trying to say.

"I will," Barak told him decisively.

Several days later, Barak found Beker sitting outside his cave watching those who traveled the roads nearby. His ragged clothes hung on his lanky frame, his white beard shaggy and unclipped.

"I've been expecting you, young Barak."

Stopping in front of him, Barak lifted a brow in inquiry.

"Adonijah said you would come."

Surprised, Barak slowly eased himself to the rocky ground. "You speak with Adonijah?"

The old man's lips tipped up slightly in a mysterious grin. He cocked his head sideways as he studied Barak.

"What is it you wish to know?"

Flustered, Barak tried to regain his thoughts after having them scattered by Beker's announcement. What was Adonijah doing coming to Beker? He would ask him later, but for now, he had other things on his mind.

"I understand that you know most of the scriptures concerning the Messiah."

The weathered old face creased into a smile. "I know *all* of the scriptures concerning the Messiah," he corrected.

Barak's narrowed gaze settled on the old man, but he realized that Beker was not boasting. He looked away.

"I wish to know about this man named Jesus."

A soft light entered the old man's eyes, and his face seemed to glow. "Then we must start at the beginning."

Barak frowned. "I don't understand."

"You will," Beker told him softly and then reiterated, "You will."

The sun had reached its zenith, and still Barak lingered, talking and arguing with old Beker. The old man had begun with a scripture Barak had learned from his youth: " 'I will put enmity between you and the woman, and between your offspring and hers; he will crush your head, and you will strike his heel.' "

Barak understood that this meant the Messiah would be born of woman. But then, everyone knew that. *All* children were born of women. But Beker explained how this proved that the Messiah would be human. Barak agreed, but then this Jesus claimed to be the Son of God.

"All nations will be blessed through him."

That was already becoming clear to him. He hadn't realized just how many scriptures there were that spoke of salvation to the Gentiles.

"He will reign on David's throne."

There was no longer any throne of David. There were no longer even twelve tribes of Israel. Beker explained how this foretold of the Messiah being of the house of David and that he would be "upholding it with justice and righteousness from that time on and forever."

From the prophecies of Micah, Beker quoted, " 'But you, Bethlehem Ephrathah, though you are small among the clans of Judah, out of you will come for me one who will be ruler over Israel, whose origins are from of old, from ancient times.' "

Barak shivered at the power of the words. Someone today, but also from ancient times? How could this be so?

"Was not this Jesus from Nazareth?"

Beker smiled. "This is true, but he was born in Bethlehem at the time of the census during Quirinius's time. It's a matter of public record."

"Who were his parents?"

Leaning back against the stone of the hillside, Beker studied Barak thoughtfully before he answered. "His mother was a woman named Mary." He paused. "His father was Jehovah."

Barak rose swiftly to his feet. "That's impossible! You sound like the Romans with their half gods."

" 'Therefore the Lord himself will give you a sign: The virgin will be with child and will give birth to a son, and will call him Immanuel.' "

Barak recognized Isaiah's prophecy. *Immanuel. God with us.* How was it possible?

"But he died," Barak told him flatly.

Beker nodded, tears in his eyes. "This was foretold, also. The Jews want land and power. The Lord wants *souls*. Jesus wanted His people." Beker gazed off into the distance. "When He was a child, Jesus was brought gifts of gold, frankincense, and myrrh. His earthly father was a carpenter, as was Jesus Himself, an occupation of no little worth. Yet He gave it all up and died with only the robe that He wore."

"Then where is the power?" Barak demanded angrily.

Beker's eyes came back to his, and Barak felt the hair rise on the back of his neck. "He rose again. There have been over five hundred witnesses to this fact.

People who saw Him hang on the tree also saw Him later as He walked among them." His voice grew soft. "I was one of them."

Barak turned in surprise and stared down at the old man. Surely the man had truly lost all reason.

Beker's eyes lifted to his, and Barak saw nothing but the shine of truth. He seated himself again slowly.

"There are those alive who can tell you this now, myself included, and perhaps we can convince you. But in the future we will all be dead and there will be no one to vow to the truth of His Resurrection. It will have to be believed here," he pointed to his head, "and here," he pointed to his heart, "and accepted on faith alone."

Barak shook his head. "It is hard to believe."

"You believe in Moses. Have you ever seen him?"

No. He had not. Why, exactly, *did* he believe in a man who had lived so long ago? There were his writings, of course. Those same writings that spoke of the Messiah to come.

The afternoon was waning, but still Barak could not bring himself to leave.

"Tell me more."

Beker complied. "Isaiah told us that He would be 'despised and rejected by men.' I think you can see the significance of that statement in relationship to Jesus. King David himself predicted that He would be betrayed by a friend. Jesus' friend, Judas Iscariot, not only fulfilled that prophecy, but one by Zechariah as well. 'So they paid me thirty pieces of silver.' "

"This Judas," Barak asked. "He knew that Jesus was the Son of God?"

Beker nodded, lifting a blade of grass and beginning to chew on it.

There were no words to express his anger over such perfidy. Barak glared at the old man but held his tongue. Son of God or no, to be betrayed by a friend was the foulest of circumstances.

"Isaiah told us that 'He was oppressed and afflicted, yet he did not open his mouth; he was led like a lamb to the slaughter, and as a sheep before her shearers is silent, so he did not open his mouth.' "

"I remember that now," Barak told him, his heart beating faster. "Uncle Simon spoke of the man Jesus and how He refused to speak in His defense except to declare that He was the Son of God."

"There are other pieces of scripture," Beker told him. "He 'was numbered with the transgressors,' He 'did not hide my face from mocking,' 'They have pierced my hands and my feet.' So many scriptures, if we would only open our eyes."

Could it possibly be true? "If the Messiah's mission was not to free our people, then what was it?"

" 'Surely he took up our infirmities and carried our sorrows, yet we considered him stricken by God, smitten by him, and afflicted. But he was pierced for our transgressions, he was crushed for our iniquities; the punishment that brought us peace was upon him, and by his wounds we are healed.' "

"The sacrificial lamb," Barak murmured.

"It is as you say," Beker agreed.

Barak watched the sky take on a purple hue, orange streaks blazoned across its surface.

"It's getting late. I must go."

Beker said nothing.

Barak rose to his feet but smiled down at the old man. "You have given me much to think on, old man."

Beker nodded, a twinkle in his eyes. "Be careful, young Barak. Seek out the truth, but know that in doing so you will find many enemies. The Lord Jesus Himself said, 'I have come to turn "a man against his father, a daughter against her mother, a daughter-in-law against her mother-in-law—a man's enemies will be the members of his own household." ' "

"The prophet Micah said this," Barak told him, and Beker dipped his head in agreement.

"Surely if we know the scriptures and can see that they are true, others will listen."

Beker smiled sadly. "First they must open their hearts."

"I have never known Uncle Simon to run from the truth."

"Your truth, or his?"

Barak had no answer. He said his good-byes and retreated down the hill, his mind more confused than ever. He had to know the truth, and there was only one way to find out. He must return to Jerusalem.

"We have found Amman."

The words struck terror in Anna's heart. She clutched her tunic, her eyes flying to her father.

"Is he. . ."

"He is alive, but barely. It would seem that those he owed money to couldn't wait for their pound of flesh."

Anna shivered. "What do we do now?"

"With Amman out of the way, you are free again." He took a seat on the couch across from her. "Perhaps you can regain some of the sparkle you are missing, hmm?"

Anna felt the color climb to her cheeks. It was not the threat of Amman that had her feeling as though the world had ended. Truth be told, she had scarce given the man a thought the past few weeks.

"Bithnia will be coming for you in two days. I have sent her word."

Jerking her head up, she stared at her father in surprise. "There is no need."

"There is every need," he argued. "You have become a shallow shadow of yourself lately. I think you need to get away. To forget."

She knew he understood, for he had never forgotten her mother. His love had remained true all these years, as Anna knew hers would be for Barak. There was something intransigent in the bond that had been formed between them, something she couldn't define.

"It's not so easy, is it, Father?"

He got up from his seat and crossed to her side, sitting down next to her. Wrapping an arm around her shoulders, he leaned back against the cushions, hugging her close. Anna nestled close to him, tears not far from the surface. For the first time, she understood his pain.

"My little girl," he murmured softly. "If only there were something I could do for you. Some way to relieve your hurt."

"What of Amman?"

He hesitated a moment, then shrugging his shoulders, he told her, "I didn't want to worry you further. They do not expect Amman to last the night."

Anna supposed she should be glad, but she realized that God loved Amman as much as anyone else. Jesus had died for him, as well as for her. Anna's heart felt heavy as she realized that she had missed a golden opportunity to witness to the Arab. Perhaps she could have won him to the Lord.

"I will pray for him."

Tirinus turned to her in surprise. "Pray for him?"

She lifted her face from his shoulder and nodded. "God loves Amman, Father. I have forgotten this."

Tirinus shook his head. "I don't see how Jehovah could love such a creature."

"He is Amman's Father, as well as ours." Her eyes twinkled up at him. "Would you love me any less if I were not an obedient daughter?"

He tweaked her nose. "Perhaps. Who knows?"

Anna knew. The love in her father's eyes was so strong, she doubted anything could remove it.

Pushing her to her feet, he commanded, "Get ready to return to Jerusalem. I am sending Emnon with you."

"Is that necessary?"

"I will not take any more chances with your safety."

"As you wish."

Tirinus watched her walk away and sighed. Life had been so much simpler when she was but a child. Now that she had grown into a woman, he knew his life would never be the same. Someday Barak would return to claim her, and he would lose her forever. He knew it as surely as he knew the sun would rise in the morning. The same magnetism that had flowed between Tirinus and his wife now flowed between his daughter and the Jew. Nothing could stand in the way of such a powerful love.

He would send her back to Jerusalem until that time, but he would miss her as though a part of him were gone. It had always been this way.

Sighing again, he went in search of Emnon.

"Uncle Simon, I wish to return to Jerusalem for Shavuot."

Simon lifted his head from where he sat mulling over the accounts of the grain harvest. His eyebrows went upward.

"What of your mother?"

"I have hired a village girl to look after her. It's just for a few weeks." Barak dropped into the seat across from him. The lamps had been lit against the fast-falling darkness, and Barak studied his uncle through the smoke drifting in the room.

Simon leaned back in his seat, watching Barak intently. "You have not been yourself since returning from Sychar. Does this desire to visit Jerusalem again so soon have anything to do with that?"

For a moment, Barak was tempted to lie. But only for a moment.

"I intend to seek news of the Messiah. I wish to find out, once and for all, if this Jesus could possibly have been Him."

Simon's face took on the hue of a thundercloud as he glared across at his nephew. "Don't be ridiculous. The man was a fraud."

Barak leaned forward. "How can you be so certain?"

"He's dead, isn't He? A dead man cannot rule on the throne of David."

"There *is* no throne of David!" Barak argued hotly.

"There will be again," his uncle answered, his voice lacking conviction.

"I have to know, Uncle Simon. I have to be certain."

Simon rose to his feet, flipping the chair back in his anger. "No! Even Saul of Tarsus was taken in by these miscreants, and he was far more zealous than you."

"I'm going."

There was the same inflexible tone in his voice that he had used in dealing with Ahaz and Miriam about their marriage. The breach it had caused between Simon and his friend was only now beginning to heal. Still, he knew his nephew, and there would be no stopping him.

"Go then. But know this. If you return here spouting some nonsense about this Jesus having been the Messiah, I will disown you before everyone. You will have *nothing*."

"Nothing but the truth," Barak refuted and saw his uncle's face darken further.

"Remember what I said," he spat, turning back to his table.

Barak retrieved his uncle's overturned chair and set it beside the table. "I will remember."

As he passed through the door, he saw Adonijah waiting for him.

"I'm going with you."

Barak shook his head negatively. "I need you to stay with Mother."

"I *have* to go," Adonijah argued, and Barak saw the same determination in his friend's eyes that he knew dwelt in his own.

A long look passed between them, a message sent and a message received. Barak nodded.

"Get your things."

Chapter 12

Once again the streets of Jerusalem were crowded with Jews who had made the pilgrimage for Shavuot, the Feast of Weeks. The babble of voices grew louder as Anna and Pisgah neared the temple area. For Anna, it held bittersweet memories, and she felt the ache in her heart that was never far away.

As she did any time she walked the streets of Jerusalem, she found herself searching for a familiar face among the crowd. It was futile, she knew, but somehow she was unable to control her wandering eyes. Or the way her heart would increase its pace when she saw someone who closely resembled Barak. The pain of disappointment was always as sharp each time she was proved wrong.

As Anna ambled along in the warm afternoon sun, Pisgah fluttered along at her side, full of enthusiasm and excitement.

"Look, Anna. The temple is crowded today." She wrinkled her nose impishly. "Should we go inside? At least to the Court of Gentiles?"

Anna shook her head. "Not today, Pisgah. Some other time."

"Oh, please," she begged. "We never did get to go the last time you were here." She closed her mouth suddenly, her eyes full of contrition. "I'm sorry. That was thoughtless of me. That couldn't have been a happy time for you."

Anna didn't answer. Was it an unhappy experience? In many ways, yes, but she wouldn't have missed the chance to know Barak for all the gold in Jerusalem. It was better to have known love than to have married and never known what love could be.

A huge crowd spilled over from the Court of Gentiles past the outside gates and beyond. People were trying to move forward to get a better look at what was inside.

Curious, Anna and Pisgah crossed the street and tried to move closer to the gate. Jostled by the seething crowd, Anna wrinkled her nose at the smell of unwashed bodies. Above the chatter of voices, they heard one lone voice, strong and clear.

Anna asked a woman standing near, "What is happening?"

The woman's face was full of eagerness. "The apostle Paul is speaking to the crowd. He is telling them of Jesus and how He fulfilled the prophecies of the Messiah."

Anna felt a little thrill of fear. The apostle Peter had been arrested only a short time ago for preaching the same message. King Herod Agrippa had had the apostle James slain with a sword and threatened the same with Peter. Only a miracle of God had saved him.

Since King Herod's death, the new procurator, Cuspius Fadus, hadn't bothered with the Christian community, but the worry was always there.

Still, to hear the apostle Paul himself would be worth the risk.

"Can you see anything?" Pisgah asked, craning her head for a better view.

"No."

Frustrated, Anna tried to hear the voice and its message. She could hear the voice, but the words were still indistinct.

The murmur of the crowd grew into an angry babble as devout Jews argued with Paul. The multitude was divided in its opinion of the apostle. Many believed his message; many did not.

As the mob of people began to take sides, a riot threatened to break out. Anna could hear Paul's voice begging for attention, but the crowd was in a frenzy.

Anna felt a firm hand latch onto her arm.

"Come," Emnon ordered, beginning to pull her from the crowded area.

"Wait!"

Emnon was firm in his refusal. "I have orders from your father to see that nothing happens to you. Soon there will be a riot, and Roman guards will come. You come with me now."

He hurried her away from the temple and back toward the market street, Pisgah running to keep up with them. Anna was almost out of breath when Emnon stopped.

"You should be safe here," he told her, glancing down at her gloomy face. His mouth tilted up into a rare smile. "It was for your own good. Yours and Mistress Pisgah's."

Anna sighed. "I know, Emnon. But I hoped to get a chance to hear the apostle Paul."

"Another time, perhaps."

Would there ever be such a time again? Anna felt frustrated at this missed opportunity. The trio wandered around the merchant booths, but much of the pleasure was ruined for Anna. Even Pisgah seemed more subdued, and by mutual consent, they agreed to return to Aunt Bithnia's villa.

As they were crossing the street to return to the Upper City, Anna stopped, her heart suddenly lodging in her throat.

There, coming from the temple area, was Barak, and close by his side was Adonijah. They were deep in discussion with each other and failed to notice anyone around them.

For a moment, Anna was tempted to call out to him, but then she rebuked herself for such a foolish thought. Still, she watched the two until they were out of sight. Barak's tall form had regained some of its color, and she knew it must be because of days spent in harvesting the grain. He looked healthy again, more handsome than ever, and Anna praised God for his healing.

Pisgah had not missed the direction of her cousin's look and knew the reason for the longing in Anna's eyes. She laid an understanding hand on her cousin's arm, silently offering her sympathy.

"Let's go home," Anna whispered.

Barak strode along with Adonijah by his side. "Do you believe what he says?"

Adonijah shrugged. "I'm not certain. There is still much that needs to be investigated."

Nodding, Barak told him, "I agree. How do we go about it?"

A group of Roman soldiers hurried in the direction they had just come from. For a moment, both men stopped to watch, then turned and proceeded on their way.

"Trouble," Adonijah suggested.

Barak agreed, but his mind was not on the soldiers. Instead, it was on the man they had just heard speak—Saul of Tarsus, now known throughout the Roman realm as Paul. "To hear the man speak. . .there is power in his words."

"He believes what he says, that's for certain. But how do *we* go about searching out the truth?"

Turning to his friend, Barak met his eyes seriously. "Let's start at the beginning."

"You mean go to Bethlehem?"

"No. To Nazareth."

Dismayed, Adonijah could only stare at him. "Are we going on a long pilgrimage, my friend? Are we going to trace the steps of this Jesus?"

"We are."

Adonijah knew that tone of voice and the set of those broad shoulders. Sighing, he shook his head. "We will need supplies. This could be dangerous, you know. Two men alone are obvious prey."

"Then we'll travel with a caravan," Barak told him, remembering another time. "One should be leaving tomorrow, at the end of Shavuot."

"I hope you know what you're doing."

Barak stopped, turning to his friend. "You don't have to go."

Adonijah shifted away from those assessing eyes. "Yes, I do," he disagreed. "Like you, I have to know." He had an odd premonition that his life was about to change forever. When he turned back to Barak, he could see the same thought reflected in his eyes.

"Let's make arrangements."

Anna was tempted to sneak back to the temple in hopes of a chance to hear Paul speak but then thought better of it. Probably by now he had left, if he hadn't been arrested.

She sat in the peristyle watching a butterfly moving from one flower to another. Summer was almost upon them in full bloom, and the flowers more than matched the season. The little garden was full of the beauty and wonder of the warming weather.

She snapped a hibiscus from the bush closest to her, lifting it to her nose and inhaling deeply. Her thoughts, as usual, were on Barak. She was beginning to grow aggravated with herself for not being able to banish him from her mind.

A thought suddenly occurred to her. Barak had been among the crowd listening to the apostle Paul. He had to have heard the apostle's message. A sudden smile lit her features. What had Barak thought of the message? Would he believe it?

She closed her eyes, and instantly Barak's face was there. Her heart still throbbed at the passionate intensity of his voice the last time they had been together. He cared. She knew he cared, though she could not understand how it could be so.

And what of the beautiful Miriam? Had their marriage been arranged by now? Her stomach clutched tightly at the thought.

Moaning, she threw herself to her feet and strode into the coolness of the villa. She *had* to forget him. Easier said than done, she knew, because she had been trying to exorcise him from her mind for weeks.

Pisgah met her at the door, and they went into the triclinium together. Servants were arranging the table for the coming supper. Tomorrow would be the Lord's Day, and there would be others to share it with; tonight there would be only the three of them.

Anna was greatly looking forward to tomorrow's fellowship. Each Lord's Day brought her joy, and if not full happiness, then at least peace. God was in charge of her life. She had given it to Him willingly, and she would not take it back now.

"We have been invited to Lucius's villa for a party tomorrow night," Pisgah told Anna, and Anna wondered at the sudden color that bloomed in her cousin's cheeks.

Anna felt a sudden niggle of worry. Lucius Castus was one of the most wealthy Romans in Jerusalem. It was said that he had the ear of the emperor himself.

"What did your mother say?"

Anna couldn't believe that her aunt would agree to such a thing. All of Jerusalem knew about Lucius's parties, and they were not for young innocents.

"I haven't told her yet," Pisgah admitted, avoiding Anna's searching eyes.

Anna sighed. "You know she will never agree to let you go. Besides, you shouldn't even *want* to go. Lucius is. . .is. . ."

"Handsome. Charming. Witty," Pisgah finished for her.

Anna frowned. "That's *not* what I was going to say."

Pisgah raised serious eyes to her cousin. "Why don't you like him?"

Studying Pisgah's sober expression, Anna wondered just how much she knew of the man.

"He's not a Christian, for one thing," she finally answered.

Pisgah's eyes took fire. "Well, neither is Barak."

Anna felt a pain wrench her heart. "Exactly," she answered softly. "That's why he is where he is, and I am where I am."

For a moment, Anna could see the desire to argue reflected in her cousin's eyes, but then their amber brown turned dark with puzzlement.

"You love him, don't you?"

Anna pulled Pisgah down to the couch beside her. "Yes, I love him, but I love God more."

Pisgah flopped back among the cushions. "Well, I don't see why you can't have both."

"Someone like Lucius would never understand a love such as I have for Jesus. He is full of the pleasures of this world."

"You and Mother have always been this way, but *I'm* different. I don't believe in the same things you do."

Anna glanced at her in surprise. "You don't believe in God?"

Flushing with color, Pisgah motioned disparagingly with one hand. "I. . .I believe in God, yes. I suppose. But if He created the world, then He must mean for us to enjoy it."

"A union between a man and woman is a beautiful thing. God instituted marriage Himself. He even said it wasn't good for man to be alone, but there is a time and a place for everything." She smiled gently. "You want things *now*, but your time will come. There is a special man waiting for you, but you must, in turn, wait for him."

"Lucius makes my heart sing," she told Anna with a deep sigh.

"And how many times have you told me this in the past?"

Pisgah colored hotly, dipping her head.

"Your mother would not countenance this relationship, especially since Lucius is old enough to be your father."

"A slight exaggeration," Pisgah commented sarcastically.

"He's forty-five years old."

Pisgah turned to her in surprise. "That's not true. He told me he was thirty."

"My father has done business with him for years. Trust me, he is forty-five."

"He *lied* to me!" She got up and began pacing. Anna watched her warily.

"Pisgah, if he were a Christian, you would never have that worry."

She flopped once more to the seat beside Anna. "Christians are so boring! They never want to have any fun."

Anna thought of a friend who would be just right for her young cousin. She would introduce them tomorrow, and then maybe Jamin could help Anna reach

Pisgah for the Lord.

Was Pisgah's comment justified? Were Christians boring? Although Barak was a Jew, he was a devout one. What would he be like as a Christian? Dull? Remembering his kiss and the warmth of his arms, she thought not.

Wherever he was right now, she wished him Godspeed.

As they traveled throughout Galilee, Barak and Adonijah spent long hours in the synagogues of each town they visited. It was the same everywhere. As tensions with Rome mounted, more and more of the Jewish leaders argued over the Messianic scriptures, hoping that the Messiah would return soon to free them of the Gentile rule.

They had questioned people in Nazareth and Bethlehem. Some acknowledged Jesus as the Messiah, while others denied Him. Either way, they conceded the man's existence.

The two were resting in the synagogue of Cana, having heard an incredible story of the man Jesus turning water into wine. Dubiously they had questioned several people. Of those who remembered, they were adamant in their endorsement. Jesus had turned water into fine wine.

"Well," Adonijah questioned, "do you believe this story?"

Barak shook his head slightly. "It's hard to accept, but these people have nothing to gain by such a wild tale."

"There is also the story about the royal official's son. This Jesus supposedly healed him without even seeing the boy."

Barak nodded. "Not many people seem to believe that story."

Adonijah turned to Barak, one dark brow lifting upward. "So what now?"

"We find this royal official."

Anna introduced her cousin to Jamin, who was immediately smitten. Anna hoped that the young man could see past the exterior beauty to the beauty that she knew lived inside. Pisgah was still so young and craving adventure.

At the same time, she hoped Jamin would be able to influence Pisgah, and not the other way around. She bit her lip as she watched the two.

"Now there is a young man I would welcome for my daughter," Bithnia told her niece as she followed the two with her gaze.

Anna agreed, but she was still concerned. Had she done right in introducing the two?

"I forgot to tell you. Tirinus is coming to Jerusalem in two weeks."

Anna's face brightened, and she turned to her aunt with a big smile. "I am so glad. I have missed him terribly. Not that I haven't enjoyed being here," she hastily assured her aunt.

Bithnia smiled. "I understand. Now, let us go into the triclinium and enjoy our meal and some Christian fellowship. Adama managed to persuade the apostle Paul to come and speak with us while he was visiting the city."

Heart leaping with joy, Anna quickly followed her aunt into the room. Praise God! She would hear the great apostle after all.

After trudging through the Judaean and Galilean countrysides for several months, Barak came to one conclusion. This man Jesus had a definite wanderlust.

From Nazareth to Bethlehem, Cana to Capernaum, Bethsaida to Nain, Jesus' footsteps were everywhere among the towns and villages.

And everywhere they went, they were met with stories of miraculous healings. What Barak was having a hard time understanding was the man's gentle message of love.

For years he had believed the Messiah would come and help the Jews conquer the world. Now he was beginning to wonder if that were so.

Adonijah stood staring at the Jordan River. He had been quiet the last several miles of their journey, ever since they had spoken with several people in the town of Bethany, where Jesus supposedly raised a man named Lazarus from the dead. Listening to the people talk of the story had raised his flesh. They had not been able to speak to the man or his family, but there were those who swore they had seen the event occur.

Adonijah's soft voice interrupted Barak's wandering thoughts.

"I want to be baptized."

For a long time, Barak stood there, oblivious of the sound of the water lapping gently against the shore. The birds calling in the trees went unheeded as he stared at his friend.

"Do you know what you're saying?" Barak's voice was hoarse with emotion.

"I know." He turned to Barak. "And if you are honest with yourself, you know, too."

Feelings of doubt warred with Jewish tradition. To give in to this urging meant to give up all he had ever known. And what would happen to his mother? What would she do if he claimed that he believed the Christ had come and been crucified on a cross? Disown him? The thought made his blood go cold.

"I am going to find a believer to baptize me. I wish to be baptized in the same river as the Messiah."

Barak struggled with feelings of misgiving. He knew that if he committed his life, there would be no turning back. He would be as zealous as was Saul of Tarsus, or should he call him Paul?

He followed Adonijah as he went in search of someone to perform the baptismal ceremony that would cleanse him from sin. Peter had commanded it, and for the first time, Barak understood the significance of the sacrificial lamb.

Jesus died once and for all, and there would never be need of such animal sacrifices again. *"I desire mercy, not sacrifice."* The words echoed around in his head until he thought he would go mad.

Three days Jesus had lain in the tomb, and on the third day He rose forever. Many even in this part of the world had witnessed the event and spread out to tell others of the good news.

As Adonijah said, he knew the truth. It was time to take a stand, to bury himself with the Lord through baptism. Let tomorrow take care of itself, for today was the Lord's. He hurried to catch up with his friend.

Anna missed hearing the apostle speak to their group, but he was off on another missionary journey. For two weeks he had spent time with them, but the need to spread the good news had given his feet wanderlust. She felt guilty that she was not filled with the same zeal to spread the message. It was what the Lord wanted her to do, but she was reluctant to stray far from the familiar surroundings of her home.

Still, it was possible to win converts in even this city. She smiled as she considered her cousin Pisgah's case. Anna's fears had been unfounded. Jamin had stood firm in his faith to his Lord, and Pisgah had slowly come to accept the truth through him. It wouldn't surprise Anna if there were a wedding on the horizon.

She sighed as she helped the servants lay the tables for the coming meeting. Communion with fellow believers had become the focal point of her week.

The thought of a marriage between her cousin and young Jamin left Anna feeling melancholy. She was not getting any younger, and though she knew her father could arrange a marriage for her in an instant, the thought of being married for her father's wealth left a sour taste in her mouth—not to mention the odious thought of belonging to someone other than Barak.

Her father had sent her several suitors over the past few months, and she was growing weary of fending them off. She knew her father was only trying to help her forget Barak, but she wished he would realize that her feelings went much deeper than that.

Anna filled bowls with flowers and set them around the room. She then made sure all the braziers were filled for the night and added incense to the stands. Glancing around her with satisfaction, she determined that everything was ready.

When Jamin arrived, Anna noticed he quickly searched the room until he found Pisgah sitting beside an elderly gentleman, laughing with him over some story they had just shared. His frown was obvious even from that distance.

Instead of going to Pisgah as Anna expected, he made his way across the room to Anna's side. His eyes were alive with some inner glow.

"Anna. I have just returned from the synagogue. I met some new converts there, and I invited them to share our Lord's Supper. Do you think Bithnia will mind?"

Anna shook her head. "Aunt Bithnia will be delighted. Who are these new converts?"

He opened his mouth to explain, then looking past her shoulder, he smiled widely.

"Here they are now."

Anna turned slowly, a ready smile upon her lips for the visitors. Barak stood just inside the doorway, his eyes fixed firmly upon Anna. There was nothing in his eyes to even give a hint to his feelings.

The color drained from Anna's face. Her look rested briefly on Adonijah but returned quickly to Barak.

"Anna. This is Barak and Adonijah. They have only recently found the Lord."

His voice seemed to come from a great distance. Anna felt it must be time to light the lamps because the room was growing dim around her.

Barak caught her as she fainted.

Anna opened her eyes slowly, the lids feeling as though they had bronze weights attached to them. She frowned as she tried to focus on the figure across from her.

"Aunt Bithnia?"

She heard her aunt's sigh of relief. "Child, you had us worried."

Anna came fully awake. "What happened?"

"You fainted."

Everything came rushing back to her, and her eyes grew large. "Barak?"

Her aunt got up from her chair and came to where Anna lay on the couch. "Waiting just outside. He's very concerned." She crossed the room to open the door.

"You may come in," she told the young man waiting on the outside.

Barak came quickly into the room, his worried brown eyes fixing on Anna. He gave her a hard, searching look that she returned with friendly but veiled eyes.

Bithnia looked from one to the other. "I will leave you alone. I must return to my other guests."

Anna gave a brief thought to the others in the outer room, but her attention was for the man standing near her.

"You are a believer?" she asked him softly.

Barak nodded, the lump in his throat making it hard to speak. He was uncertain of his welcome, and Anna had learned in the past months to keep her thoughts hidden. He found this extremely disquieting.

She rose to her feet, and he wrapped an arm around her when she swayed slightly. She pushed out of his hold and went to stare out the window into the courtyard beyond.

Darkness had come and with it a cooling breeze. The crickets chirped just beyond the window, a soothing cadence that relaxed Barak slightly.

"I had to come and let you know," he told her, his voice barely above a whisper.

"I'm glad."

Anna's thoughts were in total disorder. What did Barak's presence here mean? She could read any number of things into it, but she didn't wish to be hurt again. He would have to make the first move.

Which he did.

She could feel his presence behind her and felt her breath quicken in response. He curled his fingers around her shoulders, turning her to face him.

"I have missed you," he told her huskily.

She looked up into eyes dark with emotion and swallowed hard. "And I have missed you." So much so, that for the last several weeks she had felt only half alive.

He pulled her close, burying his face against her shoulder. They stood thus a long time before Barak could bring himself to speak.

"Is it possible that you care for me?"

She pulled back from him and smiled into his eyes. "It is not only possible, but very, very probable."

He didn't return her smile. "I have nothing to offer you. When Adonijah and I return home, my uncle will disinherit us. I can't ask you to marry me."

She opened her mouth to argue, but he closed his lips over hers. She clung to him, wishing he would never let her go again.

When he pulled back, there was a slight quirk to his lips. "That seems to be the only effective way of silencing you."

"My father. . ." she began, but he was already shaking his head.

"No, Anna."

Angry at his refusal, irritated by his pride, she could only stare at him. A voice from the doorway wrenched them apart.

"No, Anna, what? You cannot accept a gift from me?"

Anna quickly left Barak's side and went to her father, hugging him tightly. "Father, I have missed you."

"As I have missed you, my dear." His look went to Barak. "Now suppose you tell me what is going on here?"

The room grew uncomfortably quiet as Tirinus searched first one face, then the other. "Then let me," he suggested as the silence continued. "Barak would like to marry you now that he no longer considers you a heathen."

Tirinus watched the color come to the Jew's face, but he had to give the lad credit for never breaking eye contact.

"Regardless," he continued. "Anna was about to tell you that she has property of her own. Her dowry, you might say. Her aunt gave it to her before she died, since she had no offspring of her own. I have had to hire a man to farm it for years until Anna should either sell it or choose to live there."

When Barak gave no sign, Tirinus frowned. "Perhaps you cannot bring yourself to live in Sychar."

Barak lifted his hand impatiently. "I have nothing to offer her."

Anna wanted to tell him that all she wanted was him, but he hadn't yet declared his love for her.

Tirinus rightly guessed at the look his daughter gave him. "You have love," he disagreed softly. "And strength. And knowledge. You have my blessings if you can work this out between you. I want only my daughter's happiness."

The door closed behind him, and Anna knew her father hadn't heard Barak's soft, "As do I."

He came to her then, taking both of her hands in his own. "I have been so wrong about so many things. I still have much to learn."

Anna smiled. "We all do."

His voice grew soft, husky. "I would wish to learn them with you by my side."

She willed him to say the words she was waiting to hear, but he didn't. Frowning, she pulled her hands away.

"You would be willing to live in Samaria? To accept a dowry of land?"

He smiled then. "I am willing to accept such a dowry, but only if it includes you. There are many of the Way in Sychar. I have seen for myself that they are a good people, and I no longer see them as enemies, but allies. You taught me this."

"I still can't believe that you have accepted the Lord. My prayers for you have been answered."

"Anna. Look at me."

Reluctantly she did as he bid.

"All of this dancing around the issue is getting us nowhere. Tell me one thing. Do you love me?"

Words would not come past the tightness in her throat. All she could do was nod.

He crossed to her quickly, taking her in his arms and holding her close. "And I love you."

She closed her eyes, wrapping her arms around his waist. She had so longed to hear those words. Now she was almost frightened by them.

"Are you certain?"

For answer, he closed his lips over hers in a long kiss that left her shaken to her very core.

"I have never been more certain of anything in my life. Marry me."

"And you can live in Sychar?"

"I can live anywhere where you are. I will never let my pride come between us again."

He slid his palms across her cheeks and met her eyes seriously. "It will be hard," he warned.

Anna smiled. "With God, all things are possible."

Epilogue

Simon glared from one man to the other, then fastened his eyes coldly on the girl beside Barak.

"Take your heathen wife and leave. You are no longer my nephew."

Anna flinched under his angry perusal. Barak had decided that it would be better for them to marry before coming back to Jotapata. Perhaps that decision had been unwise.

"Simon!"

Barak motioned his mother to silence. He fixed an equally angry glare on his uncle.

"Saying it will not make it so. I will *always* be your nephew."

"No! No longer."

Adonijah stepped forward. "Uncle Simon, if you would only hear us out."

Simon slapped Adonijah across the face, spinning the boy aside. "Never use that title for me again," he hissed. "You were welcomed to this house as one of us, but now that is not so. Get out. All of you."

"I won't leave without my mother," Barak told him inflexibly.

"Tamar will stay here. *She* has not turned her back on the Lord."

"And who would care for her?"

"I will take her into my house, as the law commands. She will be my wife."

Tamar gasped at this declaration. Her eyes lifted to her son. Lips pressed tightly together, he told her, "The choice is yours, Mother. I cannot ask you to give up everything, but know this: You are welcome in my home."

Anna nodded. "We would be pleased to have you with us. Adonijah has already agreed to come."

Snarling, Simon moved toward Anna, but Barak stepped into his path. Glaring brown eyes met glittering brown eyes, and Simon stopped.

"Get her out of here," he told Barak. "Get her out of my house."

"We're going," Barak told him, his voice soft with warning. "As soon as I have Mother's decision."

Simon's face purpled with rage. "I tell you, she will stay here."

Barak ignored him. "Mother?"

Tamar looked from one to the other in indecision. To give up everything she had ever known and move to Samaria, of all places. Still, the thought of being separated from her only child didn't bear thinking about.

"Oh, Barak," she lamented. "Why must it be this way?"

Barak's eyes softened, and he went down on one knee before her. "Mother, the Messiah has truly come. Adonijah and I know it. We searched for the truth, and we found it."

"Blasphemy!"

Barak turned his head slightly. "No, Uncle Simon. Truth."

Adonijah had remained silent. Now he stepped forward. "If you would only let us tell you what we found." His plea was as much for Simon as for Tamar.

"I said, get out!"

"Simon." Tamar's quiet voice added balm to a fiery situation. Simon stopped, questioning her with his eyes.

"I am honored that you would be willing to have me as your wife, as the law commands, but this I cannot do. I will go with my son."

Simon sucked in an angry breath. "You can't mean it!"

Her eyes were fixed on her son. "I do. I will go with Barak."

There was silence for a full minute before Simon exploded into rage. "Go then! All of you! Get out of my house now!"

Adonijah came to Tamar and lifted her in his arms as Barak tried once more to reach his uncle.

"Search the scriptures. Seek the truth. It's there for all to see."

Simon lifted a knife from the table, shaking it threateningly at his nephew. "Be gone, I say!"

Frightened, Anna pulled at his arm. "Come, Barak."

Uncle and nephew stared into each other's eyes a long moment before Barak turned, and taking his wife by the arm, he left.

Barak stood outside the door looking around him at the home of his youth. The grapes were ripe and ready to be harvested. His fingers itched to tend the fields. He swallowed down the lump in his throat.

Anna wrapped an arm around his waist. "It's beautiful here."

He heard the uncertainty in her voice and turned and wrapped her in his arms.

"I am not sorry, Anna. You led me to Jesus, and Jesus led me to you. I am not sorry."

The firm conviction of his voice warmed her into a feeling of security.

"I told you it would be hard," he reminded.

She looked up at him, and he saw the tears in her eyes reflect the sunlight.

"I love you, Barak. For now and for always."

"Then that is all that matters," he told her, his voice rough with emotion. "As long as we have each other and Jesus as our Lord, as you said, all things are possible."

The way would indeed be difficult, but as long as they had the Lord and each other, that was all that mattered. Turning, they followed Adonijah down the hill.

A Letter to Our Readers

Dear Readers:

In order that we might better contribute to your reading enjoyment, we would appreciate your taking a few minutes to respond to the following questions. When completed, please return to the following: Fiction Editor, Barbour Publishing, Inc., P.O. Box 719, Uhrichsville, OH 44683.

1. Did you enjoy reading *Brides of the Empire* by Darlene Mindrup?
   - ❑ Very much—I would like to see more books like this.
   - ❑ Moderately—I would have enjoyed it more if ______________

____

____

2. What influenced your decision to purchase this book? (Check those that apply.)
   - ❑ Cover ❑ Back cover copy ❑ Title ❑ Price
   - ❑ Friends ❑ Publicity ❑ Other

3. Which story was your favorite?
   - ❑ *The Eagle and the Lamb* ❑ *My Enemy, My Love*
   - ❑ *Edge of Destiny*

4. Please check your age range:
   - ❑ Under 18 ❑ 18–24 ❑ 25–34
   - ❑ 35–45 ❑ 46–55 ❑ Over 55

5. How many hours per week do you read? ______________

Name ______________________________________

Occupation ______________________________________

Address ______________________________________

City______________ State__________ Zip__________

E-mail______________________________________